THE OTHER PERSUASION

AN ANTHOLOGY OF SHORT FICTION
ABOUT GAY MEN AND WOMEN

THE OTHER PERSUASION

EDITED AND WITH AN INTRODUCTION
BY SEYMOUR KLEINBERG

VINTAGE BOOKS
A DIVISION OF RANDOM HOUSE NEW YORK

A Vintage Original, May 1977

First Edition

Published in the United States by Random House, Inc., New York.

Library of Congress Cataloging in Publication Data
Main entry under title:

The other persuasion.

I. Kleinberg, Seymour, 1933–
PZ1.077 [PN6071.H724] 808.83'9'352 76–62492
ISBN 0-394-72237-X

Manufactured in the United States of America

Grateful acknowledgment is made to the following for permission to reprint previously published material:

Georges Borchardt, Inc.: "Middle Children," by Jane Rule. Copyright © 1975 by Jane Rule. Reprinted from *Theme For Diverse Instruments*, published by Talonbooks, Canada.

Curtis Brown Ltd.: Selection from pages 101–116 of *The World in the Evening*, by Christopher Isherwood. Copyright 1953 by Christopher Isherwood. Originally published by Random House, Inc.

Hallie Burnett: "The Threesome," by Helen Essary Ansell. Reprinted from *The Best College Writing in 1961*, by Whit and Hallie Burnett.

Joan Daves: "A Step Toward Gemorrah," by Ingeborg Bachmann, translated by Michael Bullock. Reprinted from *The Thirteenth Year*. English translation Copyright © 1964 by Michael Bullock. *The Thirteenth Year* was originally published in German as *Das dreissigste Jahr*. Copyright © 1961 by R. Piper & Co. Verlag, München.

H. Lovat Dickson on behalf of the Estate of Radclyffe Hall: Selection from *Miss Oglivy Finds Herself*, by Radclyffe Hall.

Harper & Row Publishers, Inc.: "Burning the Bed," by Doris Betts. Reprinted from pages

66–86 of *Beasts of the Southern Wild and Other Stories,* by Doris Betts. Copyright © 1973 by Doris Betts.

Hutchinson Publishing Group Ltd.: "My Brother Writes Poetry for an Englishman," by Marris Murray. Reprinted from pages 174–184 of *The Saturday Book 13th Year,* edited by John Hadfield.

Liveright Publishing Corporation: Book 2: "Mabel Neathe," by Gertrude Stein. Reprinted from pages 70–98 of *Fernhurst, Q.E.D., and Other Early Writings,* by Gertrude Stein. Copyright © 1971 by Daniel C. Joseph, Administrator of the Estate of Gertrude Stein.

William Morris Agency, Inc.: "Pages from an Abandoned Journal," by Gore Vidal. Reprinted from *A Thirsty Evil,* by Gore Vidal. Copyright © 1956 by Gore Vidal; "Momma," by John Horne Burns. Reprinted from *The Gallery,* by John Horne Burns. Copyright 1947 by John Horne Burns, renewed 1975 by the author; "Pages from Cold Point," by Paul Bowles. Reprinted from *The Delicate Prey,* by Paul Bowles. Copyright 1950 by Paul Bowles.

William Morrow & Company, Inc.: "Jonnie," by Joan O'Donovan. Reprinted from *Dangerous Worlds and Other Stories,* by Joan O'Donovan. Copyright © 1958 by Joan O'Donovan.

New Directions Publishing Corp.: "You May Safely Gaze," by James Purdy. Reprinted from *The Color of Darkness,* by James Purdy. Copyright © 1957 by James Purdy; "The Knife of the Times," by William Carlos Williams. Reprinted from *The Farmers' Daughters,* by William Carlos Williams. Copyright 1932, 1950 by William Carlos Williams.

W. W. Norton & Company, Inc.: "Arthur Snatchfold," by E. M. Forster. Reprinted from pages 97–112 of *The Life To Come and Other Stories,* by E. M. Forster. Copyright © 1972 by The Provost and Scholars of King's College, Cambridge.

Harold Ober Associates Incorporated: "The Wreck," by Maude Phelps Hutchins. Reprinted from *The Elevator and Other Stories,* by Maude Phelps Hutchins. Copyright © 1962 by Maude Phelps Hutchins.

Random House, Inc.: "Jurge Dulrumple," by John O'Hara. Reprinted from *The Cape Cod Lighter,* by John O'Hara. Copyright © 1961, 1962 by John O'Hara; "Divorce in Naples," by William Faulkner. Reprinted from *Collected Stories of William Faulkner.* Copyright 1931 and renewed 1959 by William Faulkner.

Charles Scribner's Sons: "The Sea Change," by Ernest Hemingway. Reprinted from *Winner Take Nothing,* by Ernest Hemingway. Copyright 1933 by Charles Scribner's Sons.

Vanguard Press, Inc.: "Just Boys," by James T. Farrell. Reprinted from *The Short Stories of James T. Farrell.* Copyright 1934 by James T. Farrell.

The Viking Press, Inc.: "Chagrin in Three Parts," by Graham Greene. Reprinted from *May We Borrow Your Husband,* by Graham Greene. Copyright © 1966 by Graham Greene; "Miss A. and Miss M.," by Elizabeth Taylor. Reprinted from *The Devastating Boys,* by Elizabeth Taylor. Copyright © 1971 by Elizabeth Taylor.

Tennessee Williams: "Two on a Party," by Tennessee Williams. Reprinted from *Hard Candy,* by Tennessee Williams. Copyright 1954 by Tennessee Williams. Reprinted by permission of the author.

CONTENTS

INSIDE: TOWARD NEW DEFINITIONS

INTRODUCTION

IN A 1976 REVIEW OF THE RITZ, A MEDIOCRE MOVIE SET IN A TURKISH BATH for homosexuals, the film critic of a sophisticated New York weekly complained that she could no longer use the words "gay" or "girl" in their *normal* contexts. She suggested that this expropriation or condemnation of "innocent" words by activists and political troublemakers not only impoverishes the English language but also inconveniences its users. The reviewer's insensitivity is, of course, much less vicious than the media's usual responses to gay activists and feminists, though I report with satisfaction that the same weekly refused me permission to reprint stories about gays (in this case, gay women) whose rights it controls.

The example illuminates two issues central to the lives of gays and feminists: the difficulty of nomenclature and the relationship of oppressed groups to each other. The relation of feminists and gay men and women is the easier issue to discuss, though it appears thornier. In the early seventies, when men and women were energetically involved in forming alliances for civil-libertarian purposes, it was clear that homosexuals and gay and straight feminists shared the sense of disenfranchisement and deprivation. At the same time, dismayingly, it was clear that the three groups, homosexual men, radical lesbians, and straight feminist women, were engaging in a great deal of denial: the men felt that the women were too "demanding" if they expected homosexuals to be more tolerant of women's needs, that men, too, were oppressed as homosexuals burdened by the anger and distrust of militant women who so often treated them as if they were straight men, i.e., oppressors. Lesbian women responded that gay oppression was a feminist issue: that male homosexuals have always been despised because they were like women, because they assumed women's roles sexually, and because they eschewed masculine stereotypes. If homosexual men were unwilling to fight for women's rights, then it was better for women to fight alone. Moreover, some women made the reluctance of homosexual men properly to identify the problem into an excuse for separatism, for an opportunity to be free from male presence, however sympathetic, since for some women all male presence was and is suspect. Ironically, radical lesbians were encountering a similar resistance from many straight women in the movement, who felt lesbian demands would deflect attention to special and sensational issues and finally usurp the seriousness of the need for solidarity with ordinary women unprepared for an identification in sisterhood with deviants. The result of these schisms has been welcomed in the heartlands: homosexuals and lesbians tend to work separately rather than together, lesbians and straight women are still in search of a dialogue, and years of mutual support, sympathy, and strength have been lost. At the moment, there are some gingerly signs of rapprochement, and it is to the creation of that *entente* that I dedicate this book.

One of the issues that immediately arose when men and women tried to organize was what to call themselves: "homosexual" was recognized by almost everyone to mean exclusively male experience (although properly speaking it does not); "lesbian" was just as gender-oriented. "Homosexual" and "lesbian," iterated constantly, became tedious. The process of elimination left little: it left "gay." Most "gays" are unhappy with the label, although no one is miserable about it. Their experiences and the stories in this anthology testify to the irony of the term. For all its limitations, "gay" is the only unpompous, unpsychological term acceptable to most men and women, one already widely used and available to heterosexuals without automatically suggesting something pejorative. Perhaps one limitation more felt than expressed is implied by grammar: used as a noun, "gay" sounds awkward; as an adjective, it is also somewhat stiff: it seems overpolite to emphasize "gay men and women." For a group in search of their identity, "gay" offers little help in self-definition.

One purpose of this collection is to assist definition by exploring some meanings of the experience that the word has connoted in the past, and by noting the changes in meaning, tentative but clear, as we approach the present. Many gays would like to believe that political exposure of gay oppression since the Stonewall years* has made a difference in the lives of

*The Stonewall Bar was the setting for the first overt rebellion by American homosexuals against police harassment. In 1969 the violent response of the men arrested in a police raid inspired the New York gay community with pride and a new awareness of the possibility of political action that they had not entertained before. In gratitude, gays mark the anniversary of the event with an annual march designated to begin Gay Pride Week.

homosexuals and lesbians. No one turns around any more, no one sneers when two men or women walk arm in arm, at least not in New York City near Bloomingdale's or in Greenwich Village. But two liberated neighborhoods in one libertine city do not a revolution make. If New York sometimes seems to be entirely gay, that is a comforting illusion: Warsaw looked very Jewish in 1940. Most gays in America do not live in New York or San Francisco, and though most do live in cities, Los Angeles and Washington and Chicago still insist that these lives be covert. In New York, where life is overt or covert by choice, the establishment's revenge is expressed by repeated failures to pass a simple, constitutionally guaranteed civil-liberties bill specifically protecting gays from prejudice in housing and employment.

I do not mean to denigrate the real and tangible changes of the past ten years. Life today is less of a hassle; it is much easier to come out than it was; there is far more support from families, peers, and lovers than before; for every taste and need, there are numerous organizations offering information, company, and counsel. But the pain of coming out is there, and the comforts are in ghettos; the sense of alienation from family and from one's own past is often traumatic. Life is still permeated by a sense of loss. For all their new freedoms, gays are still furious, and the fury turns inward as often as it did before. It is not unusual for men and women in their forties, successful in their jobs, as content with their lovers and/or sexual lives as any sane person can be these days, to admit a trifle regretfully that they still regard their homosexuality as a "weakness." After one forgets the inarticulate frustration of living under cover, after one has been out for awhile and the obsession with secrecy and publicity is diminished or forgotten, one compares the pain en route to the destination, and one wonders. Between the external oppression of duplicity and the internal oppression of self-contempt, the way is still hazardous. In the past, the common denominator has been the unique pressure of "passing," of spending a little if not a great deal of one's life masked as a heterosexual: for some, the only moments without hypocrisy were in bed; for others, the mask became the private face as well. But for all, the burden of finding out who one is as a human sexual being is a problem no amount of political freedom can solve. Most gays claim that if their social oppressions were removed, they would be happy to solve the psychological ones imposed by personality and character: "Let us be as neurotic as everyone else." Perhaps. Perhaps without the miasma of guilt hanging more or less heavily over most gay lives, adult life would be no more difficult for homosexuals and lesbians than it is for everyone else. Given the emotional quality of ordinary life these days, that is not a very grandiose hope. But the day gays can assert who they are without penalty is still a long way off. Meanwhile, the question implicit in that assertion remains to be answered: Who are we?

"Obsession," "compulsion," and "arrestment" are no longer fashionable terms; even "deviance" is called politically naïve, psychologically suspect. "Difference" and "preference" are both more polite and truly more just, but not very clear. Today, there seem to be fewer guidelines for definition than ever before, though most of the images we've inherited we can do without. Who needs to be told by heterosexual doctors what our psyches and our sexuality mean? But gays have only recently learned to turn deaf ears to conventional and authoritarian experts, unlike women, who have long been suspicious about what men have said their sexuality means. Nowadays, feminists everywhere are testifying to their own sexuality, and their discoveries are revolutionary. Women are turning to their own collective past, to the documents of women's lives, in order to rewrite their history. For gays, that history is still unwritten: the documents are often lost or invisible or were never written, and the past is filled with contradictory testimony and homophobic authority. It is possible to define oneself without the past but not very probable, and infinitely more difficult.

If history is reluctant to speak, literature is not. Here is a collection of testimonies, some still touched by sentimental tragedy or romance, some still content with revelations verging on prurience, but all seeing the plight of gay men and women in serious ways.

Proust's "Before Dark" is a new translation of material not reprinted since 1893 until *The Ladder,* a lesbian periodical, rediscovered it in 1960. Here one notes certain themes archetypal in gay fiction: the issue of confession, later to be called coming out, is as central to the story as it is to the gay experience. This is the first clue to the nature of gayness: it is, of course, a social stance, as the act of confession is a social act, a way of defining one's relations to others. Alone, one is neither gay nor gloomy—one is oneself. Proust infers that the protagonist's honesty is a necessary, painful absolution, that her duplicity has not only falsified her relation to the young man by permitting him to think their platonism has been a mutual choice, when in fact her aversion to heterosexuality has determined their relationship, but that her secrecy has somehow poisoned her psychically as well. It is not clear whether her suicidal guilt is about her lesbianism or her dishonesty, and while both are treated sympathetically, they are not separate issues. Associated with this theme is the question of romantic relations between gays and straights, a dominant motif of lesbian fiction, much of which concerns women who have been heterosexual for part of their adult lives.

Though erotic desire may limit one's choice of a partner to a single sex, and within that to ever narrowing possibilities depending on taste and need and other implausibilities, romantic yearning with its diffused sexuality and psychological ambivalences is even more eccentric in its choices, preferring in fact to select the beloved where he or she is most unavailable. Though the plot's melodrama obscures the tragic misalliance of the two characters, Proust articulates a conventional view that is to echo in much early fiction: the shame of one's deviance destroys all possibilities of happiness in love.

Gertrude Stein, on the other hand, offers the unconventional as early as 1903. "Mabel Neathe" from *Q.E.D.* explores three gay women in a triangle and assumes that misery between people is characterological, not biological, in origin. Compared to Proust's naïve tragedy, Stein offers us three women, one unsympathetic, one ambiguous, and one (Adele/Stein) the innocent voice of both reason and feeling. Stein's women are in a universal situation, and its overtones are characteristic of the fiction of many women who do not see their lesbian heroines as alienated from society in general and from themselves and their desires in particular. It is interesting that Stein is quite clear about the women's lesbianism but never explicit, a trend among women writers well into the 1950's. Usually, women examine their themes in the social and psychological context of ordinary life far more than men, who are more moralistic, and who often see gay life as tragically alienated.

The fiction of the twenties by D. H. Lawrence, Radclyffe Hall, and E. M. Forster offers a much wider range of themes. Not surprisingly, Lawrence's is the most complex, exploring the issue of romantic homoeroticism between men who think of themselves as heterosexual, and Forster's the most contemporary, presenting a totally unjudgmental view of casual sexuality, which is shown as neither promiscuous nor amoral. Both writers seem to agree that erotic feelings between men are natural and spontaneous, apparently rooted far deeper than our knowledge of the "psychological" has yet revealed. Though Lawrence emphasizes the emotional bonding between men and Forster the physical bonding (a reversal of what their literary reputations would lead us to assume), for both the desirability of such bonding is never questioned, though the possibilities for permanence and fulfillment are. Coincidentally, both pieces were suppressed by their authors. In Forster's case, the suppression is discussed in the preface he wrote to *Maurice.* Lawrence does not seem to have spoken of why this original chapter was not only dropped but never used elsewhere in the novel in the same way. In the final version of *Women in Love,* Rupert and Gerald try but fail to achieve an intense full relationship, but this is seen against the background of the men's already established relations to their lovers, Ursula and Gudrun, and to their families and pasts. The fullness of such a background diminishes the particularity of their need for each other. Both men are complex, and their need for each other is part of that complexity. But if *Women in Love* had opened with this Prologue, where we know nothing of the men except their attraction to each other, the impact of their homoeroticism would be much more powerful, particularly when contrasted to Rupert's stifling affair with Hermione.

Radclyffe Hall is a sentimental writer whose central theme is the tragedy of lesbianism. In all her work lesbianism is regarded as an error of biology: lesbians are really men in women's bodies. Though Hall's notion is repudiated today, unfortunately it was commonplace in her time among various sexual authorities (from whom no doubt the view was borrowed) and many gay women themselves. Male-identified women are not necessarily butch dykes, of course, nor do "masculine" women necessarily feel entrapped by femaleness. The image of the woman who loves women as she imagines men do is one of great pathos, but the lives of many women in our century have been shadowed by just such feelings and illusions. Though contemporary lesbians correctly insist that women love women uniquely, one does not need to apologize for the limitations of Radclyffe Hall. More than any other woman writer in the first fifty years of this century, she gave gay women, and often men, an imagery that corresponded to their own sense of tragedy and dislocation.

However, though Hall is dated, Joan O'Donovan's "Johnnie" perpetuates the same stereotype. What was tragic in the twenties becomes pathetic in the fifties. O'Donovan is concerned with the pathology of male identification, particularly when it is supported by an immediate reality that is psychopathic: both stories take place during wars, when women's roles were less prescribed, when *de facto* equality was necessary, when women were not only tolerated in "men's" work, but welcomed. Modern history has told us how Pyrrhic that equality was: women were later not only deprived of the jobs they so confidently showed they could do as well as men, but many were coerced into believing that deprivation was just.

The stories from the thirties extend the theme of sexual identity, particularly the journey from heterosexuality to homosexuality. William Carlos Williams in "A Knife of the Times" and Ernest Hemingway in "A Sea Change" give sympathetic if somewhat nervous approbation to heroines about to enter their first lesbian relationships, leaving a world of men and family not because heterosexual relationships are untenable, but because they are inadequate. Williams writes about a woman who has been closeted all her life in her intense desire and love for one other woman, a friend from childhood. Despite an adequate marriage and six children, Ethel cannot "outgrow" her feelings, which intensify to an irrepressible romantic passion in her middle age. The image of lesbianism as monogamous, as the fixed unalterable feeling of one woman for one other is an attractive romantic notion, if a somewhat patronizing one. It is also a handy rationalization for men to explain to *their* satisfaction what is often inexplicable to all men. This mystery is the premise of Hemingway's treatment of the same situation: a beautiful young woman leaving a man she has loved (and claims to love still) for a woman. The man is angry, bewildered, contemptuous, and helpless. His acquiescence is a graceless gesture of defeat, but it is also believable and intricately human. What is the proper response when one's lover falls in love with someone else? For some, self-pity is their consolation, for others, fury. Does one blame oneself, one's beloved, or the third party? Obviously, there are no adult standards; one adopts, if one is lucky, the most expedient attitude for survival. If the loss of a lover always seems incredible, it is inconceivable to men that the victorious rival should be a woman, and stirs up a tumult of feelings not only about these specific women, but about all women and their image of their own masculinity as well. These issues are painfully difficult to examine honestly, and perhaps impossible to resolve.

James T. Farrell and William Faulkner articulate two highly specialized worlds of gay men, worlds that have in common the exclusion of women or their relegation to the brothel: rough trade and men at sea. While Faulkner explores homoerotic feelings between men somewhat as Lawrence did, his proletarian men lack Rupert Birkin's driving introspection. It is a little simple-minded to equate introspectiveness with class origin, but it is as accurate a generalization as most about the proletariat, upon which all writers project their fantasies, except perhaps those who remain within it. In Faulkner's story of men who live at sea without women, we are not given the anthropological platitude about men turning to other men in the absence of "natural outlets" (see T. E. Lawrence). On the contrary, the whores of Naples are omnipresent in the story. It is the sordidness of relations with women that sustains the innocence of the two men's eroticized friendship. Farrell also gives us a society of men that is totally eroticized, though violent and debased. "Just Boys" is precocious in its image of the self-destructiveness and despair of that underworld Genet would find so interesting philosophically. If the sexual politics of Genet's vision is too nightmarish and too offensive to most gays, Farrell's Chicago with its black studs and bitchy queens is quite real in all its unpleasantness. While Farrell seems more interested in the sensationalism and violence of this fringe of the city than in the psychological or political value of these men's lives, that is a question of the reader's biases, not the writer's. Men who define what is sexually desirable for themselves exclusively in terms of hypermasculinity and a potentially violent machoism are by no means vestiges of the past.

The wide range of fiction in the forties and fifties illuminates the narrow world of gay life even more thoroughly. John Horne Burns's "Momma" is perhaps the first story to use the setting of a gay bar as its locus and meaning. That the bar is in Naples and that the story is as much concerned with its exploitative straight owner, Momma herself, are not irrelevancies. From their inception to the present day, gay bars are almost universally owned by straights, often with strong ties to the criminal world and to police corruption and bribery; these same owners, however superficially tolerant, act exclusively from venal motives. The homey neighborhood refuge is as rare as the private club; both are exceptions to the rule of the bar world, which is devoted to an ambiance of anonymity that facilitates easy pickups and transient contacts. The speciality of the bar in Burns's story is that it is as social as it is sexual; perhaps for that reason it is closed by the police. The bar as the surrogate for the brothel seems acceptable to most societies as long as the police are complacent and paid off, and the bars themselves hidden or discreet. But the bar that offers social solace, that provides companionship as well as company for the night, is more threatening and poses questions for police authority. The sexual bar with its lucrative traffic in liquor, drugs, and flesh is easily accommodated by a contemptuous urban authority. The gay world, in America at least, is the only classless society, although its egalitarianism is hardly utopian. What replaces money and education as the basis of privilege is youth and beauty, two far more fragile commodities. It would be nice but stupid to say that these values are almost universally accepted by gay men and women because their society is materialistic or shallow. It is true that the obsession with youth and beauty is excessively American, but the fact that gays unquestionably accept and intensify these values is undeniably part of their history. In New York's discreetly hidden waterfront bars, the only patrons who "belong" are the pretty young whores. It is an irony that under capitalism, where money and property have safeguarded practically anyone who has them, regardless of how he got them, the bourgeois gay is as vulnerable as the impoverished prostitute.

The social bar attracts people with diverse needs; it permits talk and perhaps criticism, the very conditions under which people gather a sense of community and mutual support necessary for social action, if not the open defiance of their exploitation. The fury that erupted at the Stonewall Bar in Greenwich Village was not premeditated; it resulted from years of contemptuous toleration by police and bar owners whom gays had made rich and from whom they received little except the opportunity to reinforce their self-contempt and feelings of helplessness.

The attraction of the bar is the freedom it offers one to act as outrageously as one wishes, not merely to be aggressive in sexual pursuit but to be as assertive as one can manage in one's social behavior—what would later be called "camping." Susan Sontag in her 1964 essay on camp was the first to try to give an extended description of the term. What she noted was that this form of behavior and the particular ironic point of view it implied were already widespread among homosexuals *and* heterosexuals, especially at those levels of society where the two mixed freely and somewhat openly. No one disputes that camp is a homosexual invention, a primary defense of gays against a hostile, intrusive society which keeps them ghettoed in boring bars. Christopher Isherwood's "Letters and Life" gives us that society in its most benevolent guise.

Camping is seen where gays feel sufficiently at ease to parody themselves without fear of the outsider's derision. What they are parodying in their lives is the artifice of their disguises; thus, gays camp by exaggerating into a self-conscious vulgarity the very attributes of femininity and masculinity they have eschewed. Men behaving in a flamboyantly effeminate manner, women aping the most machoistic stances are parodying those heterosexual values and attitudes that have been most socially oppressive to them and most erotically attractive. Men pretending to be a kind of woman who in fact has never existed (except ironically, as the product of homosexual imagination) often camp only in the absence of women; women disguised as butch he-men act out their fantasies toward other women. Thus the very exclusiveness of most gay life, the segregation of men and women into their own bars and social circles seems to create a need for the illusion of two sexes in a unisex world. Men who imitate the mannerisms of those women who most slavishly acquiesce to their own oppression have their equivalents in women whose behavior most resembles those men who brutishly despise women. The ironies are obvious; perhaps these reversals and inversions are the final camp statement about artifice and illusion; they certainly are the direst version of that duality.

That camp expresses self-contempt and simultaneously releases a contempt for straightness is one of the ambivalences gays have felt toward their oppression: to hate it and so to incorporate it. Though Isherwood treated the idea of camp before anyone else in popular fiction, he takes only a glance at it. Clearer examples of camp sensibility are found in the characters of Tennessee Williams' fiction and drama. Blanche and Stanley are probably his best-known examples; in Blanche's insufferable femininity, her obsessive artifice and illusions, and Stanley's posturings, we have images of tragicomic camp. In "Two on a Party," Williams gives us that sensibility as it transforms the entire world into a theater of sexual farce: two people exist solely for their pursuit of dubious pleasures, and only their drunkenness protects them from realizing the impoverishment of their choice. The gay man and the straight woman who have made an alliance of convenience in pursuit of the stud never experience any reciprocation of tenderness or desire, except with each other. There the tenderness and desire are riven into an impotence they finally cannot tolerate.

James Purdy's comedy "You May Safely Gaze" is a variation on the image of macho camp. Two men discussing a third, who is clearly homosexual, are suspect in their irritation with him. What upsets the speaker is not the obvious albeit unacknowledged homosexuality of Milo, but his exhibitionism, his childlike display of his body. Comic homoeroticism is a welcome relief after so much direness. Perhaps the most glaring absence in fiction about gay life is the sense of the comic; the subject seems not to lend itself easily to comedy, however much the life lends itself the sense of the absurd. Purdy depicts his awareness of the absurdity of so much posturing and so much moral outrage about it. In a world apparently imperiled on all fronts, it seems that only comedy can come to terms with a puritanism that is really trivial.

This sense of the absurd enlivens the fiction of Gore Vidal, John O'Hara, Graham Greene, and Edmund White. Vidal and White both deal with gay society abroad, though hardly the same one. Vidal's milieu is Paris in the forties, that small coterie world of expatriate Americans in the pleasure spas of Capri and Deauville, a world speckled with such forbidden pleasures as opium and kept boys. White gives a more proletarian version of the same sins in Puerto Rico, where both the drugs and the boys are coarser and cheaper.

O'Hara and Greene give us lesbian comedies, satires on heterosexual credulity, creating situations about fully drawn women who discover their solace and success with other women. These two pieces are the sixties counterpart to the very somber treatment William Carlos Williams and Ernest Hemingway gave to the theme of women awakening to a new sense of self.

The popularity of adolescence as the psychological setting of many stories is appropriate to a genre whose major theme is the search for sexual identity. The stories of Paul Bowles, Marris Murray, Maude Hutchins, and Elizabeth Taylor are neither banally psychoanalytic nor sentimentally tragic. In "Pages from Cold Point," Bowles is concerned with decadence and moral horror. His story of a gay father who discovers that his adolescent son is both homosexual and completely corrupt, but who fails to discover his own emotional bankruptcy and moral vacancy, is appalling and powerful. Maude Hutchins in "The Wreck" gives us an extraordinary vignette about adolescent sexuality gone awry, so that it verges on the pathological and becomes vulnerable to the passing adult marauder. Marris Murray's "My Brother Writes Poetry for an Englishman" provides a refreshing variation: her adolescent sees too much, but morally profits from it. What the young girl learns is not only that homosexuality is an adult choice, but that heterosexual adults are cruelly irrational when confronted with it. The endurance of this theme is illustrated in Elizabeth Taylor's study of a young girl's discovery of the lesbian relationship between two women, one of whom she adores, a discovery that is treated as comparatively uneventful for her. In "Miss A. and Miss M.", what the innocent protagonist learns is not that these two women who seem to live such idyllic and autonomous lives are lesbians, but that their lives are filled with conflict. Reversing the theme of the once heterosexual woman now abandoning that identity, Taylor explores the moral and emotional havoc that results when one woman deserts her lover for a straight marriage of convenience. The fall from innocence in this story resembles Marris Murray's: the child learns essentially ethical, not sexual information. She is never the same, because she has prematurely discovered adult callousness and disloyalty, rather than sexual difference, in those she has believed to be perfect models.

The remaining stories are as varied as my choice could make them. Helen Essary Ansell and Ingeborg Bachmann are both compassionate about characters who are confused and conflicted, though not necessarily about their lesbianism. Though the two most recent stories in the collection, Doris Betts's "Burning the Bed" and Jane Rule's "Middle Children," are about gays, gayness is no longer the central issue. Instead, Betts pessimistically examines the alienation of father and daughter in that final obligation of all children, to bury their parents, and Rule understatedly explores how two people of the same sex commit themselves with honesty without having to forgo all the benefits of conventional life, and without pretending that what they are trying to achieve is what everyone else has.

Whether gays can sustain ongoing relationships without the bedrock of institutionalized marriage and family and without imitating the patterns of their families is an open question. Some, of course, have monogamous relationships of lifelong duration that are as conventional as those of their heterosexual counterparts. But for most, the models of marriage and family life teach little that brings any sense of fulfillment. To live all one's life being told that one is different does not make for a life chosen to look like everyone else's. I don't question those who have managed to be gay and live straight and get away with it. Few of us have had the chance to try, and fewer of us want to. What heterosexual men and women today complain about most vociferously is their disaffection with the institutions of marriage and family; this hardly seems the time to ape them. What gays' choices are is less clear but, strangely, less problematic. Heterosexuals say that marriage is untenable but that there seems to be no imaginable alternative for most of them; serial monogamy may be an improvement, but it is hardly a qualitative difference. Both men and women claim that the traditional obligations of motherhood and fatherhood are no longer gratifying to them or viable for their children, yet the alternative of having no children is open only in those enlightened societies where fertility and barrenness no longer represent moral values. Most gays have already learned to live without children, though many learned first the grief of having none. It is interesting that the only story of a gay parent, though certainly not a typical one, is Paul Bowles's. In 1950, part of the shocking nature of his story was merely the admission that homosexuals sometimes have sons. Today the gay parent is not an anomaly. Gay men and women are exploring the possibilities of satisfying and "unorthodox" relationships, fully conscious of the universal difficulty all people have of committing themselves to one another.

If traditions are under fire, they still have the authority of the past. The courage to experiment and explore alternatives is not a facile one, for new standards must be created by which to judge old needs. Perhaps gays have a singular advantage: if the old needs are recognized as untenable, they are easier to forgo. If heterosexuals cannot imagine what their new choices are going to be, neither can gays. The difference is that straights are hopeful there will be other choices. Gays are now demanding an equal opportunity to hope. No one expects life to be more successful or less problematic once the possibility of choice exists, but we are certain that without such an option, our lives will continue to be as intolerable as our history testifies them to have been. We are of another persuasion; without the freedom to explore that persuasion, what remains is coercion and its consuming effects: rage, confusion, and self-contempt.

It is no help that homosexuality and lesbianism are "acceptable" and exploitable subjects for popular fiction, the theater, and the media, although one may be more pleased than sorry that our existence is acknowledged. But *The Boys in the Band* and *The Ritz,* if they do little harm, do little good. They are too sentimental, too vulgar to help us understand where we have been. In the testimony of literature, we can learn where we have been, and perhaps that will help us choose where we are going.

SEYMOUR KLEINBERG

PROLOGUE: UNDERGROUND

MARCEL PROUST

before dark

"THOUGH I'M STILL QUITE STRONG, YOU KNOW" (SHE SAID TO ME WITH something more intimate in her voice, the way we use our inflections to attenuate something we must tell those we love, something too harsh), "I might die from one day to the next—yet I'm still capable of living several months more. So I don't want to wait any longer to tell you something that's weighing on my conscience; you'll understand later how painful it was for me to speak of it." Her pupils, symbolic blue flowers, paled as if they were withering. I thought she was about to cry, but no tears came. "I know I'm deliberately destroying all hope of being admired by my best friend after I die, tarnishing the memory I sometimes imagine he might have kept of my life—a life lovelier, more harmonious than it has really been. But the claims of an esthetic arrangement"—she smiled, uttering the phrase with the tiny ironical exaggeration that always came into her voice at such moments, rare though they were in her conversation—"cannot suppress the need for truth that forces me to speak. Listen to me, Leslie, I must tell you . . . But before I do, give me my coat—it's chilly out here on the terrace, and the doctor doesn't want me getting up and down, if I can help it."

I put her coat around her. The sun had set, and the sea, glimpsed through the apple trees, was mauve. Fragile as withered wreathes and persistent as regrets, tiny pink and blue clouds were floating on the horizon. A melancholy row of poplars led away into the shadows, heads bowed in a churchly pink, resigned. The last rays of the sun, without touching their trunks, tinged their branches, fastening garlands of light to those balustrades of shadow. The breeze mingled three odors: the sea, wet leaves, milk. Never had the Norman countryside sweetened the evening sadness with a more voluptuous touch, but I had no taste for it, so stirred was I by my friend's mysterious words.

"I have loved you a great deal, but I have given you very little, my poor friend—"

"—Forgive me, Françoise, if I break all the rules of this literary form and interrupt a confession I should have heard out in silence," I exclaimed, trying to make a joke to calm her a little, but in reality deadly sad. "How can you say you have given me very little? You have given me all the more in that I asked you for less—much more in fact than if the senses had had a share in our affection. I have adored you, and you have tended me, supernatural as a madonna, gentle as a nurse. I have loved you with an affection whose sagacity was troubled by no hope of carnal pleasure. And in exchange, did you not bring me, over an exquisite tea-table, an incomparable friendship, a conversation embellished by nature herself, as well as by how many bunches of fresh roses. Only you, with your motherly and expressive hands, could have soothed my fevered brow, poured honey between my burning lips, set noble images in my life. Dear friend, I should rather not hear this absurd confession. Give me your hands, let me kiss them. It is chilly out here—let's go inside and talk about something else."

"Leslie, you must hear me out, even so, my poor darling. It must be done. Have you never wondered why I remained a widow, since I was widowed at twenty . . ."

"Suppose I had, it was none of my affair. You are a person so superior to all the rest that what in you was a weakness would have a quality of beauty and nobility lacking in other people's fine actions. You have done as you saw fit, and I am certain you have never done anything but what was delicate and pure."

"Pure! Leslie, your confidence pains me like an anticipated reproach. Listen . . . I don't know how to tell you this. It's much worse than if I had loved you, for instance, or even someone else, yes truly, anyone else."

I turned pale—pale as a sheet, pale as she was, alas, and trembling lest she notice, I tried to laugh and repeated without quite knowing what I was saying, "Oh, 'anyone else'—you really are the strangest creature! . . ."

"I said 'much worse', Leslie, and I'm completely in the dark about it, luminous though the moment is. Evenings, we see things more calmly, but I do not see this thing clearly, and there are exorbitant shadows upon my life. But if in my heart of hearts I believe this was not the worst, why should I be ashamed to tell it to you?—Was it the worst?"

I didn't understand, but at grips with a horrible agitation impossible to conceal, I began to tremble with fear, as if in a nightmare. I dared not look down the row of trees now filled with darkness and dread that stretched before us, and yet I dared not close my eyes. Her voice, which had grown lower, breaking with ever more intense sadness, suddenly rose again, and in quite a natural tone, almost brightly, she said, "You remember when my poor friend Dorothy was caught with a singer—I've forgotten the woman's name . . ." (I was relieved by this digression, which I hoped would distract us from the account of her sufferings) "how you explained to me at the time that we had no right to despise her. I recall your words: How can we be offended by behavior which Socrates—it concerned men in his case, but comes down to the same thing—who drank hemlock rather than commit an injustice, gaily approved in his chosen friends? If love that is fruitful, destined to perpetuate the race, honored as a family duty, a social duty, a human duty, is superior to a purely voluptuous love, on the other hand there is no hierarchy among the sterile loves, and it is not less moral—or rather, no more immoral—that a woman should take pleasure with another woman rather than with a being of another sex. The cause of such love lies in a nervous alteration which is too exclusively nervous to involve a moral content. We cannot say that because most people see things we call red as red that those who see them as violet are mistaken. Moreover—you added, if we refine pleasure to the point of making it aesthetic, since the body of a man and the body of a woman can each be quite as beautiful in its own way as the other, who can say why a really artistic woman would not be in love with another woman. In truly artistic natures, physical attraction or repulsion is modified by contemplation of the beautiful. Most people turn from jellyfish with disgust. Michelet, sensitive to their colors, gathered them with delight. Despite my repulsion for oysters, after I had thought of their life in the sea which their taste would now evoke for me, they have become—especially when I was some distance from the sea—a suggestive treat. Hence with the physical aptitudes, pleasures of contact, cravings for food, delight of the senses—all return to be grafted onto the place where our taste for the beautiful has taken root . . . Don't you suppose such arguments could help a woman physically predisposed to this kind of love to become aware of her vague curiosity, if certain statuettes by Rodin, for instance, had already triumphed—artistically—over her repugnances . . . that such arguments would excuse her in her own eyes, would reassure her conscience: and that this might be a great misfortune!"

I don't know how I kept from crying out, then—simultaneously the meaning of her confession and the sentiment of my dreadful responsibility flashed upon me. But letting myself be directed blindly by one of those higher inspirations which, when we are too far beneath ourselves, too inadequate to play our part in life, suddenly assume our mask and play our role quite eagerly, I said almost calmly: "I assure you I should feel no remorse, for truly I have no feeling of scorn or even of pity for such women."

Mysteriously, with an infinite sweetness of gratitude, she said to me, "You are generous." Then a little lower, and quickly, with a weary expression, as one disdains even while expressing certain earthy details, she added: "You know, I realized perfectly well for all your secret ways with everyone, that the bullet they could not remove and which has determined my illness —that you are still trying to find who shot it at me. And I've always hoped that bullet would never be discovered. Well, since medicine seems so sure of itself nowadays, and because you might suspect certain people who are innocent, I am confessing. But I prefer to tell you the truth . . ." She added, with that sweetness she had in her voice when she began to speak of her imminent death, in order to comfort the pain which what she was saying would cause by the way in which she spoke, "It was I, in one of those moments of despair which are so natural to anyone who really *lives,* it was I who . . . shot myself."

I wanted to go over and embrace her, but though I tried to contain myself, as I stood beside her, an irresistible force choked me, my eyes filled with tears, and I began to sob. At first she wiped my eyes, laughed a little, gently consoled me as she used to do, with a thousand graces. But deep within her a tremendous self-pity—no, a pity for herself and for me as well, welled up, brimming out of her eyes and falling in scalding tears. We wept together: concord of a wide and melancholy harmony! Our mingled pities now had as their object something larger than ourselves and over which we wept gladly, freely. I tried to drink her poor tears out of her hands, but others kept falling, by which she let herself become as if hypnotized. Her hands turned cold as the pale leaves which had fallen into the fountain basin. And never had we had so much pain, so much pleasure.

1893

TRANSLATED FROM THE FRENCH BY RICHARD HOWARD

1976

GERTRUDE STEIN

::

MABEL NEATHE

1

MABEL NEATHE'S ROOM FULLY MET THE HABIT OF MANY HOURS OF UNAGgressive lounging. She had command of an exceptional talent for atmosphere. The room with its very good shape, dark walls but mediocre furnishings and decorations was more than successfully unobtrusive, it had perfect quality. It had always just the amount of light necessary to make mutual observation pleasant and yet to leave the decorations in obscurity or rather to inspire a faith in their being good.

It is true of rooms as of human beings that they are bound to have one good feature and as a Frenchwoman dresses to that feature in such fashion that the observer must see that and notice nothing else, so Mabel Neathe had arranged her room so that one enjoyed one's companions and observed consciously only the pleasant fire-place.

But the important element in the success of the room as atmosphere consisted in Mabel's personality. The average guest expressed it in the simple comment that she was a perfect hostess, but the more sympathetic observers put it that it was not that she had the manners of a perfect hostess but the more unobtrusive good manners of a gentleman.

The chosen and they were a few individuals rather than a set found this statement inadequate although it was abundantly difficult for them to explain their feeling. Such an Italian type frustrated by its setting in an unimpassioned and moral community was of necessity misinterpreted although its charm was valued. Mabel's ancestry did not supply any explanation of her character. Her kinship with decadent Italy was purely spiritual.

The capacity for composing herself with her room in unaccented and perfect values was the most complete attribute of that kinship that her modern environment had developed. As for the rest it after all amounted to failure, failure as power, failure as an individual. Her passions in spite of their intensity failed to take effective hold on the objects of her desire. The subtlety and impersonality of her atmosphere which in a position of recognised power would have had compelling attraction, here in a community of equals where there could be no mystery as the seeker had complete liberty in seeking she lacked the vital force necessary to win. Although she was unscrupulous the weapons she used were too brittle, they could always be broken in pieces by a vigorous guard.

Modern situations never endure for a long enough time to allow subtle and elaborate methods to succeed. By the time they are beginning to bring about results the incident is forgotten. Subtlety moreover in order to command efficient power must be realised as dangerous and the modern world is a difficult place in which to be subtly dangerous, the risks are too great. Mabel might now compel by inspiring pity, she could never in her world compel by inspiring fear.

Adele had been for some time one of Mabel's selected few. Her enjoyment of ease and her habit of infinite leisure, combined with her vigorous personality and a capacity for endless and picturesque analysis of all things human had established a claim which her instinct for intimacy without familiarity and her ready adjustment to the necessary impersonality which a relation with Mabel demanded, had confirmed.

"It's more or less of a bore getting back for we are all agreed that Baltimore isn't much of a town to live in, but this old habit is certainly very pleasant" she remarked as she stretched herself comfortably on the couch "and after all, it is much more possible to cultivate such joys when a town isn't wildly exciting. No my tea isn't quite right" she continued. "It's worth while making a fuss you know when there is a possibility of obtaining perfection, otherwise any old tea is good enough. Anyhow what's the use of anything as long as it isn't Spain? You must really go there some time." They continued to make the most of their recent experiences in this their first meeting.

"Did you stay long in New York after you landed?" Mabel finally asked. "Only a few days" Adele replied "I suppose Helen wrote you that I saw her for a little while. We lunched together before I took my train," she added with a consciousness of the embarrassment that that meeting had caused her. "You didn't expect to like her so much, did you?" Mabel suggested. "I remember you used to say that she impressed you as almost coarse and rather decadent and that you didn't even find her interesting. And you know" she added "how much you dislike decadence."

Adele met her with frank bravado. "Of course I said that and as yet I don't retract it. I am far from sure that she is not both coarse and decadent and I don't approve of either of those qualities. I do grant you however that she is interesting, at least as a character, her talk interests me no more than it ever did" and then facing the game more boldly, she continued "but you know I really know very little about her except that she dislikes her parents and goes in for society a good deal. What else is there?"

Mabel drew a very unpleasant picture of that parentage. Her description of the father a successful lawyer and judge, and an excessively brutal and at the same time small-minded man who exercised great ingenuity in making himself unpleasant was not alluring, nor that of the mother who was very religious and spent most of her time mourning that it was not Helen that had been taken instead of the others a girl and boy whom she remembered as sweet gentle children.

One day, when Helen was a young girl she heard her mother say to the father "Isn't it sad that Helen should have been the one to be left."

Mabel described their attempts to break Helen's spirit and their anger at their lack of success. "And now" Mabel went on "they object to everything that she does, to her friends and to everything she is interested in. Mrs. T. always sides with her husband. Of course they are proud of her good looks, her cleverness and social success but she won't get married and she doesn't care to please the people her mother wants her to belong to. They don't dare to say anything to her now because she is so much better able to say things that hurt than they are."

"I suppose there is very little doubt that Helen can be uncommonly nasty when she wants to be," laughed Adele, "and if she isn't sensitive to other people's pain, a talent for being successful in bitter repartee might become a habit that would make her a most uncomfortable daughter. I believe I might condole with the elders if they were to confide their sorrows to me. By the way doesn't Helen address them the way children commonly do their parents, she always speaks of them as Mr. and Mrs. T." "Oh yes" Mabel explained, "they observe the usual forms."

"It's a queer game," Adele commented, "coming as I do from a community where all no matter how much they may quarrel and disagree have strong family affection and great respect for the ties of blood, I find it difficult to realise." "Yes there you come in with your middle-class ideals again" retorted Mabel.

She then lauded Helen's courage and daring. "Whenever there is any difficulty with the horses or anything dangerous to be done they always call in Helen. Her father is also very small-minded in money matters. He gives her so little and whenever anything happens to the carriage if she is out in it, he makes her pay and she has to get the money as best she can. Her courage never fails and that is what makes her father so bitter, that she never gives any sign of yielding and if she decides to do a thing she is perfectly reckless, nothing stops her."

"That sounds very awful" mocked Adele "not being myself of an heroic breed, I don't somehow realise that type much outside of story-books. That sort of person in real life doesn't seem very real, but I guess it's alright. Helen has courage I don't doubt that."

Mabel then described Helen's remarkable endurance of pain. She fell from a haystack one day and broke her arm. After she got home, her father was so angry that he wouldn't for some time have it attended to and she faced him boldly to the end. "She never winces or complains no matter how much she is hurt," Mabel concluded. "Yes I can believe that" Adele answered thoughtfully.

Throughout the whole of Mabel's talk of Helen, there was an implication of ownership that Adele found singularly irritating. She supposed that Mabel had a right to it but in that thought she found little comfort.

::

AS THE WINTER ADVANCED, ADELE TOOK FREQUENT TRIPS TO NEW YORK. SHE always spent some of her time with Helen. For some undefined reason a convention of secrecy governed their relations. They seemed in this way to emphasise their intention of working the thing out completely between them. To Adele's consciousness the necessity of this secrecy was only apparent when they were together. She felt no obligation to conceal this relation from her friends.

They arranged their meetings in the museums or in the park and sometimes they varied it by lunching together and taking interminable walks in the long straight streets. Adele was always staying with relatives and friends and although there was no reason why Helen should not have come to see her there, something seemed somehow to serve as one. As for Helen's house it seemed tacitly agreed between them that they should not complicate the situation by any relations with Helen's family and so they continued their homeless wanderings.

Adele spent much of their time together in announcing with great interest the result of her endless meditations. She would criticise and examine herself and her ideas with tireless interest. "Helen," she said one day, "I always had an impression that you talked a great deal but apparently you are a most silent being. What is it? Do I talk so hopelessly much that you get discouraged with it as a habit?" "No," answered Helen, "although I admit one might look upon you in the light of a warning, but really I am very silent when I know people well. I only talk when I am with superficial acquaintances." Adele laughed. "I am tempted to say for the sake of picturesque effect, that in that respect I am your complete opposite, but honesty compels me to admit in myself an admirable consistency. I don't know that the quantity is much affected by any conditions in which I find myself, but really Helen why don't you talk more to me?" "Because you know well enough that you are not interested in my ideas, in fact that they bore you. It's always been very evident. You know" Helen continued affectionately, "that you haven't much talent for concealing your feelings and impressions." Adele smiled, "Yes you are certainly right about most of your talk, it does bore me," she admitted. "But that is because it's about stuff that you are not really interested in. You don't really care about general ideas and art values and musical development and surgical operations and Heaven knows what all and naturally your talk about those things doesn't interest me. No talking is interesting that one hasn't hammered out oneself. I know I always bore myself unutterably when I talk the thoughts that I hammered out some time ago and that are no longer meaningful to me, for quoting even oneself lacks a flavor of reality, but you, you always make me feel that at no period did you ever have the thoughts that you converse with. Surely one has to hit you awfully hard to shake your realler things to the surface."

::

THESE MEETINGS SOON BECAME IMPOSSIBLE. IT WAS GETTING COLD AND unpleasant and it obviously wouldn't do to continue in that fashion and yet neither of them undertook to break the convention of silence whieh they had so completely adopted concerning the conditions of their relation.

One day after they had been lunching together they both felt strongly that restaurants had ceased to be amusing. They didn't want to stay there any longer but outside there was an unpleasant wet snow-storm, it was dark and gloomy and the streets were slushy. Helen had a sudden inspiration. "Let us go and see Jane Fairfield," she said, "you don't know her of course but that makes no difference. She is queer and will interest you and you are queer and will interest her. Oh! I don't want to listen to your protests, you are queer and interesting even if you don't know it and you like queer and interesting people even if you think you don't and you are not a bit bashful in spite of your convictions to the contrary, so come along." Adele laughed and agreed.

They wandered up to the very top of an interminable New York apartment house. It was one of the variety made up apparently of an endless number of unfinished boxes of all sizes piled up in a great oblong leaving an elevator shaft in the centre. There is a strange effect of bare wood and uncovered nails about these houses and no amount of upholstery really seems to cover their hollow nakedness.

Jane Fairfield was not at home but the elevator boy trustingly let them in to wait. They looked out of the windows at the city all gloomy and wet and white stretching down to the river, and they watched the long tracks of the elevated making such wonderful perspective that it never really seemed to disappear, it just infinitely met.

Finally they sat down on the couch to give their hostess just another quarter of an hour in which to return, and then for the first time in Adele's experience something happened in which she had no definite consciousness of beginnings. She found herself at the end of a passionate embrace.

::

SOME WEEKS AFTER WHEN ADELE CAME AGAIN TO NEW YORK THEY AGREED to meet at Helen's house. It had been arranged quite as a matter of course as if no objection to such a proceeding had ever been entertained. Adele laughed to herself as she thought of it. "Why we didn't before and why we do now are to me equally mysterious" she said shrugging her shoulders. "Great is Allah, Mohammed is no Shodah! though I dimly suspect that sometimes he is."

When the time came for keeping her engagement Adele for some time delayed going and remained lying on her friend's couch begging to be detained. She realised that her certain hold on her own frank joyousness and happy serenity was weakened. She almost longed to back out, she did so dread emotional complexities. "Oh for peace and a quiet life!" she groaned as she rang Helen's door-bell.

In Helen's room she found a note explaining that being worried as it was so much past the hour of appointment, she had gone to the Museum as Adele had perhaps misunderstood the arrangement. If she came in she was to wait. "It was very bad of me to fool around so long" Adele said to herself gravely and then sat down very peacefully to read.

"I am awfully sorry" Adele greeted Helen as she came into the room somewhat intensely, "it never occurred to me that you would be bothered, it was just dilatoriness on my part," and then they sat down. After a while Helen came and sat on the arm of Adele's chair. She took her head between tense arms and sent deep into her eyes a long straight look of concentrated question. "Haven't you anything to say to me?" she asked at last. "Why no, nothing in particular," Adele answered slowly. She met Helen's glance for a moment, returned it with simple friendliness and then withdrew from it.

"You are very chivalrous," Helen said with sad self-defiance. "You realise that there ought to be shame somewhere between us and as I have none, you generously undertake it all." "No I am not chivalrous" Adele answered, "but I realise my deficiencies. I know that I always take an everlasting time to arrive anywhere really and that the rapidity of my superficial observation keeps it from being realised. It is certainly all my fault. I am so very deceptive. I arouse false expectations. You see," she continued meeting her again with pleasant friendliness, "you haven't yet learned that I am at once impetuous and slow-minded."

::

TIME PASSED AND THEY RENEWED THEIR HABIT OF DESULTORY MEETINGS AT public places, but these were not the same as before. There was between them now a consciousness of strain, a sense of new adjustments, of uncertain standards and of changing values.

Helen was patient but occasionally moved to trenchant criticism, Adele was irritable and discursive but always ended with a frank almost bald apology for her inadequacy.

In the course of time they again arranged to meet in Helen's room. It was a wet rainy, sleety day and Adele felt chilly and unresponsive. Throwing off her hat and coat, she sat down after a cursory greeting and looked meditatively into the fire. "How completely we exemplify entirely different types" she began at last without looking at her companion. "You are a blooming Anglo-Saxon. You know what you want and you go and get it without spending your days and nights changing backwards and forwards from yes to no. If you want to stick a knife into a man you just naturally go and stick straight and hard. You would probably kill him but it would soon be over while I, I would have so many compunctions and considerations that I would cut up all his surface anatomy and make it a long drawn agony but unless he should bleed to death quite by accident, I wouldn't do him any serious injury. No you are the very brave man, passionate but not emotional, capable of great sacrifice but not tender-hearted.

"And then you really want things badly enough to go out and get them and that seems to me very strange. I want things too but only in order to understand them and I never go and get them. I am a hopeless coward, I hate to risk hurting myself or anybody else. All I want to do is to meditate endlessly and think and talk. I know you object because you believe it necessary to feel something to think about and you contend that I don't give myself time to find it. I recognise the justice of that criticism and I am doing my best these days to let it come."

She relapsed into silence and sat there smiling ironically into the fire. The silence grew longer and her smile turned into a look almost of disgust. Finally she wearily drew breath, shook her head and got up. "Ah! don't go," came from Helen in quick appeal. Adele answered the words. "No I am not going. I just want to look at these books." She wandered about a little. Finally she stopped by Helen's side and stood looking down at her with a gentle irony that wavered on the edge of scorn.

"Do you know" she began in her usual tone of dispassionate inquiry "you are a wonderful example of double personality. The you that I used to know and didn't like, and the occasional you that when I do catch a glimpse of it seems to me so very wonderful, haven't any possible connection with each other. It isn't as if my conception of you had gradually changed because it hasn't. I realise always one whole you consisting of a laugh so hard that it rattles, a voice that suggests a certain brutal coarseness and a point of view that is aggressively unsympathetic, and all that is one whole you and it alternates with another you that possesses a purity and intensity of feeling that leaves me quite awestruck and a gentleness of voice and manner and an infinitely tender patience that entirely overmasters me. Now the question which is really you because these two don't seem to have any connections. Perhaps when I really know something about you, the whole will come together but at present it is always either the one or the other and I haven't the least idea which is reallest. You certainly are one too many for me." She shrugged her shoulders, threw out her hands helplessly and sat down again before the fire. She roused at last and became conscious that Helen was trembling bitterly. All hesitations were swept away by Adele's instant passionate sympathy for a creature obviously in pain and she took her into her arms with pure maternal tenderness. Helen gave way utterly. "I tried to be adequate to your experiments" she said at last "but you have no mercy. You were not content until you had dissected out every nerve in my body and left it quite exposed and it was too much, too much. You should give your subjects occasional respite even in the ardor of research." She said it without bitterness. "Good God" cried Adele utterly dumbfounded "did you think that I was deliberately making you suffer in order to study results? Heavens and earth what do you take me for! Do you suppose that I for a moment realised that you were in pain. No! no! it is only my cursed habit of being concerned only with my own thoughts, and then you know I never for a moment believed that you really cared about me, that is one of the things that with all my conceit I never can believe. Helen how could you have had any use for me if you thought me capable of such wanton cruelty?" "I didn't know," she answered "I was willing that you should do what you liked if it interested you and I would stand it as well as I could." "Oh! Oh!" groaned Adele yearning over her with remorseful sympathy "surely dear you believe that I had no idea of your pain and that my brutality was due to ignorance and not intention." "Yes! yes! I know" whispered Helen, nestling to her. After a while she went on, "You know dear you mean so very much to me for with all your inveterate egotism you are the only person with whom I have ever come into close contact, whom I could continue to respect." "Faith" said Adele ruefully "I confess I can't see why. After all even at my best I am only tolerably decent. There are plenty of others, your experience has been unfortunate that's all, and then you know you have always shut yourself off by that fatal illusion of yours that you could stand completely alone." And then she chanted with tender mockery, "And the very strong man Kwasind and he was a very strong man" she went on "even if being an unconquerable solitary wasn't entirely a success."

2

ALL THROUGH THE WINTER HELEN AT INTERVALS SPENT A FEW DAYS WITH Mabel Neathe in Baltimore. Adele was always more or less with them on these occasions. On the surface they preserved the same relations as had existed on the steamer. The only evidence that Mabel gave of a realisation of a difference was in never if she could avoid it leaving them alone together.

It was tacitly understood between them that on these rare occasions they should give each other no sign. As the time drew near when Adele was once more to leave for Europe this time for an extended absence, the tension of this self-imposed inhibition became unendurable and they as tacitly ceased to respect it.

Some weeks before her intended departure Adele was one afternoon as usual taking tea with Mabel. "You have never met Mr. and Mrs. T. have you?" Mabel asked quite out of the air. They had never definitely avoided talking of Helen but they had not spoken of her unnecessarily. "No" Adele answered, "I haven't wanted to. I don't like perfunctory civilities and I know that I belong to the number of Helen's friends of whom they do not approve." "You would not be burdened by their civility, they never take the trouble to be as amiable as that." "Are your experiences so very unpleasant when you are stopping there? I shouldn't think that you would care to do it often." "Sometimes I feel as if it couldn't be endured but if I didn't, Helen would leave them and I think she would regret that and so I don't want her to do it. I have only to say the word and she would leave them at once and sometimes I think she will do it anyway. If she once makes up her mind she won't reconsider it. Of course I wouldn't say such things to any one but you, you know." "I can quite believe that," said Adele rather grimly, "isn't there anything else that you would like to tell me just because I am I. If so don't let me get in your way." "I have never told you about our early relations," Mabel continued. "You know Helen cared for me long before I knew anything about it. We used to be together a great deal at College and every now and then she would disappear for a long time into the country and it wasn't until long afterwards that I found out the reason of it. You know Helen never gives way. You have no idea how wonderful she is. I have been so worried lately" she went on "lest she should think it necessary to leave home for my sake because it is so uncomfortable for me in the summer when I spend a month with her." "Well then why don't you make a noble sacrifice and stay away? Apparently Helen's heroism is great enough to carry her through the ordeal." Adele felt herself to be quite satisfactorily vulgar. Mabel accepted it literally. "Do you really advise it?" she asked. "Oh yes" said Adele "there is nothing so good for the soul as self-imposed periods of total abstinence." "Well, I will think about it" Mabel answered "it is such a comfort that you understand everything and one can speak to you openly about it all." "That's where you are entirely mistaken" Adele said decisively, "I understand nothing. But after all" she added, "it isn't any of my business anyway. Adios," and she left.

When she got home she saw a letter of Helen's on the table. She felt no impulse to read it. She put it well away. "Not that it is any of my business whether she is bound and if so how," she said to herself. "That is entirely for her to work out with her own conscience. For me it is only a question of what exists between us two. I owe Mabel nothing"; and she resolutely relegated it all quite to the background of her mind.

Mabel however did not allow the subject to rest. At the very next opportunity she again asked Adele for advice. "Oh hang it all" Adele broke out "what do I know about it? I understand nothing of the nature of the bond between you." "Don't you really?" Mabel was seriously incredulous. "No I don't." Adele answered with decision, and the subject dropped.

Adele communed with herself dismally. "I was strongminded to put it out of my head once, but this time apparently it has come to stay. I can't deny that I do badly want to know and I know well enough that if I continue to want to know the only decent thing for me to do is to ask the information of Helen. But I do so hate to do that. Why? well I suppose because it would hurt so to hear her admit that she was bound. It would be infinitely pleasanter to have Mabel explain it but it certainly would be very contemptible of me to get it from her. Helen is right, it's not easy this business of really caring about people. I seem to be pretty deeply in it" and she smiled to herself "because now I don't regret the bother and the pain. I wonder if I am really beginning to care" and she lost herself in a revery.

::

MABEL'S ROOM WAS NOW FOR ADELE ALWAYS FILLED WITH THE ATMOSPHERE of the unasked question. She could dismiss it when alone but Mabel was clothed with it as with a garment although nothing concerning it passed between them.

Adele now received a letter from Helen asking why she had not written, whether it was that faith had again failed her. Adele at first found it impossible to answer; finally she wrote a note at once ambiguous and bitter.

At last the tension snapped. "Tell me then" Adele said to Mabel abruptly one evening. Mabel made no attempt to misunderstand but she did attempt to delay. "Oh well if you want to go through the farce of a refusal and an insistence, why help yourself," Adele broke out harshly, "but supposing all that done, I say again tell me." Mabel was dismayed by Adele's hot directness and she vaguely fluttered about as if to escape. "Drop your intricate delicacy" Adele said sternly "you wanted to tell, now tell." Mabel was cowed. She sat down and explained.

The room grew large and portentous and to Mabel's eyes Adele's figure grew almost dreadful in its concentrated repulsion. There was a long silence that seemed to roar and menace and Mabel grew afraid. "Good-night" said Adele and left her.

Adele had now at last learned to stop thinking. She went home and lay motionless a long time. At last she got up and sat at her desk. "I guess I must really care a good deal about Helen" she said at last, "but oh Lord," she groaned and it was very bitter pain. Finally she roused herself. "Poor Mabel" she said "I could almost find it in my heart to be sorry for her. I must have looked very dreadful."

On the next few occasions nothing was said. Finally Mabel began again. "I really supposed Adele that you knew, or else I wouldn't have said anything about it at all and after I once mentioned it, you know you made me tell." "Oh yes I made you tell." Adele could admit it quite cheerfully; Mabel seemed so trivial. "And then you know," Mabel continued "I never would have mentioned it if I had not been so fond of you." Adele laughed, "Yes it's wonderful what an amount of devotion to me there is lying around the universe; but what will Helen think of the results of this devotion of yours?" "That is what worries me" Mabel admitted "I must tell her that I have told you and I am afraid she won't like it." "I rather suspect she won't" and Adele laughed again "but there is nothing like seizing an opportunity before your courage has a chance to ooze. Helen will be down next week, you know, and that will give you your chance but I guess now there has been enough said," and she definitely dismissed the matter.

Adele found it impossible to write to Helen, she felt too sore and bitter but even in spite of her intense revulsion of feeling, she realised that she did still believe in that other Helen that she had attempted once to describe to her. In spite of all evidence she was convinced that something real existed there, something that she was bound to reverence.

She spent a painful week struggling between revulsion and respect. Finally two days before Helen's visit, she heard from her. "I am afraid I can bear it no longer" Helen wrote. "As long as I believed there was a chance of your learning to be something more than your petty complacent self, I could willingly endure everything, but now you remind me of an ignorant mob. You trample everything ruthlessly under your feet without considering whether or not you kill something precious and without being changed or influenced by what you so brutally destroy. I am like Diogenes in quest of an honest man; I want so badly to find some one I can respect and I find them all worthy of nothing but contempt. You have done your best. I am sorry."

For some time Adele was wholly possessed by hot anger, but that changed to intense sympathy for Helen's pain. She realised the torment she might be enduring and so sat down at once to answer. "Perhaps though she really no longer cares" she thought to herself and hesitated. "Well whether she does or not makes no difference I will at least do my part."

"I can make no defence" she wrote "except only that in spite of all my variations there has grown within me steadily an increasing respect and devotion to you. I am not surprised at your bitterness but your conclusions from it are not justified. It is hardly to be expected that such a changed estimate of values, such a complete departure from established convictions as I have lately undergone could take place without many revulsions. That you have been very patient I fully realise but on the other hand you should recognise that I too have done my best and your word to the contrary notwithstanding that best has not been contemptible. So don't talk any more nonsense about mobs. If your endurance is not equal to this task, why admit it and have done with it; if it is I will try to be adequate."

Adele knew that Helen would receive her letter but there would not be time to answer it as she was to arrive in Baltimore the following evening. They were all three to meet at the opera that night so for a whole day Adele would be uncertain of Helen's feeling toward her. She spent all her strength throughout the day in endeavoring to prepare herself to find that Helen still held her in contempt. It had always been her habit to force herself to realise the worst that was likely to befall her and to submit herself before the event. She was never content with simply thinking that the worst might happen and having said it to still expect the best, but she had always accustomed herself to bring her mind again and again to this worst possibility until she had really mastered herself to bear it. She did this because she always doubted her own courage and distrusted her capacity to meet a difficulty if she had not inured herself to it beforehand.

All through this day she struggled for her accustomed definite resignation and the tremendous difficulty of accomplishment made her keenly realise how much she valued Helen's regard.

She did not arrive at the opera until after it had commenced. She knew how little command she had of her expression when deeply moved and she preferred that the first greeting should take place in the dark. She came in quietly to her place. Helen leaned across Mabel and greeted her. There was nothing in her manner to indicate anything and Adele realised by her sensation of sick disappointment that she had really not prepared herself at all. Now that the necessity was more imperative she struggled again for resignation and by the time the act was over she had pretty well gained it. She had at least mastered herself enough to entertain Mabel with elaborate discussion of music and knife fights. She avoided noticing Helen but that was comparatively simple as Mabel sat between them.

Carmen that night was to her at once the longest and the shortest performance that she had ever sat through. It was short because the end brought her nearer to hopeless certainty. It was long because she could only fill it with suspense.

The opera was at last or already over, Adele was uncertain which phrase expressed her feeling most accurately, and then they went for a little while to Mabel's room. Adele was by this time convinced that all her relation with Helen was at an end.

"You look very tired to-night, what's the matter?" Mabel asked her. "Oh!" she explained "there's been a lot of packing and arranging and good-bys to say and farewell lunches and dinners to eat. How I hate baked shad, it's a particular delicacy now and I have lunched and dined on it for three days running so I think it's quite reasonable for me to be worn out. Good-by no don't come downstairs with me. Hullo Helen has started down already to do the honors. Good-by I will see you again to-morrow." Mabel went back to her room and Helen was already lost in the darkness of the lower hall. Adele slowly descended the stairs impressing herself with the necessity of self-restraint.

"Can you forgive me?" and Helen held her close. "I haven't anything to forgive if you still care," Adele answered. They were silent together a long time. "We will certainly have earned our friendship when it is finally accomplished," Adele said at last.

::

"WELL GOOD-BY," MABEL BEGAN AS THE NEXT DAY ADELE WAS LEAVING FOR good. "Oh! before you go I want to tell you that it's alright. Helen was angry but it's alright now. You will be in New York for a few days before you sail" she continued. "I know you won't be gone for a whole year, you will be certain to come back to us before long. I will think of your advice" she concluded. "You know it carries so much weight coming from you." "Oh of course" answered Adele and thought to herself, "What sort of a fool does Mabel take me for anyway."

::

ADELE WAS IN HELEN'S ROOM THE EVE OF HER DEPARTURE. THEY HAD BEEN together a long time. Adele was sitting on the floor her head resting against Helen's knee. She looked up at Helen and then broke the silence with some effort. "Before I go" she said "I want to tell you myself what I suppose you know already, that Mabel has told me of the relations existing between you." Helen's arms dropped away. "No I didn't know." She was very still. "Mabel didn't tell you then?" Adele asked. "No" replied Helen. There was a sombre silence. "If you were not wholly selfish, you would have exercised self-restraint enough to spare me this," Helen said. Adele hardly heard the words, but the power of the mood that possessed Helen awed her. She broke through it at last and began with slow resolution.

"I do not admit" she said, "that I was wrong in wanting to know. I suppose one might in a spirit of quixotic generosity deny oneself such a right but as a reasonable being, I feel that I had a right to know. I realise perfectly that it was hopelessly wrong to learn it from Mabel instead of from you. I admit I was a coward, I was simply afraid to ask you." Helen laughed harshly. "You need not have been," she said "I would have told you nothing." "I think you are wrong, I am quite sure that you would have told me and I wanted to spare myself that pain, perhaps spare you it too, I don't know. I repeat I cannot believe that I was wrong in wanting to know."

They remained there together in an unyielding silence. When an irresistible force meets an immovable body what happens? Nothing. The shadow of a long struggle inevitable as their different natures lay drearily upon them. This incident however decided was only the beginning. All that had gone before was only a preliminary. They had just gotten into position.

The silence was not oppressive but it lasted a long time. "I am very fond of you Adele" Helen said at last with a deep embrace..

It was an hour later when Adele drew a deep breath of resolution, "What foolish people those poets are who say that parting is such sweet sorrow. Although it isn't for ever I can't find a bit of sweetness in it not one tiny little speck. Helen I don't like at all this business of leaving you." "And I" Helen exclaimed "when in you I seem to be taking farewell of parents, brothers sisters my own child, everything at once. No dear you are quite right there is nothing pleasant in it."

"Then why do they put it into the books?" Adele asked with dismal petulance. "Oh dear! but at least it's some comfort to have found out that they are wrong. It's one fact discovered anyway. Dear we are neither of us sorry that we know enough to find it out, are we?" "No," Helen answered "we are neither of us sorry."

::

ON THE STEAMER ADELE RECEIVED A NOTE OF FAREWELL FROM MABEL IN which she again explained that nothing but her great regard for Adele would have made it possible for her to speak as she had done. Adele lost her temper. "I am willing to fight in any way that Mabel likes" she said to herself "underhand or overhand, in the dark, or in the light, in a room or out of doors but at this I protest. She unquestionably did that for a purpose even if the game was not successful. I don't blame her for the game, a weak man must fight with such weapons as he can hold but I don't owe it to her to endure the hypocrisy of a special affection. I can't under the circumstances be very straight but I'll not be unnecessarily crooked. I'll make it clear to her but I'll complicate it in the fashion that she loves."

"My dear Mabel" she wrote, "either you are duller than I would like to think you or you give me credit for more good-natured stupidity than I possess. If the first supposition is correct then you have nothing to say and I need say nothing; if the second then nothing that you would say would carry weight so it is equally unnecessary for you to say anything. If you don't understand what I am talking about then I am talking about nothing and it makes no difference, if you do then there's enough said." Mabel did not answer for several months and then began again to write friendly letters.

::

IT SEEMED INCREDIBLE TO ADELE THIS SUMMER THAT IT WAS ONLY ONE YEAR ago that she had seemed to herself so simple and all morality so easily reducible to formula. In these long lazy Italian days she did not discuss these matters with herself. She realized that at present morally and mentally she was too complex, and that complexity too much astir. It would take much time and strength to make it all settle again. It might, she thought, be eventually understood, it might even in a great deal of time again become simple but at present it gave little promise.

She poured herself out fully and freely to Helen in their ardent correspondence. At first she had had some hesitation about this. She knew that Helen and Mabel were to be together the greater part of the summer and she thought it possible that both the quantity and the matter of the correspondence, if it should come to Mabel's notice would give Helen a great deal of bother. She hesitated a long time whether to suggest this to Helen and to let her decide as to the expediency of being more guarded.

There were many reasons for not mentioning the matter. She realised that not alone Helen but that she herself was still uncertain as to the fidelity of her own feeling. She could not as yet trust herself and hesitated to leave herself alone with a possible relapse.

"After all," she said to herself, "it is Helen's affair and not mine. I have undertaken to follow her lead even into very devious and underground ways but I don't know that it is necessary for me to warn her. She knows Mabel as well as I do. Perhaps she really won't be sorry if the thing is brought to a head."

She remembered the reluctance that Helen always showed to taking precautions or to making any explicit statement of conditions. She seemed to satisfy her conscience and keep herself from all sense of wrong-doing by never allowing herself to expect a difficulty. When it actually arrived the active necessity of using whatever deception was necessary to cover it, drowned her conscience in the violence of action. Adele did not as yet realise this quality definitely but she was vaguely aware that Helen would shut her mind to any explicit statement of probabilities, that she would take no precautions and would thus avoid all sense of guilt. In this fashion she could safeguard herself from her own conscience.

Adele recognised all this dimly. She did not formulate it but it aided to keep her from making any statement to Helen.

She herself could not so avoid her conscience, she simply had to admit a change in moral basis. She knew what she was doing, she realised what was likely to happen and the way in which the new developments would have to be met.

She acknowledged to herself that her own defence lay simply in the fact that she thought the game was worth the candle. "After all" she concluded, "there is still the most important reason for saying nothing. The stopping of the correspondence would make me very sad and lonely. In other words I simply don't want to stop it and so I guess I won't."

For several months the correspondence contiuned with vigor and ardour on both sides. Then there came a three weeks' interval and no word from Helen then a simple friendly letter and then another long silence.

Adele lying on the green earth on a sunny English hillside communed with herself on these matters day after day. She had no real misgiving but she was deeply unhappy. Her unhappiness was the unhappiness of loneliness not of doubt. She saved herself from intense misery only by realising that the sky was still so blue and the country-side so green and beautiful. The pain of passionate longing was very hard to bear. Again and again she would bury her face in the cool grass to recover the sense of life in the midst of her sick despondency.

"There are many possibilities but to me only one probability," she said to herself. "I am not a trustful person in spite of an optimistic temperament but I am absolutely certain in the face of all the facts that Helen is unchanged. Unquestionably there has been some complication. Mabel has gotten hold of some letters and there has been trouble. I can't blame Mabel much. The point of honor would be a difficult one to decide between the three of us."

As time passed she did not doubt Helen but she began to be much troubled about her responsibility in the matter. She felt uncertain as to the attitude she should take.

"As for Mabel" she said to herself "I admit quite completely that I simply don't care. I owe her nothing. She wanted me when it was pleasant to have me and so we are quits. She entered the fight and must be ready to bear the results. We were never bound to each other, we never trusted each other and so there had been no breach of faith. She would show me no mercy and I need grant her none, particularly as she would wholly misunderstand it. It is very strange how very different one's morality and one's temper are when one wants something really badly. Here I, who have always been hopelessly soft-hearted and good-natured and who have always really preferred letting the other man win, find myself quite cold-blooded and relentless. It's a lovely morality that in which we believe even in serious matters when we are not deeply stirred, it's so delightfully noble and gentle." She sighed and then laughed. "Well, I hope some day to find a morality that can stand the wear and tear of real desire to take the place of the nice one that I have lost, but morality or no morality the fact remains that I have no compunctions on the score of Mabel.

"About Helen that's a very different matter. I unquestionably do owe her a great deal but just how to pay it is the difficult point to discover. I can't forget that to me she can never be the first consideration as she is to Mabel for I have other claims that I would always recognise as more important. I have neither the inclination or the power to take Mabel's place and I feel therefore that I have no right to step in between them. On the other hand morally and mentally she is in urgent need of a strong comrade and such in spite of all evidence I believe myself to be. Some day if we continue she will in spite of herself be compelled to choose between us and what have I to offer? Nothing but an elevating influence.

"Bah! what is the use of an elevating influence if one hasn't bread and butter. Her possible want of butter if not of bread, considering her dubious relations with her family must be kept in mind. Mabel could and would always supply them and I neither can nor will. Alas for an unbuttered influence say I. What a grovelling human I am anyway. But I do have occasional sparkling glimpses of faith and those when they come I truly believe to be worth much bread and butter. Perhaps Helen also finds them more delectable. Well I will state the case to her and abide by her decision."

She timed her letter to arrive when Helen would be once more at home alone. "I can say to you now" she wrote "what I found impossible in the early summer. I am now convinced and I think you are too that my feeling for you is genuine and loyal and whatever may be our future difficulties we are now at least on a basis of understanding and trust. I know therefore that you will not misunderstand when I beg you to consider carefully whether on the whole you had not better give me up. I can really amount to so little for you and yet will inevitably cause you so much trouble. That I dread your giving me up I do not deny but I dread more being the cause of serious annoyance to you. Please believe that this statement is sincere and is to be taken quite literally."

"Hush little one" Helen answered "oh you stupid child, don't you realize that you are the only thing in the world that makes anything seem real or worth while to me. I have had a dreadful time this summer. Mabel read a letter of mine to you and it upset her completely. She said that she found it but I can hardly believe that. She asked me if you cared for me and I told her that I didn't know and I really don't dearest. She did not ask me if I cared for you. The thing upset her completely and she was jealous of my every thought and I could not find a moment even to feel alone with you. But don't please don't say any more about giving you up. You are not any trouble to me if you will only not leave me. It's alright now with Mabel, she says that she will never be jealous again." "Oh Lord!" groaned Adele "well if she isn't she would be a hopeless fool. Anyhow I said I would abide by Helen's decision and I certainly will but how so proud a woman can permit such control is more than I can understand."

1903

ON THE FRINGE: FROM TRAGEDY TO CAMP

D. H. LAWRENCE

::

PROLOGUE TO WOMEN IN LOVE

THE ACQUAINTANCE BETWEEN THE TWO MEN WAS SLIGHT AND INSIGNIFICANT. Yet there was a subtle bond that connected them.

They had met four years ago, brought together by a common friend, Hosken, a naval man. The three, Rupert Birkin, William Hosken, and Gerald Crich had then spent a week in the Tyrol together, mountain-climbing.

Birkin and Gerald Crich felt take place between them, the moment they saw each other, that sudden connection which sometimes springs up between men who are very different in temper. There had been a subterranean kindling in each man. Each looked towards the other, and knew the trembling nearness.

Yet they had maintained complete reserve, their relations had been, to all knowledge, entirely casual and trivial. Because of the inward kindled connection, they were even more distant and slight than men usually are, one towards the other.

There was, however, a certain tenderness in their politeness, an almost uncomfortable understanding lurked under their formal, reserved behaviour. They were vividly aware of each other's presence, and each was just as vividly aware of himself, in presence of the other.

The week of mountain-climbing passed like an intense brief lifetime. The three men were very close together, and lifted into an abstract isolation, among the upper rocks and the snow. The world that lay below, the whole field of human activity, was sunk and subordinated, they had trespassed into the upper silence and loneliness. The three of them had reached another state of being, they were enkindled in the upper silences into a rare, unspoken intimacy, an intimacy that took no expression, but which was between them like a transfiguration. As if thrown into the strange fire of abstraction, up in the mountains, they knew and were known to each other. It was another world, another life, transfigured, and yet most vividly corporeal, the senses all raised till each felt his own body, and the presence of his companions, like an essential flame, they radiated to one enkindled, transcendent fire, in the upper world.

Then had come the sudden falling down to earth, the sudden extinction. At Innsbruck they had parted, Birkin to go to Munich, Gerald Crich and Hosken to take the train for Paris and London. On the station they shook hands, and went asunder, having spoken no word and given no sign of the transcendent intimacy which had roused them beyond the everyday life. They shook hands and took leave casually, as mere acquaintances going their separate ways. Yet there remained always, for Birkin and for Gerald Crich, the absolute recognition that had passed between them then, the knowledge that was in their eyes as they met at the moment of parting. They knew they loved each other, that each would die for the other.

Yet all this knowledge was kept submerged in the soul of the two men. Outwardly they would have none of it. Outwardly they only stiffened themselves away from it. They took leave from each other even more coldly and casually than is usual.

And for a year they had seen nothing of each other, neither had they exchanged any word. They passed away from each other, and, superficially, forgot.

But when they met again, in a country house in Derbyshire, the enkindled sensitiveness sprang up again like a strange, embarrassing fire. They scarcely knew each other, yet here was this strange, unacknowledged, inflammable intimacy between them. It made them uneasy.

Rupert Birkin, however, strongly centred in himself, never gave way in his soul, to anyone. He remained in the last issue detached, self-responsible, having no communion with any other soul. Therefore Gerald Crich remained intact in his own form.

The two men were very different. Gerald Crich was the fair, keen-eyed Englishman of medium stature, hard in his muscles and full of energy as a machine. He was a hunter, a traveller, a soldier, always active, always moving vigorously, and giving orders to some subordinate.

Birkin on the other hand was quiet and unobtrusive. In stature he was long and very thin, and yet not bony, close-knit, flexible, and full of repose, like a steel wire. His energy was not evident, he seemed almost weak, passive, insignificant. He was delicate in health. His face was pale and rather ugly, his hair dun-coloured, his eyes were of a yellowish-grey, full of life and warmth. They were the only noticeable thing about him, to the ordinary observer, being very warm and sudden and attractive, alive like fires. But this chief attraction of Birkin's was a false one. Those that knew him best knew that his lovable eyes were, in the last issue, estranged and unsoftening like the eyes of a wolf. In the last issue he was callous, and without feeling, confident, just as Gerald Crich in the last issue was wavering and lost.

The two men were staying in the house of Sir Charles Roddice, Gerald Crich as friend of the host, Rupert Birkin as friend of his host's daughter, Hermione* Roddice. Sir Charles would have been glad for Gerald Crich to marry the daughter of the house, because this young man was a well-set young Englishman of strong conservative temperament, and heir to considerable wealth. But Gerald Crich did not care for Hermione Roddice, and Hermione Roddice disliked Gerald Crich.

She was a rather beautiful woman of twenty-five, fair, tall, slender, graceful, and of some learning. She had known Rupert Birkin in Oxford. He was a year her senior. He was a fellow of Magdalen College, and had been, at twenty-one, one of the young lights of the place, a coming somebody. His essays on Education were brilliant, and he became an inspector of schools.

Hermione Roddice loved him. When she had listened to his passionate declamations, in his rooms in the Blackhorse Road, and when she had heard the respect with which he was spoken of, five years ago, she being a girl of twenty, reading political economy, and he a youth of twenty-one, holding forth against Nietzsche, then she devoted herself to his name and fame. She added herself to his mental and spiritual flame.

Sir Charles thought they would marry. He considered that Birkin, hanging on year after year, was spoiling all his daughter's chances, and without pledging himself in the least. It irked the soldierly knight considerably. But he was somewhat afraid of the quiet, always-civil Birkin. And Hermione, when Sir Charles mentioned that he thought of speaking to the young man, in order to know his intentions, fell into such a white and overweening, contemptuous passion, that her father was nonplussed and reduced to irritated silence.

"How vulgar you are!" cried the young woman. "You are not to dare to say a word to him. It is a friendship, and it is not to be broken-in upon in this fashion. Why should you want to rush me into marriage? I am more than happy as I am."

Her liquid grey eyes swam dark with fury and pain and resentment, her

*Lawrence substituted the name *Hermione* in place of the name *Ethel.*

beautiful face was convulsed. She seemed like a prophetess violated. Her father withdrew, cold and huffed.

So the relationship between the young woman and Birkin continued. He was an inspector of schools, she studied Education. He wrote also harsh, jarring poetry, very real and painful, under which she suffered; and sometimes, shallower, gentle lyrics, which she treasured as drops of manna. Like a priestess she kept his records and his oracles, he was like a god who would be nothing if his worship were neglected.

Hermione could not understand the affection between the two men. They would sit together in the hall, at evening, and talk without any depth. What did Rupert find to take him up, in Gerald Crich's conversation? She, Hermione, was only rather bored, and puzzled. Yet the two men seemed happy, holding their commonplace discussion. Hermione was impatient. She knew that Birkin was, as usual, belittling his own mind and talent, for the sake of something that she felt unworthy. Some common correspondence which she knew demeaned and belied him. Why would he always come down so eagerly to the level of common people, why was he always so anxious to vulgarize and betray himself? She bit her lip in torment. It was as if he were anxious to deny all that was fine and rare in himself.

Birkin knew what she was feeling and thinking. Yet he continued almost spitefully against her. He *did* want to betray the heights and depths of nearly religious intercourse which he had with her. He, the God, turned round upon his priestess, and became the common vulgar man who turned her to scorn. He performed some strange metamorphosis of soul, and from being a pure, incandescent spirit burning intense with the presence of God, he became a lustful, shallow, insignificant fellow running in all the common ruts. Even there was some vindictiveness in him now, something jeering and spiteful and low, unendurable. It drove her mad. She had given him all her trembling, naked soul, and now he turned mongrel, and triumphed in his own degeneration. It was his deep desire, to be common, vulgar, a little gross. She could not bear the look of almost sordid jeering with which he turned on her, when she reached out her hand, imploring. It was as if some rat bit her, she felt she was going insane. And he jeered at her, at the spiritual woman who waited at the tomb, in her sandals and her mourning robes. He jeered at her horribly, knowing her secrets. And she was insane, she knew she was going mad.

But he plunged on triumphant into intimacy with Gerald Crich, excluding the woman, tormenting her. He knew how to pitch himself into tune with another person. He could adjust his mind, his consciousness, almost perfectly to that of Gerald Crich, lighting up the edge of the other man's limitation with a glimmering light that was the essence of exquisite adventure and liberation to the confined intelligence. The two men talked together for hours, Birkin watching the hard limbs and the rather stiff face of the traveller in unknown countries, Gerald Crich catching the pale, luminous face opposite him, lit up over the edge of the unknown regions of the soul, trembling into new being, quivering with new intelligence.

To Hermione, it was insupportable degradation that Rupert Birkin should maintain this correspondence, prostituting his mind and his understanding to the coarser stupidity of the other man. She felt confusion gathering upon her, she was unanchored on the edge of madness. Why did he do it? Why was he, whom she knew as her leader, star-like and pure, why was he the lowest betrayer and the ugliest of blasphemers? She held her temples, feeling herself reel towards the bottomless pit.

For Birkin did get a greater satisfaction, at least for the time being, from his intercourse with the other man, than from his spiritual relation with her. It satisfied him to have to do with Gerald Crich, it fulfilled him to have this other man, this hard-limbed traveller and sportsman, following implicitly, held as it were consummated within the spell of a more powerful understanding. Birkin felt a passion of desire for Gerald Crich, for the clumsier, cruder intelligence and the limited soul, and for the striving, unlightened body of his friend. And Gerald Crich, not understanding, was transfused with pleasure. He did not even know he loved Birkin. He thought him marvellous in understanding, almost unnatural, and on the other hand pitiful and delicate in body. He felt a great tenderness towards him, of superior physical strength, and at the same time some reverence for his delicacy and fineness of being.

All the same, there was no profession of friendship, no open mark of intimacy. They remained to all intents and purposes distant, mere acquaintances. It was in the other world of the subconsciousness that the interplay took place, the interchange of spiritual and physical richness, the relieving of physical and spiritual poverty, without any intrinsic change of state in either man.

Hermione could not understand it at all. She was mortified and in despair. In his lapses, she despised and revolted from Birkin. Her mistrust of him pierced to the quick of her soul. If his intense and pure flame of spirituality only sank to this guttering prostration, a low, degraded heat, servile to a clumsy Gerald Crich, fawning on a coarse, unsusceptible being, such as was Gerald Crich and all the multitudes of Gerald Criches of this world, then nothing was anything. The transcendent star of one evening was the putrescent phosphorescence of the next, and glory and corruptibility were interchangeable. Her soul was convulsed with cynicism. She despised her God and her angel. Yet she could not do without him. She believed in herself as a priestess, and that was all. Though there were no God to serve, still she was a priestess. Yet having no altar to kindle, no sacrifice to burn, she would be barren and useless. So she adhered to her God in him, which she claimed almost violently, whilst her soul turned in bitter cynicism from the prostitute man in him. She did not believe in him, she only believed in that which she could gather from him, as one gathers silk from the corrupt worm. She was the maker of gods.

So, after a few days, Gerald Crich went away and Birkin was left to Hermione Roddice. It is true, Crich said to Birkin: "Come and see us, if ever you are near enough, will you?", and Birkin had said yes. But for some reason, it was concluded beforehand that this visit would never be made, deliberately.

Sick, helpless, Birkin swung back to Hermione. In the garden, at evening, looking over the silvery hills, he sat near to her, or lay with his head on her bosom, while the moonlight came gently upon the trees, and they talked, quietly, gently as dew distilling, their two disembodied voices distilled in the silvery air, two voices moving and ceasing like ghosts, like spirits. And they talked of life, and of death, but chiefly of death, his words turning strange and phosphorescent, like dark water suddenly shaken alight, whilst she held his head against her breast, infinitely satisfied and completed by its weight upon her, and her hand travelled gently, finely, oh, with such exquisite quivering adjustment, over his hair. The pain of tenderness he felt for her was almost unendurable, as her hand fluttered and came near, scarcely touching him, so light and sensitive it was, as it passed over his hair, rhythmically. And still his voice moved and thrilled through her like the keenest pangs of embrace, she remained possessed by him, possessed by the spirit. And the sense of beauty and perfect, blade-keen ecstasy was balanced to perfection, she passed away, was transported.

After these nights of superfine ecstasy of beauty, after all was consumed in the silver fire of moonlight, all the soul caught up in the universal chill-blazing bonfire of the moonlit night, there came the morning, and the ash, when his body was grey and consumed, and his soul ill. Why should the sun shine, and hot gay flowers come out, when the kingdom of reality was the silver-cold night of death, lovely and perfect.

She, like a priestess, was fulfilled and rich. But he became more hollow and ghastly to look at. There was no escape, they penetrated further and further into the regions of death, and soon the connection with life would be broken.

Then came his revulsion against her. After he loved her with a tenderness that was anguish, a love that was all pain, or else transcendent white ecstasy, he turned upon her savagely, like a maddened dog. And like a priestess who is rended for sacrifice, she submitted and endured. She would serve the God she possessed, even though he should turn periodically into a fierce dog, to rend her.

So he went away, to his duties, and his work. He had made a passionate study of education, only to come, gradually, to the knowledge that education is nothing but the process of building up, gradually, a complete unit of consciousness. And each unit of consciousness is the living unit of that great social, religious, philosophic idea towards which mankind, like an organism seeking its final form, is laboriously growing. But if there *be* no great philosophic idea, if, for the time being, mankind, instead of going through a period of growth, is going through a corresponding process of decay and decomposition from some old, fulfilled, obsolete idea, then what is the good of educating? Decay and decomposition will take their own way. It is impossible to educate for this end, impossible to teach the world how to die away from its achieved, nullified form. The autumn must take place in every individual soul, as well as in all the people, all must die, individually and socially. But education is a process of striving to a new, unanimous being, a whole organic form. But when winter has set in, when the frosts are strangling the leaves off the trees and the birds are silent knots of darkness, how can there be a unanimous movement towards a whole summer of florescence? There can be none of this, only submission to the death of this nature, in the winter that has come upon mankind, and a cherishing of the unknown that is unknown for many a day yet, buds that may not open till a far off season comes, when the season of death has passed away.

And Birkin was just coming to a knowledge of the essential futility of all attempt at social unanimity in constructiveness. In the winter, there can only be unanimity of disintegration, the leaves fall unanimously, the plants die down, each creature is a soft-slumbering grave, as the adder and the dormouse in winter are the soft tombs of the adder and the dormouse, which slip about like rays of brindled darkness, in summer.

How to get away from this process of reduction, how escape this phosphorescent passage into the tomb, which was universal though unacknowledged, this was the unconscious problem which tortured Birkin day and night. He came to Hermione, and found with her the pure, translucent regions of death itself, of ecstasy. In the world the autumn was setting in. What should a man add himself on to?—to science, to social reform, to aestheticism, to sensationalism? The whole world's constructive activity was a fiction, a lie, to hide the great process of decomposition, which had set in. What then to adhere to?

He ran about from death to death. Work was terrible, horrible because he did not believe in it. It was almost a horror to him, to think of going from school to school, making reports and giving suggestions, when the whole process to his soul was pure futility, a process of mechanical activity entirely purposeless, sham growth which was entirely rootless. Nowhere more than in education did a man feel the horror of false, rootless, spasmodic activity more acutely. The whole business was like dementia. It created in him a feeling of nausea and horror. He recoiled from it. And yet, where should a man repair, what should he do?

In his private life the same horror of futility and wrongness dogged him. Leaving alone all ideas, religious or philosophic, all of which are mere sounds, old repetitions, or else novel, dexterous, sham permutations and combinations of old repetitions, leaving alone all the things of the mind and the consciousness, what remained in a man's life? There is his emotional and his sensuous activity, is not this enough?

Birkin started with madness from this question, for it touched the quick of torture. There was his love for Hermione, a love based entirely on ecstasy and on pain, and ultimate death. He *knew* he did not love her with any living, creative love. He did not even desire her: he had no passion for her, there was no hot impulse of growth between them, only this terrible reducing activity of phosphorescent consciousness, the consciousness ever liberated more and more into the void, at the expense of the flesh, which was burnt down like dead grey ash.

He did not call this love. Yet he was bound to her, and it was agony to leave her. And he did not love anyone else. He did not love any woman. He *wanted* to love. But between wanting to love, and loving, is the whole difference between life and death.

The incapacity to love, the incapacity to desire any woman, positively, with body and soul, this was a real torture, a deep torture indeed. Never to be able to love spontaneously, never to be moved by a power greater than oneself, but always to be within one's own control, deliberate, having the choice, this was horrifying, more deadly than death. Yet how was one to escape? How could a man escape from being deliberate and unloving, except a greater power, an impersonal, imperative love should take hold of him? And if the greater power should not take hold of him, what could he do but continue in his deliberateness, without any fundamental spontaneity?

He did not love Hermione, he did not desire her. But he wanted to force himself to love her and to desire her. He was consumed by sexual desire, and he wanted to be fulfilled. Yet he did not desire Hermione. She repelled him rather. Yet he *would* have this physical fulfilment, he would have the sexual activity. So he forced himself towards her.

She was hopeless from the start. Yet she resigned herself to him. In her soul, she knew this was not the way. And yet even she was ashamed, as of some physical deficiency. She did not want him either. But with all her soul, she *wanted* to want him. She would do anything to give him what he wanted, that which he was raging for, this physical fulfilment he insisted on. She was wise; she thought for the best. She prepared herself like a perfect sacrifice to him. She offered herself gladly to him, gave herself into his will.

And oh, it was all such a cruel failure, just a failure. This last act of love which he had demanded of her was the keenest grief of all, it was so insignificant, so null. He had no pleasure of her, only some mortification. And her heart almost broke with grief.

She wanted him to take her. She wanted him to take her, to break her with his passion, to destroy her with his desire, so long as he got satisfaction. She looked forward, tremulous, to a kind of death at his hands, she gave herself up. She would be broken and dying, destroyed, if only he would rise fulfilled.

But he was not capable of it, he failed. He could not take her and destroy her. He could not forget her. They had too rare a spiritual intimacy, he could not now tear himself away from all this, and come like a brute to take its satisfaction. He was too much aware of her, and of her fear, and of her writhing torment, as she lay in sacrifice. He had too much deference for her feeling. He could not, as she madly wanted, destroy her, trample her, and crush a satisfaction from her. He was not experienced enough, not hardened enough. He was always aware of *her* feelings, so that he had none of his own. Which made this last love-making between them an ignominious failure, very, very cruel to bear.

And it was this failure which broke the love between them. He hated her, for her incapacity in love, for her lack of desire for him, her complete and almost perfect lack of any physical desire towards him. Her desire was all spiritual, all in the consciousness. She wanted him all, all through the consciousness, never through the senses.

And she hated him, and despised him, for his incapacity to wreak his desire upon her, his lack of strength to crush his satisfaction from her. If only he could have taken her, destroyed her, used her all up, and been satisfied, she would be at last free. She might be killed, but it would be the death which gave her consummation.

It was a failure, a bitter, final failure. He could not take from her what he wanted, because he could not, bare-handed, destroy her. And she despised him that he could not destroy her.

Still, though they had failed, finally, they did not go apart. Their relation was too deep-established. He was by this time twenty-eight years old, and she twenty-seven. Still, for his spiritual delight, for a companion in his conscious life, for someone to share and heighten his joy in thinking, or in reading, or in feeling beautiful things, or in knowing landscape intimately and poignantly, he turned to her. For all these things, she was still with him, she made up the greater part of his life. And he, she knew to her anguish and mortification, he was still the master-key to almost all life, for her. She wanted it not to be so, she wanted to be free of him, of the strange, terrible bondage of his domination. But as yet, she could not free herself from him.

He went to other women, to women of purely sensual, sensational attraction, he prostituted his spirit with them. And he got *some* satisfaction. She watched him go, sadly, and yet not without a measure of relief. For he would torment her less, now.

She knew he would come back to her. She knew, inevitably as the dawn would rise, he would come back to her, half-exultant and triumphant over her, half-bitter against her for letting him go and wanting her now, wanting the communion with her. It was as if he went to the other, the dark, sensual, almost bestial woman thoroughly and fully to degrade himself. He despised himself, essentially, in his attempts at sensuality, she knew that. So she let him be. It was only his rather vulgar arrogance of a sinner that she found hard to bear. For before her, he wore his sins with braggadocio, flaunted them a little in front of her. And this alone drove her to exasperation to the point of uttering her contempt for his childishness and his instability.

But as yet, she forbore, because of the deference he still felt towards her. Intrinsically, in his spirit, he still served her. And this service she cherished.

But he was becoming gnawed and bitter, a little mad. His whole system was inflamed to a pitch of mad irritability, he became blind, unconscious to the greater half of life, only a few things he saw with feverish acuteness. And she, she kept the key to him, all the while.

The only thing she dreaded was his making up his mind. She dreaded his way of seeing some particular things vividly and feverishly, and of his acting upon this special sight. For once he decided a thing, it became a reigning universal truth to him, and he was completely inhuman.

He was, in his own way, quite honest with himself. But every man has his own truths, and is honest with himself according to them. The terrible thing about Birkin, for Hermoine, was that when once he decided upon a truth, he acted upon it, cost what it might. If he decided that his eye did really offend him, he would in truth pluck it out. And this seemed to her so inhuman, so abstract, that it chilled her to the depths of her soul, and made him seem to her inhuman, something between a monster and a complete fool. For might not she herself easily be found to be this eye which much needs be plucked out?

He had stuck fast over this question of love and of physical fulfilment in love, till it had become like a monomania. All his thought turned upon it. For he wanted to keep his integrity of being, he would not consent to sacrifice one half of himself to the other. He would not sacrifice the sensual to the spiritual half of himself, and he could not sacrifice the spiritual to the sensual half. Neither could he obtain fulfilment in both, the two halves always reacted from each other. To be spiritual, he must have a Hermione, completely without desire: to be sensual, he must have a slightly bestial woman, the very scent of whose skin soon disgusted him, whose manners nauseated him beyond bearing, so that Hermione, always chaste and always stretching out her hands for beauty, seemed to him the purest and most desirable thing on earth.

He knew he obtained no real fulfilment in sensuality, he became disgusted and despised the whole process as if it were dirty. And he knew that he had no real fulfilment in his spiritual and aesthetic intercourse with Hermione. That process he also despised, with considerable cynicism.

And he recognized that he was on the point either of breaking, becoming a thing, losing his integral being, or else of becoming insane. He was now nothing but a series of reactions from dark to light, from light to dark, almost mechanical, without unity or meaning.

This was the most insufferable bondage, the most tormenting affliction, that he could not save himself from these extreme reactions, the vibration between two poles, one of which was Hermione, the centre of social virtue, the other of which was a prostitute, anti-social, almost criminal. He knew that in the end, subject to this extreme vibration, he would be shattered, would die, or else, worse still, would become a mere disordered set of processes, without purpose or integral being. He knew this, and dreaded it. Yet he could not save himself.

To save himself, he must unite the two halves of himself, spiritual and sensual. And this is what no man can do at once, deliberately. It must happen to him. Birkin willed to be sensual, as well as spiritual, with Hermione. He might will it, he might act according to his will, but he did not bring to pass that which he willed. A man cannot create desire in himself, nor cease at will from desiring. Desire, in any shape or form, is primal, whereas the will is secondary, derived. The will can destroy, but it cannot create.

So the more he tried with his will, to force his senses towards Hermione, the greater misery he produced. On the other hand his pride never ceased to contemn his profligate intercourse elsewhere. After all, it was *not* that which he wanted. He did not want libertine pleasures, not fundamentally. His fundamental desire was, to be able to love completely, in one and the same act: both body and soul at once, struck into a complete oneness in contact with a complete woman.

And he failed in this desire. It was always a case of one or the other, of spirit or of senses, and each, alone, was deadly. All history, almost all art, seemed the story of this deadly half-love: either passion, like Cleopatra, or else spirit, like Mary of Bethany or Vittoria Colonna.

He pondered on the subject endlessly, and knew himself in his reactions. But self-knowledge is not everything. No man, by taking thought, can add one cubit to his stature. He can but know his own height and limitation.

He knew that he loved no woman, that in nothing was he really complete, really himself. In his most passionate moments of spiritual enlightenment, when like a saviour of mankind he would pour out his soul for the world, there was in him a capacity to jeer at all his own righteousness and spirituality, justly and sincerely to make a mock of it all. And the mockery was so true, it bit to the very core of his righteousness, and showed it rotten, shining with phosphorescence. But at the same time, whilst quivering in the climax-thrill of sensual pangs, some cold voice could say in him: "You are not really moved; you could rise up and go away from this pleasure quite coldly and calmly; it is not radical, your enjoyment."

He knew he had not loved, could not love. The only thing then was to make the best of it, have the two things separate, and over them all, a calm detached mind. But to this he would not acquiesce. "I should be like a

Neckan," he said to himself, "like a sea-water being, I should have no soul." And he pondered the stories of the wistful, limpid creatures who watched ceaselessly, hoping to gain a soul.

So the trouble went on, he became more hollow and deathly, more like a spectre with hollow bones. He knew that he was not very far from dissolution.

All the time, he recognized that, although he was always drawn to women, feeling more at home with a woman than with a man, yet it was for men that he felt the hot, flushing, roused attraction which a man is supposed to feel for the other sex. Although nearly all his living interchange went on with one woman or another, although he was always terribly intimate with at least one woman, and practically never intimate with a man, yet the male physique had a fascination for him, and for the female physique he felt only a fondness, a sort of sacred love, as for a sister.

In the street, it was the men who roused him by their flesh and their manly, vigorous movement, quite apart from all the individual character, whilst he studied the women as sisters, knowing their meaning and their intents. It was the men's physique which held the passion and the mystery to him. The women he seemed to be kin to, he looked for the soul in them. The soul of a woman and the physique of a man, these were the two things he watched for, in the street.

And this was a new torture to him. Why did not the face of a woman move him in the same manner, with the same sense of handsome desirability, as the face of a man? Why was a man's beauty, the beauté mâle, so vivid and intoxicating a thing to him, whilst female beauty was something quite unsubstantial, consisting all of look and gesture and revelation of intuitive intelligence? He thought women beautiful purely because of their expression. But it was plastic form that fascinated him in men, the contour and movement of the flesh itself.

He wanted all the time to love women. He wanted all the while to feel this kindled, loving attraction towards a beautiful woman, that he would often feel towards a handsome man. But he could not. Whenever it was a case of a woman, there entered in too much spiritual, sisterly love; or else, in reaction, there was only a brutal, callous sort of lust.

This was an entanglement from which there seemed no escape. How can a man *create* his own feelings? He cannot. It is only in his power to suppress them, to bind them in the chain of the will. And what is suppression but a mere negation of life, and of living.

He had several friendships wherein this passion entered, friendships with men of no very great intelligence, but of pleasant appearance: ruddy, well-nourished fellows, good-natured and easy, who protected him in his delicate health more gently than a woman would protect him. He loved his friend, the beauty of whose manly limbs made him tremble with pleasure. He wanted to caress him.

But reserve, which was as strong as a chain of iron in him, kept him from any demonstration. And if he were away for any length of time from the man he loved so hotly, then he forgot him, the flame which invested the beloved like a transfiguration passed away, and Birkin remembered his friend as tedious. He could not go back to him, to talk as tediously as he would have to talk, to take such a level of intelligence as he would have to take. He forgot his men friends completely, as one forgets the candle one has blown out. They remained as quite extraneous and uninteresting persons living their life in their own sphere, and having not the slightest relation to himself, even though they themselves maintained a real warmth of affection, almost of love for him. He paid not the slightest heed to this love which was constant to him, he felt it sincerely to be just nothing, valueless.

So he left his old friends completely, even those to whom he had been attached passionately, like David to Jonathan. Men whose presence he had waited for cravingly, the touch of whose shoulder suffused him with a vibration of physical love, became to him mere figures, as nonexistent as is the waiter who sets the table in a restaurant.

He wondered very slightly at this, but dismissed it with hardly a thought. Yet, every now and again, would come over him the same passionate desire to have near him some man he saw, to exchange intimacy, to unburden himself of love of this new beloved.

It might be any man, a policeman who suddenly looked up at him, as he inquired the way, or a soldier who sat next to him in a railway carriage. How vividly, months afterwards, he would recall the soldier who had sat pressed up close to him on a journey from Charing Cross to Westerham; the shapely, motionless body, the large, dumb, coarsely-beautiful hands that rested helpless upon the strong knees, the dark brown eyes, vulnerable in the erect body. Or a young man in flannels on the sands at Margate, flaxen and ruddy, like a Viking of twenty-three, with clean, rounded contours, pure as the contours of snow, playing with some young children, building a castle in sand, intent and abstract, like a seagull or a keen white bear.

In his mind was a small gallery of such men: men whom he had never spoken to, but who had flashed themselves upon his senses unforgettably, men whom he apprehended intoxicatingly in his blood. They divided themselves roughly into two classes: these white-skinned, keen-limbed men with eyes like blue-flashing ice and hair like crystals of winter sunshine, the northmen, inhuman as sharp-crying gulls, distinct like splinters of ice, like crystals, isolated, individual; and then the men with dark eyes that one can enter and plunge into, bathe in, as in a liquid darkness, dark-skinned, supple, night-smelling men, who are the living substance of the viscous, universal heavy darkness.

His senses surged towards these men, towards the perfect and beautiful representatives of these two halves. And he knew them, by seeing them and by apprehending them sensuously, he knew their very blood, its weight and savour; the blood of the northmen sharp and red and light, tending to be keenly acrid, like cranberries, the blood of the dark-limbed men heavy and luscious, and in the end nauseating, revolting.

He asked himself, often, as he grew older, and more unearthly, when he was twenty-eight and twenty-nine years old, would he ever be appeased, would he ever cease to desire these two sorts of men. And a wan kind of hopelessness would come over him, as if he would never escape from this attraction, which was a bondage.

For he would never acquiesce to it. He could never acquiesce to his own feelings, to his own passion. He could never grant that it should be so, that it was well for him to feel this keen desire to have and to possess the bodies of such men, the passion to bathe in the very substance of such men, the substance of living, eternal light, like eternal snow, and the flux of heavy, rank-smelling darkness.

He wanted to cast out these desires, he wanted not to know them. Yet a man can no more slay a living desire in him, than he can prevent his body from feeling heat and cold. He can put himself into bondage, to prevent the fulfilment of the desire, that is all. But the desire is there, as the travelling of the blood itself is there, until it is fulfilled or until the body is dead.

So he went on, month after month, year after year, divided against himself, striving for the day when the beauty of men should not be so acutely attractive to him, when the beauty of woman should move him instead.

But that day came no nearer, rather it went further away. His deep dread was that it would always be so, that he would never be free. His life would have been one long torture of struggle against his own innate desire, his own innate being. But to be so divided against oneself, this is terrible, a nullification of all being.

He went into violent excess with a mistress whom, in a rather anti-social, ashamed spirit, he loved. And so for a long time he forgot about this attraction that men had for him. He forgot about it entirely. And then he grew stronger, surer.

But then, inevitably, it would recur again. There would come into a restaurant a strange Cornish type of man, with dark eyes like holes in his head, or like the eyes of a rat, and with dark, fine, rather stiff hair, and full, heavy, softly-strong limbs. Then again Birkin would feel the desire spring up in him, the desire to know this man, to have him, as it were to eat him, to take the very substance of him. And watching the strange, rather furtive, rabbit-like way in which the strong, softly-built man ate, Birkin would feel the rousedness burning in his own breast, as if this were what he wanted, as if the satisfaction of his desire lay in the body of the young, strong man opposite.

And then in his soul would succeed a sort of despair, because this passion for a man had recurred in him. It was a deep misery to him. And it would seem as if he had always loved men, always and only loved men. And this was the greatest suffering to him.

But it was not so, that he always loved men. For weeks it would be all gone from him, this passionate admiration of the rich body of a man. For weeks he was free, active, and living. But he had such a dread of his own feelings and desires, that when they recurred again, the interval vanished, and it seemed the bondage and the torment had been continuous.

This was the one and only secret he kept to himself, this secret of his passionate and sudden, spasmodic affinity for men he saw. He kept this secret even from himself. He knew what he felt, but he always kept the knowledge at bay. His a priori were: "I *should not* feel like this," and "It is the ultimate mark of my own deficiency, that I feel like this." Therefore, though he admitted everything, he never really faced the question. He never accepted the desire, and received it as part of himself. He always tried to keep it expelled from him.*

Gerald Crich was the one towards whom Birkin felt most strongly that immediate, roused attraction which transfigured the person of the attracter with such a glow and such a desirable beauty. The two men had met once or twice, and then Gerald Crich went abroad, to South America. Birkin forgot him, all connection died down. But it was not finally dead. In both men were the seeds of a strong, inflammable affinity.

*At one time the Prologue chapter ended here, for the next page of the manuscript is headed *Chapter II The Wedding*. This heading is cancelled and the direction "Run on" is twice inserted.

Therefore, when Birkin found himself pledged to act as best man at the wedding of Hosken, the friend of the mountain-climbing holiday, and of Laura Crich, sister of Gerald, the old affection sprang awake in a moment. He wondered what Gerald would be like now.

Hermione, knowing of Hosken's request to Birkin, at once secured for herself the position of bridesmaid to Laura Crich. It was inevitable. She and Rupert Birkin were running to the end of their friendship. He was now thirty years of age, and she twenty-nine. His feeling of hostility towards Hermione had grown now to an almost constant dislike. Still she held him in her power. But the hold became weaker and weaker. "If he breaks loose," she said, "he will fall into the abyss."

Nevertheless he was bound to break loose, because his reaction against Hermione was the strongest movement in his life, now. He was thrusting her off, fighting her off all the while, thrusting himself clear, although he had no other foothold, although he was breaking away from her, his one rock, to fall into a bottomless sea.

1921

RADCLYFFE HALL

::

MISS OGILVY FINDS HERSELF

MISS OGILVY STOOD ON THE QUAY AT CALAIS AND SURVEYED THE DISBANDing of her Unit, the Unit that together with the coming of war had completely altered the complexion of her life, at all events for three years.

Miss Ogilvy's thin, pale lips were set sternly and her forehead was puckered in an effort of attention, in an effort to memorise every small detail of every old war-weary battered motor on whose side still appeared the merciful emblem that had set Miss Ogilvy free.

Miss Ogilvy's mind was jerking a little, trying to regain its accustomed balance, trying to readjust itself quickly to this sudden and paralysing change. Her tall, awkward body with its queer look of strength, its broad, flat bosom and thick legs and ankles, as though in response to her jerking mind, moved uneasily, rocking backwards and forwards. She had this trick of rocking on her feet in moments of controlled agitation. As usual, her hands were thrust deep into her pockets, they seldom seemed to come out of her pockets unless it were to light a cigarette, and as though she were still standing firm under fire while the wounded were placed in her ambulances, she suddenly straddled her legs very slightly and lifted her head and listened. She was standing firm under fire at that moment, the fire of a desperate regret.

Some girls came towards her, young, tired-looking creatures whose eyes were too bright from long strain and excitement. They had all been members of that glorious Unit, and they still wore the queer little forage-caps and the short, clumsy tunics of the French Militaire. They still slouched in walking and smoked Caporals in emulation of the Poilus. Like their founder and leader these girls were all English, but like her they had chosen to serve England's ally, fearlessly thrusting right up to the trenches in search of the wounded and dying. They had seen some fine things in the course of three years, not the least fine of which was the cold, hard-faced woman who, commanding, domineering, even hectoring at times, had yet been possessed of so dauntless a courage and of so insistent a vitality that it vitalised the whole Unit.

"It's rotten!" Miss Ogilvy heard someone saying. "It's rotten, this breaking up of our Unit!" And the high, rather childish voice of the speaker sounded perilously near to tears.

Miss Ogilvy looked at the girl almost gently, and it seemed, for a moment, as though some deep feeling were about to find expression in words. But Miss Ogilvy's feelings had been held in abeyance so long that they seldom dared become vocal, so she merely said "Oh?" on a rising inflection —her method of checking emotion.

They were swinging the ambulance cars in midair, those of them that were destined to go back to England, swinging them up like sacks of potatoes, then lowering them with much clanging of chains to the deck of the waiting steamer. The porters were shoving and shouting and quarrelling, pausing now and again to make meaningless gestures; while a pompous official was becoming quite angry as he pointed at Miss Ogilvy's own special car—it annoyed him, it was bulky and difficult to move.

"Bon Dieu! Mais dépêchez-vous donc!" he bawled, as though he were bullying the motor.

Then Miss Ogilvy's heart gave a sudden, thick thud to see this undignified, pitiful ending; and she turned and patted the gallant old car as though she were patting a well-beloved horse, as though she would say: "Yes, I know how it feels—never mind, we'll go down together."

2

MISS OGILVY SAT IN THE RAILWAY CARRIAGE ON HER WAY FROM DOVER TO London. The soft English landscape sped smoothly past: small homesteads, small churches, small pastures, small lanes with small hedges; all small like England itself, all small like Miss Ogilvy's future. And sitting there still arrayed in her tunic, with her forage-cap resting on her knees, she was conscious of a sense of complete frustration; thinking less of those glorious years at the Front and of all that had gone to the making of her, than of all that had gone to the marring of her from the days of her earliest childhood.

She saw herself as a queer little girl, aggressive and awkward because of her shyness; a queer little girl who loathed sisters and dolls, preferring the stable-boys as companions, preferring to play with footballs and tops, and occasional catapults. She saw herself climbing the tallest beech trees, arrayed in old breeches illicitly come by. She remembered insisting with tears and some temper that her real name was William and not Wilhelmina. All these childish pretences and illusions she remembered, and the bitterness that came after. For Miss Ogilvy had found as her life went on that in this world it is better to be one with the herd, that the world has no wish to understand those who cannot conform to its stereotyped pattern. True enough, in her youth she had gloried in her strength, lifting weights, swinging clubs and developing muscles, but presently this had grown irksome to her; it had seemed to lead nowhere, she being a woman, and then as her mother had often protested: muscles looked so appalling in evening dress—a young girl ought not to have muscles.

Miss Ogilvy's relation to the opposite sex was unusual and at that time added much to her worries, for no less than three men had wished to propose, to the genuine amazement of the world and her mother. Miss Ogilvy's instinct made her like and trust men, for whom she had a pronounced fellow-feeling; she would always have chosen them as her friends and companions in preference to girls or women; she would dearly have loved to share in their sports, their business, their ideals and their wide-flung interests. But men had not wanted her, except the three who had found in her strangeness a definite attraction, and those would-be suitors she had actually feared, regarding them with aversion. Towards young girls and women she was shy and respectful, apologetic and sometimes admiring. But their fads and their foibles, none of which she could share, while amusing her very often in secret, set her outside the sphere of their intimate lives, so that in the end she must blaze a lone trail through the difficulties of her nature.

"I can't understand you," her mother had said, "you're a very odd creature—now when I was your age . . ."

And her daughter had nodded, feeling sympathetic. There were two younger girls who also gave trouble, though in their case the trouble was fighting for husbands who were scarce enough even in those days. It was finally decided, at Miss Ogilvy's request, to allow her to leave the field clear for her sisters. She would remain in the country with her father when the others went up for the Season.

Followed long, uneventful years spent in sport, while Sarah and Fanny toiled, sweated and gambled in the matrimonial market. Neither ever succeeded in netting a husband, and when the Squire died leaving very little money, Miss Ogilvy found to her great surprise that they looked upon her as a brother. They had so often jibed at her in the past, that at first she could scarcely believe her senses, but before very long it became all too real: she it was who must straighten out endless muddles, who must make the dreary arrangements for the move, who must find a cheap but genteel house in London and, once there, who must cope with the family accounts which she only, it seemed, could balance.

It would be: "You might see to that, Wilhelmina; you write, you've got such a good head for business." Or: "I wish you'd go down and explain to that man that we really can't pay his account till next quarter." Or: "This money for the grocer is five shillings short. Do run over my sum, Wilhelmina."

Her mother, grown feeble, discovered in this daughter a staff upon which she could lean with safety. Miss Ogilvy genuinely loved her mother, and was therefore quite prepared to be leaned on; but when Sarah and Fanny began to lean too with the full weight of endless neurotic symptoms incubated in resentful virginity, Miss Ogilvy found herself staggering a little. For Sarah and Fanny were grown hard to bear, with their mania for telling their symptoms to doctors, with their unstable nerves and their acrid tongues and the secret dislike they now felt for their mother. Indeed, when old Mrs. Ogilvy died, she was unmourned except by her eldest daughter who actually felt a void in her life—the unforeseen void that the ailing and weak will not infrequently leave behind them.

At about this time an aunt also died, bequeathing her fortune to her niece Wilhelmina who, however, was too weary to gird up her loins and set forth in search of exciting adventure—all she did was to move her protesting sisters to a little estate she had purchased in Surrey. This experiment was only a partial success, for Miss Ogilvy failed to make friends of her neighbours; thus at fifty-five she had grown rather dour, as is often the way with shy, lonely people.

When the war came she had just begun settling down—people do settle down in their fifty-sixth year—she was feeling quite glad that her hair was grey, that the garden took up so much of her time, that, in fact, the beat of her blood was slowing. But all this was changed when war was declared; on that day Miss Ogilvy's pulses throbbed wildly.

"My God! If only I were a man!" she burst out, as she glared at Sarah and Fanny, "if only I had been born a man!" Something in her was feeling deeply defrauded.

Sarah and Fanny were soon knitting socks and mittens and mufflers and

Jaeger trench-helmets. Other ladies were busily working at depots, making swabs at the Squire's, or splints at the Parson's; but Miss Ogilvy scowled and did none of these things—she was not at all like other ladies.

For nearly twelve months she worried officials with a view to getting a job out in France—not in their way but in hers, and that was the trouble. She wished to go up to the front-line trenches, she wished to be actually under fire, she informed the harassed officials.

To all her enquiries she received the same answer: "We regret that we cannot accept your offer." But once thoroughly roused she was hard to subdue, for her shyness had left her as though by magic.

Sarah and Fanny shrugged angular shoulders: "There's plenty of work here at home," they remarked, "though of course it's not quite so melodramatic!"

"Oh . . . ?" queried their sister on a rising note of impatience—and she promptly cut off her hair: "That'll jar them!" she thought with satisfaction.

Then she went up to London, formed her admirable unit and finally got it accepted by the French, despite renewed opposition.

In London she had found herself quite at her ease, for many another of her kind was in London doing excellent work for the nation. It was really surprising how many cropped heads had suddenly appeared as it were out of space; how many Miss Ogilvies, losing their shyness, had come forward asserting their right to serve, asserting their claim to attention.

There followed those turbulent years at the front, full of courage and hardship and high endeavour; and during those years Miss Ogilvy forgot the bad joke that Nature seemed to have played her. She was given the rank of a French lieutenant and she lived in a kind of blissful illusion; appalling reality lay on all sides and yet she managed to live in illusion. She was competent, fearless, devoted and untiring. What then? Could any man hope to do better? She was nearly fifty-eight, yet she walked with a stride, and at times she even swaggered a little.

Poor Miss Ogilvy sitting so glumly in the train with her manly trench-boots and her forage-cap! Poor all the Miss Ogilvies back from the war with their tunics, their trench-boots, and their childish illusions! Wars come and wars go but the world does not change: it will always forget an indebtedness which it thinks it expedient not to remember.

3

WHEN MISS OGILVY RETURNED TO HER HOME IN SURREY IT WAS ONLY TO find that her sisters were ailing from the usual imaginary causes, and this to a woman who had seen the real thing was intolerable, so that she looked with distaste at Sarah and then at Fanny. Fanny was certainly not prepossessing, she was suffering from a spurious attack of hay fever.

"Stop sneezing!" commanded Miss Ogilvy, in the voice that had so much impressed the Unit. But as Fanny was not in the least impressed, she naturally went on sneezing.

Miss Ogilvy's desk was piled mountain-high with endless tiresome letters and papers: circulars, bills, months-old correspondence, the gardener's accounts, an agent's report on some fields that required land-draining. She seated herself before this collection; then she sighed, it all seemed so absurdly trivial.

"Will you let your hair grow again?" Fanny enquired . . . she and Sarah had followed her into the study. "I'm certain the Vicar would be glad if you did."

"Oh?" murmured Miss Ogilvy, rather too blandly.

"Wilhelmina!"

"Yes?"

"You will do it, won't you?"

"Do what?"

"Let your hair grow; we all wish you would."

"Why should I?"

"Oh, well, it will look less odd, especially now that the war is over—in a small place like this people notice such things."

"I entirely agree with Fanny;" announced Sarah.

Sarah had become very self-assertive, no doubt through having mismanaged the estate during the years of her sister's absence. They had quite a heated dispute one morning over the south herbaceous border.

"Whose garden is this?" Miss Ogilvy asked sharply. "I insist on auricula-eyed sweet Williams! I even took the trouble to write from France, but it seems that my letter has been ignored."

"Don't shout," rebuked Sarah, "you're not in France now!"

Miss Ogilvy could gladly have boxed her ears: "I only wish to God I were," she muttered.

Another dispute followed close on its heels, and this time it happened to be over the dinner. Sarah and Fanny were living on weeds—at least that was the way Miss Ogilvy put it.

"We've become vegetarians," Sarah said grandly.

"You've become two damn tiresome cranks!" snapped their sister.

Now it never had been Miss Ogilvy's way to indulge in acid recriminations, but somehow, these days, she forgot to say: "Oh?" quite so often as expediency demanded. It may have been Fanny's perpetual sneezing that had got on her nerves; or it may have been Sarah, or the gardener, or the Vicar, or even the canary; though it really did not matter very much what it was just so long as she found a convenient peg upon which to hang her growing irritation.

"This won't do at all," Miss Ogilvy thought sternly, "life's not worth so much fuss, I must pull myself together." But it seemed this was easier said than done; not a day passed without her losing her temper and that over some trifle: "No, this won't do at all—it just mustn't be," she thought sternly.

Everyone pitied Sarah and Fanny: "Such a dreadful, violent old thing," said the neighbours.

But Sarah and Fanny had their revenge: "Poor darling, it's shell shock, you know," they murmured.

Thus Miss Ogilvy's prowess was whittled away until she herself was beginning to doubt it. Had she ever been that courageous person who had faced death in France with such perfect composure? Had she ever stood tranquilly under fire, without turning a hair, while she issued her orders? Had she ever been treated with marked respect? She herself was beginning to doubt it.

Sometimes she would see an old member of the Unit, a girl who, more faithful to her than the others, would take the trouble to run down to Surrey. These visits, however, were seldom enlivening.

"Oh, well . . . here we are . . ." Miss Ogilvy would mutter.

But one day the girl smiled and shook her blond head: "I'm not—I'm going to be married."

Strange thoughts had come to Miss Ogilvy, unbidden, thoughts that had stayed for many an hour after the girl's departure. Alone in her study she had suddenly shivered, feeling a sense of complete desolation. With cold hands she had lighted a cigarette.

"I must be ill or something," she had mused, as she stared at her trembling fingers.

After this she would sometimes cry out in her sleep, living over in dreams God knows what emotions; returning, maybe, to the battlefields of France. Her hair turned snow-white; it was not unbecoming yet she fretted about it.

"I'm growing very old," she would sigh as she brushed her thick mop before the glass; and then she would peer at her wrinkles.

For now that it had happened she hated being old; it no longer appeared such an easy solution of those difficulties that had always beset her. And this she resented most bitterly, so that she became the prey of self-pity, and of other undesirable states in which the body will torment the mind, and the mind, in its turn, the body. Then Miss Ogilvy straightened her ageing back, in spite of the fact that of late it had ached with muscular rheumatism, and she faced herself squarely and came to a resolve.

"I'm off!" she announced abruptly one day; and that evening she packed her kit-bag.

4

NEAR THE SOUTH COAST OF DEVON THERE EXISTS A SMALL ISLAND THAT IS still very little known to the world, but which nevertheless can boast an hotel, the only building upon it. Miss Ogilvy had chosen this place quite at random, it was marked on her map by scarcely more than a dot, but somehow she had liked the look of that dot and had set forth alone to explore it.

She found herself standing on the mainland one morning looking at a vague blur of green through the mist, a vague blur of green that rose out of the Channel like a tidal wave suddenly suspended. Miss Ogilvy was filled with a sense of adventure; she had not felt like this since the ending of war.

"I was right to come here, very right indeed. I'm going to shake off all my troubles," she decided.

A fisherman's boat was parting the mist, and before it was properly beached, in she bundled.

"I hope they're expecting me?" she said gaily.

"They du be expecting you," the man answered.

The sea, which is generally rough off that coast, was indulging itself in an oily ground-swell; the broad, glossy swells struck the side of the boat, then broke and sprayed over Miss Ogilvy's ankles.

The fisherman grinned: "Feeling all right?" he queried. "It du be tiresome most times about these parts." But the mist had suddenly drifted away and Miss Ogilvy was staring wide-eyed at the island.

She saw a long shoal of jagged black rocks, and between them the curve of a small sloping beach, and above that the lift of the island itself, and above that again, blue heaven. Near the beach stood the little two-storied hotel which was thatched, and built entirely of timber; for the rest she could make out no signs of life apart from a host of white sea-gulls.

Then Miss Ogilvy said a curious thing. She said: "On the south-west side of that place there was once a cave—a very large cave. I remember that it was some way from the sea."

"There du be a cave still," the fisherman told her, "but it's just above highwater level."

"A-ah," murmured Miss Ogilvy thoughtfully, as though to herself; then she looked embarrassed.

The little hotel proved both comfortable and clean, the hostess both pleasant and comely. Miss Ogilvy started unpacking her bag, changed her mind and went for a stroll round the island. The island was covered with turf and thistles and traversed by narrow green paths thick with daisies. It had four rock-bound coves of which the south-western was by far the most difficult of access. For just here the island descended abruptly as though it were hurtling down to the water; and just here the shale was most treacherous and the tide-swept rocks most aggressively pointed. Here it was that the seagulls, grown fearless of man by reason of his absurd limitations, built their nests on the ledges and reared countless young who multiplied, in their turn, every season. Yes, and here it was that Miss Ogilvy, greatly marvelling, stood and stared across at a cave; much too near the crumbling edge for her safety, but by now completely indifferent to caution.

"I remember . . . I remember . . ." she kept repeating. Then: "That's all very well, but what do I remember?"

She was conscious of somehow remembering all wrong, of her memory being distorted and coloured—perhaps by the endless things she had seen since her eyes had last rested upon that cave. This worried her sorely, far more than the fact that she should be remembering the cave at all, she who had never set foot on the island before that actual morning. Indeed, except for the sense of wrongness when she struggled to piece her memories together, she was steeped in a very profound contentment which surged over her spirit, wave upon wave.

"It's extremely odd," pondered Miss Ogilvy. Then she laughed, so pleased did she feel with its oddness.

5

THAT NIGHT AFTER SUPPER SHE TALKED TO HER HOSTESS WHO WAS ONLY TOO glad, it seemed, to be questioned. She owned the whole island and was proud of the fact, as she very well might be, decided her boarder. Some curious things had been found on the island, according to comely Mrs.

Nanceskivel: bronze arrow-heads, pieces of ancient stone celts; and once they had dug up a man's skull and thigh-bone—this had happened while they were sinking a well. Would Miss Ogilvy care to have a look at the bones? They were kept in a cupboard in the scullery.

Miss Ogilvy nodded.

"Then I'll fetch him this moment," said Mrs. Nanceskivel, briskly.

In less than two minutes she was back with the box that contained those poor remnants of a man, and Miss Ogilvy, who had risen from her chair, was gazing down at those remnants. As she did so her mouth was sternly compressed, but her face and her neck flushed darkly.

Mrs. Nanceskivel was pointing to the skull: "Look, miss, he was killed," she remarked rather proudly, "and they tell me that the axe that killed him was bronze. He's thousands and thousands of years old, they tell me. Our local doctor knows a lot about such things and he wants me to send these bones to an expert; they ought to belong to the Nation, he says. But I know what would happen, they'd come digging up my island, and I won't have people digging up my island, I've got enough worry with the rabbits as it is." But Miss Ogilvy could no longer hear the words for the pounding of the blood in her temples.

She was filled with a sudden, inexplicable fury against the innocent Mrs. Nanceskivel: "You . . . *you* . . ." she began, then checked herself, fearful of what she might say to the woman.

For her sense of outrage was overwhelming as she stared at those bones that were kept in the scullery; moreover, she knew how such men had been buried, which made the outrage seem all the more shameful. They had buried such men in deep, well-dug pits surmounted by four stout stones at their corners—four stout stones there had been and a covering stone. And all this Miss Ogilvy knew as by instinct, having no concrete knowledge on which to draw. But she knew it right down in the depths of her soul, and she hated Mrs. Nanceskivel.

And now she was swept by another emotion that was even more strange and more devastating: such a grief as she had not conceived could exist; a terrible unassuageable grief, without hope, without respite, without palliation, so that with something akin to despair she touched the long gash in the skull. Then her eyes, that had never wept since her childhood, filled slowly with large, hot, difficult tears. She must blink very hard, then close her eyelids, turn away from the lamp and say rather loudly:

"Thanks, Mrs. Nanceskivel. It's past eleven—I think I'll be going upstairs."

6

MISS OGILVY CLOSED THE DOOR OF HER BEDROOM, AFTER WHICH SHE stood quite still to consider: "Is it shell shock?" she muttered incredulously. "I wonder, can it be shell shock?"

She began to pace slowly about the room, smoking a Caporal. As usual her hands were deep in her pockets; she could feel small, familiar things in those pockets and she gripped them, glad of their presence. Then all of a sudden she was terribly tired, so tired that she flung herself down on the bed, unable to stand any longer.

She thought that she lay there struggling to reason, that her eyes were closed in the painful effort, and that as she closed them she continued to puff the inevitable cigarette. At least that was what she thought at one moment—the next, she was out in a sunset evening, and a large red sun was sinking slowly to the rim of a distant sea.

Miss Ogilvy knew that she was herself, that is to say she was conscious of her being, and yet she was not Miss Ogilvy at all, nor had she a memory of her. All that she now saw was very familiar, all that she now did was what she should do, and all that she now was seemed perfectly natural. Indeed, she did not think of these things; there seemed no reason for thinking about them.

She was walking with bare feet on turf that felt springy and was greatly enjoying the sensation; she had always enjoyed it, ever since as an infant she had learned to crawl on this turf. On either hand stretched rolling green uplands, while at her back she knew that there were forests; but in front, far away, lay the gleam of the sea towards which the big sun was sinking. The air was cool and intensely still, with never so much as a ripple or bird song. It was wonderfully pure—one might almost say young—but Miss Ogilvy thought of it merely as air. Having always breathed it she took it for granted, as she took the soft turf and the uplands.

She pictured herself as immensely tall; she was feeling immensely tall at that moment. As a matter of fact she was five feet eight which, however, was quite a considerable height when compared to that of her fellow tribesmen. She was wearing a single garment of pelts which came to her knees and left her arms sleeveless. Her arms and her legs, which were closely tattooed with blue zig-zag lines, were extremely hairy. From a leathern thong twisted about her waist there hung a clumsily made stone weapon, a celt, which in spite of its clumsiness was strongly hafted and useful for killing.

Miss Ogilvy wanted to shout aloud from a glorious sense of physical well-being, but instead she picked up a heavy, round stone which she hurled with great force at some distant rocks.

"Good! Strong!" she exclaimed. "See how far it goes!"

"Yes, strong. There is no one so strong as you. You are surely the strongest man in our tribe," replied her little companion.

Miss Ogilvy glanced at this little companion and rejoiced that they two were alone together. The girl at her side had a smooth brownish skin, oblique black eyes and short, sturdy limbs. Miss Ogilvy marvelled because of her beauty. She also was wearing a single garment of pelts, new pelts, she had made it that morning. She had stitched at it diligently for hours with short lengths of gut and her best bone needle. A strand of black hair hung over her bosom, and this she was constantly stroking and fondling; then she lifted the strand and examined her hair.

"Pretty," she remarked with childish complacence.

"Pretty," echoed the young man at her side.

"For you," she told him, "all of me is for you and none other. For you this body has ripened."

He shook back his own coarse hair from his eyes; he had sad brown eyes like those of a monkey. For the rest he was lean and steel-strong of loin, broad of chest, and with features not too uncomely. His prominent cheek-bones were set rather high, his nose was blunt, his jaw somewhat bestial; but his mouth, though full-lipped, contradicted his jaw, being very gentle and sweet in expression. And now he smiled, showing big, square, white teeth.

"You . . . woman," he murmured contentedly, and the sound seemed to come from the depths of his being.

His speech was slow and lacking in words when it came to expressing a vital emotion, so one word must suffice and this he now spoke, and the word that he spoke had a number of meanings. It meant: "Little spring of exceedingly pure water." It meant: "Hut of peace for a man after battle." It meant: "Ripe red berry sweet to the taste." It meant: "Happy small home of future generations." All these things he must try to express by a word, and because of their loving she understood him.

They paused, and lifting her up he kissed her. Then he rubbed his large shaggy head on her shoulder; and when he released her she knelt at his feet.

"My master; blood of my body," she whispered. For with her it was different, love had taught her love's speech, so that she might turn her heart into sounds that her primitive tongue could utter.

After she had pressed her lips to his hands, and her cheek to his hairy and powerful forearm, she stood up and they gazed at the setting sun, but with bowed heads, gazing under their lids, because this was very sacred.

A couple of mating bears padded towards them from a thicket, and the female rose to her haunches. But the man drew his celt and menaced the beast, so that she dropped down noiselessly and fled, and her mate also fled, for here was the power that few dared to withstand by day or by night, on the uplands or in the forests. And now from across to the left where a river would presently lose itself in the marshes, came a rhythmical thudding, as a herd of red deer with wide nostrils and starting eyes thundered past, disturbed in their drinking by the bears.

After this the evening returned to its silence, and the spell of its silence descended on the lovers, so that each felt very much alone, yet withal more closely united to the other. But the man became restless under that spell, and he suddenly laughed; then grasping the woman he tossed her above his head and caught her. This he did many times for his own amusement and because he knew that his strength gave her joy. In this manner they played together for a while, he with his strength and she with her weakness. And they cried out, and made many guttural sounds which were meaningless save only to themselves. And the tunic of pelts slipped down from her breasts, and her two little breasts were pear-shaped.

Presently, he grew tired of their playing, and he pointed towards a cluster of huts and earthworks that lay to the eastward. The smoke from these huts rose in thick straight lines, bending neither to right nor left in its rising, and the thought of sweet burning rushes and brushwood touched his consciousness, making him feel sentimental.

"Smoke," he said.

And she answered: "Blue smoke."

He nodded: "Yes, blue smoke—home."

Then she said: "I have ground much corn since the full moon. My stones are too smooth. You make me new stones."

"All you have need of, I make," he told her.

She stole closer to him, taking his hand: "My father is still a black cloud full of thunder. He thinks that you wish to be head of our tribe in his place, because he is now very old. He must not hear of these meetings of ours, if he did I think he would beat me!"

So he asked her: "Are you unhappy, small berry?"

But at this she smiled: "What is being unhappy? I do not know what that means any more."

"I do not either," he answered.

Then as though some invisible force had drawn him, his body swung round and he stared at the forests where they lay and darkened, fold upon fold; and his eyes dilated with wonder and terror, and he moved his head quickly from side to side as a wild thing will do that is held between bars and whose mind is pitifully bewildered.

"Water!" he cried hoarsely, "great water—look, look! Over there. This land is surrounded by water!"

"What water?" she questioned.

He answered: "The sea." And he covered his face with his hands.

"Not so," she consoled, "big forests, good hunting. Big forests in which you hunt boar and aurochs. No sea over there but only the trees."

He took his trembling hands from his face: "You are right . . . only trees," he said dully.

But now his face had grown heavy and brooding and he started to speak of a thing that oppressed him: "The Roundheaded-ones, they are devils," he growled, while his bushy black brows met over his eyes, and when this happened it changed his expression which became a little sub-human.

"No matter," she protested, for she saw that he forgot her and she wished him to think and talk only of love. "No matter. My father laughs at your fears. Are we not friends with the Roundheaded-ones? We are friends, so why should we fear them?"

"Our forts, very old, very weak," he went on, "and the Roundheaded-ones have terrible weapons. Their weapons are not made of good stone like ours, but of some dark, devilish substance."

"What of that?" she said lightly. "They would fight on our side, so why need we trouble about their weapons?"

But he looked away, not appearing to hear her. "We must barter all, all for their celts and arrows and spears, and then we must learn their secret. They lust after our women, they lust after our lands. We must barter all, all for their sly brown celts."

"Me . . . bartered?" she queried, very sure of his answer, otherwise she had not dared to say this.

"The Roundheaded-ones may destroy my tribe and yet I will not part with you," he told her. Then he spoke very gravely: "But I think they desire to slay us, and me they will try to slay first because they well know how much I mistrust them—they have seen my eyes fixed many times on their camps."

She cried: "I will bite out the throats of these people if they so much as scratch your skin!"

And at this his mood changed and he roared with amusement: "You . . . woman!" he roared. "Little foolish white teeth. Your teeth were made for nibbling wild cherries, not for tearing the throats of the Roundheaded-ones!"

"Thoughts of war always make me afraid," she whimpered, still wishing him to talk about love.

He turned his sorrowful eyes upon her, the eyes that were sad even when he was merry, and although his mind was often obtuse, yet he clearly perceived how it was with her then. And his blood caught fire from the flame in her blood, so that he strained her against his body.

"You . . . mine . . ." he stammered.

"Love," she said, trembling, "this is love."

And he answered: "Love."

Then their faces grew melancholy for a moment, because dimly, very dimly in their dawning souls, they were conscious of a longing for something more vast than this earthly passion could compass.

Presently, he lifted her like a child and carried her quickly southward and westward till they came to a place where a gentle descent led down to a marshy valley. Far away, at the line where the marshes ended, they discerned the misty line of the sea; but the sea and the marshes were become as one substance, merging, blending, folding together; and since they were lovers they also would be one, even as the sea and the marshes.

And now they had reached the mouth of a cave that was set in the quiet hillside. There was bright green verdure beside the cave, and a number of small, pink, thick-stemmed flowers that when they were crushed smelt of spices. And within the cave there was bracken newly gathered and heaped together for a bed; while beyond, from some rocks, came a low liquid sound as a spring dripped out through a crevice. Abruptly, he set the girl on her feet, and she knew that the days of her innocence were over. And she thought of the anxious virgin soil that was rent and sown to bring forth fruit in season, and she gave a quick little gasp of fear:

"No . . . no . . ." she gasped. For, divining his need, she was weak with the longing to be possessed, yet the terror of love lay heavy upon her. "No . . . no . . ." she gasped.

But he caught her wrist and she felt the great strength of his rough, gnarled fingers, the great strength of the urge that leapt in his loins, and again she must give that quick gasp of fear, the while she clung close to him lest he should spare her.

The twilight was engulfed and possessed by darkness, which in turn was transfigured by the moonrise, which in turn was fulfilled and consumed by dawn. A mighty eagle soared up from his eyrie, cleaving the air with his masterful wings, and beneath him from the rushes that harboured their nests, rose other great birds, crying loudly. Then the heavy-horned elks appeared on the uplands, bending their burdened heads to the sod; while beyond in the forests the fierce wild aurochs stamped as they bellowed their love songs.

But within the dim cave the lord of these creatures had put by his weapon and his instinct for slaying. And he lay there defenceless with tenderness, thinking no longer of death but of life as he murmured the word that had so many meanings. That meant: "Little spring of exceedingly pure water." That meant: "Hut of peace for a man after battle." That meant: "Ripe red berry sweet to the taste." That meant: "Happy small home of future generations."

7

THEY FOUND MISS OGILVY THE NEXT MORNING; THE FISHERMAN SAW HER and climbed to the ledge. She was sitting at the mouth of the cave. She was dead, with her hands thrust deep into her pockets.

1926

E. M. FORSTER

::

ARTHUR SNATCHFOLD

1

CONWAY (SIR RICHARD CONWAY) WOKE EARLY, AND WENT TO THE WINDOW to have a look at the Trevor Donaldsons' garden. Too green. A flight of mossy steps led up from the drive to a turfed amphitheatre. This contained a number of trees of the lead-pencil persuasion, and a number of flower-beds, profuse with herbaceous promises which would certainly not be fulfilled that weekend. The summer was heavy-leaved and at a moment between flowerings, and the gardener, though evidently expensive, had been caught bending. Bounding the amphitheatre was a high yew hedge, an imposing background had there been any foreground, and behind the hedge a heavy wood shut the sky out. Of course what was wanted was colour. Delphinium, salvia, red-hot-poker, zinnias, tobacco-plant, anything. Leaning out of the baronial casement, Conway considered this, while he waited for his tea. He was not an artist, nor a philosopher, but he liked exercising his mind when he had nothing else to do, as on this Sunday morning, this country morning, with so much ahead to be eaten, and so little to be said.

The visit, like the view, threatened monotony. Dinner had been dull. His own spruce gray head, gleaming in the mirrors, really seemed the brightest object about. Trevor Donaldson's head was mangy, Mrs Donaldson's combed up into bastions of iron. He did not get unduly fussed at the prospect of boredom. He was a man of experience with plenty of resources and plenty of armour, and he was a decent human being too. The Donaldsons were his inferiors—they had not travelled or read or gone in for sport or love, they were merely his business allies, linked to him by a common interest in aluminium. Still, he must try to make things nice, since they had been so good as to invite him down.

"But it's not so easy to make things nice for us business people," he reflected, as he listened to the chonk of a blackbird, the clink of a milk-can, and the distant self-communings of an electric pump. "We're not stupid or uncultivated, we can use our minds when required, we can go to concerts when we're not too tired, we've invested—even Trevor Donaldson has—in the sense of humour. But I'm afraid we don't get much pleasure out of it all. No. Pleasure's been left out of our packet." Business occupied him increasingly since his wife's death. He brought an active mind to bear on it, and was quickly becoming rich.

He looked at the dull costly garden. It improved. A man had come into it from the back of the yew hedge. He had on a canary-coloured shirt, and the effect was exactly right. The whole scene blazed. *That* was what the place wanted—not a flower-bed, but a man, who advanced with a confident tread down the amphitheatre, and as he came nearer Conway saw that besides being proper to the colour scheme he was a very proper youth. His shoulders were broad, his face sensuous and open, his eyes, screwed up against the light, promised good temper. One arm shot out at an angle, the other supported a milk-can. "Good morning, nice morning," he called, and he sounded happy.

"Good morning, nice morning," he called back. The man continued at a steady pace, turned left, and disappeared in the direction of the servants' entrance, where an outburst of laughter welcomed him.

Conway hoped he might return by the same route, and waited. "That is a nice-looking fellow, I do like the way he holds himself, and probably no nonsense about him," he thought. But the vision had departed, the sunlight stopped, the garden turned stodgy and green again, and the maid came in with his tea. She said, "I'm sorry to be late, we were waiting for the milk, sir." The man had not called him sir, and the omission flattered him. "Good morning, sir" would have been the more natural salutation to an elderly stranger, a wealthy customer's guest. But the vigorous voice had shouted "Good morning, nice morning," as if they were equals.

Where had he gone off to now, he and his voice? To finish his round, welcomed at house after house, and then for a bathe perhaps, his shirt golden on the grass beside him. Ruddy brown to the waist he would show now. . . . What was his name? Was he a local? Sir Richard put these questions to himself as he dressed, but not vehemently. He was not a sentimentalist, there was no danger of him being shattered for the day. He would have liked to meet the vision again, and spend the whole of Sunday with it, giving it a slap-up lunch at the hotel, hiring a car, which they would drive alternately, treating it to the pictures in the neighbouring town, and returning with it, after one drink too much, through dusky lanes. But that was sheer nonsense, even if the vision had been agreeable to the programme. He was staying with the Trevor Donaldsons; and he must not repay their hospitality by moping. Dressed in a cheerful gray, he ran downstairs to the breakfast-room. Mrs Donaldson was already there, and she asked him how his daughters were getting on at their school.

Then his host followed, rubbing his hands together, and saying "Aha, aha!" and when they had eaten they went into the other garden, the one which sloped towards the water, and started talking business. They had not intended to do this, but there was also of their company a Mr Clifford Clarke, and when Trevor Donaldson, Clifford Clarke and Richard Conway got together it was impossible that aluminium should escape. Their voices deepened, their heads nodded or shook as they recalled vast sums that had been lost through unsound investments or misapplied advice. Conway found himself the most intelligent of the three, the quickest at taking a point, the strongest at following an argument. The moments passed, the blackbird chonk-chonked unheeded, unnoticed was the failure of the gardener to produce anything but tightly furled geraniums, unnoticed the ladies on the lawn, who wanted to get some golf. At last the hostess called, "Trevor! Is this a holiday or isn't it?" and they stopped, feeling rather ashamed. The cars came round, and soon they were five miles away, on the course, taking their turn in a queue of fellow merry-makers. Conway was good at golf, and got what excitement he could from it, but as soon as the ball flew off he was aware of a slight sinking feeling. This occupied them till lunch. After coffee they walked down to the water, and played with the dogs—Mrs Donaldson bred Sealyhams. Several neighbours came to tea, and now the animation rested with Donaldson, for he fancied himself as a country magnate, and wanted to show how well he was settling into the part. There was a good deal of talk about local conditions, women's institutes, education through discipline, and poaching. Conway found all this quite nonsensical and unreal. People who are not feudal should not play at feudalism, and all magistrates (this he said aloud) ought to be trained and ought to be paid. Since he was well-bred, he said it in a form which did not give offence. Thus the day wore away, and they filled in the interval before dinner by driving to see a ruined monastery. What on earth had they got to do with a monastery? Nothing at all. Nothing at all. He caught sight of Clifford Clarke looking mournfully at a rose-window, and he got the feeling that they were all of them looking for something which was not there, that there was an empty chair at the table, a card missing from the bridge-pack, a ball lost in the gorse, a stitch dropped in the shirt; that the chief guest had not come. On their way out they passed through the village, on their way back past a cinema, which was giving a Wild West stunt. They returned through darkling lanes. They did not say, "Thank you! What a delightful day!" That would be saved up for tomorrow morning, and for the final gratitude of departure. Every word would be needed then. "I *have* enjoyed myself, *I have,* absolutely marvellous!" the women would chant, and the men would grunt, as if moved beyond words, and the host and hostess would cry, "Oh but come again, then, come again." Into the void the little unmemorable visit would fall, like a leaf it would fall upon similar leaves, but Conway wondered whether it hadn't been, so to speak, specially negative, out of the way unflowering, whether a champion, one bare arm at an angle, hadn't carried away to the servants' quarters some refreshment which was badly needed in the smoking-room.

"Well, perhaps we shall see, we may yet find out," he thought, as he went up to bed, carrying with him his raincoat.

For he was not one to give in and grumble. He believed in pleasure; he had a free mind and an active body, and he knew that pleasure cannot be won without courage and coolness. The Donaldsons were all very well, but they were not the whole of his life. His daughters were all very well, but the same held good of them. The female sex was all very well and he was addicted to it, but permitted himself an occasional deviation. He set his alarm watch for an hour slightly earlier than the hour at which he had woken in the morning, and he put it under his pillow, and he fell asleep looking quite young.

Seven o'clock tinkled. He glanced into the passage, then put on his raincoat and thick slippers, and went to the window.

It was a silent sunless morning, and seemed earlier than it actually was. The green of the garden and of the trees was filmed with grey, as if it wanted wiping. Presently the electric pump started. He looked at his watch again, slipped down the stairs, out of the house, across the amphitheatre and through the yew hedge. He did not run, in case he was seen and had to explain. He moved at the maximum pace possible for a gentleman, known to be an original, who fancies an early stroll in his pyjamas. "I thought I'd have a look at your formal garden, there wouldn't have been time after breakfast" would have been the line. He had of course looked at it the day before, also at the wood. The wood lay before him now, and the sun was just tipping into it. There were two paths through the bracken, a broad and a narrow. He waited until he heard the milk-can approaching down the narrow path. Then he moved quickly, and they met, well out of sight of the Donaldsonian demesne.

"Hullo!" he called in his easy out-of-doors voice; he had several voices, and knew by instinct which was wanted.

"Hullo! Somebody's out early!"

"You're early yourself."

"Me? Whor'd the milk be if I worn't?" the milkman grinned, throwing his head back and coming to a standstill. Seen at close quarters he was coarse, very much of the people and of the thick-fingered earth; a hundred years ago his type was trodden into the mud, now it burst and flowered and didn't care a damn.

"You're the morning delivery, eh?"

"Looks like it." He evidently proposed to be facetious—the clumsy fun which can be so delightful when it falls from the proper lips. "I'm not the evening delivery anyway, and I'm not the butcher nor the grocer, nor'm I the coals."

"Live around here?"

"Maybe. Maybe I don't. Maybe I flop about in them planes."

"You live around here, I bet."

"What if I do?"

"If you do you do. And if I don't I don't."

This fatuous retort was a success, and was greeted with doubled-up laughter. "If you don't you don't! Ho, you're a funny one! There's a thing to say! If you don't you don't! Walking about in yer night things, too, you'll ketch a cold you will, that'll be the end of you! Stopping back in the 'otel, I suppose?"

"No. Donaldson's. You saw me there yesterday."

"Oh, Donaldson's, that's it. You was the old granfa' at the upstairs window."

"Old granfa' indeed. . . . I'll granfa' you," and he tweaked at the impudent nose. It dodged, it seemed used to this sort of thing. There was probably nothing the lad wouldn't consent to if properly handled, partly out of mischief, partly to oblige. "Oh, by the way . . ." and he felt the shirt as if interested in the quality of its material. "What was I going to say?" and he gave the zip at the throat a downward pull. Much slid into view. "Oh, I know—when's this round of yours over?"

" 'Bout eleven. Why?"

"Why not?"

" 'Bout eleven *at night*. Ha ha. Got yer there. Eleven at night. What you want to arst all them questions for? We're strangers, aren't we?"

"How old are you?"

"Ninety, same as yourself."

"What's your address?"

"There you go on! Hi! I like that. Arstin questions after I tell you No."

"Got a girl? Ever heard of a pint? Ever heard of two?"

"Go on. Get out." But he suffered his forearm to be worked between massaging fingers, and he set down his milk-can. He was amused. He was charmed. He was hooked, and a touch would land him.

"You look like a boy who looks all right," the elder man breathed.

"Oh, *stop* it. . . . All right, I'll go with you."

Conway was entranced. Thus, exactly thus, should the smaller pleasures of life be approached. They understood one another with a precision impossible for lovers. He laid his face on the warm skin over the clavicle, hands nudged him behind, and presently the sensation for which he had planned so cleverly was over. It was part of the past. It had fallen like a flower upon similar flowers.

He heard "You all right?" It was over there too, part of a different past. They were lying deeper in the wood, where the fern was highest. He did not reply, for it was pleasant to lie stretched thus and to gaze up through bracken fronds at the distant treetops and the pale blue sky, and feel the exquisite pleasure fade.

"That was what you wanted, wasn't it?" Propped on his elbows the young man looked down anxiously. All his roughness and pertness had gone, and he only wanted to know whether he had been a success.

"Yes. . . . Lovely."

"Lovely? You say lovely?" he beamed, prodding gently with his stomach.

"Nice boy, nice shirt, nice everything."

"That a fact?"

Conway guessed that he was vain, the better sort often are, and laid on the flattery thick to please him, praised his comeliness, his thrusting thrashing strength; there was plenty to praise. He liked to do this and to see the broad face grinning and feel the heavy body on him. There was no cynicism in the flattery, he was genuinely admiring and gratified.

"So you enjoyed that?"

"Who wouldn't?"

"Pity you didn't tell me yesterday."

"I didn't know how to."

"I'd a met you down where I have my swim. You could 'elped me strip, you'd like that. Still, we mustn't grumble." He gave Conway a hand and pulled him up, and brushed and tidied the raincoat like an old friend. "We could get seven years for this, couldn't we?"

"Not seven years, still we'd get something nasty. Madness, isn't it? What can it matter to anyone else if you and I don't mind?"

"Oh, I suppose they've to occupy themselves with somethink or other," and he took up the milk-can to go on.

"Half a minute, boy—do take this and get yourself some trifle with it." He produced a note which he had brought on the chance.

"I didn't do it fer that."

"I know you didn't."

"Naow, we was each as bad as the other. . . . Naow . . . keep yer money."

"I'd be pleased if you would take it. I expect I'm better off than you and it might come in useful. To take out your girl, say, or towards your next new suit. However, please yourself, of course."

"Can you honestly afford it?"

"Honestly."

"Well, I'll find a way to spend it, no doubt. People don't always behave as nice as you, you know."

Conway could have returned the compliment. The affair had been trivial and crude, and yet they both had behaved perfectly. They would never meet again, and they did not exchange names. After a hearty handshake, the young man swung away down the path, the sunlight and shadow rushing over his back. He did not turn round, but his arm, jerking sideways to balance him, waved an acceptable farewell. The green flowed over his brightness, the path bent, he disappeared. Back he went to his own life, and through the quiet of the morning his laugh could be heard as he whooped at the maids.

Conway waited for a few moments, as arranged, and then he went back too. His luck held. He met no one, either in the amphitheatre garden or on the stairs, and after he had been in his room for a minute the maid arrived with his early tea. "I'm sorry the milk was late again, sir," she said. He enjoyed it, bathed and shaved and dressed himself for town. It was the figure of a superior city-man which was reflected in the mirror as he tripped downstairs. The car came round after breakfast to take him to the station, and he was completely sincere when he told the Trevor Donaldsons that he had had an out-of-the-way pleasant weekend. They believed him, and their faces grew brighter. "Come again then, come by all means again," they cried as he slid off. In the train he read the papers rather less than usual and smiled to himself rather more. It was so pleasant to have been completely right over a stranger, even down to little details like the texture of the skin. It flattered his vanity. It increased his sense of power.

2

HE DID NOT SEE TREVOR DONALDSON AGAIN FOR SOME WEEKS. THEN THEY met in London at his club, for a business talk and a spot of lunch. Circumstances which they could not control had rendered them less friendly. Owing to regrouping in the financial world, their interests were now opposed, and if one of them stood to make money out of aluminium the other stood to lose. So the talk had been cautious. Donaldson, the weaker man, felt tired and worried after it. He had not, to his knowledge, made a mistake, but he might have slipped unwittingly, and be poorer, and have to give up his county state. He looked at his host with hostility and wished he could harm him. Sir Richard was aware of this, but felt no hostility in return. For one thing, he was going to win, for another, hating never interested him. This was probably the last occasion on which they would foregather socially; but he exercised his usual charm. He wanted, too, to find out during lunch how far Donaldson was aware of his own danger. Clifford Clarke (who was allied with him) had failed to do this.

After adjourning to the cloakroom and washing their hands at adjacent basins, they sat opposite each other at a little table. Down the long room sat other pairs of elderly men, eating, drinking, talking quietly, instructing the waiters. Inquiries were exchanged about Mrs Donaldson and the young Miss Conways, and there were some humorous references to golf. Then Donaldson said, with a change in his voice: "Golf's all you say, and the great advantage of it in these days is that you get it practically anywhere. I used to think our course was good, for a little country course, but it is far below the average. This is somewhat of a disappointment to us both, since we settled down there specially for the golf. The fact is, the country is not at all what it seems when first you go there."

"So I've always heard."

"My wife likes it, of course, she has her Sealyhams, she has her flowers, she has her local charities—though in these days one's not supposed to speak of 'charity'. I don't know why. I should have thought it was a good word, charity. She runs the Women's Institute, so far as it consents to be run, but Conway, Conway, you'd never believe how offhand the village women are in these days. They don't elect Mrs Donaldson president yearly as a matter of course. She takes turn and turn with cottagers."

"Oh, that's the spirit of the age, of course. One's always running into it in some form or other. For instance, I don't get nearly the deference I did from my clerks."

"But better work from them, no doubt," said Donaldson gloomily.

"No. But probably they're better men."

"Well, perhaps the ladies at the Women's Institute are becoming better women. But my wife doubts it. Of course our village is particularly unfortunate, owing to that deplorable hotel. It has had such a bad influence. We had an extraordinary case before us on the Bench recently, connected with it."

"That hotel did look too flash—it would attract the wrong crowd."

"I've also had bother bother bother with the Rural District Council over the removal of tins, and another bother—a really maddening one—over a right of way through the church meadows. That almost made me lose my patience. And I really sometimes wonder whether I've been sensible in digging myself in in the country, and trying to make myself useful in local affairs. There is no gratitude. There is no warmth of welcome."

"I quite believe it, Donaldson, and I know I'd never have a country place myself, even if the scenery is as pleasant as yours is, and even if I could afford it. I make do with a service flat in town, and I retain a small furnished cottage for my girls' holidays, and when they leave school I shall partly take them and partly send them abroad. I don't believe in undiluted England, nice as are sometimes the English. Shall we go up and have coffee?"

He ran up the staircase briskly, for he had found out what he wanted to know: Donaldson was feeling poor. He stuck him in a low leathern armchair, and had a look at him as he closed his eyes. That was it: he felt he couldn't afford his "little place", and was running it down, so that no one should be surprised when he gave it up. Meanwhile, there was one point in the conversation it amused him to take up now that business was finished with: the reference to that "extraordinary case" connected with the local hotel.

Donaldson opened his eyes when asked, and they had gone prawn-like. "Oh, that was a case, it was a really really," he said. "I knew such things existed, of course, but I assumed in my innocence they were confined to Piccadilly. However, it has all been traced back to the hotel, the proprietress has had a thorough fright, and I don't think there will be any trouble in the future. Indecency between males."

"Oh, good Lord!" said Sir Richard coolly. "Black or white?"

"White, please, it's an awful nuisance, but I can't take black coffee now, although I greatly prefer it. You see, some of the hotel guests—there was a bar, and some of the villagers used to go in there after cricket because they thought it smarter than that charming old thatched pub by the church —you remember that old thatched pub. Villagers are terrific snobs, that's one of the disappointing discoveries one makes. The bar got a bad reputation of a certain type, especially at weekends, someone complained to the police, a watch was set, and the result was this quite extraordinary case. . . . Really, really, I wouldn't have believed it. A *little* milk, please, Conway, if I may, just a little; I'm not allowed to take my coffee black."

"So sorry. Have a liqueur."

"No, no thanks, I'm not allowed that even, especially after lunch."

"Come on, do—I will if you will. Waiter, can we have two double cognacs?"

"He hasn't heard you. Don't bother."

Conway had not wanted the waiter to hear him, he had wanted an excuse to be out of the room and have a minute alone. He was suddenly worried in case that milkman had got into a scrape. He had scarcely thought about him since—he had a very full life, and it included an intrigue with a cultivated woman, which was gradually ripening—but nobody could have been more decent and honest, or more physically attractive in a particular way. It had been a charming little adventure, and a remarkably lively one. And their parting had been perfect. Wretched if the lad had come to grief! Enough to make one cry. He offered up a sort of prayer, ordered the cognacs, and rejoined Donaldson with his usual briskness. He put on the Renaissance armour that suited him so well, and "How did the hotel case end?" he asked.

"We committed him for trial."

"Oh! As bad as that?"

"Well, we thought so. Actually a gang of about half a dozen were involved, but we only caught one of them. His mother, if you please, is president of the Women's Institute, and hasn't had the decency to resign! I tell you, Conway, these people aren't the same flesh and blood as oneself. One pretends they are, but they aren't. And what with this disillusionment, and what with the right of way, I've a good mind to clear out next year, and leave the so-called country to stew in its own juice. It's utterly corrupt. This man made an awfully bad impression on the Bench and we didn't feel that six months, which is the maximum we are allowed to impose, was adequate to the offence. And it was all so revoltingly commercial—his only motive was money."

Conway felt relieved; it couldn't be his own friend, for anyone less grasping . . .

"And another unpleasant feature—at least for me—is that he had the habit of taking his clients into my grounds."

"How most vexatious for you!"

"It suited his convenience, and of what else should he think? I have a little wood—you didn't see it—which stretches up to the hotel, so he could easily bring people in. A path my wife was particularly fond of—a mass of bluebells in springtime—it was there they were caught. You may well imagine this has helped to put me off the place."

"Who caught them?" he asked, holding his glass up to the light; their cognacs had arrived.

"Our local bobby. For we do possess that extraordinary rarity, a policeman who keeps his eyes open. He sometimes commits errors of judgement—he did on this occasion—but he's certainly observant, and as he was coming down one of the other paths, a public one, he saw a bright yellow shirt through the bracken—upsa! Take care!"

"Upsa!" were some drops of brandy, which Conway had spilt. Alas, alas, there could be no doubt about it. He felt deeply distressed, and rather guilty. The young man must have decided after their successful encounter to use the wood as a rendez-vous. It was a cruel stupid world, and he was countenancing it more than he should. Wretched, wretched, to think of that good-tempered, harmless chap being bruised and ruined . . . the whole thing so unnecessary—betrayed by the shirt he was so proud of. . . . Conway was not often moved, but this time he felt much regret and compassion.

"Well, he recognized that shirt at once. He had particular reasons for keeping a watch on its wearer. And he got him, he got him. But he lost the other man. He didn't charge them straight away, as he ought to have done. I think he was genuinely startled and could scarcely believe his eyes. For one thing, it was so early in the morning—barely seven o'clock."

"A strange hour!" said Conway, and put his glass down, and folded his hands on his knee.

"He caught sight of them as they were getting up after committing the indecency, also he saw money pass, but instead of rushing in there and then he made an elaborate and totally unnecessary plan for interrupting the youth on the further side of my house, and of course he could have got him any time, any time. A stupid error of judgement. A great pity. He never arrested him until 7.45."

"Was there then sufficient evidence for an arrest?"

"There was abundant evidence of a medical character, if you follow me —what a case, oh, what a case!—also there was the money on him, which clinched his guilt."

"Mayn't the money have been in connection with his round?"

"No. It was a note, and he only had small change in connection with his round. We established that from his employer. But how ever did you guess he was on a round?"

"You told me," said Conway, who never became flustered when he made a slip. "You mentioned that he had a milk round and that the mother was connected with some local organization which Mrs Donaldson takes an interest in."

"Yes, yes, the Women's Institute. Well, having fixed all that up, our policeman then went on to the hotel, but it was far too late by that time, some of the guests were breakfasting, others had left, he couldn't go round cross-questioning everyone, and no one corresponded to the description of the person whom he saw being hauled up out of the fern."

"What was the description?"

"An old man in pyjamas and a mackintosh—our Chairman was awfully anxious to get hold of him—oh, you remember our Chairman, Ernest Dray, you met him at my little place. He's determined to stamp this sort of thing out, once and for all. Hullo, it's past three, I must be getting back to my grindstone. Many thanks for lunch. I don't know why I've discoursed on this somewhat unsavoury topic. I'd have done better to consult you about the right of way."

"You must another time. I did look up the subject once."

"How about a spot of lunch with me this day week?" said Donaldson, remembering their business feud, and becoming uneasily jolly.

"This day week? Now can I? No, I can't. I've promised this day week to go and see my little girls. Not that they're little any longer. Time flies, doesn't it? We're none of us younger."

"Sad but true," said Donaldson, heaving himself out of the deep leather chair. Similar chairs, empty or filled with similar men, receded down the room, and far away a small fire smoked under a heavy mantelpiece. "But aren't you going to drink your cognac? It's excellent cognac."

"I suddenly took against it—I do indulge in caprices." Getting up, he felt faint, the blood rushed to his head and he thought he was going to fall. "Tell me," he said, taking his enemy's arm and conducting him to the door, "this old man in the mackintosh—how was it the fellow you caught never put you on his track?"

"He tried to."

"Oh, did he?"

"Yes indeed, and he was all the more anxious to do so, because we made it clear that he would be let off if he helped us to make the major arrest. But all he could say was what we knew already—that it was someone from the hotel."

"Oh, he said that, did he? From the hotel."

"Said it again and again. Scarcely said anything else, indeed almost went into a sort of fit. There he stood with his head thrown back and his eyes shut, barking at us, 'Th'otel. Keep to th'otel. I tell you he come from th'otel.' We advised him not to get so excited, whereupon he became insolent, which did him no good with Ernest Dray, as you may well imagine, and called the Bench a row of interfering bastards. He was instantly removed from the court and as he went he shouted back at us—you'll never credit this—that if he and the old grandfather didn't mind it why should anyone else. We talked the case over carefully and came to the conclusion it must go to Assizes."

"What was his name?"

"But we don't know, I tell you, we never caught him."

"I mean the name of the one you did catch, the village boy."

"Arthur Snatchfold."

They had reached the top of the club staircase. Conway saw the reflection of his face once more in a mirror, and it was the face of an old man. He pushed Trevor Donaldson off abruptly, and went back to sit down by his liqueur-glass. He was safe, safe, he could go forward with his career as planned. But waves of shame came over him. Oh for prayer!—but whom had he to pray to, and what about? He saw that little things can turn into great ones, and he did not want greatness. He was not up to it. For a moment he considered giving himself up and standing his trial, however what possible good would that do? He would ruin himself and his daughters, he would delight his enemies, and he would not save his saviour. He recalled his clever manoeuvres for a little fun, and the good-humoured response, the mischievous face, the obliging body. It had all seemed so trivial. Taking a notebook from his pocket, he wrote down the name of his lover, yes, his lover who was going to prison to save him, in order that he might not forget it. Arthur Snatchfold. He had only heard the name once, and he would never hear it again.

1928

WILLIAM FAULKNER

DIVORCE IN NAPLES

I

WE WERE SITTING AT A TABLE INSIDE: MONCKTON AND THE BOSUN AND CARL and George and me and the women, the three women of that abject glittering kind that seamen know or that know seamen. We were talking English and they were not talking at all. By that means they could speak constantly to us above and below the sound of our voices in a tongue older than recorded speech and time too. Older than the thirty-four days of sea time which we had but completed, anyway. Now and then they spoke to one another in Italian. The women in Italian, the men in English, as if language might be the sex difference, the functioning of the vocal cords the inner biding until the dark pairing time. The men in English, the women in Italian: a decorum as of two parallel streams separated by a levee for a little while.

We were talking about Carl, to George.

"Why did you bring him here, then?" the bosun said.

"Yes," Monckton said. "I sure wouldn't bring my wife to a place like this."

George cursed Monckton: not with a word or even a sentence; a paragraph. He was a Greek, big and black, a full head taller than Carl; his eyebrows looked like two crows in overlapping flight. He cursed us all with immediate thoroughness and in well-nigh faultless classic Anglo-Saxon, who at other times functioned in the vocabulary of an eight-year-old by-blow of a vaudeville comedian and a horse, say.

"Yes, sir," the bosun said. He was smoking an Italian cigar and drinking ginger beer; the same tumbler of which, incidentally, he had been engaged with for about two hours and which now must have been about the temperature of a ship's showerbath. "I sure wouldn't bring my girl to a dive like this, even if he did wear pants."

Carl meanwhile had not stirred. He sat serene among us, with his round yellow head and his round eyes, looking like a sophisticated baby against the noise and the glitter, with his glass of thin Italian beer and the women murmuring to one another and watching us and then Carl with that biding and inscrutable foreknowledge which they do not appear to know that they possess. *"Èinnocente,"* one said; again they murmured, contemplating Carl with musing, secret looks. "He may have fooled you already," the bosun said. "He may have slipped through a porthole on you any time these three years."

George glared at the bosun, his mouth open for cursing. But he didn't curse. Instead he looked at Carl, his mouth still open. His mouth closed slowly. We all looked at Carl. Beneath our eyes he raised his glass and drank with contained deliberation.

"Are you still pure?" George said. "I mean, sho enough."

Beneath our fourteen eyes Carl emptied the glass of thin, bitter, three per cent beer. "I been to sea three years," he said. "All over Europe."

George glared at him, his face baffled and outraged. He had just shaved; his close blue jowls lay flat and hard as a prizefighter's or a pirate's, up to the black explosion of his hair. He was our second cook. "You damn lying little bastard," he said.

The bosun raised his glass of ginger beer with an exact replica of Carl's drinking. Steadily and deliberately, his body thrown a little back and his head tilted, he poured the ginger beer over his right shoulder at the exact speed of swallowing, still with that air of Carl's, that grave and cosmopolitan swagger. He set the glass down, and rose. "Come on," he said to Monckton and me; "let's go. Might as well be board ship if we're going to spend the evening in one place."

Monckton and I rose. He was smoking a short pipe. One of the women was his, another the bosun's. The third one had a lot of gold teeth. She could have been thirty, but maybe she wasn't. We left her with George and Carl. When I looked back from the door, the waiter was just fetching them some more beer.

II

THEY CAME INTO THE SHIP TOGETHER AT GALVESTON, GEORGE CARRYING A portable victrola and a small parcel wrapped in paper bearing the imprint of a well-known ten-cent store, and Carl carrying two bulging imitation leather bags that looked like they might weigh forty pounds apiece. George appropriated two berths, one above the other like a Pullman section, cursing Carl in a harsh, concatenant voice a little overburred with *v*'s and *r*'s and ordering him about like a nigger, while Carl stowed their effects away with the meticulousness of an old maid, producing from one of the bags a stack of freshly laundered drill serving jackets that must have numbered a dozen. For the next thirty-four days (he was the messboy) he wore a fresh one for each meal in the saloon, and there were always two or three recently washed ones drying under the poop awning. And for thirty-four evenings, after the galley was closed, we watched the two of them in pants and undershirts, dancing to the victrola on the after well deck above a hold full of Texas cotton and Georgia resin. They had only one record for the machine and it had a crack in it, and each time the needle clucked George would stamp on the deck. I don't think that either one of them was aware that he did it.

It was George who told us about Carl. Carl was eighteen, from Philadelphia. They both called it Philly; George in a proprietorial tone, as if he had created Philadelphia in order to produce Carl, though it later appeared that George had not discovered Carl until Carl had been to sea for a year already. And Carl himself told some of it: a fourth or fifth child of a first generation of Scandinavian-American shipwrights, brought up in one of an identical series of small frame houses a good trolley ride from salt water, by a mother or an older sister: this whom, at the age of fifteen and weighing perhaps a little less than a hundred pounds, some ancestor long knocking his quiet bones together at the bottom of the sea (or perhaps havened by accident in dry earth and become restive with ease and quiet) had sent back to the old dream and the old unrest three or maybe four generations late.

"I was a kid, then," Carl told us, who had yet to experience or need a shave. "I thought about everything but going to sea. I thought once I'd be a ballplayer or maybe a prize fighter. They had pictures of them on the walls, see, when Sis would send me down to the corner after the old man on a Saturday night. Jeez, I'd stand outside on the street and watch them go in, and I could see their legs under the door and hear them and smell the sawdust and see the pictures of them on the walls through the smoke. I was a kid then, see. I hadn't been nowheres then."

We asked George how he had ever got a berth, even as a messman, standing even now about four inches over five feet and with yet a face that should have followed monstrances up church aisles, if not looked down from one of the colored windows themselves.

"Why shouldn't he have come to sea?" George said. "Ain't this a free country? Even if he ain't nothing but a damn mess." He looked at us, black, serious. "He's a virgin, see? Do you know what that means?" He told us what it meant. Someone had evidently told him what it meant not so long ago, told him what he used to be himself, if he could remember that far back, and he thought that perhaps we didn't know the man, or maybe he thought it was a new word they had just invented. So he told us what it meant. It was in the first night watch and we were on the poop after supper, two days out of Gibraltar, listening to Monckton talking about cauliflower. Carl was taking a shower (he always took a bath after he had cleared the saloon after supper. George, who only cooked, never bathed until we were in port and the petite cleared) and George told us what it meant.

Then he began to curse. He cursed for a long time.

"Well, George," the bosun said, "suppose you were one, then? What would you do?"

"What would I do?" George said. "What wouldn't I do?" He cursed for some time, steadily. "It's like the first cigarette in the morning," he said. "By noon, when you remember how it tasted, how you felt when you was waiting for the match to get to the end of it, and when that first drag—" He cursed, long, impersonal, like a chant.

Monckton watched him: not listened; watched, nursing his pipe. "Why, George," he said, "you're by way of being almost a poet."

There was a swipe, some West India Docks crum; I forget his name. "Call that lobbing the tongue?" he said. "You should hear a Lymus mate laying into a fo'c'sle of bloody Portygee ginneys."

"Monckton wasn't talking about the language," the bosun said. "Any man can swear." He looked at George. "You're not the first man that ever wished that, George. That's something that has to be *was* because you don't know you are when you are." Then he paraphrased unwitting and with unprintable aptness Byron's epigram about women's mouths. "But what are you saving him for? What good will it do you when he stops being?"

George cursed, looking from face to face, baffled and outraged.

"Maybe Carl will let George hold his hand at the time," Monckton said. He reached a match from his pocket. "Now, you take Brussels sprouts—"

"You might get the Old Man to quarantine him when we reach Naples," the bosun said.

George cursed.

"Now, you take Brussels sprouts," Monckton said.

III

It took us some time that night, to get either started or settled down. We—Monckton and the bosun and the two women and I—visited four more cafés, each like the other one and like the one where we had left George and Carl—same people, same music, same thin, colored drinks. The two women accompanied us, with us but not of us, biding and acquiescent, saying constantly and patiently and without words that it was time to go to bed. So after a while I left them and went back to the ship. George and Carl were not aboard.

The next morning they were not there either, though Monckton and the bosun were, and the cook and the steward swearing up and down the galley; it seemed that the cook was planning to spend the day ashore himself. So they had to stay aboard all day. Along toward midafternoon there came aboard a smallish man in a soiled suit who looked like one of those Columbia day students that go up each morning on the East Side subway from around Chatham Square. He was hatless, with an oiled pompadour. He had not shaved recently, and he spoke no English in a pleasant, deprecatory way that was all teeth. But he had found the right ship and he had a note from George, written on the edge of a dirty scrap of newspaper, and we found where George was. He was in jail.

The steward hadn't stopped cursing all day, anyhow. He didn't stop now, either. He and the messenger went off to the consul's. The steward returned a little after six o'clock, with George. George didn't look so much like he had been drunk; he looked dazed, quiet, with his wild hair and a blue stubble on his jaw. He went straight to Carl's bunk and he began to turn Carl's meticulous covers back one by one like a traveler examining the bed in a third-class European hotel, as if he expected to find Carl hidden among them. "You mean," he said, "he ain't been back? He ain't been back a-*tall?*"

"We haven't seen him," we told George. "The steward hasn't seen him either. We thought he was in jail with you."

He began to replace the covers; that is, he made an attempt to draw them one by one up the bed again in a kind of detached way, as if he were not conscious, sentient. "They run," he said in a dull tone. "They ducked out on me. I never thought he'd a done it. I never thought he'd a done me this way. It was her. She was the one made him done it. She knew what he was, and how I . . ." Then he began to cry, quietly, in that dull, detached way.

"He must have been sitting there with his hand in her lap all the time. And I never suspicioned. She kept on moving her chair closer and closer to his. But I trusted him. I never suspicioned nothing. I thought he wouldn't a done nothing serious without asking me first, let alone . . . I trusted him."

It appeared that the bottom of George's glass had distorted their shapes enough to create in George the illusion that Carl and the woman were drinking as he drank, in a serious but celibate way. He left them at the table and went back to the lavatory; or rather, he said that he realized suddenly that he was in the lavatory and that he had better be getting back, concerned not over what might transpire while he was away, but over the lapse, over his failure to be present at his own doings which the getting to the lavatory inferred. So he returned to the table, not yet alarmed; merely concerned and amused. He said he was having a fine time.

So at first he believed that he was still having such a good time that he could not find his own table. He found the one which he believed should be his, but it was vacant save for three stacks of saucers, so he made one round of the room, still amused, still enjoying himself; he was still enjoying himself when he repaired to the center of the dance floor where, a head above the dancers, he began to shout "Porteus ahoy!" in a loud voice, and continued to do so until a waiter who spoke English came and removed him and led him back to that same vacant table bearing the three stacks of saucers and the three glasses, one of which he now recognized as his own.

But he was still enjoying himself, though not so much now, believing himself to be the victim of a practical joke, first on the part of the management, and it appeared that he must have created some little disturbance, enjoying himself less and less all the while, the center of an augmenting clump of waiters and patrons.

When at last he did realize, accept the fact, that they were gone, it must have been pretty bad for him: the outrage, the despair, the sense of elapsed time, an unfamiliar city at night in which Carl must be found, and that quickly if it was to do any good. He tried to leave, to break through the crowd, without paying the score. Not that he would have beaten the bill; he just didn't have time. If he could have found Carl within the next ten minutes, he would have returned and paid the score twice over: I am sure of that.

And so they held him, the wild American, a cordon of waiters and clients —women and men both—and he dragging a handful of coins from his pockets ringing onto the tile floor. Then he said it was like having your legs swarmed by a pack of dogs: waiters, clients, men and women, on hands and knees on the floor, scrabbling after the rolling coins, and George slapping about with his big feet, trying to stamp the hands away.

Then he was standing in the center of an abrupt wide circle, breathing a little hard, with the two Napoleons in their swords and pallbearer gloves and Knights of Pythias bonnets on either side of him. He did not know what he had done; he only knew that he was under arrest. It was not until they reached the Prefecture, where there was an interpreter, that he learned that he was a political prisoner, having insulted the king's majesty by placing foot on the king's effigy on a coin. They put him in a forty-foot dungeon, with seven other political prisoners, one of whom was the messenger.

"They taken my belt and my necktie and the strings out of my shoes," he told us dully. "There wasn't nothing in the room but a barrel fastened in the middle of the floor and a wooden bench running all the way around the walls. I knew what the barrel was for right off, because they had already been using it for that for some time. You was expected to sleep on the bench when you couldn't stay on your feet no longer. When I stooped over and looked at it close, it was like looking down at Forty-second Street from a airplane. They looked just like Yellow cabs. Then I went and used the barrel. But I used it with the end of me it wasn't intended to be used with."

Then he told about the messenger. Truly, Despair, like Poverty, looks after its own. There they were: the Italian who spoke no English, and George who scarcely spoke any language at all; certainly not Italian. That was about four o'clock in the morning. Yet by daylight George had found the one man out of the seven who could have served him or probably would have.

"He told me he was going to get out at noon, and I told him I would give him ten lire as soon as I got out, and he got me the scrap of paper and the pencil (this, in a bare dungeon, from among the seven men stripped to the skin of everything save the simplest residue of clothing necessary for warmth: of money, knives, shoelaces, even pins and loose buttons) and I wrote the note and he hid it and they left him out and after about four hours they come and got me and there was the steward."

"How did you talk to him, George?" the bosun said. "Even the steward couldn't find out anything until they got to the consul's."

"I don't know," George said. "We just talked. That was the only way I could tell anybody where I was at."

We tried to get him to go to bed, but he wouldn't do it. He didn't even shave. He got something to eat in the galley and went ashore. We watched him go down the side.

"Poor bastard," Monckton said.

"Why?" the bosun said. "What did he take Carl there for? They could have gone to the movies."

"I wasn't thinking about George," Monckton said.

"Oh," the bosun said. "Well, a man can't keep on going ashore anywhere, let alone Europe, all his life without getting ravaged now and then."

"Good God," Monckton said. "I should hope not."

George returned at six o'clock the next morning. He still looked dazed, though still quite sober, quite calm. Overnight his beard had grown another quarter inch. "I couldn't find them," he said quietly. "I couldn't find them nowheres." He had to act as messman now, taking Carl's place at the officer's table, but as soon as breakfast was done, he disappeared; we heard the steward cursing him up and down the ship until noon, trying to find him. Just before noon he returned, got through dinner, departed again. He came back just before dark.

"Found him yet?" I said. He didn't answer. He stared at me for a while with that blank look. Then he went to their bunks and hauled one of the imitation leather bags down and tumbled all of Carl's things into it and crushed down the lid upon the dangling sleeves and socks and hurled the bag out onto the well deck, where it tumbled once and burst open, vomiting the white jackets and the mute socks and the underclothes. Then he went to bed, fully dressed, and slept fourteen hours. The cook tried to get him up for breakfast, but it was like trying to rouse up a dead man.

When he waked he looked better. He borrowed a cigarette of me and went and shaved and came back and borrowed another cigarette. "Hell with him," he said. "Leave the bastard go. I don't give a damn."

That afternoon he put Carl's things back into his bunk. Not carefully and not uncarefully: he just gathered them up and dumped them into the berth and paused for a moment to see if any of them were going to fall out, before turning away.

IV

IT WAS JUST BEFORE DAYLIGHT. WHEN I RETURNED TO THE SHIP ABOUT midnight, the quarters were empty. When I waked just before daylight, all the bunks save my own were still vacant. I was lying in a halfdoze, when I heard Carl in the passage. He was coming quietly; I had scarcely heard him before he appeared in the door. He stood there for a while, looking no larger than an adolescent boy in the halflight, before he entered. I closed my eyes quickly. I heard him, still on tiptoe, come to my bunk and stand above me for a while. Then I heard him turn away. I opened my eyes just enough to watch him.

He undressed swiftly, ripping his clothes off, ripping off a button that struck the bulkhead with a faint click. Naked, in the wan light, he looked smaller and frailer than ever as he dug a towel from his bunk where George had tumbled his things, flinging the other garments aside with a kind of dreadful haste. Then he went out, his bare feet whispering in the passage.

I could hear the shower beyond the bulkhead running for a long time; it would be cold now, too. But it ran for a long time, then it ceased and I closed my eyes again until he had entered. Then I watched him lift from the floor the undergarment which he had removed and thrust it through a porthole quickly, with something of the air of a recovered drunkard putting out of sight an empty bottle. He dressed and put on a fresh white jacket and combed his hair, leaning to the small mirror, looking at his face for a long time.

And then he went to work. He worked about the bridge deck all day long; what he could have found to do there we could not imagine. But the crew's quarters never saw him until after dark. All day long we watched the white jacket flitting back and forth beyond the open doors or kneeling as he polished the brightwork about the companions. He seemed to work with a kind of fury. And when he was forced by his duties to come topside during the day, we noticed that it was always on the port side, and we lay with our starboard to the dock. And about the galley or the after deck George worked a little and loafed a good deal, not looking toward the bridge at all.

"That's the reason he stays up there, polishing that brightwork all day long," the bosun said. "He knows George can't come up there."

"It don't look to me like George wants to," I said.

"That's right," Monckton said. "For a dollar George would go up to the binnacle and ask the Old Man for a cigarette."

"But not for curiosity," the bosun said.

"You think that's all it is?" Monckton said. "Just curiosity?"

"Sure," the bosun said. "Why not?"

"Monckton's right," I said. "This is the most difficult moment in marriage: the day after your wife has stayed out all night."

"You mean the easiest," the bosun said. "George can quit him now."

"Do you think so?" Monckton said.

We lay there five days. Carl was still polishing the brightwork in the bridge-deck companions. The steward would send him out on deck, and go away; he would return and find Carl still working on the port side and he would make him go to starboard, above the dock and the Italian boys in bright, soiled jerseys and the venders of pornographic postcards. But it didn't take him long there, and then we would see him below again, sitting quietly in his white jacket in the stale gloom, waiting for suppertime. Usually he would be darning socks.

George had not yet said one word to him; Carl might not have been aboard at all, the very displacement of space which was his body, impedeless and breathable air. It was now George's turn to stay away from the ship most of the day and all of the night, returning a little drunk at three and four o'clock, to waken everyone by hand, save Carl, and talk in gross and loud recapitulation of recent and always different women before climbing into his bunk. As far as we knew, they did not even look at one another until we were well on our way to Gibraltar.

Then Carl's fury of work slacked somewhat. Yet he worked steadily all day, then, bathed, his blond hair wet and smooth, his slight body in a cotton singlet, we would see him leaning alone in the long twilight upon the rail midships or forward. But never about the poop where we smoked and talked and where George had begun again to play the single record on the victrola, committing, unrequested and anathemaed, cold-blooded encore after encore.

Then one night we saw them together. They were leaning side by side on the poop rail. That was the first time Carl had looked astern, looked toward Naples since that morning when he returned to the ship, and even now it was the evening on which the Gates of Hercules had sunk into the waxing twilight and the River Ocean began to flow down into the darkling sea and overhead the crosstrees swayed in measured and slow recover against the tall night and the low new moon.

"He's all right now," Monckton said. "The dog's gone back to his vomit."

"I said he was all right all the time," the bosun said. "George didn't give a damn."

"I wasn't talking about George," Monckton said. "George hasn't made the grade yet."

V

GEORGE TOLD US. "HE'D KEEP ON MOPING AND MOONING, SEE, AND I'D keep on trying to talk to him, to tell him I wasn't mad no more. Jeez, it had to come some day; a man can't be a angel all your life. But he wouldn't even look back that way. Until all of a sudden he says one night:

" 'What do you do to them?' I looked at him. 'How does a man treat them?'

" 'You mean to tell me,' I says, 'that you spent three days with her and she ain't showed you that?'

" 'I mean, give them,' he says. 'Don't men give—'

" 'Jeez Christ,' I says, 'you done already give her something they would have paid you money for it in Siam. Would have made you the prince or the prime minister at the least. What do you mean?'

" 'I don't mean money,' he says. 'I mean . . .'

" 'Well,' I says, 'if you was going to see her again, if she was going to be your girl, you'd give her something. Bring it back to her. Like something to wear or something: they don't care much what, them foreign women, hustling them wops all their life that wouldn't give them a full breath if they was a toy balloon; they don't care much what it is. But you ain't going to see her again, are you?'

" 'No,' he says. 'No,' he says. 'No.' And he looked like he was fixing to jump off the boat and swim on ahead and wait for us at Hatteras.

" 'So you don't want to worry about that,' I says. Then I went and played the vic again, thinking that might cheer him up, because he ain't the first, for Christ's sake; he never invented it. But it was the next night; we was at the poop rail then—the first time he had looked back—watching the phosrus along the logline, when he says:

" 'Maybe I got her into trouble.'

" 'Doing what?' I says. 'With what? With the police? Didn't you make her show you her petite?' Like she would have needed a ticket, with that face full of gold; Jeez, she could have rode the train on her face alone; maybe that was her savings bank instead of using her stocking.

" 'What ticket?' he says. So I told him. For a minute I thought he was crying, then I seen that he was just trying to not puke. So I knew what the trouble was, what had been worrying him. I remember the first time it come as a surprise to me. 'Oh,' I says, 'the smell. It don't mean nothing,' I says; 'you don't want to let that worry you. It ain't that they smell bad,' I says, 'that's just the Italian national air.' "

And then we thought that at last he really was sick. He worked all day long, coming to bed only after the rest of us were asleep and snoring, and I saw him in the night get up and go topside again, and I followed and saw him sitting on a windlass. He looked like a little boy, still, small, motionless in his underclothes. But he was young, and even an old man can't be sick very long with nothing but work to do and salt air to breathe; and so two weeks later we were watching him and George dancing again in their undershirts after supper on the after well deck while the victrola lifted its fatuous and reiterant ego against the waxing moon and the ship snored and hissed through the long seas off Hatteras. They didn't talk; they just danced, gravely and tirelessly as the nightly moon stood higher and higher up the sky. Then we turned south, and the Gulf Stream ran like blue ink alongside, bubbled with fire by night in the softening latitudes, and one night off Tortugas the ship began to tread the moon's silver train like an awkward and eager courtier, and Carl spoke for the first time after almost twenty days.

"George," he said, "do me a favor, will you?"

"Sure, bud," George said, stamping on the deck each time the needle clucked, his black head shoulders above Carl's sleek pale one, the two of them in decorous embrace, their canvas shoes hissing in unison: "Sure," George said. "Spit it out."

"When we get to Galveston, I want you to buy me a suit of these pink silk teddybears that ladies use. A little bigger than I'd wear, see?"

1931

JAMES T. FARRELL

::

just boys

I

BABY FACE WAS BLUE. AT THE PUBLIC HEALTH INSTITUTE, HE HAD JUST received another shot. The doctor had told him that he was making slow progress toward a cure, and that it should take at least another year. He rode out on a Jackson Park Express elevated train, sorrowing as he gazed through the window. He smiled, recalling the man with whom he had ridden down on the building elevator after his treatment. He had been small, and disgustingly unattractive, and he had had a scabby, unshaven face. He'd been wearing a khaki shirt, and perhaps he had been an ex-soldier, but he was most certainly not the type of soldier boy whom Baby Face liked. But Baby Face continued to smile, recalling the man's ebullience, when he had said:

"Damn it, kid, I've been having Wassermann's taken for seven years, and this is the first goddamn one that's been negative."

Baby Face's delicate profile clouded, and he wondered when he would be able to show a negative reaction in a test. The train swept on, overhead the tumbling buildings of the Chicago black belt. Baby Face stared at them, twisting about like a jumpy awkward girl. He almost could have cried disgracefully, right out in public. He had a thin sensitive face, with deep blue eyes, a short nose, powdered cherry-red cheeks, and thin, artfully rouged lips. And he was blue. He told himself that he didn't care, he was just not going to be celibate like a nun until he was cured.

He thought of Kenneth, and his blue eyes changed to an emotion which he described for himself as sheer fury. He would just like to scratch Kenneth's yellowish face until the blood poured from it like a river flooding over a dam. And he would like to rip Kenneth's eyes out, and just choke him until he fell gasping, and dead, and then he would stand over him and laugh, yes laugh hysterically. For Kenneth was nothing but a poaching black bitch, and Kenneth had had no right to take Caesar away from him. He thought of Caesar, a strong, husky, magnificent-looking coppery brown boy of twenty-one, with such a handsome innocent face, and such a manly torso. He remembered that scene with Caesar when Caesar had lost his temper and struck him. Baby Face visualized Caesar's face, just before he had punched; tense, sweating, contracted. And after that first punch, he had taunted Caesar, demanded that he be struck again and again, and he had screamed while Caesar had discolored his eyes and split his lips. Baby Face determined that he was going to write that poem he had been intending to write, describing his wild night with Caesar. And he would name it: *Purple Madness.* It made him furious, too, to think how those black bitches at the Princess Amy's would taunt and flaunt him because he had lost his big man to Kenneth, who was nothing but a disgraceful black trollop. And they would laugh at him for having contracted such a vile, perfectly disgusting, and obnoxious disease from that marine he had met at the Blue Eagle Cabaret on South State Street. If Kenneth had not stolen Caesar from him, he never would have gone there that night. Well, he did not care, he was not going to be celibate. The world had been unfair to him, and it had placed a tragic load upon his shoulders. He was going to repay the world. And Kenneth, too. He studied his thin, effeminate hands, with their tapering fingers, and long, polished finger nails. He imagined himself sticking the nail of his right index finger straight in Kenneth's eye.

He got off the elevated train at Fifty-eighth Street, and lightly pranced down the station steps to the street. He decided not to go to the Princess Amy's until he had found himself a big, husky black boy who would cause Kenneth to squirm with spite and envy. He turned his steps toward Washington Park. He had been cruising about the park when he had first met Caesar. He might have better luck on such a fine spring day as this one.

II

SAMMY WAS A MUSCULAR AND BROAD-SHOULDERED NEGRO OF ABOUT twenty. He was close to six feet tall, and his skin was dark and oily. He had high cheek-bones, large, even white teeth, and a pleasing smile. He strolled around the southern bend of the park lagoon, wistful and lonesome. He hoped that he would meet a girl, and his mind was choked with images of crude sex. Since he had split up with Annie Jones, he had not had any girls, and that had been at least a month ago. If he found a hot mama, he would feel more at peace with himself. He had also just lost his job, and he had very little money left. His room rent was paid up only until Saturday. After that, he did not know what he was going to do.

"Hello, there!" Baby Face lisped, falling into pace with Sammy, and rolling those well-practiced eyes of his.

"Hello!" Sammy abstractedly replied; he looked at the stranger, and immediately reflected that this flapper of a white boy was queer. He determined that he would have nothing to do with him.

Baby Face held out a package of perfumed Turkish cigarettes, and Sammy, tempted, accepted one. Baby Face lit it for Sammy. Sammy obliviously kicked his foot at the gravel walk. Baby Face held his puny shoulders back firmly, and swayed his narrow hips as he walked. He asked Sammy his name, and whether he lived in the vicinity. Not intending to reply, Sammy nevertheless answered.

"Well, I say, Sammy Lincoln, did you ever get your kitchen scrubbed?"

Sammy stared at Baby Face with open-mouthed bewilderment. The whites of his eyes showed. Baby Face laughed nervously. Sammy shook his head, and could not understand why this white boy asked such a peculiar question.

Sammy drawled that when he had been young, and living with his mammy, he had used to scrub the kitchen often while his mammy was out working for white folks. But that was a long time ago, and now, his mammy was dead, and his father was in jail. And he had never liked to scrub the kitchen because it was a wet job. Baby Face smiled. He questioned Sammy about sweet dark girls, and as they passed over the stone bridge, onto the wooded island, offered him a second perfumed cigarette. Sammy wanted to talk about girls, and about Annie Jones. He described her with simple eloquence. He sighed and said, with obvious and rather child-like regret, that Annie and he had gone and had a quarrel and split up, and that now, some white pimp down around Forty-third and Grand Boulevard had her working for him. Baby Face discreetly suggested that it was a poor policy to trust a girl. Sammy countered that he had been to blame in the quarrel. Baby Face asked Sammy if he worked. Sammy told him that he had been working, running an elevator in a building down on South Dearborn Street, but his boss had done gone and fired him because it was hard times. Now, he had no work, and he was tired of sitting around the pool room, so he had come for a walk in the park. Baby Face smiled coyly, and asked him if he were not out looking for a girl.

"Well . . ." Sammy drawled, commencing to answer.

Baby Face interrupted to tell him that girls were treacherous and lecherous bitches, who ruined clean-minded boys. As he spoke he laughed with a nervous subjective laugh that puzzled Sammy. Baby Face continued by advising Sammy that the only thing to do with girls was to put them on the block. Sammy did not understand this white boy's language. He thought of Annie, while Baby Face told him a story of how a black boy he had known had gone cruising around Washington Park, looking for a girl, and that he had found one. Five days later, he learned that he had contracted something that was perfectly disgusting.

"You like boys . . . too?" Baby Face asked, posing and posturing, rolling his eyes and concluding his pantomime with a suggestive wink.

Sammy wanted to say no. The words did not come out of his mouth. He thought that he knew what this queer white boy meant. His friend, Albert, always had bragged about the way such white boys chased after him, and how they gave him clothes and liquor, and took him out for good times at cabarets. He also thought of how he had lost his job, how he was almost without money, and how on Saturday when his room rent was due, he would not have it, and his landlady would probably tell him to clear out. Very soon that stomach of his was going to start tantalizing him, and ask him: Sammy, how about some pork chops? And Sammy would have to tell it: Stomach, we ain't gonna have no pork chops.

"Sammy, with me it's searing purple passions," Baby Face said, acting strangely, his voice jerky.

Sammy covertly observed Baby Face, liking the clothes he wore, particularly his purple tie.

"Well, white boy, that all . . . depends," Sammy said, speaking very slowly.

They sat on the bench, and after questioning Sammy further, Baby Face learned that he was jobless and broke. He told Sammy that he might be able to help him. It commenced to grow dark, and Baby Face took Sammy down to the Golden Lily on Garfield Boulevard for supper. After they had eaten, Baby Face asked Sammy if he would like to walk over to his room, and look at some of his ties.

They crossed the park toward Cottage Grove Avenue, and went to Baby Face's room in a run-down apartment hotel near the University, where Baby Face had been a student until he had been flunked out. Sammy was suddenly struck by the whiteness and rosiness of Baby Face's complexion. He was as pretty as a girl, with skin as tender. And he might take care of Sammy.

III

ON THE FOLLOWING SATURDAY EVENING, BABY FACE BROUGHT SAMMY TO a party at the Princess Amy's. Baby Face wore a blue flannel shirt, with brilliantly flaming red cravat, crystal earrings, and two imitation diamond rings from a five-and-ten-cent store. Sammy wore a purple tie which Baby Face had given him.

The Princess Amy had an apartment in a three-story building, a few doors north of the Prairie Theatre at Fifty-eighth and Prairie. The Princess was in his thirties, a coal black, corpulent, perspiring Negro, with small fat bags of flesh under his eyes. For his Saturday evening party, he was wearing a trailing green formal dress and artificial breasts.

There was a Negro group already gathered in the parlor when Baby Face and Sammy arrived. The parlor was rectangular, with shaded lamps, a plush carpet wine red in the lighting, a large overstuffed divan, several wing chairs with leather seats and claw feet, an electric victrola, and red satin pillows that had been scattered indiscriminately about the floor. The room was odored with incense, and with the perfumes which most of those present had applied to their persons. The only female in the group was Louise, a washed-out Negro prostitute with a drawn mulatto face. She was attempting to reform Kenneth, and sat on a pillow near the victrola, frowning while Kenneth, a wiry twenty-one year old Negro with blue velvet coat, a red-and-black checkered lumberman's shirt, and an orange tie, danced with the Princess.

Baby Face's entrance heralded giddy greetings, and several references to his disease. Sammy Lincoln was introduced around, and appraised by the various and effeminate black boys. Baby Face immediately asked why they did not have candles lit instead of lights. The Princess Amy touched the electric button, and the room was in darkness. Those present made various smacking noises with their lips, shouted and laughed, and jovially complained of wandering hands. Soon there were several candles lit, and the Princess Amy waddled about the room, lighting and arranging additional ones. Kenneth started a victrola record going, and the room was filled with the sounds of hot Negro jazz. The Princess and Kenneth shimmied in the center of the floor, scarcely moving their feet. Louise frowned at them. One of the boys pointed to them and loudly smacked his lips.

Sammy sat next to Baby Face on the divan, casting his eyes around the room, looking frequently and questioningly at Louise, lost. He could not understand the others in the room, but he was slightly complimented by the attention he received from them. Baby Face danced with Sammy, and several other boys succeeded Baby Face. Princess Amy, sitting in a winged armchair as if it were a throne, suggested that Kenneth dance with Sammy, and there was responsive laughter. Kenneth said that he didn't care to, if Baby Face had gotten to him first. Baby Face wasted a hateful look on Kenneth, who turned his back, and spoke with Caesar. Sammy next danced with a mulatto boy who was called Marie; he was wearing wide bell-bottom trousers, with a red patch of flannel and pearl buttons just above the pants cuffs. Sammy was relieved when the record was ended. He quickly approached Louise and asked her to dance. She seemed bored, and in the dance did not give him a tumble. Baby Face and Princess Amy kept ragging at her, telling her that she had no right to go hustling now, scabbing on them.

Drinks were served. The atmosphere of the room thickened. The perfume odors commenced to stale, and they mingled with the odors of incense, gin, and perspiration. The room was clouded in unwholesomely thick curtains of cigarette smoke. A number of the guests started clamoring for a game of *Truth.* Kenneth fetched a leather-covered Bible, and commenced to pass it from person to person, each one improvising a mock oath, swearing to tell the truth to all questions asked him in the game. The Bible passed around the room very slowly, because the oaths were made an occasion of wit, and each occasion of wit produced additional wit and high-pitched laughter. In the midst of the mock oath-taking, two boys arose from pillows, and, arm in arm, crossed toward the hallway. They could not be persuaded to remain for the game, and while they stood at the entrance way of the room, bandying jokes, Kenneth rushed to the rear of the house, and quickly reappeared with a knife, fork, and plate. He handed the implements to the two boys who were bent on leaving, and the room was convulsed. Sammy sat scratching his head, trying vainly to understand the joke. The boys went down the hallway toward another part of the apartment. The oath-taking finally was concluded. Kenneth stood at one end of the room, and opened the questioning.

"Marie?" he asked of the boy with the pearl button sewn in his trousers, "Marie, what was you and the Princess doing on the back porch, just before Baby Face and Sammy came?"

There was more laughter.

"Well, you see, it was thissaway . . ."

Another outburst of laughter interrupted him.

"I done stood up and . . ."

They laughed so loudly and interpolated so many comments that the answer went unheard.

"Sammy," Kenneth continued when there was enough quiet to permit speaking, "how many fish has you on the block?"

"What? . . . What's 'at?" Sammy asked, slowly shaking a troublingly confused head from side to side.

"He's asking you how many women you have working for you?" Baby Face whispered.

"Why, me . . . ah . . . no one. Ah ain't even got a job for myself," Sammy said, much to their amusement.

"Baby Face, has you all told Sammy Lincoln what you has got wrong with that hot blood of yours?" Kenneth asked with unmasked malice.

As they laughed, Baby Face dabbed aside a tear, leaped to his feet, and said tensely:

"Kenneth, you're just a jealous, viperish no-account lying bitch."

"Is I?"

"I'm as pure and as white as a lily," Baby Face hastily said before Kenneth could say more, and the laughter and comments drowned out Kenneth's words.

"What's at? What's he mean?" Sammy quietly asked Baby Face. Baby Face answered that Kenneth was just trying to insinuate lies out of jealousy. Sammy scratched the poll of his kinky head. He was sorry he was present with these people.

"Clara, what kind does you prefer the most?" Kenneth asked, continuing the Truth game.

"Whatever my big man says," Clara, a frail dark boy in a gray suit replied, and they went into fresh paroxysms.

The truth game proceeded until Kenneth finally got them to change to a game of kiss-the-pillow. Baby Face frowned at Kenneth, arose, and left the room in an angry flounce. He went out to the back porch to have a good cry by himself. He drooled tears. In the parlor, Kenneth postured in the center of the room, holding one of the red pillows in his hands, while he audibly wondered where he should drop it. He exclaimed, to their amusement, that Baby Face should be paged, and the pillow dropped at Sammy's feet. Sammy pointed his finger against his chest, and asked if it meant that he was supposed to do something. Kenneth knelt on the pillow and smiled up at him. He was told to kneel on the pillow, and he complied. Kenneth embraced him, and planted a long, wet, slobbering kiss on his lips, much to everyone's amusement. Sammy arose startled, and Kenneth placed the pillow in his hands. Sammy was told to close his eyes, twirl around and drop the pillow. It fell before Louise, and she knelt and kissed him casually. The game of kiss-the-pillow was punctuated with prolonged, salivary, sometimes smacking, and sometimes sloppy, osculations. It broke up when Princess Amy bestirred himself to produce a tray full of highballs. They drank slowly, discussed their lives, likes, inclinations and problems, and cordially teased and insulted one another. Every insult, every smutty joke, every sexual reference was a source of delight. More drinks were furnished. Slowly, some of them commenced getting drunk.

Baby Face went to the bathroom and studied his red-eyed face in the key of tragedy. He made his face up, and then quietly sneaked into the Princess Amy's bedroom. He donned one of the Princess' red silk dresses, and his appearance in the parlor occasioned hilarity. He and the Princess shimmy-danced while the hilarity persisted.

"Baby Face, if you all wasn't a diseased bitch, I could kiss you and make up," Kenneth said, mischievously.

Baby Face emitted a hysteric scream, and sprang for Kenneth, sinking his nails into Kenneth's cheeks. Princess Amy, fearful of his dress, separated Baby Face from Kenneth. Kenneth, in tears, applied a silk handkerchief to his scratched, bleeding face. Baby Face raved ignoring all consolation, and refusing the drink which the Princess offered him.

"Kenneth, as long as I live, I'll never forgive you!" Baby Face declared, his voice cracked, tense.

Caesar led Kenneth to the rear of the apartment.

Sammy, in mounting perplexion, arose from the divan.

"Tell me, white boy, has you all got one of them diseases?" he asked haltingly, over-emphasizing the final word of his question.

"He's just a lying, jealous bitch," Baby Face said.

Princess Amy placed a fat, restraining hand on Sammy's shoulder. Sammy shook it off.

"Tell me, white boy, has you?"

Baby Face crumpled himself on the divan, sobbed. Sammy, the center of attention in the suddenly excited room, stood over him, his face hard and determined.

"Has you all got a disease, and gone and given it to me?"

Sammy did not know much about diseases, but he knew that they were quite terrible, and that getting one cost a lot of money.

He jerked Baby Face to his feet, gripped his throat, and stared into his watering eyes. Baby Face went limp. His arms flung above his head, and he fell into Sammy's arms in a faint. Princess Amy revived him with smelling salts. He asked, his voice throbbing, to speak alone with Sammy. Sammy followed him into Princess Amy's bedroom, pushing the button to switch on the electricity. Baby Face asked for darkness, but Sammy ignored his request. Baby Face fell into Sammy's arms.

"Sammy, I can't live without you."

In a firm but slowly deliberate manner, Sammy removed Baby Face's arms from his own neck. He held him off at arm's length, and stared at him intently.

"Look me in de eye, white boy, and tell me, has you all given me one of them diseases?"

"No!" Baby Face whimpered.

Sammy shoved Baby Face, who, losing his equilibrium, tumbled back onto Princess Amy's high-poster bed. Sammy left the room, and searched for Kenneth. He found him on the back porch in Caesar's arms. Kenneth told Sammy that Baby Face was diseased, and described how it had been contracted. Caesar confirmed Kenneth's statement.

Sammy seemed to petrify on the spot. He blew instead of breathed. He was a simple and ignorant young Negro boy, with little education, and with only crude experiences in living. Back of him were whirlpools of superstition and fear, and they cluttered his consciousness like a sudden rush of blood to the head, focusing themselves through his sudden discovery. He slowly returned to the bedroom, where Baby Face lay, head downward, in tears.

Methodically, he dragged Baby Face to his feet by the neck of Princess Amy's dress. The silk split and ripped. With equal methodicalness, he knocked Baby Face down with a calculated, timed punch in the jaw. An insane ecstatic gleam lit in Baby Face's eyes. He crawled on his hands and knees to Sammy, and tightly clutched him below the knees. Looking up insanely, he screamed:

"Hit me! Hit me again!"

He jumped to his feet, and thrust his face forward.

"Hit me! Beat me! Kill me!"

"White boy, has you all gone and . . . diseased me?"

"Kill me! Kill me for it!" Baby Face shouted, emitting saliva which struck Sammy's cheek.

All awareness of the situation was gone from Sammy. He saw, like an object in a dream, the tender face and soft white neck of Baby Face. He was an automation driven on by a whole heredity of superstitions and ignorance, which caused him to be almost paralyzed with fear. In an unwitting trice, and fighting with this fear, he flashed a razor, and with one stroke, slit Baby Face's throat. Blood spurted onto Sammy's clothes, as if from a pump. Baby Face's head, half-severed, unsupportedly dropped forward, chin striking chest, and he fell to the floor. His blood pooled over the carpet, soaked in.

Sammy stood over him without any realization of what had happened; tightly grasped the handle of his now bloodied razor. His head was in a sweltering circle of confusion. His motor centers seemed unable to function. Perspiration arose in great beads upon his forehead. He sat on the bed like a somnambulist, and stared at the green lizards painted over the wall paper. Princess Amy appeared in the doorway, screamed, and fell in a hefty heap on the floor. Others appeared, and by the time Princess Amy was revived, the room was in an uproar of shrieks, outcries, and fainting boys. Sammy continued to sit ghost-like in their midst, clutching his razor, and no one dared approach him or the dead Baby Face.

Coats and wraps were suddenly grabbed, and there was a determined cluttering attempt for an exodus. Before anyone escaped, policemen, having heard so many shrieks and outcries, were hammering at the door. Princess Amy opened it, and the two policemen did not understand him, as he confusedly tried to explain what had happened, and how he was totally unresponsible.

The police patrol was called, and they were loaded into the wagon. A small crowd collected, and curiously gaped, as they were marched into it. When Sammy placed his foot on the lower step to the entrance of the rear of the car, the policeman by the door sneered and shoved him at the neck. Sammy lurched, tumbled onto the floor of the aisle inside of the car. He sat there whimpering, afraid. He began to moan and to pray in a sing-song fashion, and the police told him to shut up. He continued, and a policeman stepped inside and belted him in the jaw. He cowered and grovelled on the floor aisle.

A passing detective observed the crowd and wagon and asked one of the policemen what was the trouble.

"Just a nigger fairy party, and one of the shines slashed a white pansy's throat. Christ, you should have seen them when we broke in. Like a regiment of hysterical old women."

"That the one who did it?" the detective asked, pointing at Sammy within the automobile.

"Yeh, and he'll make nice frying on the hot chair."

"The boys are getting rough," the detective said.

"Yeh, just boys," the policeman said, sardonically.

1931–1934

WILLIAM CARLOS WILLIAMS

::

THE KNIFE OF THE TIMES

AS THE YEARS PASSED THE GIRLS WHO HAD BEEN SUCH INTIMATES AS CHILDREN still remained true to one another.

Ethel by now had married. Maura had married; the one having removed to Harrisburg, the other to New York City. And both began to bring up families. Ethel especially went in for children. Within a very brief period, comparatively speaking, she had three of them, then four, then five and finally six. And through it all, she kept in constant touch with her girlhood friend, dark-eyed Maura, by writing long intimate letters.

At first these had been newsy chit chat, ending always however in continued protestations of that love which the women had enjoyed during their childhood. Maura showed them to her husband and both enjoyed their full newsy quality dealing as they did with people and scenes with which both were familiar.

But after several years, as these letters continued to flow, there came a change in them. First the personal note grew more confidential. Ethel told about her children, how she had had one after the other—to divert her mind, to distract her thoughts from their constant brooding. Each child would raise her hopes of relief, each anticipated delivery brought only renewed disappointment. She confided more and more in Maura. She loved her husband; it was not that. In fact, she didn't know what it was save that she, Ethel, could never get her old friend Maura out of her mind.

Until at last the secret was out. It is you, Maura, that I want. Nothing but you. Nobody but you can appease my grief. Forgive me if I distress you with this confession. It is the last thing in this world that I desire. But I cannot contain myself longer.

Thicker and faster came the letters. Full love missives they were now without the least restraint.

Ethel wrote letters now such as Maura wished she might at some time in her life have received from a man. She was told that all these years she had been dreamed of, passionately without rival, without relief. Now, surely, Maura did not dare show the letters any longer to her husband. He would not understand.

They affected her strangely, they frightened her, but they caused a shrewd look to come into her dark eyes and she packed them carefully away where none should ever come upon them. She herself was occupied otherwise but she felt tenderly toward Ethel, loved her in an old remembered manner—but that was all. She was disturbed by the turn Ethel's mind had taken and thanked providence her friend and she lived far enough apart to keep them from embarrassing encounters.

But, in spite of the lack of adequate response to her advances, Ethel never wavered, never altered in her passionate appeals. She begged her friend to visit her, to come to her, to live with her. She spoke of her longings, to touch the velvet flesh of her darling's breasts, her thighs. She longed to kiss her to sleep, to hold her in her arms. Franker and franker became her outspoken lusts. For which she begged indulgence.

Once she implored Maura to wear a silk chemise which she was sending, to wear it for a week and to return it to her, to Ethel, unwashed, that she might wear it in her turn constantly upon her.

Then, after twenty years, one day Maura received a letter from Ethel asking her to meet her—and her mother, in New York. They were expecting a sister back from Europe on the Mauretania and they wanted Maura to be there—for old times' sake.

Maura consented. With strange feelings of curiosity and not a little fear, she stood at the gate of the Pennsylvania station waiting for her friend to come out at the wicket on the arrival of the Harrisburg express. Would she be alone? Would her mother be with her really? Was it a hoax? Was the woman crazy after all? And, finally, would she recognize her?

There she was and her mother along with her. After the first stare, the greetings on all sides were quiet, courteous and friendly. The mother dominated the moment. Her keen eyes looked Maura up and down once and then she asked the time, when would the steamer dock, how far was the pier and had they time for lunch first?

There was plenty of time. Yes, let's lunch. But first Ethel had a small need to satisfy and asked Maura if she would show her the way. Maura led her friend to the Pay Toilets and there, after inserting the coin, Ethel opened the door and, before Maura could find the voice to protest, drew her in with herself and closed the door after her.

What a meeting! What a release! Ethel took her friend into her arms and between tears and kisses, tried in some way, as best she could, to tell her of her happiness. She fondled her old playmate, hugged her, lifted her off her feet in the eager impressment of her desire, whispering into her ear, stroking her hair, her face, touching her lips, her eyes; holding her, holding her about as if she could never again release her.

No one could remain cold to such an appeal, as pathetic to Maura as it was understandable and sincere, she tried her best to modify its fury, to abate it, to control. But, failing that, she did what she could to appease her old friend. She loved Ethel, truly, but all this show was beyond her. She did not understand it, she did not know how to return it. But she was not angry, she found herself in fact in tears, her heart touched, her lips willing.

Time was slipping by and they had to go.

At lunch Ethel kept her foot upon the toe of Maura's slipper. It was a delirious meal for Maura with thinking of old times, watching the heroic beauty of the old lady and, while keeping up a chatter of small conversation, intermixed with recollections, to respond secretly as best she could to Ethel's insistent pressures.

At the pier there was a long line waiting to be admitted to the enclosure. It was no use—Ethel from behind constantly pressed her body against her embarrassed friend, embarrassed not from lack of understanding or sympathy, but for fear lest one of the officers and Customs inspectors who were constantly watching them should detect something out of the ordinary.

But the steamer was met, the sister saluted; the day came to an end and the hour of parting found Ethel still keeping close, close to the object of her lifelong adoration.

What shall I do? thought Maura afterward on her way home, on the train alone. Ethel had begged her to visit her, to go to her, to spend a week at least with her, to sleep with her. Why not?

1932

ERNEST HEMINGWAY

::

THE SEA CHANGE

"ALL RIGHT," SAID THE MAN. "WHAT ABOUT IT?"

"No," said the girl, "I can't."

"You mean you won't."

"I can't," said the girl. "That's all that I mean."

"You mean that you won't."

"All right," said the girl. "You have it your own way."

"I don't have it my own way. I wish to God I did."

"You did for a long time," the girl said.

It was early, and there was no one in the café except the barman and these two who sat together at a table in the corner. It was the end of the summer and they were both tanned, so that they looked out of place in Paris. The girl wore a tweed suit, her skin was a smooth golden brown, her blonde hair was cut short and grew beautifully away from her forehead. The man looked at her.

"I'll kill her," he said.

"Please don't," the girl said. She had very fine hands and the man looked at them. They were slim and brown and very beautiful.

"I will. I swear to God I will."

"It won't make you happy."

"Couldn't you have gotten into something else? Couldn't you have gotten into some other jam?"

"It seems not," the girl said. "What are you going to do about it?"

"I told you."

"No; I mean really."

"I don't know," he said. She looked at him and put out her hand. "Poor old Phil," she said. He looked at her hands, but he did not touch her hand with his.

"No, thanks," he said.

"It doesn't do any good to say I'm sorry?"

"No."

"Nor to tell you how it is?"

"I'd rather not hear."

"I love you very much."

"Yes, this proves it."

"I'm sorry," she said, "if you don't understand."

"I understand. That's the trouble. I understand."

"You do," she said. "That makes it worse, of course."

"Sure," he said, looking at her. "I'll understand all the time. All day and all night. Especially all night. I'll understand. You don't have to worry about that."

"I'm sorry," she said.

"If it was a man—"

"Don't say that. It wouldn't be a man. You know that. Don't you trust me?"

"That's funny," he said. "Trust you. That's really funny."

"I'm sorry," she said. "That's all I seem to say. But when we do understand each other there's no use to pretend we don't."

"No," he said. "I suppose not."

"I'll come back if you want me."

"No. I don't want you."

Then they did not say anything for a while.

"You don't believe I love you, do you?" the girl asked.

"Let's not talk rot," the man said.

"Don't you really believe I love you?"

"Why don't you prove it?"

"You didn't used to be that way. You never asked me to prove anything. That isn't polite."

"You're a funny girl."

"You're not. You're a fine man and it breaks my heart to go off and leave you—"

"You have to, of course."

"Yes," she said. "I have to and you know it."

He did not say anything and she looked at him and put her hand out again. The barman was at the far end of the bar. His face was white and so was his jacket. He knew these two and thought them a handsome young couple. He had seen many handsome young couples break up and new couples form that were never so handsome long. He was not thinking about this, but about a horse. In half an hour he could send across the street to find if the horse had won.

"Couldn't you just be good to me and let me go?" the girl asked.

"What do you think I'm going to do?"

Two people came in the door and went up to the bar.

"Yes, sir," the barman took the orders.

"You can't forgive me? When you know about it?" the girl asked.

"No."

"You don't think things we've had and done should make any difference in understanding?"

" 'Vice is a monster of such fearful mien,' " the young man said bitterly, "that to be something or other needs but to be seen. Then we something, something, then embrace." He could not remember the words. "I can't quote," he said.

"Let's not say vice," she said. "That's not very polite."

"Perversion," he said.

"James," one of the clients addressed the barman, "you're looking very well."

"You're looking very well yourself," the barman said.

"Old James," the other client said. "You're fatter, James."

"It's terrible," the barman said, "the way I put it on."

"Don't neglect to insert the brandy, James," the first client said.

"No, sir," said the barman. "Trust me."

The two at the bar looked over at the two at the table, then looked back at the barman again. Towards the barman was the comfortable direction.

"I'd like it better if you didn't use words like that," the girl said. "There's no necessity to use a word like that."

"What do you want me to call it?"

"You don't have to call it. You don't have to put any name to it."

"That's the name for it."

"No," she said. "We're made up of all sorts of things. You've known that. You've used it well enough."

"You don't have to say that again."

"Because that explains it to you."

"All right," he said. "All right."

"You mean all wrong. I know. It's all wrong. But I'll come back. I told you I'd come back. I'll come back right away."

"No, you won't. Not to me."

"You'll see."

"Yes," he said. "That's the hell of it. You probably will."

"Of course I will."

"Go on, then."

"Really?" She could not believe him, but her voice was happy.

"Go on," his voice sounded strange to him. He was looking at her, at the way her mouth went and the curve of her cheek bones, at her eyes and at the way her hair grew on her forehead and at the edge of her ear and at her neck.

"Not really. Oh, you're too sweet," she said. "You're too good to me."

"And when you come back tell me all about it." His voice sounded very strange. He did not recognize it. She looked at him quickly. He was settled into something.

"You want me to go?" she asked seriously.

"Yes," he said seriously. "Right away." His voice was not the same, and his mouth was very dry. "Now," he said.

She stood up and went out quickly. She did not look back at him. He watched her go. He was not the same-looking man as he had been before he had told her to go. He got up from the table, picked up the two checks and went over to the bar with them.

"I'm a different man, James," he said to the barman. "You see in me quite a different man."

"Yes, sir?" said James.

"Vice," said the brown young man, "is a very strange thing, James." He looked out the door. He saw her going down the street. As he looked in the glass, he saw he was really quite a different-looking man. The other two at the bar moved down to make room for him.

"You're right there, sir," James said.

The other two moved down a little more, so that he would be quite comfortable. The young man saw himself in the mirror behind the bar. "I said I was a different man, James," he said. Looking into the mirror he saw that this was quite true.

"You look very well, sir," James said. "You must have had a very good summer."

1933

JOHN HORNE BURNS

::

MOMMA

MOMMA ALWAYS LAY A WHILE IN HER BED WHEN SHE AWOKE. POPPA WAS up four hours earlier and went out into the streets of Naples for a walk, to buy *Risorgimento* and to drink his caffè espresso. He said it made him nervous to lie beside her because she cooed to herself as she slept.

That love which Poppa no longer desired of her Momma showered on the clientele of her bar. One reason she cooed in her sleep was that she was one of the richest women in Naples. She could afford to buy black market food at two thousand lire a day. She ate better than the Americans. She had furs and lovely dresses and patent leather pumps which even the countesses in the Vomero couldn't afford. Momma had come from a poor family in Milan, but she'd made herself into one of the great ladies of Naples. And the merchants of Naples, when they sent her monthly bills, instead of writing signora before her name, wrote N.D., standing for nobil donna.

As the churches of Naples struck noon, Momma got out of her bed. She was wearing a lace nightie brought her from Cairo by an American flier. Momma knew that the flier had made money on the deal, but no other woman in Naples had one like it. In the old days she'd have driven Poppa mad with this lace nightie. But now he simply crawled in beside her, felt the sheer stuff, and clucked his tongue in disapproval. Poppa was first and last a Neapolitan. Even in the early days of their marriage he'd never grasped the fineness of Momma's grain. But she was beyond such bitterness now. She loved the world, and the world returned her love in her bar in the Galleria Umberto.

Beneath a colored picture of the Madonna of Pompei, flanked by two tapers and a pot of pinks, Momma said her morning prayers. She thanked the Virgin for saving her during the bombardments of Naples. But the

Virgin hadn't spared that lovely appartamento in Piazza Garibaldi. And Momma prayed for all the sweet boys who came to her bar, that they might soon be returned to their families—but not too soon, for Momma loved their company. And she prayed also for the future of poor Italy, that the line up by Florence might soon be smashed by the American Fifth Army. And she prayed that Il Duce and his mistress Claretta Petacci might see the error of their ways. Finally Momma prayed that all the world might be as prosperous and happy as she herself was.

With the bombing of her apartment in Piazza Garibaldi in March, 1943, Momma'd been able to salvage only her frigidaire. Everything else had been destroyed—the lovely linens she'd brought Poppa with her dowry from Milan, her fragile plate, her genteel furniture. Only the frigidaire was to be found among the rubble, pert and smiling as a bomb shelter. Momma'd wept the whole day; then she and Poppa had moved into a dreary set of rooms on the third floor of the Galleria Umberto. Momma'd got the rooms cleaned, set the frigidaire in the kitchen, and bought secondhand furniture by cautious shopping in Piazza Dante. But her heart as a homemaker had died in the ruins of that appartamento to which Poppa had brought her as a bride.

She lived now only for her bar and for the Allied soldiers who came there every night except Sunday. In fact Momma was only treading water all day long until 1630 hours, at which time the provost marshal of Naples allowed her to open her bar. At 1930 MP's came to make sure it was closed. Three hours. Yet in those three hours Momma lived more than most folks do in twenty-four.

She'd opened her bar the night after Naples fell to the Allies, in October, 1943. Some American of the 34th Division had christened her Momma, and the name stuck. And because Momma had an instinctive knack for entertaining people, her bar was the most celebrated in Naples. Indeed a Kiwi had once told her that it was famous all over the world, that everyone in the Allied armies told everyone else about it. Momma rejoiced. Her only selfish desire was to be renowned as a great hostess. She was happy that she made money in her bar, but that wasn't her be-and-end-all. She knew that she was going down in history with Lili Marlene and the Mademoiselle of Armentières—though for a different reason.

::

MOMMA BRUSHED HER TEETH WITH AMERICAN DENTRIFICE WHILE THE WATER ran into her tub. She studied her hair in the mirror. For ten years she'd been hennaing it. But she was too honest to go on kidding the world. She was forty-six. In the face of that sacred title, Momma, it seemed to her sacrilegious to sit every night behind her cash register with crimson hair glowing in the lights. So she'd stopped using the rinse. Now her hair was in that transitional stage, with gray and white and henna streaked through it. But the momentary ugliness of her hair was worth her title. At closing time in her bar, some of her boys, a bit brilli, would cry on her shoulder and tell her that she looked just like some elderly lady in Arkansas or Lyon or North Wales or the Transvaal or Sydney. Then she'd pat their hands and say:

—Ah, mio caro! Se fosse qui la Sua mamma! . . .

She'd never been able to learn English, though she understood nearly everything that was said to her in it.

Momma climbed into the tub after she'd sprinkled in some salts a merchant seaman had brought her from New York. Her body was getting a little chunky, but she tried her best to keep it trim, the way a Momma's should be. At first she'd worn a pince-nez until Poppa had told her she looked like a Sicilian carthorse with blinders. So she had reverted to her gold-rimmed spectacles. She doted on American black market steaks, her pasta asciutta, her risotti, and her peperoni. She knew that a Momma musn't be skinny either.

She dressed herself in black silk and laid out a quaint straw hat on which a stuffed bird sprawled eating cherries. She opened her drawerful of silk stockings. You could count on the fingers of one hand the women in Naples of August, 1944, who owned silk stockings—were they prostitutes on the Toledo or marchese in villas at Bagnoli. But Momma had em; she averaged a pair a week from her American admirers. Momma considered herself one of the luckiest ladies in the world. She knew that no woman gets presents for nothing.

Finally dressed and fragrant and cool in spite of the furnace that was Naples in August, 1944, Momma took up her purse and looked around the apartment before locking it. She checked the ice in the frigidaire. Sometimes, after she was compelled to close her bar, she invited her favorite boys up for extra drinks. She didn't charge for this hospitality.

She walked through the Galleria Umberto. At this hour it was empty of Neapolitans because of the heat. But the Allied soldiery was already out in full force. The bars weren't open, so they just loitered against the walls reading their *Stars and Stripes* or whistling at the signorine. A few waved to Momma, and she bowed to them. Then she went onto the Toledo, which Il Duce had vulgarized into Via Roma. Here she clutched her bag more tightly. Like anybody else born in Milan, she had no use for Neapolitans or Sicilians. They thought the world owed them a living, so they preyed on one another with a malicious vitality, like monkeys removing one another's fleas. And now that the Allies were in Naples, the Neapolitans were united in milking them. Momma knew that the Neapolitans hated her because she was rich and because she refused to speak their dialect. She walked through them all with her head in the air, clutching her purse. Some who knew her called out vulgar names in dialect and cracks about Napoli Milionaria, but she paid them no attention.

She and Poppa usually lunched together at a black market restaurant on Via Chiaia, patronized by Americans and those few Italians who could afford the price of a meal there. Today Poppa was out campaigning for public office at the Municipio, so Momma ate alone at her special table. Sometimes she suspected that Poppa had a mistress. But then he wouldn't stand a chance at snapping up anything really good, what with all the Allies in Naples.

The treatment Momma got at this restaurant was in a class by itself. Naturally the Americans got fawned on, but then they didn't know what the waiters said about them in the kitchen. Whereas Momma, as an Italian who'd made a success in the hardiest times Naples had ever known, always got a welcome as though she were Queen Margherita. There were flowers on her table and special wines rustled up from the cellar, although the Allies got watered vino ordinario. And when Momma entered, the orchestra stopped playing American jazz, picked up their violins, and did her favorite tune, "Mazzolin di Fiori." Momma tapped her chin with her white glove and hummed appreciatively.

While she picked at her whitefish and sipped her white wine and peeped around the restaurant from under the shadow of the red bird that forever ate cherries on her hat, Momma observed an American sergeant wrestling with an American black market steak. He was quite drunk, and to Momma, who knew all the symptoms so well, he seemed ready to cry. She debated inviting him to her table and treating him to his lunch. But he gave her the I-hate-Italians scowl, so she thought better of it. He wasn't the sort who came to her bar anyhow. Momma was basically shy, except with people she thought needed affection. Then she'd open up like all the great hostesses of the world. However, she did take out of her purse a little pasteboard card advertising her bar. She sent it by a waiter over to the sergeant, plus a bottle of Chianti. He scowled at her again, and Momma decided basta, she'd gone more than halfway. Then he tore up her card and began to guzzle her wine.

She finished her lunch and smoked a cigarette. There seemed to be a rope about her neck pulled taut by all the evil fingers of the world. She wanted to go somewhere and have a good cry. She needed a friend. Poppa had never been close to her since, in the first year of their marriage, he discovered that she wasn't going to be fertile, like all the other women of Italy. Momma had conceived just once. In her Fallopian tubes. After the medico had curetted her out and she'd all but died, he'd told her she could never have a child of her own. And Poppa in disgust had taken to politics and reading the papers. Momma'd only begun to love again since the night in October, 1943, when she'd opened her bar in the Galleria Umberto. . . .

She arose from table and drew on her white gloves. As she walked to the door, she saw herself pass by in the gilded mirror, a dumpy figure holding in its chin, a scudding straw hat under a bird chewing cherries. She knew that if she didn't get outside soon, she'd bawl right there in front of the waiters, and the drama she'd built up of a great lady would collapse forever. On Via Chiaia she debated what movie she'd go to. Since she went every afternoon, she'd seen them all. A few American films were beginning to dribble into Naples, and Momma'd enjoyed Greer Garson or Ginger Rogers with an Italian sound track. Yet movies bored her unless there was lots of music and color. The truth was that she went every afternoon because she'd nothing else to do; she was just killing time till the hour to open her bar. She decided on the Cinema Regina Elena off Via Santa Brigida.

She found a seat three-quarters of the way back from the screen, put on her glasses, and watched the show. It was an Italian film made in Rome on a budget of a few thousand lire. Momma was used to the tempo of American movies, so she found herself nodding. There wasn't even anything worth crying over. She eased her feet out of their patent leather pumps, cursed the pinching of her girdle, and settled down. Sometimes she drew a peppermint patty out of her bag and sucked it thoughtfully. Every half-hour the lights came up for an intervallo; the windows were opened, and people came in or out or changed their seats for various reasons. Momma'd have liked an Allied soldier to be sitting beside her. But to these the cinemas of Naples were off limits because of the danger of typhus and because of certain nuisances they'd committed in the dark just after the city fell. During the intervalli Momma stayed in her seat and smoked a cigarette. She wasn't going to force her feet back into her pumps.

The Italian film went on and on; Momma fell asleep and dreamed in the moldy dark. Her dreams were always the same, of the boys who came to her bar. There was a heterogeneous quality about them. They had an air of being tremendously wise, older than the human race. They understood one another, as though from France and New Zealand and America they all had membership cards in some occult freemasonry. And they had a refinement of manner, an intuitive appreciation of her as a woman. Their conversation was flashing, bitter, and lucid. More than other men they'd laughed much together, laughing at life itself perhaps. Momma'd never seen anything like her boys. Some were extraordinarily handsome, but not as other men were handsome. They had an acuteness in their eyes and a predatory richness of the mouth as though they'd bitten into a pomegranate. Momma dreamed that she was queen of some gay exclusive club.

She awoke and glanced at her watch. It was time to go. She'd seen almost nothing of the film. But she didn't care. She felt more rested than she did by Poppa's side. A silver hammer in her heart kept tapping out that in fifteen minutes more her life for the day would begin. She had the yearning hectic panic of a child going to a show. She shot her feet into her pumps. As the lights came up for the secondo tempo Momma left the theater. She looked a little disdainfully at the audience, contrasting it with what she'd shortly be seeing. Peaked Neopolitan girls on the afternoon of their giorno di festa, holding tightly to the arms of their fidanzati wearing GI undershirts; sailors of the Regia Marina and the Squadra Navale in their patched blue and whites; housewives from the vichi and the off-limits areas who'd come in with a houseful of children to peer at the screen and lose themselves in its shadowy life.

Her patent leather pumps hurt Momma's feet, but she sprinted up Santa Brigida. She turned left at Via Giuseppe Verdi. Once in the Galleria Momma all but flew. She wondered if she looked spruce, if her hat was chic. The Galleria was milling and humming, for all the bars opened within a few seconds of one another, just as clocks stagger their striking the hour throughout a great city. Momma had a presentiment that today was going to be especially glamorous.

The 1630 shift of troie were coming into the arcade with the promptness of factory girls. From now until curfew time the Galleria would be a concentrated fever of bargaining and merchandising peculiar to Naples in August, 1944.

The rolling steel shutters of Momma's bar were already up. Gaetano was polishing the mirrors. He greeted Momma and went back to thinking about his wife and thirteen children and how it wasn't fair that a man who'd never signed the Fascist tessera should live like a dog under the Allies. Vincenzo was wearing a spotted apron, so Momma lashed him with her tongue and forced him into the gabinetto to put on a fresh one. She stitched them up herself out of American potato bags. Momma also inspected the glassware, the taps on the wine casks, the alignment of the bottles. She was kilometers ahead of the sanitation standards set by the PBS surgeon and the provost marshal.

She seated herself behind the cassa, unlocked the cash drawer, and counted her soldi. At this moment the old feeling of ecstasy returned. For Momma loved her bar: the mirrors in which everyone could watch everyone else, the shining Carrara marble, the urns for making caffè espresso. Behind her on the mirror she'd fastened a price list. She offered excellent white wine, vermouth, and cherry brandy. She hoped soon to be licensed to sell gin and cognac, which were what the Allies really wanted. When stronger liquors were available, the tone of her place would go sky-high, along with the moods of her clientele.

No one had yet turned up. Momma knew with racecourse certainty the exact order in which her habitués came. Her patrons were of three types: some came only to look, some with a thinly veiled purpose of meeting someone else, some just happened in.

A shadow cut the fierce light of the Galleria bouncing around the mirrors. It was Poppa treading warily and carrying his straw hat. Momma flinched. She had no desire to see Poppa now. If he addressed her in dialect, she'd refuse to answer. He had rings under his eyes, and through his brown teeth came the perfume of onions. Momma told him that there was half a chicken waiting in the frigidaire. But he seemed to want to talk. Momma got as peeved as though someone tried to explain a movie to her. So Poppa, after a few more attempts to talk, put on his straw hat and went out. But he called back to her from the entrance:

—Attenzione, cara. . . .

—Perchè? Momma cried, but he was gone.

Nettled and distracted, she settled herself behind the cash register and folded her hands. Where *were* they? All behind schedule tonight. She began to wonder if some of the other bar owners had sabotaged her by passing around the rumor that she was selling methyl alcohol such as would cause blindness.

The husky figure of a major entered the bar. Momma smelled a rat because this major was wearing the crossed pistols of an MP officer. On his left shoulder he wore the inverted chamber pot with the inset blue star, symbolizing the Peninsular Base Section. The major set his jaw like one asking for trouble. He ran his hands through some of the wineglasses and blew on the wine spigots for dust.

—Ees clean the glass, the wine, everything! Momma cried cheerily. Bar molto buono, molto pulito. . . .

The major advanced upon her. She was beginning to tremble behind her desk. He walked with the burly tread of one accustomed to cuff and kick. Momma remembered that some of the Germans, when they'd been in Naples, had walked like that.

—Lissen to me, signorina, the major said, dropping a porky hand on her desk.

—Signora, scusi, said Momma with dignity.

—I don't give a damn one way or the other, the major said. But don't try an play dumb with me, see, paesan?

—Ees molto buono my bar, Momma twittered, offering the major a cigarette.

Vincenzo and Gaetano were watching the proceedings like cats.

—Molto buono, my eye. You're gettin away with murder in this joint. . . . Now you can just take your choice. Either you get rid of most of the people who come here, or we'll put you off limits. And you know we damn well can, don't you?

Momma quailed as she lit the major's cigarette. The words "off limits" were understood by any Neopolitan who wanted to keep his shop open. Nothing could withstand the MP's closing a place, unless you were friendly with some colonel of PBS.

—You know as well as I do, said the major. An old doll like yourself ain't as dumb as she looks. We don't want any more Eyeties comin in here to mix with the soldiers. Do I make myself clear? And you gotta refuse to serve some of the other characters. . . . Don't come whinin around that you ain't been warned.

Momma motioned to Vincenzo and Gaetano to bring out a glass of that fine cognac from which she gave her favorites shots after closing time. It was set at the major's elbow. He drank it off, glaring at her the while, set down the glass with a click, and left.

—Capeesh? he cried as he belched like a balloon out into the sunlight of the Galleria.

Momma couldn't decide what grudge the MP's had against her. There had been occasional fights in her bar, yet the other bars of Naples had even more of them. Her soldiers were gentle. All she was trying to do was run a clean bar where people could gather with other congenial people. Her crowd had something that other groups hadn't. Momma's boys had an awareness of having been born alone and sequestered by some deep difference from other men. For this she loved them. And Momma knew something of those four freedoms the Allies were forever preaching. She believed that a minority should be let alone. . . .

In came the Desert Rat. He took off his black beret and pushed a hand through his rich inky hair. He said good evening to Momma and bought his quota of six chits for double white wines. It would take him three hours to drink these. He was always the first to arrive and the last to leave. He never spoke to a soul. He was the handsomest and silentest boy Momma'd ever seen. Why did he come at all? His manners were so perfect and soft that at a greeting from another, he'd reply and recede into himself. Momma wondered if at Tobruk or El Alamein someone in the desert night had cut his soul to pieces. He'd loved once—perfectly—someone, somewhere. Momma would cheerfully have slain whoever had hurt him so.

The face of the Desert Rat was an oval of light brown. His short-sleeved shirt showed the cleft in his neck just above the hair of his chest. He wore the tightest and shortest pair of shorts he could get into, and he leaned lost and dreaming against the bar with his ankles scraping one another in their low socks and canvas gaiters. Those legs were part of the poetry of the Desert Rat for Momma—the long firm legs of Germans, but tanned and covered from thigh to calf with thick soft hair. For three hours this English boy would stand in Momma's bar, doped and dozing in maddening relaxation and grace from the white wine.

Momma tore six chits out of the cash register and gave the Desert Rat four lire back out of his one hundred. Tonight she went so far as to pat his wrist, a thing she'd been longing to do for months.

—Ees warm tonight, no?

—Oh very, madam, the Desert Rat said.

It was the first time she'd seen his smile. And Momma suddenly saw him in someone's arms by moonlight in the Egyptian desert, in the midst of that love which had sliced the boy's heart in two. . . . He left her and went to the bar. In the next three hours it was usually at him that Momma'd look when she wasn't making change. She saw him from all perspectives in the mirrors, all the loveliness of his majestic body.

Next to arrive was a Negro second lieutenant of the American quartermaster corps. Momma smiled to herself as the Negro made an entrance.

He seemed to have the idea he was stepping onto some lighted stage. He moved his hips ever so slightly and carried his pink-insided hands tightly against his thighs. For some dramatic reason he wore combat boots, though Momma knew he'd never been farther north than the docks of Naples.

—Hulllllo, darling, he said to Momma, kissing her fingers. He had a suave overeducated voice. You look simpppply wonderful tonight. Who does your hats? Queen Mary? . . . uh-huh, uh-huh, uh-huh. . . .

Then he stationed himself at the bar quite close to the Desert Rat. They looked at each other for a swift appraising instant. Then the Negro lieutenant began to talk a blue streak at the Desert Rat.

—It's going to be brilliant here tonight, absolutely brrrrilliant. I feel it way down inside. . . . My aunt, you know, is a social worker in Richmond, Virginia. But do you think I'm ever going back there? No, indeed, baby. I found a home in Italy, where the human plant can't help but thrive. I like the Italians, you know. They're like me, refined animals, which of course doesn't bar the utmost in subtlety and human development. . . . They talk about French love. . . . Well, the Italians know all the French do, and have a tenderness besides. . . . My God, why doesn't everybody just live for love? That's all there is, baby. And out of bed you have to be simply brilllllllliant. . . .

Momma sometimes pondered to herself the reason for the wild rhetoric talk by some of the people who came to her bar. It wasn't like Italian rhetoric, which makes good Italian conversation a sort of shimmering badminton. At Momma's most of her customers talked like literate salesmen who cunningly invite you out to dinner—all the time you knew that they were selling something, but their propaganda was sparkling and insidious. At Momma's there were people who talked constantly for the whole three hours. There were others who simply listened to the talkers, smiling and accepting, as though they'd tacitly agreed to play audience. And Momma could tell the precise time in her bar by the level of the noise, by the speed with which the words shot through the air like molten needles, by the ever mounting bubbles of laughter and derision. Under this conversation Momma sensed a vacuum of pain, as though her guests jabbered at one another to get their minds off themselves, to convince themselves of the reality of something or other.

There now arrived the only two Momma didn't rejoice to see, two British sergeants wearing shorts draped like an old maid's flannels. They were almost twins, had peaked noses and spectacles that caused them to peer at everyone as though they were having difficulty in threading a needle from their rocking chairs. Momma wished they wouldn't stand so close to her desk, blocking her view. But stand there they did until the bar closed. Their conversation was a series of laments and groans and criticisms of everyone else present. They called this dishing the joint. Momma thought that they came to her bar because they couldn't stay away. They were disdainful and envious and balefully curious all at the same time. They reminded her of old women who take out their false teeth and contemplate their photograph of forty years ago. These sergeants bought some chits, took off their berets, and primped a little in the mirror behind Momma.

—Esther, my coiffure! Used to be so thick and lustrous. . . . We're not getting any younger, are we? We'll have to start paying for it soon. Shall we live together and take in tatting?

And the other sergeant said, giving himself a finger wave:

—Well, I've read that the end of all this is exhaustion and ennui. As we've agreed steen times before, Magda, the problem is bottomless, simply bottomless. No one but ourselves understands it, or is even interested. You put your hand into a cleft tree to your own peril, Magda. When you take out the wedge, the tree snaps together and breaks your hand. . . . And you cry your eyes out at night, but it doesn't do any good. . . . It keeps coming back on you because it's in you. Even though you don't get any satisfaction, you go back to it like a dog to his vomit. . . . That's what it is, Magda, vomit. Why kid ourselves and talk of love? Love is a constructive force. . . . We only want to destroy ourselves in others because we hate ourselves. . . .

At 1700 hours Rhoda appeared after she'd had evening chow at the WAC-ery. Rhoda was the only woman who came to Momma's bar. No one ever spoke to Rhoda, who did her drinking standing at the far end of the counter, reading a thick book. She always made it a point to show Momma what she was reading. Rhoda worried about the state of the world. She studied theories of leisure classes and patterns behind governments.

—I'm not good for much of anything, Rhoda once said, except to talk up a storm.

To Momma's Italian ear Rhoda had a voice like a baritone; everything she said carried about a kilometer.

—What am I? Rhoda said once. The reincarnation of L'Aiglon.

It seemed to Momma that Rhoda was happy in her WAC uniform—the neat tie, the coat, the stripes on the sleeve, the skirt that didn't call attention to the fact that it was a skirt. Under her overseas cap Rhoda wore an exceptional hairdo. It was something like the pageboy bob of twenty years ago cut still more boyishly. And under this cropped poll were Rhoda's stark face, thin lips, weasel eyes. Rhoda looked as though she were lying in ambush for something. She bought a slew of tickets from Momma and went to her accustomed place, reading and drinking. She turned the pages by moistening her forefinger and looking quickly at the other persons in the bar.

Rhoda was the only American girl whom Momma knew well, but she was a symbol. Momma had a theory that romantic love was on the wane in America because if all the women were like Rhoda, American girls were mighty emancipated and intellectual. Since Rhoda was so cool and unfeminine, Momma foresaw a day in the United States when all the old graceful concepts of love would have perished. The women would have brought it on themselves by insisting on equality with the men. To Momma, thinking of her girlhood in Milan, this wasn't an inviting picture. . . .

—Why don't signorine come here? Rhoda asked authoritatively of Momma. Intellectual Italian women, I mean. I'd spread the gospel to them. I'm the best little proselytizer in the world. I'd make them socially conscious. We'd read the *Nation* and John Dos Passos. I might even pass out copies of *Consumers' Research* to help Italian girls buy wisely.

Momma smiled. She knew quite well that if signorine started coming to her bar, most of her patrons would go away. It was an easy matter to get a signorina anywhere else in the Galleria Umberto or on the Toledo. Momma had indeed been ill at ease when Rhoda had first appeared, but the boys had accepted Rhoda while ignoring her. And so long as there was harmony, Momma didn't care who came to her bar. . . .

—Oh this place of yours, Rhoda boomed with a thick shiver. It's positively electric here, Momma. I get so much thinking and reading done in this stimulating atmosphere. . . . Just like a salon.

The two British sergeants eyed Rhoda. Momma'd been expecting them to accost one another for the past week. And tonight the bubble was going to burst.

—We've been asking one another why you come here, the sergeant called Esther said. You must have a Saint Francis of Assisi complex. Or else you're a Messalina. . . . If you want to give us a good laugh, why don't you bring one of your Warm Sisters with you and make a gruesome twosome? You shouldn't come here alone, darling. Momma's bar is like nature, which abhors vacuums and solitary people.

—I'm not answerable to the likes of you, Rhoda roared back, bristling with delight. But I will say I've always sought out milieux that vibrate in tune with me. . . . So you two just get back to your knitting. Just because you two are jaded and joaded, that's no sign I should be too.

—Magda, she's a tigress, the other British sergeant said, but a veritable tigress. We must have her to our next Caserta party.

—Don't think I don't know those parties, Rhoda rumbled. The height of sterility. Everybody sits around tearing everybody else to pieces, thinking, My God, ain't we brilliant. Everybody gets stinking drunk. Then somebody makes an entrance down the stairs in ostrich feathers and a boa. . . . No thank you, my pretty chicks.

—Well, get you, Mabel, the first British sergeant tittered.

Momma cleared her throat. She hated the turn things were taking by her cash desk. It was as though the three were armed with talons, raking at one another's faces.

—We understand one another all too well, don't we? Rhoda said triumphantly. I pity you two from the bottom of my swelling heart. If you had a little more of what I have, or I had a little more of what you have, what beautiful music we could make . . . a trio. . . .

—Darling, I see you in London, the second sergeant said. A sensation. But you aren't quite Bankhead, darling. But you are happy in the WAC's, aren't you, dear? Your postwar plans are to run a smart little night club . . . wearing a white tuxedo . . . but darling, you just haven't the figger for it.

—It's no use trying to scratch my eyes out, Rhoda rumbled in her open diapason. I have a perfect armorplating against elderly queans.

—Pleasa, Momma murmured, clearing her throat again, pleasa. . . .

In her bar things moved by fits and starts. Incidents in the course of three hours followed some secret natural rhythm of fission and quiescence, like earthquakes and Vesuvio. Each time the climaxes grew fuller. This first was only a ripple to what she knew would happen later.

Rhoda and the two British sergeants glared at one another. She reopened her thick book and retreated into it like an elephant hulking off into the jungle. The two sergeants put arms about each other's waists and executed a little congratulatory dance.

After the first incident the Desert Rat raised his fine dark head, looked into the mirror, and ordered another white wine. The Negro second lieutenant stopped his monologue and called out:

—Everyone's still wearing their veil . . . but wait. . . .

An Italian contingent always came to Momma's on schedule. They entered with the furtive gaiety of those who know they aren't wanted, but have set their hearts on coming anyhow. They wore shorts and sandals and whimsical little coats which they carried like wraps around their shoulders, neglecting to put their arms into the sleeves. Momma knew that her Allied clientele didn't care for them. And besides they never drank more than two glasses apiece, if they drank that much. They just sat around and mimicked one another and sniggered and looked hard at the Allied soldiery. Each evening they had a fresh set of photos and letters to show one another. Momma thought of nothing so much as a bevy of Milan shopgirls having a reunion after the day's work. She knew them all so well. The Italians treated Momma with a skeptical deference, as though to say, Well, here we are again, dearie; your bar is in the public domain; so what are you going to do with us if we don't make a nuisance of ourselves?

There was Armando, who worked in a drygoods store. He was led in by his shepherd dog on a leather thong. This dog was Armando's lure for introduction to many people. He had tight curls like a Greek statue's, a long brown face, and an air of distinction learned from the films. He wore powder-blue shorts. It was Armando who translated all his little friends' English letters for them.

There was Vittorio, with the blue eyes of a doll and gorgeous clothes such as Momma'd seen on young ingegneri in the old days in Milan. Vittorio worked as a typist at Navy House on Via Caracciolo. He worked so well and conscientiously that the British gave him soap and food rations. Sunday afternoons he walked by the aquarium with an English ensign who murmured in his ear. Vittorio had arrogance and bitterness. He was the leader of the others. All evening long at Momma's he lectured on literature and life and the sad fate of handsome young Neapolitans in Naples of August, 1944. In Momma's hearing he said that he'd continue his present career till he was thirty. Then he'd marry a contessa and retire to her villa at Amalfi.

There was Enzo, who'd been a carabiniere directing traffic until the Allies had liberated Naples. Now Enzo led the life of a gaga, strolling the town in a T-shirt, inviting his friends to coffee in the afternoon, and singing at dusk in dark corners. Momma thought Enzo the apogee of brutal refinement. Over his shorts he wore shirts of scented silk or pongee. Under these the muscles of his back shimmered like salmon. The nostrils in his almost black face showed like pits, flaring with his breathing.

There was also a tiny sergente maggiore of the Italian Army. He held himself off from the rest, though he always came in with them. He used them as air-umbrella protection for his own debarking operations. The name of this sergente maggiore was Giulio. His eyes darted warily about, and once in a while he'd call out something in a barking voice, to show that he was accustomed to command. He insisted on wearing his smart fascist peaked cap, the visor of which he would nervously tug when he got an unexpected answer.

The last Italian to arrive at Momma's was the only one she respected. He was a count, but he permitted himself to be known only as Gianni. Besides his title he had a spacious apartment in the Vomero. Momma respected his rank, and she hoped some day to be presented to his mother the countess. Momma liked Gianni as a person too. He was always dressed in black, with a white stiff collar and a black knitted tie. His black eyes smoldered with a remote nostalgia. For some months now he'd come to Momma's drunk a little, and gone away. But tonight he seemed purposeful. He greeted Momma with a tender wretchedness. Momma knew his disease. He was a Neapolitan conte, dying of love. Gianni avoided the other Italians, who had perched themselves on a counter at the rear of the bar, and went straight up to the Desert Rat. Momma leaned over her cash desk and watched with popping eyes.

—May I speak to you, sir? Gianni said to the Desert Rat.

His English was as slow and exquisite as that melancholy that lay over him like a cloud.

—Speak up, chum, the Desert Rat said in his almost inaudible voice.

—Do you like me a little, sir?

The Desert Rat didn't answer, but his tall body stiffened.

—I had a friend once, Gianni said, almost crying. He was a German officer. He taught me German, you see. He was kind to me. And I think I was kind to him. I think I am a good person, sir. I am a rich count, but of course to you that does not import. . . . I seek nothing from you, sir . . . like the others. . . . You look so much like the German officer. I was happy with him. He said he was happy with me. . . . Would you like sometimes to come to my house in the Vomero, sir?

The two British sergeants set up a screaming like parrots. Gianni fled. Momma put her hand to her heart, which had given one vast jump. The Desert Rat quietly put down his wineglass. He took the two British sergeants and knocked their heads together. Then he ran out through the bar. Momma watched him stand outside, peering up and down the Galleria and shielding his eyes against the sun. After a while he returned to his place and fell into his old reverie. He seemed as stirred and angry as a true and passionate boy.

The two British sergeants were shrieking and sobbing and looking at their reddened faces in the mirror. Then they repaired to the gabinetto. Momma could hear them inside splashing water on their faces and gibbering like chickens being bathed by a hen.

Rhoda looked over her book at the silent Desert Rat. The second incident rolled through the bar like the aftertones of a bell. Momma just held onto her cash register and prayed, for she knew that this was going to be an evening. The Negro second lieutenant began to sing something about "Strange Fruit." The Italians footnoted the incident to one another. Momma's bar wasn't nearly full yet, but it was buzzing like a bomb.

Presently the two British sergeants swept out of the gabinetto, their faces swollen and their eyes flushed from weeping. They looked like hawks for someone to prey on. Enzo stepped easily up to them, placed a hand on his hip, and extended his powerful jeweled hand:

—Buona sera, ragazze.

—You go straight to hell! the first British sergeant screeched. Why do you come here at all, you sordid little tramps in your dirty old finery? Do you think we feel sorry for you? Go on Via Roma and peddle your stuff and stop trying to act like trade. . . . We see through you, two-shilling belles. All of you get out, do you hear? Nobody here wants anything you've got. The Allies are quite self-sufficient, thank you. We did all right before Naples fell. . . . Why the nerve of you wop queans! Glamor!? Why you've all got as much allure as Gracie Fields in drag. . . . Go find some drunken Yank along the port. . . . But get the hell out of here!

The Italians replied to the sally of the British sergeants in their own indirect but effective way. Momma decided that the Italians were more deeply rooted in life, that they accepted themselves. For the Italian contingent merely sent up a merry carol of laughter. If they'd had fans, they'd have retreated behind them. This laughter hadn't a hollow ring. It was based on the assumption that anything in life can be laughed out of existence. Momma had never admired the Italian element in her bar. Now she did. They shook with the silveriest laughter, lolling over one another like cats at play. Their limbs gleamed in their shorts. Even the tiny sergente maggiore joined in the badinage. And the two British sergeants stepped back by Momma's cash desk and resumed their jeremiad.

—What will become of us, Esther? When we were young, we could laugh off the whole business. You and I both know that's what camping is. It's a Greek mask to hide the fact that our souls are being castrated and drawn and quartered with each fresh affair. What started as a seduction at twelve goes on till we're senile old aunties, doing it just as a reflex action. . . .

—And we're at the menopause now, Magda. . . . O God, if some hormone would just shrivel up in me and leave me in peace! I hate the thought of making a fool of myself when I turn forty. I'll see something gorgeous walking down Piccadilly and I'll make a pass and all England will read of my trial at the Old Bailey. . . . Do you think we would have been happier in Athens, Magda?

—Esther, let's face facts. You can't argue yourself out of your own time and dimension. You and I don't look like the Greeks and we don't think like them. We were born in England under a late Victorian morality, and so we'll die. . . . The end is the same anyhow, Greek or English. Don't you see, Esther? We've spent our youth looking for something that doesn't really exist. Therefore none of us is ever at peace with herself. All bitchery adds up to an attempt to get away from yourself by playing a variety of poses, each one more gruesome and leering than the last. . . . I'm sick to death of it, Esther. I can think of more reasons for not having been born than I can for living. . . . Is there perhaps some nobility stirring in my bones?

—Then is there no solution, Magda? the second British sergeant asked wistfully.

He cast his eyes about the bar like a novice about to take the veil.

—Millions, Esther. But rarely in the thing itself. That's what tantalizes us all. We play with the thing till it makes of us what we swear we'll never become, cold-blooded sex machines, dead to love. There are so many ways of sublimating, Esther. . . . But are they truly satisfying either? For some hours I've known, though they'll never come again, I'd cheerfully pass all eternity in hell.

—And I too, Magda. That's the hell of it. We all have known moments, days, weeks that were perfect.

—All part of the baggage of deceit, Esther. God lets us have those moments the way you'd give poisoned candy to a child. And we look back on those wonderful nights with far fiercer resentment than an old lady counting the medals of her dead son.

—But we've had them, Magda; we've had them. No one can take them away from us.

The two British sergeants lapsed into silence, for which Momma was grateful. Their conversation was a long swish of hissing *s*'s and flying eyebrows. They began to scratch their chevrons in a troubled and preoccupied way, and their faces fell into the same sort of introspective emptiness that Momma'd observed on old actresses sitting alone in a café. There was a lost air about them that made her prefer not to look at them, as though the devil had put her a riddle admitting of no solution, and a forfeit any way she answered it.

::

IT WAS 1830 HOURS IN MOMMA'S BAR, THE TIME OF THE BREATHING SPELL. She was quite aware that, gathered under her roof and drinking her white wine and vermouth, there was a great deal of energy that didn't quite know how to spend itself. And since there's some rhythm in life, in bars, and in war, everybody at once stopped talking and ordered fresh drinks. She could see them all looking at their wrist watches and telling themselves: I have another hour to go—what will it bring me?

Momma's sixth sense told her there was trouble brewing. A group of soldiers and sailors entered her bar. From the way they shot around their half-closed eyes she knew that this wasn't the place for them. They had an easiness and a superiority about them as though they were looking for trouble with infinite condescension. Cigars lolled from their mouths.

—Gracious, the Negro second lieutenant said, men!

—Look, Esther, said the first of the British sergeants, look at the essence of our sorrow. . . . What we seek and can never have. . . . And each side hates the other. The twain never meet except in case of necessity. And they part with tension on both sides.

For there were two American parachutists who lounged insolently, taking up more cubic space than they should have. And with them were two drunken American sailors, singing and holding one another up. Momma now wished that Poppa were here to order this foursome out summarily, under threat of the MP's. Vincenzo and Gaetano were no help at all in such circumstances. Then what she feared happened. Someone of her regular clientele let up a soft scream like a pigeon being strangled. At once a parachutist stiffened, flipped a wrist, and bawled:

—Oh saaaay, Nellie!

This was the moment the Italians had been waiting for. They picked themselves off the flat-topped counter where they'd been idling and padded toward the four newcomers. They were cajoling and tender and satiric and gay. They lit cigarettes for the parachutists and the sailors, and took some themselves. It became a swirling ballet of hands and light and rippling voices and the thickened accents of the sailors and the parachutists.

—Jesus, baby, those bedroom eyes! someone said to Vittorio.

—I hateya and I loveya, ya beast, one of the sailors said.

—Coo, it teases me right out of my mind, one of the British sergeants said. So simple and complex. Masculine and feminine. All gradations and all degrees and all nuances.

—The basis of life and love and cruelty and death, said the other British sergeant, looking as though he would faint. And in the long run, Magda, who is master and who mistress?

From a tension that was surely building up, Momma was distracted by the appearance of an assorted horde. In the final hour of the evening her bar filled until there were forty wedged in, six to eight deep from the mirrors to the bar. Her eyes had a mad skipping time to follow all that went on. It was like trying to watch a circus with a thousand shows simultaneous in as many rings.

First came an Aussie in a fedora hat, to which his invention had added flowers and feathers. Tonight he was more than usually drunk. He slunk in with the slow detachment of a mannequin modeling clothes. He waved a lace handkerchief at all:

—Oh my pets, my pets! Your mother's awfully late tonight, but she'll try and make it up to you!

—Ella's out of this world, some one said. She's brilliant, brilliant.

A glazed look came over the sailors' eyes like snakes asleep. Ella the Aussie kissed their hands and bustled off while they were still collecting themselves.

—Don't call *me* your sister! Ella shrieked, waving at his public while buying chits from Momma. He kissed Momma on both her cheeks, leaving a stench of alcohol and perfume.

There was a rich hollow thud. Momma at first feared that someone had planted a fist on someone else's chin. But it was only Rhoda, the WAC corporal, closing her book. That evening she read no further. It was getting too crowded in there even to turn pages.

Next to appear at Momma's was a British marine, sullen in his red and black, with a hulking beret. Momma knew he was a boxer, but not the sort who made trouble. He'd a red slim face, pockmarked and dour; the muscles in his calves stood out like knots. While drinking he teetered up and down on his toes and was a master at engineering newcomers into conversation. He observed everyone with a cool devotion. Often he'd invited Momma to his bouts at the Teatro delle Palme, but she hadn't gone because she couldn't bear to see him beating and being beaten in the ring. This British marine was on the most basic and genial terms with himself and the world.

Next came a plump South African lance corporal with red pips, and a Grenadier Guardsman, tall and reserved and mustached. The South African lance corporal was a favorite of Momma's because he made so much of her. She knew he didn't mean a word of it, but the whole ceremony was so much fun to her.

—Old girl, I've finally got married, said the plump lance corporal, presenting her to the Grenadier Guardsman, who looked terrified and bulwarky at the same time. This is Bert. You'll love Bert. He save my life in Tunisia. And he understands me. So he's not as stupid as he looks. And his devotion, darling! Coo! Just like a Saint Bernard Bert is. He knows how to cook, you know. . . . Bert's essence is in his mustaches. The traditionalism, the stolidity, and the stupidity of the British people produced those mustaches of Bert's.

Momma was in such a whirl of happiness that she gave the guardsman a chit for a drink on the house. Meanwhile the South African lance corporal whirled about the bar, burbling to everyone and formally announcing his marriage to Bert.

Momma was beginning to believe that she wasn't going to have any trouble from the parachutists and the sailors. They and the Italians were lazily drinking and mooing at one another. Momma tried to spell out for herself some theory of good and evil, but the older she got and the more she saw, the less clear cut the boundaries became to her. She could only conclude that these boys who drank at her bar were exceptional human beings. The masculine and the feminine weren't nicely divided in Momma's mind as they are to a biologist. They overlapped and blurred in life. This trait was what kept life and Momma's bar from being black and white. If everything were so clear cut, there'd be nothing to learn after the age of six and arithmetic.

::

AMONG THE LATER COMERS TO MOMMA'S WERE CERTAIN PERSONS FROM THE port battalion that sweated loading and unloading ships in the Bay of Naples. They turned up in her bar in the Galleria Umberto as soon as the afternoon shift got off, just as the truck drivers make a beeline for coffee and doughnuts. They usually came with fatigues damp with their sweat, with green-visored caps askew on their knotted hair. Because they were out of uniform Momma feared trouble with the MP's. But some of these port battalion GI's were Momma's favorites since they brought her many odds and ends they'd taken from the holds of Liberty ships: tidbits destined for generals' villas and the like. They knew Momma's nature as a curio collector of things and people.

There was Eddie, an American corporal. Momma loved Eddie the way she'd love a child of her own who was born not quite all there. Eddie'd been a garage mechanic in Vermont. He squirmed with that twisted tenderness often acquired by people who spend their lives lying under motors and having axle grease drip on them. Eddie had misty lonely eyes; his mouth was that of one who has never made the transition out of babyhood. His red hair yielded to no comb, and there was always a thick mechanical residue under his fingernails, which Momma sometimes cleaned herself. Eddie was drunk on duty and off. As he bought his chits, he leaned over Momma and patted her clumsily on her hair.

—Come stai, figlio mio? Momma asked.

—Bene, bene, Momma, he replied.

Eddie would caress people in a soft frightened way and then run his tongue over his lips. After he'd got good and tight, he'd go through the crowded bar playing games, pulling neckties, snapping belt buckles, and thrusting his knee between people's legs. He was like a little dog that has got mixed up in society and desires to find a master.

Then there was a supply sergeant of the port battalion, with his vulture face. His every movement seemed to Momma a raucous suppression of some deeper inferiority sense. He talked constantly like a supply catalogue, reeling off lists of things in his warehouse for the potent music of their names. Then he would shoot out his jaw and the blood would capillate into his eyes. Momma got him rooms around Naples with spinster acquaintances of hers. He stayed in these rooms on his one night off a week. This sergeant loved to sally into off-limits areas and wet-smelling vichi.

—Color and glamour, the sergeant said, all there is to life, baby. . . .

Eddie meanwhile had drunk three glasses of vermouth and came and stood by Momma, slipping cakes of soap into her hand behind the cash desk.

—Jees, I tink I got da scabies, Momma . . .

The last delegate from the port battalion was one of its tech sergeants named Wilbur. He treated Momma like a serving girl and spent his time going over everyone with his eyes. Wilbur should have been born a lynx, for he draped his length over any available area with a slow rehearsed lewdness. Tonight he was growing a mustache, but it didn't camouflage his violet eyes that glowed like amethysts in his face. Momma could never get him to look her in the eyes. He simply drawled at everyone, and all the things he said lay around in gluey pools like melted lavender sherbet.

—Bonsoir, ducks, Wilbur said to the two British sergeants. When is all this blah going to end? Because it is blah, and nobody knows it better than you. . . . Done any one nice lately? What a town to cruise this is. All the belles in the States would give their eyeteeth to be in Naples tonight. And when they saw all there is here, they'd be so confused they wouldn't know what to do with it. . . . Can you imagine the smell of their breaths? . . . Blah, that's all it is.

Two of Momma's more distinguished patrons now entered from the Galleria. They did it every evening, but every evening a little hush fell over the drinkers. They came in a little flushed, as though they'd been surprised in a closet. Perhaps the momentary pall proceeded from a certain awe at their rank, or at their temerity in coming at all. For by now the party was well under way, susceptible to that hiatus in levels of euphoria when people come late to a group that is already from alcohol in a state of dubious social cohesion. One was a pasty-faced major of the American medical corps who gave Momma a free physical examination every month and got his dentist friends to clean her teeth gratis. The major's breath always boiled in an asthmatic fashion, as though he were in the last stages of love-making. With him was his crony, a not so young second lieutenant who'd been commissioned for valor in combat at Cassino. The major and the lieutenant both wore gold wedding bands on their fingers. Momma gathered that they preferred not to discuss their wives, since these little women were four thousand miles away.

—Poor pickins tonight, said the major to the lieutenant.

—I don't waste any time any more, the lieutenant grunted, paying for his chits. I just say do you and pushem into a dark corner. . . . Piss on all introductions and flourishes. . . . Who started this way anyhow? Not me, buddy. . . .

Momma looked at the half-bald head of the lieutenant under the crazy angle of his cap. She knew that he'd been most heroic in battle—that was how he'd got his commission. There was strife in his low grating voice. Once he'd told her of last winter in battle, of an Italian boy sewing by moonlight in the arch of a bombed house near Formia:

—I was drinking vino with my GI's. . . . And he just sits there looking at me. Fifteen, he said he was . . . white skin. I remember his eyes over his needle. . . . I wonder where he is now.

As the lieutenant fumbled to pay her for their chits, a woman's picture fell on Momma's counter out of his pocket:

—Ees your wife in Stati Uniti? Momma said, trying to turn the glossy print over.

He covered it from her gaze with a hand pocked with sandfly bites and umber with cigarette stains. His eyes were close to hers, yellow and protruding.

—Never mind that, Momma, he said, restoring the picture to his pocket.

Momma knew that the bravest and coolest entered her bar alone. They entered with a curt functionalism that informed everyone that hadn't come just to drink or to watch or to brood. Still others came in specious twosomes, talked together a little, and spent most of the time ignoring one another and looking into the mirrors in a sort of reconnoitering restlessness. And a few came in groups of twos and threes for protection. When Momma's bar was full, it was like a peacock's tail because she could see nothing but eyes through the cigarette smoke. Restless and unsocketed eyes that wheeled all around, wholly taken up in the business of looking and calculating. Eyes of every color. Momma's bar when crowded was a goldfish bowl swimming with retinas and irises in motion.

Next there came two French lieutenants and two French sailors. The sailors were ubriachi and the lieutenants were icily sober. In the two French officers Momma'd always noted an excellence in the little braided pips through their shoulder loops, their American khaki shirts, and their tailored shorts. Their conversation played over the heads of their sailors with a silvery irony. Momma understood their tongue decently enough, that perfect language which gave all their remarks a literary quality beyond even the intelligence of the speakers.

—Ainsi je noie toute mon angoisse, said the first French officer.

—C'est ma femme qui m'incite à de telles folies, said the other.

—Tilimbom, the drunken sailors said, clapping the pompons on their caps.

The French officers had a jeep which they parked at the steps of the Galleria. When Momma closed her bar, she knew that they whisked into this jeep an assorted and sparkling company and drove to the top of Naples to admire the August moonlight. Momma wondered if the ripple of their epigrams and refinements ceased even when they were making love.

—C'est une manie, Pierre.

—Bon appétit, André.

::

MOMMA HAD LESS THAN HALF AN HOUR TILL CLOSING TIME. HER BAR, INTO which people now must wedge themselves, was swimming in smoke and a terrific tempo of talk and innuendo. Under its surface there was a force of madness and a laughter of gods about to burst. Momma put her hand to her throat and swallowed hard in the strangling ecstasy of one dropping down an elevator shaft. For this was the time she loved best of her three hours: a presentiment of infinite possibilities, of hectic enchantments, of the fleeting moment that never could be again because it was too preposterous and frantic and keyed up.

The Desert Rat was finishing his fifth white wine in his prison of detachment and musing. Ella the Aussie was being removed by Gaetano and Vincenzo from the top of the bar, where he was executing a cancan. Rhoda was booming out a quotation from Spengler. The Negro second lieutenant was examining his nail polish. Eddie had put his arms around one of the French officers, talking about parlayvoo-fransay. And the two British sergeants reared up like Savonarolas.

—I'm asking you, Esther, to take a good look at all these mad people. For they are mad. And consider the subtle thread that brings them all together here. Not so subtle as that either, Esther, since their personalities are so deeply rooted in it. What an odd force to unite so many varied personalities! Something they all want . . . and when they've had it, their reactions will be different. Some will feel themselves defiled. Others will want another try at it. Others will feel that they haven't found what they were looking for and will be back here tomorrow night.

—Does either of us know what these people are looking for, Magda? the second sergeant asked with thickened tongue.

—Don't be dull, Esther. They're all looking for perfection . . . and perfection is a love of death, if you face the issue squarely. That's the reason why these people live so hysterically. Since the desire to live, in its truest sense of reproducing, isn't in them, they live for the moment more passionately than most. That makes them brazen and shortsighted. . . . In this life, Esther, when you find perfection, you either die on the spot in orgasm, or else you don't know what to do with it. . . . These people are the embodiment of the tragic principle of life. They contain tragedy as surely as a taut string contains a musical note. They're the race's own question mark on its value to survive.

—Is there any hope for them, Magda? the second sergeant whimpered, wiping a mist from his glasses.

—In the exact measure that they believe in themselves, Esther. Depending on how they control their centripetal desires. Some hold back in their minds and distrust what they're doing. In them are the seeds of schizophrenia and destruction. Others give themselves wholly up to their impulses with a dizziness and a comic sense that are revolting to the more serious ones. . . . Lastly there's a group which sees that they can profit by everything in this world. These are the sane. The Orientals are wiser in these matters than we or Queen Victoria. No phase of human life is evil in itself, provided the whole doesn't grow static or subservient to the part. . . . But beware, Esther, of the bright psychiatrists who try to demarcate clearly the normal from the abnormal. In the Middle Ages people suffered themselves to be burnt as witches because it gave them such satisfaction to keep up their act. It was just a harmless expression of their ego. And children allow themselves to be pinked by hot stoves just to get a little sympathy out of their parents.

—What does God think of all this, Magda? mourned the second sergeant.

—Thank Him, if He exists, that we don't know. . . . A new morality may come into existence in our time, Esther. That's one of the few facts that thrills me, old bitch that I am. Some distinction may be made between public and private sins, between economic and ethical issues. In 1944 you find the most incredible intermingling, a porridge of the old and the new, of superstition and enlightenment. How can we speak of sin when thousands are cremated in German furnaces, when it isn't wrong to make a million pounds, but a crime to steal a loaf of bread? Perhaps some new code may come out of all this . . . I hope so.

—And if not?

—Why then, the first British sergeant said in drunken triumph, we shall have a chaos far worse than in Momma's bar this evening. This is merely a polite kind of anarchy, Esther. These people are expressing a desire disapproved of by society. But in relation to the world of 1944, this is just a bunch of gay people letting down their back hair . . . We mustn't go mad over details, Esther. Big issues are much more important. It is they which should drive us insane if we must be driven at all. . . . All I say is, some compromise must and will be reached. . . . Esther, I'm stinko.

Momma watched the two British sergeants embrace each other with an acid tenderness. Then they slid to the floor unconscious, in a welter of battle dress and chevrons and spectacles. They lay with their eyes closed in the quiet bliss of two spinsters who have fought out their differences at whist, falling asleep over the rubber. And it was typical of Momma's at this time of the evening that no one paid any attention to the collapse, just pushed and wedged in closer to give the corpses room.

The talk was now at its full tide of animation, like a river ravenous to reach the sea, yet a little apprehensive to lose its identity in that amorphous mass which ends everything. Momma knew the secret of an evening's drinking, that life grows sweeter as the sun sets and one gets tighter. If only drinkers knew how to hold their sights on that yellow target bobbing on their horizons! For Momma understood the drunkenness of the Nordic better than most Italians did. They drank out of impatience with details, with personalities that were centrifugal, with a certain feminine desire to have a crutch for the spirit, with a certain sluggishness of their metabolism. Momma thought it weak of them to drink, but it was a weakness as amiable as modesty, courtesy, or the desire to live at all when the odds were against them.

In a delirium Momma leaned over her cash desk and strained her ear at the hurtling shafts of talk:

—How can you possibly like actors? Every goddam one of them is constantly playing a part. Off the stage too . . .

—I am essentially an aristocrat. People must come to me. But I'm by no means passive . . .

—My aunt, a refined colored woman, brought me up most circumspectly. I come from a long line of missionaries. So don't think I don't spread the good word among the Gentiles . . .

—I don't know why our sort is always in the best jobs and the smartest . . .

—First time for me, ya see. I'm not the lowered-eyelash kind . . .

—So I told this Nellie to go peddle her fish somewhere else. And she did . . .

—Do you remember loathing your father and doting on your teachers? . . . You didn't? . . .

—. . . not responsible for anything I do tonight . . .

—Il n'y a rien au monde comme deux personnes qui s'aiment . . .

—Every time I think this is the real thing, the bottom falls right out from under me. Here I go again . . .

—. . . un vero appassionato di quelle cose misteriose . . .

—I could be faithful all night long . . .

—Ciao, cara . . .

—In the Pincio Gardens all I saw was flesh flesh flesh . . .

—Sometime we'll read the *Phaedo* together. Then you'll see what I mean . . .

—There's somethin in ya eyes. I dunno, I just know when I'm happy . . .

—Let's you and me stop beating around the bush . . .

—Don't feel you have to be elegant with me, Bella, cause your tiara's slippin over one ear . . .

—For Chrissakes, what in hell do ya take me for? . . .

—They're all suckin for a bruise . . . or somethin else . . .

—. . . am frankly revolted with the spectacle of human beings with their bobbie pins flying all over the place . . .

—And when they expect you to pay them for it . . .

—Pussunally I tink da Eyetalians is a hunnert years behind da times . . .

—Why do I wear a tie? Just to be different, that's why . . .

—. . . simply no idea of the effect of Mozart coming over a loudspeaker at the edge of the desert. The Krauts simply lovedddd ittt! . . .

—In a society predominantly militaristic . . .

—Ciao, cara . . .

—I looked at you earlier . . . but I didn't dare think . . .

A sudden silence descended on Momma's bar. There was a movement of many bodies giving way to make space. She now knew exactly what time it was and who had come. It was Captain Joe and the young Florentine. This was the climax of every evening. Captain Joe stalked cool and somber in his tank boots, a green bandanna tucked round his neck in the negligence of magnificence. He had gold hair which caught the light like bees shuttling at high noon. He had a hard intense sunburned face that smoldered like a monk in a Spanish painting. Momma knew that he was a perfect law unto himself, though gentle and courteous with all. He came only in the company of the young Florentine, whose eyes never left his face. The captain smiled with amusement and understanding at all, but he spoke only to his friend. Their faces complemented one another as a spoon shapes what it holds. The Florentine had dark thoughtful eyes and olive skin. He seemed wholly selfless. He and Captain Joe shared a delight and a comprehension that couldn't be heard. But they gave out a peace, a wild tranquillity.

—Buona sera a Lei, said Captain Joe to Momma. You keep a great circus at Naples, signora. And the miraculous thing about you is that you don't need the whip of a ringmaster. . . . You and I and Orlando are the last of a vanishing tribe. We live in the sunshine of our own nobility. A perilous charge in these days. I wonder if our time will ever come again. We give because we have to. And others try to draw us into their own common mold, reading their own defects into our virtues.

Momma signaled to Vincenzo and Gaetano to shut down the rolling steel shutter. It was closing time. Captain Joe lit her cigarette.

—Happiness, Captain Joe said, is a compromise, signora, between being what you are and not hurting others. . . . We smile, Orlando and I. . . . Genius knows its own weaknesses and hammers them into jewels. All our triumphs come from within. We've never learned to weep . . .

A shout, a thud, and screams tore the air.

—Ya will, willya! a drunken voice roared, hoarse with murder. Fists began to fly and people retreated against the walls. There was kicking and petitioning and cursing. The Desert Rat roused from his torpor and leaped in to defend the fallen. In the narrow bar persons swirled back and forth in a millrace. There were bloody noses and snapping joints. And when Momma saw the MP's break in from the Galleria, flailing their night sticks, she knew that the time had come for her to faint. So almost effortlessly she fell out and across her cash desk. She'd been practicing mentally all evening long.

1947

PAUL BOWLES

PAGES FROM COLD POINT

OUR CIVILIZATION IS DOOMED TO A SHORT LIFE: ITS COMPONENT PARTS ARE too heterogeneous. I personally am content to see everything in the process of decay. The bigger the bombs, the quicker it will be done. Life is visually too hideous for one to make the attempt to preserve it. Let it go. Perhaps some day another form of life will come along. Either way, it is of no consequence. At the same time, I am still a part of life, and I am bound by this to protect myself to whatever extent I am able. And so I am here. Here in the Islands vegetation still has the upper hand, and man has to fight even to make his presence seen at all. It is beautiful here, the trade winds blow all year, and I suspect that bombs are extremely unlikely to be wasted on this unfrequented side of the island, if indeed on any part of it.

I was loath to give up the house after Hope's death. But it was the obvious move to make. My university career always having been an utter farce (since I believe no reason inducing a man to "teach" can possibly be a valid one), I was elated by the idea of resigning, and as soon as her affairs had been settled and the money properly invested, I lost no time in doing so.

I think that week was the first time since childhood that I had managed to recapture the feeling of there being a content in existence. I went from one pleasant house to the next, making my adieux to the English quacks, the Philosophy fakirs, and so on—even to those colleagues with whom I was merely on speaking terms. I watched the envy in their faces when I announced my departure by Pan American on Saturday morning; and the greatest pleasure I felt in all this was in being able to answer, "Nothing," when I was asked, as invariably I was, what I intended to do.

When I was a boy people used to refer to Charles as "Big Brother C.", although he is only a scant year older than I. To me now he is merely "Fat

Brother C.", a successful lawyer. His thick, red face and hands, his back-slapping joviality, and his fathomless hypocritical prudery, these are the qualities which make him truly repulsive to me. There is also the fact that he once looked not unlike the way Racky does now. And after all, he still is my big brother, and disapproves openly of everything I do. The loathing I feel for him is so strong that for years I have not been able to swallow a morsel of food or a drop of liquid in his presence without making a prodigious effort. No one knows this but me—certainly not Charles, who would be the last one I should tell about it. He came up on the late train two nights before I left. He got quickly to the point—as soon as he was settled with a highball.

"So you're off for the wilds," he said, sitting forward in his chair like a salesman.

"If you can call it the wilds," I replied. "Certainly it's not wild like Mitichi." (He has a lodge in northern Quebec.) "I consider it really civilized."

He drank and smacked his lips together stiffly, bringing the glass down hard on his knee.

"And Racky. You're taking him along?"

"Of course."

"Out of school. Away. So he'll see nobody but you. You think that's good."

I looked at him. "I do," I said.

"By God, if I could stop you legally, I would!" he cried, jumping up and putting his glass on the mantel. I was trembling inwardly with excitement, but I merely sat and watched him. He went on. "You're not fit to have custody of the kid!" he shouted. He shot a stern glance at me over his spectacles.

"You think not?" I said gently.

Again he looked at me sharply. "D'ye think I've forgotten?"

I was understandably eager to get him out of the house as soon as I could. As I piled and sorted letters and magazines on the desk, I said: "Is that all you came to tell me? I have a good deal to do tomorrow and I must get some sleep. I probably shan't see you at breakfast. Agnes'll see that you eat in time to make the early train."

All he said was: "God! Wake up! Get wise to yourself! You're not fooling anybody, you know."

That kind of talk is typical of Charles. His mind is slow and obtuse; he constantly imagines that everyone he meets is playing some private game of deception with him. He is so utterly incapable of following the functioning of even a moderately evolved intellect that he finds the will to secretiveness and duplicity everywhere.

"I haven't time to listen to that sort of nonsense," I said, preparing to leave the room.

But he shouted, "You don't want to listen! No! Of course not! You just want to do what you want to do. You just want to go on off down there and live as you've a mind to, and to hell with the consequences!" At this point I heard Racky coming downstairs. C. obviously heard nothing, and he raved on. "But just remember, I've got your number all right, and if there's any trouble with the boy I'll know who's to blame."

I hurried across the room and opened the door so he could see that Racky was there in the hallway. That stopped his tirade. It was hard to know whether Racky had heard any of it or not. Although he is not a quiet young person, he is the soul of discretion, and it is almost never possible to know any more about what goes on inside his head than he intends one to know.

I was annoyed that C. should have been bellowing at me in my own house. To be sure, he is the only one from whom I would accept such behavior, but then, no father likes to have his son see him take criticism meekly. Racky simply stood there in his bathrobe, his angelic face quite devoid of expression, saying: "Tell Uncle Charley good night for me, will you? I forgot."

I said I would, and quickly shut the door. When I thought Racky was back upstairs in his room, I bade Charles good night. I have never been able to get out of his presence fast enough. The effect he has on me dates from an early period of our lives, from days I dislike to recall.

::

RACKY IS A WONDERFUL BOY. AFTER WE ARRIVED, WHEN WE FOUND IT impossible to secure a proper house near any town where he might have the company of English boys and girls his own age, he showed no sign of chagrin, although he must have been disappointed. Instead, as we went out of the renting office into the glare of the street, he grinned and said: "Well, I guess we'll have to get bikes, that's all."

The few available houses near what Charles would have called "civilization" turned out to be so ugly and so impossibly confining in atmosphere that we decided immediately on Cold Point, even though it was across the island and quite isolated on its seaside cliff. It was beyond a doubt one of the most desirable properties on the island, and Racky was as enthusiastic about its splendors as I.

"You'll get tired of being alone out there, just with me," I said to him as we walked back to the hotel.

"Aw, I'll get along all right. When do we look for the bikes?"

At his insistence we bought two the next morning. I was sure I should not make much use of mine, but I reflected that an extra bicycle might be convenient to have around the house. It turned out that the servants all had their own bicycles, without which they would not have been able to get to and from the village of Orange Walk, eight miles down the shore. So for a while I was forced to get astride mine each morning before breakfast and pedal madly along beside Racky for a half hour. We would ride through the cool early air, under the towering silk-cotton trees near the house, and out to the great curve in the shoreline where the waving palms bend landward in the stiff breeze that always blows there. Then we would make a wide turn and race back to the house, loudly discussing the degrees of our desires for the various items of breakfast we knew were awaiting us there on the terrace. Back home we would eat in the wind, looking out over the Caribbean, and talk about the news in yesterday's local paper, brought to us by Isiah each morning from Orange Walk. Then Racky would disappear for the whole morning on his bicycle, riding furiously along the road in one direction or the other until he had discovered an unfamiliar strip of sand along the shore that he could consider a new beach. At lunch he would describe it in detail to me, along with a recounting of all the physical hazards involved in hiding the bicycle in among the trees, so that natives passing along the road on foot would not spot it, or in climbing down unscalable cliffs that turned out to be much higher than they had appeared at first sight, or in measuring the depth of the water preparatory to diving from the rocks, or in judging the efficacy of the reef in barring sharks and barracuda. There is never any element of bragadoccio in Racky's relating of his exploits—only the joyous excitement he derives from telling how he satisfies his inexhaustible curiosity. And his mind shows its alertness in all directions at once. I do not mean to say that I expect him to be an "intellectual." That is no affair of mine, nor do I have any particular interest in whether he turns out to be a thinking man or not. I know he will always have a certain boldness of manner and a great purity of spirit in judging values. The former will prevent his becoming what I call a "victim": he never will be brutalized by realities. And his unerring sense of balance in ethical considerations will shield him from the paralyzing effects of present-day materialism.

For a boy of sixteen Racky has an extraordinary innocence of vision. I do not say this as a doting father, although God knows I can never even think of the boy without that familiar overwhelming sensation of delight and gratitude for being vouchsafed the privilege of sharing my life with him. What he takes so completely as a matter of course, our daily life here together, is a source of never-ending wonder to me; and I reflect upon it a good part of each day, just sitting here being conscious of my great good fortune in having him all to myself, beyond the reach of prying eyes and malicious tongues. (I suppose I am really thinking of C. when I write that.) And I believe that a part of the charm of sharing Racky's life with him consists precisely in his taking it all so utterly for granted. I have never asked him whether he likes being here—it is so patent that he does, very much. I think if he were to turn to me one day and tell me how happy he is here, that somehow, perhaps, the spell might be broken. Yet if he were to be thoughtless and inconsiderate, or even unkind to me, I feel that I should be able only to love him the more for it.

I have reread that last sentence. What does it mean? And why should I even imagine it could mean anything more than it says?

Still, much as I may try, I can never believe in the gratuitous, isolated fact. What I must mean is that I feel that Racky already has been in some way inconsiderate. But in what way? Surely I cannot resent his bicycle treks; I cannot expect him to want to stay and sit talking with me all day. And I never worry about his being in danger; I know he is more capable than most adults of taking care of himself, and that he is no more likely than any native to come to harm crawling over the cliffs or swimming in the bays. At the same time there is no doubt in my mind that something about our existence annoys me. I must resent some detail in the pattern, whatever that pattern may be. Perhaps it is just his youth, and I am envious of the lithe body, the smooth skin, the animal energy and grace.

::

FOR A LONG TIME THIS MORNING I SAT LOOKING OUT TO SEA, TRYING TO solve that small puzzle. Two white herons came and perched on a dead stump east of the garden. They stayed a long time there without stirring. I would turn my head away and accustom my eyes to the bright sea-horizon, then I would look suddenly at them to see if they had shifted position, but they would always be in the same attitude. I tried to imagine the black stump without them—a purely vegetable landscape—but it was impossible. All the while I was slowly forcing myself to accept a ridiculous explanation of my annoyance with Racky. It had made itself manifest to me only yesterday, when instead of appearing for lunch, he sent a young colored boy from Orange Walk to say that he would be lunching in the village. I could not help noticing that the boy was riding Racky's bicycle. I had been waiting lunch a good half hour for him, and I had Gloria serve immediately as the boy rode off, back to the village. I was curious to know in what sort of place and with whom Racky could be eating, since Orange Walk, as far as I know, is inhabited exclusively by Negroes, and I was sure Gloria would be able to shed some light on the matter, but I could scarcely ask her. However, as she brought on the dessert, I said: "Who was that boy that brought the message from Mister Racky?"

She shrugged her shoulders. "A young lad of Orange Walk. He's named Wilmot."

When Racky returned at dusk, flushed from his exertion (for he never rides casually), I watched him closely. His behavior struck my already suspicious eye as being one of false heartiness and a rather forced good humor. He went to his room early and read for quite a while before turning off his light. I took a long walk in the almost day-bright moonlight, listening to the songs of the night insects in the trees. And I sat for a while in the dark on the stone railing of the bridge across Black River. (It is really only a brook that rushes down over the rocks from the mountain a few miles inland, to the beach near the house.) In the night it always sounds louder and more important than it does in the daytime. The music of the water over the stones relaxed my nerves, although why I had need of such a thing I find it difficult to understand, unless I was really upset by Racky's not having come home for lunch. But if that were true it would be absurd, and moreover, dangerous—just the sort of the thing the parent of an adolescent has to beware of and fight against, unless he is indifferent to the prospect of losing the trust and affection of his offspring permanently. Racky must stay out whenever he likes, with whom he likes, and for as long as he likes, and I must not think twice about it, much less mention it to him, or in any way give the impression of prying. Lack of confidence on the part of a parent is the one unforgivable sin.

Although we still take our morning dip together on arising, it is three weeks since we have been for the early spin. One morning I found that Racky had jumped onto his bicycle in his wet trunks while I was still swimming, and gone by himself, and since then there has been an unspoken agreement between us that such is to be the procedure; he will go alone. Perhaps I held him back; he likes to ride so fast.

Young Peter, the smiling gardener from Saint Ives Cove, is Racky's special friend. It is amusing to see them together among the bushes, crouched over an ant-hill or rushing about trying to catch a lizard, almost of an age the two, yet so disparate—Racky with his tan skin looking almost white in contrast to the glistening black of the other. Today I know I shall be alone for lunch, since it is Peter's day off. On such days they usually go together on their bicycles into Saint Ives Cove, where Peter keeps a small rowboat. They fish along the coast there, but they have never returned with anything so far.

Meanwhile I am here alone, sitting on the rocks in the sun, from time to time climbing down to cool myself in the water, always conscious of the house behind me under the high palms, like a large glass boat filled with orchids and lilies. The servants are clean and quiet, and the work seems to be accomplished almost automatically. The good, black servants are another blessing of the islands; the British, born here in this paradise, have no conception of how fortunate they are. In fact, they do nothing but complain. One must have lived in the United States to appreciate the wonder of this place. Still, even here ideas are changing each day. Soon the people will decide that they want their land to be a part of today's monstrous world, and once that happens, it will be all over. As soon as you have that desire, you are infected with the deadly virus, and you begin to show the symptoms of the disease. You live in terms of time and money, and you think in terms of society and progress. Then all that is left for you is to kill the other people who think the same way, along with a good many of those who do not, since that is the final manifestation of the malady. Here for the moment at any rate, one has a feeling of staticity—existence ceases to be like those last few seconds in the hour-glass when what is left of the sand suddenly begins to rush through to the bottom all at once. For the moment, it seems suspended. And if it seems, it is. Each wave at my feet, each bird-call in the forest at my back, does *not* carry me one step nearer the final disaster. The disaster is certain, but it will suddenly have happened, that is all. Until then, time stays still.

::

I AM UPSET BY A LETTER IN THIS MORNING'S MAIL: THE ROYAL BANK OF Canada requests that I call in person at its central office to sign the deposit slips and other papers for a sum that was cabled from the bank in Boston. Since the central office is on the other side of the island, fifty miles away,

I shall have to spend the night over there and return the following day. There is no point in taking Racky along. The sight of "civilization" might awaken a longing for it in him; one never knows. I am sure it would have in me when I was his age. And if that should once start, he would merely be unhappy, since there is nothing for him but to stay here with me, at least for the next two years, when I hope to renew the lease, or, if things in New York pick up, buy the place. I am sending word by Isiah when he goes home into Orange Walk this evening, to have the McCoigh car call for me at seven-thirty tomorrow morning. It is an enormous old open Packard, and Isiah can save the ride out to work here by piling his bicycle into the back and riding with McCoigh.

::

THE TRIP ACROSS THE ISLAND WAS BEAUTIFUL, AND WOULD HAVE BEEN highly enjoyable if my imagination had not played me a strange trick at the very outset. We stopped in Orange Walk for gasoline, and while that was being seen to, I got out and went to the corner store for some cigarettes. Since it was not yet eight o'clock, the store was still closed, and I hurried up the side street to the other little shop which I thought might be open. It was, and I bought my cigarettes. On the way back to the corner I noticed a large black woman leaning with her arms on the gate in front of her tiny house, staring into the street. As I passed by her, she looked straight into my face and said something with the strange accent of the island. It was said in what seemed an unfriendly tone, and ostensibly was directed at me, but I had no notion what it was. I got back into the car and the driver started it. The sound of the words had stayed in my head, however, as a bright shape outlined by darkness is likely to stay in the mind's eye, in such a way that when one shuts one's eyes one can see the exact contour of the shape. The car was already roaring up the hill toward the overland road when I suddenly reheard the very words. And they were: "Keep your boy at home, mahn." I sat perfectly rigid for a moment as the open countryside rushed past. Why should I think she had said that? Immediately I decided that I was giving an arbitrary sense to a phrase I could not have understood even if I had been paying strict attention. And then I wondered why my subconscious should have chosen that sense, since now that I whispered the words over to myself they failed to connect with any anxiety to which my mind might have been disposed. Actually I have never given a thought to Racky's wanderings about Orange Walk. I can find no such preoccupation no matter how I put the question to myself. Then, could she really have said those words? All the way through the mountains I pondered the question, even though it was obviously a waste of energy. And soon I could no longer hear the sound of her voice in my memory: I had played the record over too many times, and worn it out.

Here in the hotel a gala dance is in progress. The abominable orchestra, comprising two saxophones and one sour violin, is playing directly under my window in the garden, and the serious-looking couples slide about on the waxed concrete floor of the terrace, in the light of strings of paper lanterns. I suppose it is meant to look Japanese.

At this moment I wonder what Racky is doing there in the house with only Peter and Ernest the watchman to keep him company. I wonder if he is asleep. The house, which I am accustomed to think of as smiling and benevolent in its airiness, could just as well be in the most sinister and remote regions of the globe, now that I am here. Sitting here with the absurd orchestra bleating downstairs, I picture it to myself, and it strikes me as terribly vulnerable in its isolation. In my mind's eye I see the moonlit point with its tall palms waving restlessly in the wind, its dark cliffs licked by the waves below. Suddenly, although I struggle against the sensation, I am inexpressibly glad to be away from the house, helpless there, far on its point of land, in the silence of the night. Then I remember that the night is seldom silent. There is the loud sea at the base of the rocks, the droning of the thousands of insects, the occasional cries of the night birds—all the familiar noises that make sleep so sound. And Racky is there surrounded by them as usual, not even hearing them. But I feel profoundly guilty for having left him, unutterably tender and sad at the thought of him, lying there alone in the house with the two Negroes the only human beings within miles. If I keep thinking of Cold Point I shall be more and more nervous.

I am not going to bed yet. They are all screaming with laughter down there, the idiots; I could never sleep anyway. The bar is still open. Fortunately it is on the street side of the hotel. For once I need a few drinks.

Much later, but I feel no better; I may be a little drunk. The dance is over and it is quiet in the garden, but the room is too hot.

::

AS I WAS FALLING ASLEEP LAST NIGHT, ALL DRESSED, AND WITH THE OVERhead light shining sordidly in my face, I heard the black woman's voice again, more clearly even than I did in the car yesterday. For some reason this morning there is no doubt in my mind that the words I heard are the words she said. I accept that and go on from there. Suppose she did tell me to keep Racky home. It could only mean that she, or someone else in Orange Walk, has had a childish altercation with him; although I must say it is hard to conceive of Racky's entering into any sort of argument or feud with those people. To set my mind at rest (for I do seem to be taking the whole thing with great seriousness), I am going to stop in the village this afternoon before going home, and try to see the woman. I am extremely curious to know what she could have meant.

::

I HAD NOT BEEN CONSCIOUS UNTIL THIS EVENING WHEN I CAME BACK TO Cold Point how powerful they are, all those physical elements that go to make up its atmosphere: the sea and wind-sounds that isolate the house from the road, the brilliancy of the water, sky and sun, the bright colors and strong odors of the flowers, the feeling of space both outside and within the house. One naturally accepts these things when one is living here. This afternoon when I returned I was conscious of them all over again, of their existence and their strength. All of them together are like a powerful drug; coming back made me feel as though I had been disintoxicated and were returning to the scene of my former indulgences. Now at eleven it is as if I had never been absent an hour. Everything is the same as always, even to the dry palm branch that scrapes against the window screen by my night table. And indeed, it is only thirty-six hours since I was here; but I always expect my absence from a place to bring about irremediable changes.

Strangely enough, now that I think of it, I feel that something *has* changed since I left yesterday morning, and that is the general attitude of the servants—their collective aura, so to speak. I noticed that difference immediately upon arriving back, but was unable to define it. Now I see it clearly. The network of common understanding which slowly spreads itself through a well-run household has been destroyed. Each person is by himself now. No unfriendliness, however, that I can see. They all behave with the utmost courtesy, excepting possibly Peter, who struck me as looking unaccustomedly glum when I encountered him in the kitchen after dinner. I meant to ask Racky if he had noticed it, but I forgot and he went to bed early.

In Orange Walk I made a brief stop on the pretext to McCoigh that

I wanted to see the seamstress in the side street. I walked up and back in front of the house where I had seen the woman, but there was no sign of anyone.

As for my absence, Racky seems to have been perfectly content, having spent most of the day swimming off the rocks below the terrace. The insect sounds are at their height now, the breeze is cooler than usual, and I shall take advantage of these favorable conditions to get a good long night's rest.

::

TODAY HAS BEEN ONE OF THE MOST DIFFICULT DAYS OF MY LIFE. I AROSE early, we had breakfast at the regular time, and Racky went off in the direction of Saint Ives Cove. I lay in the sun on the terrace for a while, listening to the noises of the household's regime. Peter was all over the property, collecting dead leaves and fallen blossoms in a huge basket and carrying them off to the compost heap. He appeared to be in an even fouler humor than last night. When he came near to me at one point on his way to another part of the garden I called to him. He set the basket down and stood looking at me; then he walked across the grass toward me slowly—reluctantly, it seemed to me.

"Peter, is everything all right with you?"

"Yes, sir."

"No trouble at home?"

"Oh, no, sir."

"Good."

"Yes, sir."

He went back to his work. But his face belied his words. Not only did he seem to be in a decidedly unpleasant temper; out here in the sunlight he looked positively ill. However, it was not my concern, if he refused to admit it.

When the heavy heat of the sun reached the unbearable point for me, I got out of my chair and went down the side of the cliff along the series of steps cut there into the rock. A level platform is below, and a diving board, for the water is deep. At each side, the rocks spread out and the waves break over them, but by the platform the wall of rock is vertical and the water merely hits against it below the springboard. The place is a tiny amphitheatre, quite cut off in sound and sight from the house. There too I like to lie in the sun; when I climb out of the water I often remove my trunks and lie stark naked on the springboard. I regularly make fun of Racky because he is embarrassed to do the same. Occasionally he will do it, but never without being coaxed. I was spread out there without a stitch on, being lulled by the slapping of the water, when an unfamiliar voice very close to me said: "Mister Norton?"

I jumped with nervousness, nearly fell off the springboard, and sat up, reaching at the same time, but in vain, for my trunks, which were lying on the rock practically at the feet of a middle-aged mulatto gentleman. He was in a white duck suit, and wore a high collar with a black tie, and it seemed to me that he was eyeing me with a certain degree of horror.

My next reaction was one of anger at being trespassed upon in this way. I rose and got the trunks, however, donning them calmly and saying nothing more meaningful than: "I didn't hear you come down the steps."

"Shall we go up?" said my caller. As he led the way, I had a definite premonition that he was here on an unpleasant errand. On the terrace we sat down, and he offered me an American cigarette which I did not accept.

"This is a delightful spot," he said, glancing out to sea and then at the end of his cigarette, which was only partially aglow. He puffed at it.

I said, "Yes," waiting for him to go on; presently he did.

"I am from the constabulary of this parish. The police, you see." And seeing my face, "This is a friendly call. But still it must be taken as a warning, Mister Norton. It is very serious. If anyone else comes to you about this it will mean trouble for you, heavy trouble. That's why I want to see you privately this way and warn you personally. You see."

I could not believe I was hearing his words. At length I said faintly: "But what about?"

"This is not an official call. You must not be upset. I have taken it upon myself to speak to you because I want to save you deep trouble."

"But I *am* upset!" I cried, finding my voice at last. "How can I help being upset, when I don't know what you're talking about?"

He moved his chair close to mine, and spoke in a very low voice.

"I have waited until the young man was away from the house so we could talk in private. You see, it is about him."

Somehow that did not surprise me. I nodded.

"I will tell you very briefly. The people here are simple country folk. They make trouble easily. Right now they are all talking about the young man you have living here with you. He is your son, I hear." His inflection here was sceptical.

"Certainly he's my son."

His expression did not change, but his voice grew indignant. "Whoever he is, that is a bad young man."

"What do you mean?" I cried, but he cut in hotly: "He may be your son; he may not be. I don't care who he is. That is not my affair. But he is bad through and through. We don't have such things going on here, sir. The people in Orange Walk and Saint Ives Cove are very cross now. You don't know what these folk do when they are aroused."

I thought it my turn to interrupt. "Please tell me why you say my son is bad. What has he done?" Perhaps the earnestness in my voice reached him, for his face assumed a gentler aspect. He leaned still closer to me and almost whispered.

"He has no shame. He does what he pleases with all the young boys, and the men too, and gives them a shilling so they won't tell about it. But they talk. Of course they talk. Every man for twenty miles up and down the coast knows about it. And the women too, they know about it." There was a silence.

I had felt myself preparing to get to my feet for the last few seconds because I wanted to go into my room and be alone, to get away from that scandalized stage whisper. I think I mumbled "Good morning" or "Thank you," as I turned away and began walking toward the house. But he was still beside me, still whispering like an eager conspirator into my ear: "Keep him home, Mister Norton. Or send him away to school, if he is your son. But make him stay out of these towns. For his own sake."

I shook hands with him and went to lie on my bed. From there I heard his car door slam, heard him drive off. I was painfully trying to formulate an opening sentence to use in speaking to Racky about this, feeling that the opening sentence would define my stand. The attempt was merely a sort of therapeutic action, to avoid thinking about the thing itself. Every attitude seemed impossible. There was no way to broach the subject. I suddenly realized that I should never be able to speak to him directly about it. With the advent of this news he had become another person—an adult, mysterious and formidable. To be sure, it did occur to me that the mulatto's story might not be true, but automatically I rejected the doubt. It was as if I wanted to believe it, almost as if I had already known it, and he had merely confirmed it.

Racky returned at midday, panting and grinning. The inevitable comb appeared and was used on the sweaty, unruly locks. Sitting down to lunch, he exclaimed: "Gosh! Did I find a swell beach this morning! But what a job to get to it!" I tried to look unconcerned as I met his gaze; it was as if our positions had been reversed, and I were hoping to stem his rebuke. He prattled on about thorns and vines and his machete. Throughout the meal I kept telling myself: "Now is the moment. You must say something."

But all I said was: "More salad? Or do you want dessert now?" So the lunch passed and nothing happened. After I had finished my coffee I went into my bedroom and looked at myself in the large mirror. I saw my eyes trying to give their reflected brothers a little courage. As I stood there I heard a commotion in the other wing of the house: voices, bumpings, the sound of a scuffle. Above the noise came Gloria's sharp voice, imperious and excited: "No, mahn! Don't strike him!" And louder: "Peter, mahn, no!"

I went quickly toward the kitchen, where the trouble seemed to be, but on the way I was run into by Racky, who staggered into the hallway with his hands in front of his face.

"What is it, Racky?" I cried.

He pushed past me into the living room without moving his hands away from his face; I turned and followed him. From there he went into his own room, leaving the door open behind him. I heard him in his bathroom running the water. I was undecided what to do. Suddenly Peter appeared in the hall doorway, his hat in his hand. When he raised his head, I was surprised to see that his cheek was bleeding. In his eyes was a strange, confused expression of transient fear and deep hostility. He looked down again.

"May I please talk with you, sir?"

"What was all the racket? What's been happening?"

"May I talk with you outside, sir?" He said it doggedly, still not looking up.

In view of the circumstances, I humored him. We walked slowly up the cinder road to the main highway, across the bridge, and through the forest while he told me his story. I said nothing.

At the end he said: "I never wanted to, sir, even the first time, but after the first time I was afraid, and Mister Racky was after me every day."

I stood still, and finally said: "If you had only told me this the first time it happened, it would have been much better for everyone."

He turned his hat in his hands, studying it intently. "Yes, sir. But I didn't know what everyone was saying about him in Orange Walk until today. You know I always go to the beach at Saint Ives Cove with Mister Racky on my free days. If I had known what they were all saying I wouldn't have been afraid, sir. And I wanted to keep on working here. I needed the money." Then he repeated what he had already said three times. "Mister Racky said you'd see about it that I was put in the jail. I'm a year older than Mister Racky, sir."

"I know, I know," I said impatiently; and deciding that severity was what Peter expected of me at this point I added: "You had better get your things together and go home. You can't work here any longer, you know."

The hostility in his face assumed terrifying proportions as he said: "If you killed me I would not work any more at Cold Point, sir."

I turned and walked briskly back to the house, leaving him standing there in the road. It seems he returned at dusk, a little while ago, and got his belongings.

In his room Racky was reading. He had stuck some adhesive tape on his chin and over his cheekbone.

"I've dismissed Peter," I announced. "He hit you, didn't he?"

He glanced up. His left eye was swollen, but not yet black.

"He sure did. But I landed him one, too. And I guess I deserved it anyway."

I rested against the table. "Why?" I asked nonchalantly.

"Oh, I had something on him from a long time back that he was afraid I'd tell you."

"And just now you threatened to tell me?"

"Oh, no! He said he was going to quit the job here, and I kidded him about being yellow."

"Why did he want to quit? I thought he liked the job."

"Well, he did, I guess, but he didn't like me." Racky's candid gaze betrayed a shade of pique. I still leaned against the table.

I persisted. "But I thought you two got on fine together. You seemed to."

"Nah. He was just scared of losing his job. I had something on him. He was a good guy, though; I liked him all right." He paused. "Has he gone yet?" A strange quaver crept into his voice as he said the last words, and I understood that for the first time Racky's heretofore impeccable histrionics were not quite equal to the occasion. He was very much upset at losing Peter.

"Yes, he's gone," I said shortly. "He's not coming back, either." And as Racky, hearing the unaccustomed inflection in my voice, looked up at me suddenly with faint astonishment in his young eyes, I realized that this was the moment to press on, to say: "What did you have on him?" But as if he had arrived at the same spot in my mind a fraction of a second earlier, he proceeded to snatch away my advantage by jumping up, bursting into loud song, and pulling off all his clothes simultaneously. As he stood before me naked, singing at the top of his lungs, and stepped into his swimming trunks, I was conscious that again I should be incapable of saying to him what I must say.

He was in and out of the house all afternoon: some of the time he read in his room, and most of the time he was down on the diving board. It is strange behavior for him; if I could only know what is in his mind. As evening approached, my problem took on a purely obsessive character. I walked to and fro in my room, always pausing at one end to look out the window over the sea, and at the other end to glance at my face in the mirror. As if that could help me! Then I took a drink. And another. I thought I might be able to do it at dinner, when I felt fortified by the whisky. But no. Soon he will have gone to bed. It is not that I expect to confront him with any accusations. That I know I never can do. But I must find a way to keep him from his wanderings, and I must offer a reason to give him, so that he will never suspect that I know.

::

WE FEAR FOR THE FUTURE OF OUR OFFSPRING. IT IS LUDICROUS, BUT ONLY a little more palpably so than anything else in life. A length of time has passed; days which I am content to have known, even if now they are over. I think that this period was what I had always been waiting for life to offer, the recompense I had unconsciously but firmly expected, in return for having been held so closely in the grip of existence all these years.

That evening seems long ago only because I have recalled its details so many times that they have taken on the color of legend. Actually my problem already had been solved for me then, but I did not know it. Because I could not perceive the pattern, I foolishly imagined that I must cudgel my brains to find the right words with which to approach Racky. But it was he who came to me. That same evening, as I was about to go out for a solitary stroll which I thought might help me hit upon a formula, he appeared at my door.

"Going for a walk?" he asked, seeing the stick in my hand.

The prospect of making an exit immediately after speaking with him made things seem simpler. "Yes," I said, "but I'd like to have a word with you first."

"Sure. What?" I did not look at him because I did not want to see the watchful light I was sure was playing in his eyes at this moment. As I spoke I tapped with my stick along the designs made by the tiles in the floor. "Racky, would you like to go back to school?"

"Are you kidding? You know I hate school."

I glanced up at him. "No, I'm not kidding. Don't look so horrified. You'd probably enjoy being with a bunch of fellows your own age." (That was not one of the arguments I had meant to use.)

"I might like to be with guys my own age, but I don't want to have to be in school to do it. I've had school enough."

I went to the door and said lamely: "I thought I'd get your reactions."

He laughed. "No, thanks."

"That doesn't mean you're not going," I said over my shoulder as I went out.

On my walk I pounded the highway's asphalt with my stick, stood on the bridge having dramatic visions which involved such eventualities as our moving back to the States, Racky's having a bad spill on his bicycle and being paralyzed for some months, and even the possibility of my letting events take their course, which would doubtless mean my having to visit him now and then in the governmental prison with gifts of food, if it meant nothing more tragic and violent. "But none of these things will happen," I said to myself, and I knew I was wasting precious time; he must not return to Orange Walk tomorrow.

I went back toward the point at a snail's pace. There was no moon and very little breeze. As I approached the house, trying to tread lightly on the cinders so as not to awaken the watchful Ernest and have to explain to him that it was only I, I saw that there were no lights in Racky's room. The house was dark save for the dim lamp on my night table. Instead of going in, I skirted the entire building, colliding with bushes and getting my face sticky with spider webs, and went to sit a while on the terrace where there seemed to be a breath of air. The sound of the sea was far out on the reef, where the breakers sighed. Here below, there were only slight watery chugs and gurgles now and then. It was unusually low tide. I smoked three cigarettes mechanically, having ceased even to think, and then, my mouth tasting bitter from the smoke, I went inside.

My room was airless. I flung my clothes onto a chair and looked at the night table to see if the carafe of water was there. Then my mouth opened. The top sheet of my bed had been stripped back to the foot. There on the far side of the bed, dark against the whiteness of the lower sheet, lay Racky asleep on his side, and naked.

I stood looking at him for a long time, probably holding my breath, for I remember feeling a little dizzy at one point. I was whispering to myself, as my eyes followed the curve of his arm, shoulder, back, thigh, leg: "A child. A child." Destiny, when one perceives it clearly from very near, has no qualities at all. The recognition of it and the consciousness of the vision's clarity leave no room on the mind's horizon. Finally I turned off the light and softly lay down. The night was absolutely black.

He lay perfectly quiet until dawn. I shall never know whether or not he was really asleep all that time. Of course he couldn't have been, and yet he lay so still. Warm and firm, but still as death. The darkness and silence were heavy around us. As the birds began to sing, I sank into a soft, enveloping slumber; when I awoke in the sunlight later, he was gone.

I found him down by the water, cavorting alone on the springboard; for the first time he had discarded his trunks without my suggesting it. All day we stayed together around the terrace and on the rocks, talking, swimming, reading, and just lying flat in the hot sun. Nor did he return to his room when night came. Instead after the servants were asleep, we brought three bottles of champagne in and set the pail on the night table.

Thus it came about that I was able to touch on the delicate subject that still preoccupied me, and profiting by the new understanding between us, I made my request in the easiest, most natural fashion.

"Racky, would you do me a tremendous favor if I asked you?"

He lay on his back, his hands beneath his head. It seemed to me his regard was circumspect, wanting in candor.

"I guess so," he said. "What is it?"

"Will you stay around the house for a few days—a week, say? Just to please me? We can take some rides together, as far as you like. Would you do that for me?"

"Sure thing," he said, smiling.

I was temporizing, but I was desperate.

Perhaps a week later—(it is only when one is not fully happy that one is meticulous about time, so that it may have been more or less)—we were having breakfast. Isiah stood by, in the shade, waiting to pour us more coffee.

"I noticed you had a letter from Uncle Charley the other day," said Racky. "Don't you think we ought to invite him down?"

My heart began to beat with great force.

"Here? He'd hate it here," I said casually. "Besides, there's no room. Where would he sleep?" Even as I heard myself saying the words, I knew that they were the wrong ones, that I was not really participating in the conversation. Again I felt the fascination of complete helplessness that comes when one is suddenly a conscious on-looker at the shaping of one's fate.

"In my room," said Racky. "It's empty."

I could see more of the pattern at that moment than I had ever suspected existed. "Nonsense," I said. "This is not the sort of place for Uncle Charley."

Racky appeared to be hitting on an excellent idea. "Maybe if I wrote and invited him," he suggested, motioning to Isiah for more coffee.

"Nonsense," I said again, watching still more of the pattern reveal itself, like a photographic print becoming constantly clearer in a tray of developing solution.

Isiah filled Racky's cup and returned to the shade. Racky drank slowly, pretending to be savoring the coffee.

"Well, it won't do any harm to try. He'd appreciate the invitation," he said speculatively.

For some reason, at this juncture I knew what to say, and as I said it, I knew what I was going to do.

"I thought we might fly over to Havana for a few days next week."

He looked guardedly interested, and then he broke into a wide grin. "Swell!" he cried. "Why wait till next week?"

::

THE NEXT MORNING THE SERVANTS CALLED "GOOD-BYE" TO US AS WE drove up the cinder road in the McCoigh car. We took off from the airport at six that evening. Racky was in high spirits; he kept the stewardess engaged in conversation all the way to Camagüey.

He was delighted also with Havana. Sitting in the bar at the Nacional, we continued to discuss the possibility of having C. pay us a visit at the island. It was not without difficulty that I eventually managed to persuade Racky that writing him would be inadvisable.

We decided to look for an apartment right there in Vedado for Racky. He did not seem to want to come back here to Cold Point. We also decided that living in Havana he would need a larger income than I. I am already having the greater part of Hope's estate transferred to his name in the form of a trust fund which I shall administer until he is of age. It was his mother's money, after all.

We bought a new convertible, and he drove me out to Rancho Boyeros in it when I took my plane. A Cuban named Claudio with very white teeth, whom Racky had met in the pool that morning, sat between us.

We were waiting in front of the landing field. An official finally unhooked the chain to let the passengers through. "If you get fed up, come to Havana," said Racky, pinching my arm.

The two of them stood together behind the rope, waving to me, their shirts flapping in the wind as the plane started to move.

::

THE WIND BLOWS BY MY HEAD; BETWEEN EACH WAVE THERE ARE THOUSANDS of tiny licking and chopping sounds as the water hurries out of the crevices and holes; and a part-floating, part-submerged feeling of being in the water haunts my mind even as the hot sun burns my face. I sit here and I read, and I wait for the pleasant feeling of repletion that follows a good meal, to turn slowly, as the hours pass along, into the even more delightful, slightly stirring sensation deep within, which accompanies the awakening of the appetite.

I am perfectly happy here in reality, because I still believe that nothing very drastic is likely to befall this part of the island in the near future.

1950

CHRISTOPHER ISHERWOOD

::

LETTERS AND LIFE

DURING THE FIRST WEEK OF MY BED-LIFE I DID HAVE ONE VISITOR, HOWEVER, who startled me right out of the reverie because he was unexpected. Both Gerda and Sarah were away that morning, and I was alone in the house. I heard steps on the stairs and along the corridor, where they seemed to hesitate, and then there was a sudden impatient knock at the door. It opened before I could answer. Bob Wood came slouching into the room.

"Hello," he said.

"Hello, there."

"What are you doing?" There was a kind of reproachful surprise in his tone.

"Just lying here on my ass. Did you expect to find me tap-dancing?"

Bob grinned. Then he seemed to lose all interest in me. He wandered restlessly around the room, picking up books and putting them down again immediately, as though he were hunting for something. I watched him, remembering how Michael Drummond used to do this, too.

"Aren't you bored?" he asked abruptly. He sounded just like Charles Kennedy.

"No. That's a funny thing—I keep expecting I will be, but I'm not."

"What do you think about, all day?"

"Oh—everything."

"I'll bet you do." Bob looked at me with sympathetic curiosity. "You know, I kind of envy you? That's just what I need, right now; to be shut up some place where I don't have anything to do but think." There was a pause. "Charles says you were raised as a Quaker. Like me."

"Yes. I was."

"Do you believe any of that, now?"

"Well—it rather depends what you mean by . . ."

"Oh, for Pete's sake, Steve," Bob interrupted impatiently, "you don't have to be cagey. You know perfectly well what I mean. To begin with, do you believe in God?" He scowled angrily as he brought the word out, and his mouth pulled down sideways into a deprecatory grimace.

"Well, yes. Yes, I guess so. Only . . ."

"I do," Bob told me aggressively, as if my answer had been No. "But the trouble is, I just can't stand the sort of people who do."

"Thanks," I said. We both laughed.

"Oh, I'm not including you, Steve. You're different. At least, I think you are. That's why I went to Meeting the other day. I hadn't been in years. I wanted to see if it was still the way I remembered."

"And was it?"

"Pretty much. It was still there, this thing I used to feel—whatever it is. And I still couldn't stand the people."

"They bothered me, too."

"They did? Good, I'm glad of that. Then you do know what I mean. . . . Jesus, you'd think the Inner Light was something they owned! And they hate like hell to admit that anyone can get any of it without joining their club and keeping all their rules. I felt like a gate crasher."

"No, Bob! That's not true. I'm certain it isn't. I used to think that myself. But I know I was wrong."

"Well, maybe I'm exaggerating. I get a bit carried away, whenever I talk about them. How did you feel about the Meeting itself?"

"The same way you did, more or less. The thing was still there."

"Isn't it amazing, how it takes hold of you again?"

"I know. I kept fighting it, though. I didn't want it to."

"Neither did I. . . . Charles couldn't possibly understand any of that. You couldn't expect him to, I guess. He doesn't have our background. . . . You know, Steve, you and I are kind of in the same boat?"

"Yes, I suppose we are."

"That's why I had to come and talk to you. You see, I've got to do an awful lot of thinking. And quick. I might be going back in the Navy, soon."

"Sarah told me."

"When I enlisted before, I was just a kid. I did it because I wanted to make a big gesture, and show the Friends what a hell of a rebel I was. Whatever they believed in, I was against, automatically. As a matter of fact, my gesture fell flat. Nobody gave a damn, either way, what I did. And I had lots of fun. But everything's different, now. . . . Are you a pacifist, Steve?"

"Kind of. I haven't ever thought about it properly."

"I hadn't, until quite lately. And I'm still all mixed up. Of course, I loathe all this wishy-washy brotherly love talk. Just the same, you know, the Friends really have got something there. If you read what Christ said—not all those alibis and double talk about what he's supposed to have meant—there aren't any two ways about it. . . . I suppose we'll get into this war, won't we, sooner or later?"

"Yes, I'm afraid we will."

"It isn't so much that I'm scared of that. Though I am, of course. But I'd be even more scared of being a conscientious objector."

"So would I."

"What did you tell them when you registered for the draft?"

"I haven't had to, yet. I'm just over age."

"You are? You don't look it. . . . If I don't go back in the Navy, I'll be drafted. I didn't register as a C.O. I couldn't make up my mind to. Now I'd just have to refuse, and go to jail. . . . Would you go to jail, Steve?"

"I'd have to be awfully sure I was right, first. And, even then, I'd try to find some excuse to wriggle out of it."

"You probably don't feel quite the same way about the Law as I do. That's natural. After all," Bob's mouth pulled down sideways again, "*you're* not a professional criminal."

"What do you mean by that?"

"Exactly what did Sarah tell you about Charles and me?"

"Not very much. Why?"

"Look, you don't have to play naïve. You're not like those old biddies in Dolgelly who keep trying to marry Charles off to their daughters. You've been around. When two guys live together, you know what that means?"

I smiled. "Not necessarily."

"Well, in our case it does." Bob looked at me with a certain hostility. "Charles said you'd know that without being told. Only I don't like leaving things vague."

"And what am I supposed to do now? Ask you to get out of the house?"

Bob grinned uncertainly. "That's up to you."

"Sure, I understand all about that, Bob. And I'm glad you told me. I mean, I appreciate your wanting to. I kind of guessed, but I wasn't sure . . ." I tried hard, but I couldn't quite keep the embarrassment out of my voice. "Naturally, I don't think it's wrong, or anything. Certainly not for people like you and Charles. You're not children. You both know what you're doing."

"You're pretty broad-minded, aren't you?"

"Oh, Bob, don't be stuffy about this, please!"

"That's what you heterosexuals always say. We'll run you out of town. We'll send you to jail. We'll stop you ever getting another job. But please don't you be stuffy about it."

"I only mean don't be so aggressive. That's what puts people against you."

"Maybe we ought to put people against us. Maybe we're too damned tactful. People just ignore us, most of the time, and we let them. We encourage them to. So this whole business never gets discussed, and the laws never get changed. There's a few people right here in the village who really know what the score is with Charles and me, but they won't admit it, not even to themselves. We're such *nice* boys, they say. So wholesome. They just refuse to imagine how nice boys like us could be arrested and locked up as crooks. They're afraid to think about it, for fear it'd trouble their tender consciences. Next thing you know, they might get a *concern*" —Bob's mouth was twitching ferociously—"and then they'd have to *do* something. Jesus, I'd like to take them and rub their noses in it!"

"That wouldn't help Charles much, in his position."

"Do you suppose I don't realize that? If it wasn't for Charles, I'd be out of this dump in five minutes, anyway."

"Let me tell you something, Bob. There was a guy I liked, once. In that way, I mean. . . ."

"Sure, I know," Bob grinned ironically. "Some kid in school. And afterwards you hated yourselves. And now he's married and got ten children."

"No. This wasn't in school. . . ."

"Well then, it was in some low bar in Port Said, and you were drunk, and you got picked up, and it was horrible. . . ."

"It wasn't in Port Said, and it wasn't in the least horrible. It didn't just happen once, either. I told you, I liked this guy. He's one of the best people I've ever known. . . . And now, will you stop treating me like a public meeting?"

"Okay, okay," said Bob, laughing. "I'm sorry. You're all right, Steve. If everyone was like you, I wouldn't get so mad."

"But you rather enjoy getting mad, don't you?"

"I do not. It makes me sick to my stomach. It's the only way I seem to be able to let off steam, though. In the service, I was always getting into fist fights, for no reason at all. I lost a couple of teeth that way, but at least there were no hard feelings afterward. It was a lot better than saying rotten things you don't mean and hurting someone you really care about. I do that to Charles, sometimes. I act like the filthiest little bitch. It's a wonder he doesn't throw me out. . . . Jesus, it's a bore being neurotic! Look, I'd better be going."

"Do you have to?"

"You don't want to listen to any more of this dreary crap."

"I'm in the mood for crap, today. The drearier the better."

"Well, I'm not."

"No, seriously, Bob, I just wish I could help you somehow. I mean, say something constructive."

"You don't have to. It does me good just to talk to someone who isn't sick in the head."

"How do you know I'm not?"

"Well, if you are, I don't want to hear about it. Don't you ever lose your wig while I'm around. I won't stand for it."

"I'll keep it glued on tight. . . . Come and see me soon again, won't you? How about tomorrow?"

"All right. If you really want me to. I'm not much of a sickbed visitor."

"You're the kind I like best. You haven't once said you were sorry for me."

"I'm not. I'm too busy being sorry for myself."

"That's the spirit!"

"Well—take it easy."

"You too."

Bob was already moving toward the door. He turned for a moment and gave me a quick smile that was both humorous and unhappy. "I sure wish I could," he said. Then he went out.

::

WHEN CHARLES KENNEDY LOOKED IN TO SEE ME, WHICH HE DID TWO OR three times a week, it would usually be around six o'clock in the evening. The day after Bob's visit, he appeared, bringing with him a contraption which he called a monkey bar. It was a kind of miniature trapeze hanging from a metal arm which was made to screw on to a bedstead. I could take hold of it and pull myself up in bed, whenever I'd slipped down too far.

"You know Bob was in to see me yesterday?" I asked, while he was installing it.

"Yes. He told me." Charles spoke in his briefest staccato. He was standing at the back of the bed where I couldn't see his face, but I knew at once that something was wrong.

"As a matter of fact," I went on, "I was expecting him to come again this morning. He promised to."

Charles was silent.

"Is there any special reason," I persisted, "why he didn't?"

Charles didn't answer at once. He shook the metal arm to make sure that it was firmly attached. Then he came around the bed and sat down on the end of it, facing me.

"It was probably my fault," he said. "Bob and I had a big argument, last night. One of the biggest we ever had since we've been together."

"What about?"

"Well, it started about you." Charles grinned at me painfully. He was obviously embarrassed. "In fact, I suppose it was a rather ordinary kind of domestic jealousy scene. As far as I was concerned."

"Jealousy? You surely don't mean that Bob . . . ?"

"No—it wasn't quite as ordinary as that. But he came home and raved about you. How wonderful and sympathetic and understanding you were. Meaning that I wasn't."

"But, Charles, that's ridiculous! If Bob does feel that about me, it's only because I'm a complete stranger. Strangers always seem to understand everything—until you get to know them."

"That's exactly what I told him." Charles smiled in a more relaxed manner. "No offense to you, Stephen! I think you *are* an understanding person. And I think you might be very good for Bob. It was idiotic of me to get mad about it. Ordinarily, I wouldn't have. Only I happen to be under quite a bit of pressure myself, right now."

"Well, yes, I can imagine. With all your work."

"It isn't the work that I mind. That's good for me. It keeps me from thinking. You see, the trouble is, Stephen, I don't really enjoy being a doctor. I'm not a bad one. As a matter of fact, I'm a lot better than average. I've got the talent for it, but no vocation. This isn't what I wanted to do in life."

"What did you want?"

"I wanted to be a writer. Isn't that a laugh?"

"Why is it a laugh?"

"Because I can't write. Vocation but no talent."

"Are you sure?"

"Absolutely sure. I found that out years ago. Oh, don't worry, I'm not about to ask you to read my stuff. There isn't any. It's all burned."

"That's too bad."

"Look, I'm not telling you this to get sympathy. I just want you to understand the situation. That's my personal problem, and ordinarily I can handle it. It's only when Bob needs help that I find I'm not on such firm ground myself. So then we're both in trouble. And when I can't help him and he turns to someone else, I get silly and jealous. . . . Bob's been going through a bad time, lately. He told you all that, didn't he?"

"About being a conscientious objector?"

"That's only part of it. There's this whole thing of having been brought up as a Quaker. You see, Bob adored his father and mother. They do seem to have been pretty wonderful people, in their own way. When he was a kid, he believed everything they believed, on trust. Then they died, and he was put into a Friends' school, where the teachers weren't quite as wonderful as his parents; so he despised them for not being, the way teenagers do sometimes, and it all went sour on him."

"He didn't tell me any of that."

"No. I suppose he wouldn't. He hardly ever mentions his parents, because they're at the root of everything. . . . Anyhow, he decided that Quakerdom stank. And he's been trying to kid himself, ever since, that it never really meant anything to him. It's been working inside him all these years and now it's starting to act up. Just like with a lapsed Catholic. The difficulty is, we get into a violent fight whenever we discuss this because he resents what he thinks is my attitude toward the Quakes. Actually, he'd resent *any* attitude I took toward them. He doesn't think I've got the right to have one."

"You don't like them, do you, Charles?"

"That's what Bob thinks. He accuses me of sneering at them. But he's quite wrong. I respect them. And I admire them in a lot of ways. They don't sit nursing guilty consciences; they go right out and work their guilt off, helping people. They've got the courage of their convictions, and they mean exactly what they say, and they've found their own answers to everything without resorting to any trick theology. What I do hate about the Quakes, though, is their lack of style. They don't know how to do things with an air. They're hopelessly tacky. They've no notion of elegance."

"But that's their great point, surely? They believe in plainness."

"Plainness doesn't exclude elegance; it only makes it all the more necessary. Anyhow, 'elegance' isn't quite what I mean. . . . In any of your *voyages au bout de la nuit,* did you ever run across the word 'camp'?"

"I've heard people use it in bars. But I thought . . ."

"You thought it meant a swishy little boy with peroxided hair, dressed in a picture hat and a feather boa, pretending to be Marlene Dietrich? Yes, in queer circles, they call *that* camping. It's all very well in its place, but it's an utterly debased form. . . ." Charles's eyes shone delightedly. He seemed to be in the best of spirits, now, and thoroughly enjoying this exposition. "What I mean by camp is something much more fundamental. You can call the other Low Camp, if you like; then what I'm talking about is High Camp. High Camp is the whole emotional basis of the ballet, for example, and of course of baroque art. You see, true High Camp always has an underlying seriousness. You can't camp about something you don't take seriously. You're not making fun of it; you're making fun out of it. You're expressing what's basically serious to you in terms of fun and artifice and elegance. Baroque art is largely camp about religion. The ballet is camp about love. . . . Do you see at all what I'm getting at?"

"I'm not sure. Give me some instances. What about Mozart?"

"Mozart's definitely a camp. Beethoven, on the other hand, isn't."

"Is Flaubert?"

"God, no!"

"And neither is Rembrandt?"

"No. Definitely not."

"But El Greco is?"

"Certainly."

"And so is Dostoevski?"

"Of course he is! In fact, he's the founder of the whole school of modern Psycho-Camp which was later developed by Freud." Charles had a sudden spasm of laughter. "Splendid, Stephen! You've really gotten the idea."

"I don't know if I have or not. It seems such an elastic expression."

"Actually, it isn't at all. But I admit it's terribly hard to define. You have to meditate on it and feel it intuitively, like Laotse's *Tao.* Once you've done that, you'll find yourself wanting to use the word whenever you discuss aesthetics or philosophy or almost anything. I never can understand how critics manage to do without it."

"I must say, I can hardly see how the Friends would apply it."

"Naturally you can't. Neither can I. That's because Quaker Camp doesn't exist, yet. Some tremendous genius will have to arise and create it. Until that happens, it's as unimaginable as Rimbaud's prose poems would have been to Keats."

"Does Bob think the Quakers need High Camp?"

"He does in his heart, but he won't admit it. He can't criticize them or discuss them objectively, at all; he can only love them or hate them. He's in a classically schizoid predicament. His conscience is split right down the middle. You know, I really believe he's unable to think about anything except in relation to a conflict of loyalties. He has to do everything on principle. . . . It's only on principle that he stays with me, really."

"You must know that isn't true, Charles."

"Yes, I do. Of course. I'm starting to talk nonsense. Sorry."

"Bob loves you very much. Even I can see that."

"Oh, I know. And I love him very much." Charles sighed. "But it isn't that simple. . . . The trouble is, I can't seem to take Bob for granted. I'm always trying to understand him. And, of course, I'm the one person who can't, ever. If I did, that'd be another kind of relationship. We wouldn't feel the way we do about each other."

"Does Bob try to understand you?"

"Gracious, no! He only tries to make me into what he wants me to be. All this respectability of mine drives him frantic. Medical etiquette. The bedside manner. Horse-and-buggy humor. Talking to the Dolgelly ladies about the weather. Sometimes he makes an effort to play along with it for a while, and then he gets furious with himself and me, too. He'd like for us to march down the street with a banner, singing 'We're queer because we're queer because we're queer because we're queer.' That's really what we keep fighting about. And the idiotic part of it is, I'm actually on his side, and he knows it."

"He's quite a crusader, isn't he?"

"That's just it. He needs an heroic setting. The best part of him just isn't functioning here, at all. He ought to be involved in some political movement, or storming barricades. Then he'd be completely alive."

"You don't call the Navy an heroic setting, do you?"

"The Navy's a very old-fashioned and occasionally very dangerous kindergarten. If Bob goes back into it, it'll do its best to turn him into a loyal anti-crusading five-year-old moron."

"Then you think he'd be better off in prison, as an objector?"

"Of course he would. But there, my attitude's completely selfish, I admit. I'm so deathly afraid of losing him for keeps. After an experience like that, he probably wouldn't need me any more. I can't see him coming back here and settling down again."

Charles walked over to the window and stood there, looking out. "All that dogwood!" he muttered. "Horrible sickly stuff. Like whipped cream."

He turned back toward the room. "I don't know what I'd do if I lost Bob. Before I knew him, I was such a mess. . . . *I'm* no crusader. I'm sick of belonging to these whining militant minorities. Everybody hates them, and pretends not to. And they hate themselves like poison. You know something funny? My father's name was Klatnik. He changed it. I used to tell myself that I'd change it back when I grew up. But I never did, of course. I found excuses not to. I didn't have the guts."

"Well, for that matter," I said, trying to get Charles out of this mood, "I belong to a minority, myself. One of the most unpopular."

"What's that?"

"I'm rich."

Charles gave a sort of scornful grunt.

"You think that's nothing?" I said. "Till you've had a lot of money, you just don't know what guilt is."

"I dare say that's absolutely true." Charles became more cheerful at once. "You must tell me all about it, some time. I had an uncle who was rich. He spent his whole life explaining why he couldn't give us more money. He actually shed tears while he was doing it, too. He died of a broken heart."

"I bet you were horrible to him."

"We certainly were! We didn't regard him as a human being, at all. We treated him as a sort of golden monster. So he turned into one. All ghoul and a yard wide. . . . Look, I must go. I've got another patient to see." Charles tapped the cast with his finger. "How's this whited sepulcher?"

"Not too bad. Except for the stink."

"Stink?" Charles bent down and sniffed at it. "My poor friend, you call *that* stinking? Wait till you've been in it another two months. Nobody will be able to come near the house. Loathsome worms and beetles will crawl out of it. Buzzards and vultures will assemble and sharpen their beaks. And then, one morning, it'll crack wide open and the most gorgeous butterfly, all dazzling white, will emerge and spread its wings and flutter away over the treetops."

"And that'll be me?"

"That'll be you, brother. Never fear." Charles laughed and patted me on the shoulder. Then, as he walked over to the door, he added, "Don't get any wrong ideas about Bob and me and that argument. If I made it sound like a big drama, I didn't mean to. It's like what they used to say about Austria: the situation's desperate but not serious. The whole thing'll simmer down in a day or two, you'll see. Actually, Stephen, if we do have any more fights, it's you who's going to bear the brunt of them, from now on. We've been needing someone to act as umpire. And you're the heaven-sent victim. You can't run out on us. I'm certainly glad you threw yourself under that truck."

"It was a pleasure," I said. "For you, I'd break one of my necks, any time."

::

BOB REAPPEARED TWO DAYS LATER, BRINGING WITH HIM A PILE OF RECORDS and a box of radio tubes, tools, wire and mechanical parts. "Just another service of your friendly neighborhood Dog People," he told me, grinning. He worked all morning, installing a record player and a radio beside my bed and a loud-speaker in a corner of the room. I couldn't help suspecting that this was his way of showing me that he didn't want any renewal of our previous conversation. During this visit, he talked very little. As he worked, he whistled softly to himself as though he were alone, and only broke off now and then to explain briefly to me what he was doing, in a gruff matter-of-fact voice.

After this, he came to see me fairly often. Sometimes he seemed to have nothing to say at all. He was capable of vast but vaguely expectant silences, during which he would sit looking at me with his mouth slightly open until I got embarrassed and started to chatter about anything that came into my head. Sometimes—especially after he had been playing tennis or getting a workout at the college gym—he would be as noisy and silly as a teen-age boy, walking around the room on his hands or hiding under the bed and grabbing at Gerda's ankles, as if the exercise had released him for a while from his tensions. And there were other times when he would talk freely and naturally, telling me funny stories of his life in the Navy or asking me questions about places I'd been to. But our talk never again got really intimate. Charles had been wrong there, apparently. Bob didn't seem to want to confide in me any more; or maybe his quarrel with Charles had somehow made that impossible for him.

What struck me chiefly about him, always, was his quality of loneliness; and this was even more apparent when he and Charles came to visit me together. When, for example, Bob was fixing our cocktails, his slim figure with its big shoulders bending over the bottles would look strangely weary and solitary, and he seemed suddenly miles away from either of us. He was like a prospector preparing a meal in the midst of the wilderness.

The cocktails gave me an added reason to look forward to their visits, for these were the only times I ever got a drink. Charles and Bob would come on evenings when Sarah and Gerda were away in Philadelphia, and they always arrived with a bag of ice cubes, a shaker and several bottles of liquor. Once, they also brought a load of Bob's paintings and held what Charles described as "Bob's first one-dog show." The paintings certainly weren't primitives, as Charles had called them; but Bob had told the truth when he said that he painted in various styles. Some of them were severe abstractions made up of rectangles in pure color, like Mondrian's. Others suggested a gloomy disorganized impressionism; they were muddy and scratchy. And there were a few gay, surprisingly humorous landscapes which owed a lot to Dufy and Matisse. None of them were very distinguished, but, as revelations of Bob's mental condition, they were most interesting. I thought I could see in them the conflict between Bob's birthright Quakerism and Charles's "High Camp." Perhaps the creation of "Quaker Camp" would be the only possible solution to Bob's problems, both as a human being and a painter.

It was probably the difficulty of making suitable and tactful comments on the pictures that caused me to drink more than usual, that night. Anyhow, I passed out cold. I woke, a couple of hours later, to find that Charles and Bob had left, taking the paintings with them. The lights were still burning. On the table beside my bed, there was a note from Charles, in very unsteady, straggling handwriting:

"So sad we had to lose our favorite patient. Here's the latest x-ray photograph of you. Things don't seem to be working out too well. Frankly, I'm alarmed. Suggest you see a specialist."

This puzzled me, until I looked down at the cast. Bob had drawn all over it in charcoal, continuing the lines of my body and turning them into a kind of hermaphroditic mermaid, with fantastic sexual organs.

A short while later, Sarah and Gerda arrived back home and came up to say good night.

"There's quite a chill in the air," Sarah told me. "Most unseasonable. Be sure to keep yourself very carefully covered, Stephen dear." In my still drunken state, this advice struck me as so funny that I had a hard time fighting back the giggles. As soon as Sarah had left the room, I pushed down the bedclothes and showed Gerda the drawing.

"Pfui!" she exclaimed, laughing. "So *eine Schweinerei!* But this is clever, no? It is something like Picasso, I find."

We agreed, regretfully, that it had to go, however. So Gerda wiped the cast clean with a wet face cloth.

1952

MARRIS MURRAY

::

my brother writes poetry for an englishman

OUR HOUSE WAS ALMOST ON THE BEACH, AND I USED TO THINK OF THE window of my small bedroom as a never-sleeping eye, that watched the bay for me, in winter and summer, by day and night. As I now remember it, that bay was never sombred, but always a radiant semi-circle filled with the purity of the invisible air and the salt freshness of the blue glass sea. Sometimes, when the wind blew, my curtains would stream out of the window, tugging on their rings, and I would feel that I ought to release them, and let them flap away like high-flying cormorants, round the bend of the coast. But when my brother's curtains tugged and flapped he would pull them in, and fasten them with drawing pins to the window sashes. Then, having given them what he called his master's glance, he would bend his head again over the book in which he had been writing. I admired this firmness, and would have liked to copy it. I thought him brilliant and ruthless, and knew that he would have been happiest in a world without women and little girls. I often heard him tell my mother so, and I felt that he resented my presence on the beach when he was there. But no knife-sharp glances, no impatiences, no shrugs nor silences could drive me out of my paradise.

And after all, the beach was large enough. Rocky, sandy, edging past great boulders, widening out and lying down under the trampling of the breakers, shrugging itself into secret coves, it wound along for miles. We did not need to meet, but of course we did. Perhaps it was because we had the same favourite places. Now it seems to me that it was not me but my passion for the shore that he resented. He alone should love it, and he would not allow that it should fill me too with mysterious imaginings, so that when we returned to the house in the evenings my eyes, like his, should be wide with a light as secret and elusive as the twilight on the glittering waters.

Lying awake at night I would think of myself as a shell in whose whorls the sea sound was never stilled; but in the mornings, when I ran down to the beach, it was as though I saw and heard the sea for the first time, and I would stand and snuff the salty air and sigh 'Ah . . .' The enchantment of the shore filled my being; I was like a seaweed that has hung, dried and darkened, from the rock's side after the ebb, but which, when the waters return, is transformed, and gleams and undulates, stroking the current. Then, brimming with life, I would begin to run. I would run towards my rock pools, along the tide line, with bird-like swoops and darts to gather up shells as I went: pale spotted cowries, Venus's ears, pink-rimmed and nacreous or, sometimes, a ribbed nautilus, white as paper, brittle as flaked sand, ridged with blue, rare, fortunate for the finder, most beautiful.

My brother was always before me, and I would see him standing at the very extremity of the rock shelf, where the pale green water swirled and bubbled round his ankles, gazing over the bay. His bare legs were as brown as the rocks, his hair bleached to the colour of the yellow foam that piled up over the stones after a gale. I would wonder, with something of the sadness of a shut-out animal in my wondering, what it was he saw with his sea-grey eyes, and what visions of strangeness formed and vanished behind his solemn brow. 'Zanzibar,' I would murmur to myself, 'Antananarivo, the Land of Fire, the River of Silver, the Magnetic Pole.' Then I would come to my pools, to my private, primitive, subaqueous world, to change into a fleckered fish, a hermit crab, a feather-star, anything other, aloof, alone, defying my solitude of a human child by the greater solitude of my secret life. But when these hours were over, when we were called into the house and sat, dreamy and silent, on each side of my mother, then I would long for my brother to speak to me with complicity. There was no ordeal that I would not have faced, darkness, octopuses, even the jaws of the shark I had once seen, dead and displayed on the quay, if he had called me through it into his secret. But he would quell me with his master's glance, and speak to my mother with a distant, condescending politeness. She too was distant, looking through the window at the sea, perhaps remembering her childhood, and counting over all the love that was owing to her, and which she would never now receive. I knew that she was always sad because she and my father lived together with coldness and quarrels. Like the hands of two unsynchronized clocks, their emotions were never at the same place at the same time: they never told the hour together. Sometimes this sadness of hers would pierce my child's indifference, and I would fling my arms round her neck and kiss her. And as she kissed me with a despairing tenderness,

I would see the tears gather in her eyes. In my embarrassment and misery I would struggle to free myself, and run out of the house, back to the burning sand of midday. Occasionally, when her dejection was most pronounced, my brother would leave the shore and wander inland to pick wild flowers for her, but I never saw him give or suffer a caress.

Then one afternoon, when the autumn sunlight was soft and iridescent, as though it were filtering through invisible eyelashes, I saw the Englishman. I was sailing my home-made schooner, or rather, although the ship was only six inches long and the reluctant captain a small hermit crab, I should say that I was sailing in my schooner, along the towering cliffs of a largish rock pool. I was, as I often found myself, strangely divided, so that I was myself, sunburned and pig-tailed, and I was also a stranger, captain of the schooner cruising in the unknown bay, explorer, and master of an empty hold, fearful of shipwreck on rocky islands, but bound by an inexorable and mysterious fate to sail forever towards lonelier, more elusive seas. A shadow fell over my sails, and looking up I saw my brother standing beside a tall stranger. The stranger smiled at me, and his lips and teeth, as I now realize, were such as mark those of boldness and appetite, whose mastery of things makes them also the captors and tamers of men. He asked: 'Where are you sailing?' and I was about to answer 'In the South Seas,' when I noticed the expression on my brother's face. Something in the set of his mouth silenced me, and I hung my head so low that my pig-tails fell into the water on each side of my schooner. The stranger laughed 'Destination secret,' and then they walked away. When I raised my head to look after them, they had gone far over the rocks, walking side by side. "A pair," I murmured, and then thought: But a pair should be the same size; how silly.

From that day, my brother was gone. He slept in his bed, came to table at meal times, answered when he was spoken to. But I saw the icefloes forming in his eyes and, tiny and half-hidden in their distended pupils, I saw the pennants of the volcanoes flicker and blaze. I tried to follow him, by accident as it were, when he went along the shore to meet the Englishman, but they always met unseen, and I arrived only to see them walking away, just out of hearing, and with something so absorbed in the carriage of their heads that I knew that I could not have caught them even had they been within arm's reach. Yet I pursued, hanging my head, and pretending to search for corks along the ribbon of flotsam, and I was so intent to catch the secret that I would see the Englishman's yellow head and blue sailcloth trousers beckoning from behind every rock. He never spoke to me again that summer; in fact, I never came close enough even to see his face. I remembered only the movement and flash of his lips and teeth, and the vibration of his voice. A week after he had gone, when the winter squalls came tearing across the bay, my brother broke his leg. Lying up on the old sofa on the stoep, watching the rain-beaten waves through the panes of the glass screen, he looked small and left behind, his master's glance forgotten. Sometimes he spoke to me, not kindly, but almost as an equal, almost as though there were no years between ten and fifteen. I waited on him, stole my father's cigarettes for him, sat beside him with my ears like shells, roaring with emptiness, waiting for the sound of his voice. He told me nothing, except once, when I asked 'What are you always writing?' and he answered 'Poetry.'

'What about?'

'Denizens.'

'What's that?'

'Don't you know? The things underneath, vulgarly called Denizens of the Deep.' I saw that he was mocking me, and tears came into my eyes. He stared at them and said, seriously, 'He told me to write it for him.'

'The Englishman?'

'Yes,' and then, shocked by his own confidingness, he commanded in an angry voice 'Go away, you bore me.'

I went down to the wind-smoothed beach and gathered seaweed, laying it out on the hard, wet sand at the waves' end. 'Fronds,' I murmured. 'Waving fronds. Torn up by the waves. You will never grow again now,' and a desolation of sadness shook me, and wordlessly the creature within me, the primitive dweller in rock pools, agreed: Life is not for laughing.

Too strange, too deep for laughing, even in childhood, even in that translucent bay. Lapped by light and water, I lived lonely, sad, secret, in a pride of solitude, and, except when I saw or thought about my brother, satisfied in my solitude. As soon as his leg was mended, he was out again along the shore, gazing seawards, or sitting with bent head upon a rock. When he was not on the shore he was in his room, at the table under the window, writing. I got back from school before he did, and sometimes I would go softly into his room and stand by the table. I would rest my forefinger on the thick black notebook that lay there and think: His poetry is inside. But I never thought to open the book. It was his, and therefore not for me. We were a reserved family, respecting each other's privacy. The Englishman had given him the curiously-formed skull of a fish, and my brother had forced a round silver bullet into each empty eye-socket. This head, all air and outlines, lay beside the notebook, and when the sunlight fell through the window, the solid silver eyes blazed in the emptiness, as though he had left his master's glance behind him, to guard his book. But it seemed to me that throughout the winter, and the next summer, and in the winter that followed, I could feel the thing growing beneath the cover. It was as though the weight and tension of what was written in the book ran up into my finger, and made it tremble with prophetic prickings, like the thumbs of witches.

It was at this time that the dream began. When I look back on it now, my whole life then seems to me like a dream—or perhaps two dreams, one by day and one by night. In the daytime I lived aloof from my school fellows, who did not interest me, and at home I wandered on the shore in the silence of my imaginings. And sometimes at night the real dream came. I was on a ship, alone in the crow's nest, and although it seemed to be my own body that contained me, in some way I knew that I was not myself; I was my brother.

The deck was so far below me that it looked like the deck of my toy schooner. The sky above me was brilliant and yet dark, composed of greens and blues so deep that they merged to black. The sea was dark too, but all flecked and worried with paws of foam. The ship plunged through the waves, and the masts went round and down, tossed, and came round and up. I hung on to the rim of the crow's nest, and as I went down and down, the foam came leaping for my face, and I could see the fishes turning, and the huge shadows of the whales came rushing to meet me. And then, with a great shake, the masts lifted up and up, and I could see again the horizon curving round, the ice cliffs towering, and the bears lurching across the floes. A ring of light burst round the pole, and then I went down and down again. I knew it was coming—I waited for it, afraid and yet confident—the moment when I was thrown out of the crow's nest and fell, down, down, down into the sea. But I never got there. Just as it seemed that the sea must have me, that I must be forever lost among the scattering fishes and the looming whales, I was standing on the deck, and the Englishman was beside me. And in that moment of ecstasy everything was all right, the presence of the Englishman made all secure. He turned his head, I saw the face I had never seen, and he kissed me. Then the ship raced forward, the sun shone, and shining white clouds raced above us. I saw the whole sphere of the earth: the ice-caps; the equator like a belt of diamonds; ships dipping over the curve into other seas; atolls; and men with sextants; and water-spouts; rainbows, and the albatross. And our ship went racing through them all.

The atmosphere of this dream would hang about me for days, and then, just when it seemed to have dissolved altogether away, I would dream it again. I did not tell my brother about it; there seemed no need. Surely, I thought, he too must dream it; surely he must share my reassurance and expectancy. And I noticed that when he was with my mother and me, although his glance was still cold and remote, it was no longer impatient, and sometimes, when I met him on the shore, I saw that he was smiling as he went.

We were a reserved family; none pried into the life of another, and I do not know what it was that made my father, one evening when my brother was out on the shore, go into his room and open his black notebook. My brother returned to find a terrible anger in the house. Sitting trembling on my bed, I heard my mother's voice, tearful and stubborn, and my father's, cold, loud, endlessly asking and accusing. And later, the sound of punishment.

For a week my brother was kept in his room, and I was forbidden to speak to him. A deeper silence than I had ever known fell on the house, but after I had gone to bed at nights I could hear my parents' voices, murmuring on and on, like the surf on the sands. It was then that my dream failed me: I fell from the crow's nest, and I did not reach the deck. I went down and down and down, the sea rushed towards me, and as I sank into the dark water, among the monstrous shadows, I awoke, standing on my bedroom floor, beating the air. I did not know who called out, I or my brother, but I ran out of my room and into his. He was half-sitting up in bed, his head and shoulders raised by the pillows. A candle burned upon the table, and by its small light I could see that his eyes were open. But he was not there: there was nothing in his grey eyes, nothing in his pallid face. He looked like a drowned boy, or an idiot. 'What is it?' I whispered. 'Wake up! Wake up!' When I spoke, his eyes moved; he looked at me, and I burst out crying. He sat up and said 'Janie. Stay on the shore. Do you hear me, Janie? Stay on the shore.' Then he leaned back on to the pillows and closed his eyes. When I sobbed and spoke his name again and again, he made no reply, and presently I tiptoed to my room, and lay on my back in the darkness with the tears falling out of the corners of my eyes.

The next morning my mother packed a trunk for him, and there was the hurry and disorder of a sudden departure. When she told me that my father was going to send him to a boarding school, I said 'If you do that, he will die.' She was angry with me then, and sent me out of the house.

About a mile westwards along the shore lay the carcass of a stranded whale. It had lain there for many months, and a nauseating smell streamed from it, shifting as the wind shifted, like a flag. People had hacked it about, removing parts of the blubber, and the spring tides had battered and moved some of the vertebrae. I often visited these sad remains, to sit on a bone larger than myself and wonder what had driven the creature to his mysterious and lonely death. This afternoon the desolation of the scene was made greater by the tones of the winter sea and sky, deep and yet cold. The beetle-like scavengers of the shore were running over and under the amber-coloured mass of the carcass, and in and out of the pools of oil, and a tern hopped along the bare white bough of a jaw-bone. I wandered around, filled with fear and pity, and thinking of the whale-shadows in my dream. I felt myself falling again among them, only now it seemed that it was in my brother's body that I fell, and over his head that the waters closed.

He was taken ill during his first week at the boarding school; a fortnight later my father brought his body back to be buried in the cemetery by the sea where my grandparents lay.

I did not go to the funeral; I was left at home with our coloured maid, who sat sobbing in the kitchen, leaving the dishes unwashed and the floors unswept. I wandered in and out of the silent house, going from room to room, listening. It was in my father's study that I heard what I should do. I pulled out all the drawers of his desk, but it was not there. Then I looked in the cupboard under the bookcase, and found it, thrust at the back of the bottom shelf among dusty newspapers and old magazines. So they had not burned it.

I pushed the black notebook up under my jersey, so that it lay hard upon my chest, and I folded my arms over it. Then I ran out of the house and along the beach to where the great jumbled boulders, leaning against each other, made passages and caves, too small for any but children. I crawled into the inmost cave and crouched on the sand under the damp granite roof. Then I opened the book and began to read.

As I read, I shivered with ecstasy, and my skin pricked up into goose-pimples. Here at last I had the secret of the beauty of things: the length and breadth and depth and tract of life; the sea, deep as the roots of agony; and the land, like a constant heart, enduring all. Love beat in every poem, wild and sad and faithful, and with it all that longing which, when the wind blew, made my heart sicken like a captive animal.

I read in an ecstasy, but in fear and trembling, like a miser over gold. From time to time I crawled out of the cave to watch how the day was going, and when I saw that the shadow of the mountain was creeping over the waves, I left the cave and stood blinking on the sands, wondering where to put the book. I began to walk westwards, and as I walked I suddenly knew what I should do. I would hide the book in the whale. No one would look there; the stench and decay would protect it, like dragons before a cave of pearls.

When I reached the carcass, I pulled off my jersey and wrapped the book in it. Then I thrust the bundle under the ribbed skin, among the odour and putrefaction of the creature's belly. No one will find it here, I told myself. It will be safe. It is like the honeycomb in the dead lion, like the pearl in the wounded oyster. It is my hidden treasure. And then I went slowly home, to lie about my missing jersey and the manner in which I had spent the day.

The dream of the Englishman never came again. Instead, I had to find my way along a lonely coast, sometimes swimming, sometimes struggling through dry sand, or balancing on a narrow rock path that overhung the waves. Often I was in danger of being cut off by the tide, or of falling from a cliff's edge. I had to reach the next bay, for there someone was waiting who would end anxiety and solitude, and set all right. Sometimes my dream allowed me almost to turn the corner and reach the bay, but always it dissolved before I could do so. And sometimes I met my brother, standing at the waves' edge, and he would give me a poem. This I would faithfully remember, and the next day I would go to the whale, take out the notebook, and copy it in.

Of course I could not have hidden the book in the whale forever. The spring tides might have had it, or the isopods devoured it, and so it was as well that I was discovered. I had gone there with a poem from the night before, and had just drawn the bundle out, and was beginning to unwrap it, when some sound caused me to look behind me. A man stood watching me, a friend of my parents, an impassioned fisherman who was often on the shore. His loose-fitting clothes shivered in the wind, the brim of his felt hat flapped against his ear. He was carrying a fishing rod, and he stared at me with surprise on his face. He asked 'What are you doing, Janie? What are you grubbing in that stinking mess for?'

I sprang up, ready to run, clasping the notebook to my chest.

'What's that you've got? A book? Show me.'

I shook my head. 'It is my brother's.'

'But Janie,' he protested, and took a step towards me. 'Your brother is dead.'

'No,' I said. 'Oh no. My brother writes poetry for an Englishman.'

'Now look here—'

But I had turned and gone, running along the shore, with my pig-tails flapping and my sandals sliding in the sand. Running, running, into the eye of the afternoon. I clasped the book tightly, my heart thudded against its cover, and as I ran I thought: Round the headland. I must get round the headland. He will come along the shore, out of the dazzle of the west, asking for his poetry. My legs ached, there was a knife in my side, and I sobbed: If he does not come soon, they will get me. Come soon, Englishman, come soon. And, O time, beat fast; O life, make haste.

1953

TENNESSEE WILLIAMS

::

TWO ON A PARTY

HE COULDN'T REALLY GUESS THE AGE OF THE WOMAN, CORA, BUT SHE WAS certainly not any younger than he, and he was almost thirty-five. There were some mornings when he thought she looked, if he wasn't flattering himself, almost old enough to be his mother, but there were evenings when the liquor was hitting her right, when her eyes were lustrous and her face becomingly flushed, and then she looked younger than he. As you get to know people, if you grow to like them, they begin to seem younger to you. The cruelty or damaging candor of the first impression is washed away like the lines in a doctored photograph, and Billy no longer remembered that the first night he met her he had thought of her as "an old bag." Of course, that night when he first met her she was not looking her best. It was in a Broadway bar; she was occupying the stool next to Billy and she had lost a diamond ear-clip and was complaining excitedly about it to the barman. She kept ducking down like a diving seal to look for it among the disgusting refuse under the brass rail, bobbing up and down and grunting and complaining, her face inflamed and swollen by the exertion, her rather heavy figure doubled into ludicrous positions. Billy had the uncomfortable feeling that she suspected him of stealing the diamond ear-clip. Each time she glanced at him his face turned hot. He always had that guilty feeling when anything valuable was lost, and it made him angry; he thought of her as an irritating old bag. Actually she wasn't accusing anybody of stealing the diamond ear-clip; in fact she kept assuring the barman that the clasp on the ear-clip was loose and she was a goddam fool to put it on.

Then Billy found the thing for her, just as he was about to leave the bar, embarrassed and annoyed beyond endurance; he noticed the sparkle of it almost under his shoe, the one on the opposite side from the ducking and puffing "old bag." With the sort of school-teacherish austerity that he assumed when annoyed, when righteously indignant over something, an air that he had picked up during his short, much earlier, career as an English instructor at a midwestern university, he picked up the clip and slammed it wordlessly down on the bar in front of her and started to walk away. Two things happened to detain him. Three sailors off a Norwegian vessel came one, two, three through the revolving door of the bar and headed straight for the vacant stools just beyond where he had been sitting, and at the same instant, the woman, Cora, grabbed hold of his arm, shouting, Oh, don't go, don't go, the least you can do is let me buy you a drink! And so he had turned right around, as quickly and precisely as the revolving door through which the glittering trio of Norsemen had entered. Okay, why not? He resumed his seat beside her, she bought him a drink, he bought her a drink, inside of five minutes they were buying beer for the sailors and it was just as if the place was suddenly lit up by a dozen big chandeliers.

Quickly she looked different to him, not an old bag at all but really sort of attractive and obviously more to the taste of the dazzling Norsemen than Billy could be. Observing the two of them in the long bar mirror, himself and Cora, he saw that they looked good together, they made a good pair, they were mutually advantageous as a team for cruising the Broadway bars. She was a good deal darker than he and more heavily built. Billy was slight and he had very blond skin that the sun turned pink. Unfortunately for Billy, the pink also showed through the silky, thin yellow hair on the crown of his head where the baldness, so fiercely but impotently resisted, was now becoming a fact that he couldn't disown. Of course, the crown of the head doesn't show in the mirror unless you bow to your image in the glass, but there is no denying that the top of a queen's head is a conspicuous area on certain occasions which are not unimportant. That was how he put it, laughing about it to Cora. She said, Honey, I swear to Jesus I think you're more self-conscious about your looks and your age than I am! She said it kindly, in fact, she said everything kindly. Cora was a kind person. She was the kindest person that Billy had ever met. She said and meant everything kindly, literally everything; she hadn't a single malicious bone in her body, not a particle of jealousy or suspicion or evil in her nature, and that was what made it so sad that Cora was a lush. Yes, after he stopped thinking of her as "an old bag," which was almost immediately after they got acquainted, he started thinking of Cora as a lush, kindly, yes, but not as kindly as Cora thought about him, for Billy was not, by nature, as kind as Cora. Nobody else could be. Her kindness was monumental, the sort that simply doesn't exist any more, at least not in the queen world.

Fortunately for Billy, Billy was fairly tall. He had formed the defensive habit of holding his head rather high so that the crown of it wouldn't be so noticeable in bars, but unfortunately for Billy, he had what doctors had told him was a calcium deposit in the ears which made him hard of hearing and which could only be corrected by a delicate and expensive operation —boring a hole in the bone. He didn't have much money; he had just saved enough to live, not frugally but carefully, for two or three more years before he would have to go back to work at something. If he had the ear operation, he would have to go back to work right away and so abandon his sybaritic existence which suited him better than the dubious glory of being a somewhat better than hack writer of Hollywood film scenarios and so forth. Yes, and so forth!

Being hard of hearing, in fact, progressively so, he would have to crouch over and bend sidewise a little to hold a conversation in a bar, that is, if he wanted to understand what the other party was saying. In a bar it's dangerous not to listen to the other party, because the way of speaking is just as important as the look of the face in distinguishing between good trade and dirt, and Billy did not at all enjoy being beaten as some queens do. So he would have to bend sidewise and expose the almost baldness on the crown of his blond head, and he would cringe and turn red instead of pink with embarrassment as he did so. He knew that it was ridiculous of him to be that sensitive about it. But as he said to Cora, age does worse things to a queen than it does to a woman.

She disagreed about that and they had great arguments about it. But it was a subject on which Billy could hold forth as eloquently as a southern Senator making a filibuster against the repeal of the poll tax, and Cora would lose the argument by default, simply not able to continue it any longer, for Cora did not like gloomy topics of conversation so much as Billy liked them.

About her own defects of appearance, however, Cora was equally distressed and humble.

You see, she would tell him, I'm really a queen myself. I mean it's the same difference, honey, I like and do the same things, sometimes I think in bed if they're drunk enough they don't even know I'm a woman, at least they don't act like they do, and I don't blame them. Look at me, I'm a mess. I'm getting so heavy in the hips and I've got these big udders on me!

Nonsense, Billy would protest, you have a healthy and beautiful female body, and you mustn't low-rate yourself all the time that way, I won't allow it!

And he would place his arm about her warm and Florida-sun-browned shoulders, exposed by her backless white gown (the little woolly-looking canary yellow jacket being deposited on a vacant bar stool beside her), for it was usually quite late, almost time for the bars to close, when they began to discuss what the years had done to them, the attritions of time. Beside Billy, too, there would be a vacant bar stool on which he had placed the hat that concealed his thinning hair from the streets. It would be one of those evenings that gradually wear out the exhilaration you start with. It would be one of those evenings when lady luck showed the bitchy streak in her nature. They would have had one or two promising encounters which had fizzled out, coming to a big fat zero at three A.M. In the game they played, the true refinement of torture is to almost pull in a catch and then the line breaks, and when that happens, each not pitying himself as much as he did the other, they would sit out the final hour before closing, talking about the wicked things time had done to them, the gradual loss of his hearing and his hair, the fatty expansion of her breasts and buttocks, forgetting that they were still fairly attractive people and still not old.

Actually, in the long run their luck broke about fifty-fifty. Just about every other night one or the other of them would be successful in the pursuit of what Billy called "the lyric quarry." One or the other or both might be successful on the good nights, and if it was a really good night, then both would be. Good nights, that is, really good nights, were by no means as rare as hen's teeth nor were they as frequent as streetcars, but they knew very well, both of them, that they did better together than they had done separately in the past. They set off something warm and good in each other that strangers responded to with something warm and good in themselves. Loneliness dissolved any reserve and suspicion, the night was a great warm comfortable meeting of people, it shone, it radiated, it had the effect of a dozen big chandeliers, oh, it was great, it was grand, you simply couldn't describe it, you got the colored lights going, and there it all was, the final pattern of it and the original pattern, all put together, made to fit exactly, no, there were simply no words good enough to describe it. And if the worst happened, if someone who looked like a Botticelli angel drew a knife, or if the law descended suddenly on you, and those were eventualities the possibility of which a queen must always consider, you still could say you'd had a good run for your money.

Like everyone whose life is conditioned by luck, they had some brilliant streaks of it and some that were dismal. For instance, that first week they operated together in Manhattan. That was really a freak; you couldn't expect a thing like that to happen twice in a lifetime. The trade was running as thick as spawning salmon up those narrow cataracts in the Rockies. Head to tail, tail to head, crowding, swarming together, seemingly driven along by some immoderate instinct. It was not a question of catching; it was simply a question of deciding which ones to keep and which to throw back in the stream, all glittering, all swift, all flowing one way which was toward you!

That week was in Manhattan, where they teamed up. It was, to be exact, in Emerald Joe's at the corner of Forty-second and Broadway that they had met each other the night of the lost diamond clip that Billy had found. It was the week of the big blizzard and the big Chinese Red offensive in North Korea. The combination seemed to make for a wildness in the air, and trade is always best when the atmosphere of a city is excited whether it be over a national election or New Year's or a championship prizefight or the World Series baseball games; anything that stirs up the whole population makes it better for cruising.

Yes, it was a lucky combination of circumstances, and that first week together had been brilliant. It was before they started actually living together. At that time, she had a room at the Hotel Pennsylvania and he had one at the Astor. But at the end of that week, the one of their first acquaintance, they gave up separate establishments and took a place together at a small East Side hotel in the Fifties, because of the fact that Cora had an old friend from her hometown in Louisiana employed there as the night clerk. This one was a gay one that she had known long ago and innocently expected to be still the same. Cora did not understand how some people turn bitter. She had never turned bitchy and it was not understandable to her that others might. She said this friend on the desk was a perfect setup; he'd be delighted to see them bringing in trade. But that was the way in which it failed to work out . . .

That second week in New York was not a good one. Cora had been exceeding her usual quota of double ryes on the rocks and it began all at once to tell on her appearance. Her system couldn't absorb any more; she had reached the saturation point, and it was no longer possible for her to pick herself up in the evenings. Her face had a bloated look and her eyes remained bloodshot all the time. They looked, as she said, like a couple of poached eggs in a sea of blood, and Billy had to agree with her that they did. She started looking her oldest and she had the shakes.

Then about Friday of that week the gay one at the desk turned bitchy on them. Billy had expected him to turn, but Cora hadn't. Sooner or later,

Billy knew, that frustrated queen was bound to get a severe attack of jaundice over the fairly continual coming and going of so much close-fitting blue wool, and Billy was not mistaken. When they brought their trade in, he would slam down the key without looking at them or speaking a word of greeting. Then one night they brought in a perfectly divine-looking pharmacist's mate of Italian extraction and his almost equally attractive buddy. The old friend of Cora's exploded, went off like a spit-devil.

I'm sorry, he hissed, but this is *not* a flea-bag! You should have stayed on Times Square where you started.

There was a scene. He refused to give them their room-key unless the two sailors withdrew from the lobby. Cora said, Fuck you, Mary, and reached across the desk and grabbed the key from the hook. The old friend seized her wrist and tried to make her let go.

Put that key down, he shrieked, or you'll be sorry!

He started twisting her wrist; then Billy hit him; he vaulted right over the desk and knocked the son-of-a-bitch into the switchboard.

Call the police, call the police, the clerk screamed to the porter.

Drunk as she was, Cora suddenly pulled herself together. She took as much command of the situation as could be taken.

You boys wait outside, she said to the sailors, there's no use in you all getting into S.P. trouble.

One of them, the Italian, wanted to stay and join in the roughhouse, but his buddy, who was the bigger one, forcibly removed him to the sidewalk. (Cora and Billy never saw them again.) By that time, Billy had the night clerk by the collar and was giving him slaps that bobbed his head right and left like something rubber, as if that night clerk was everything that he loathed in a hostile world. Cora stopped him. She had that wonderful, that really invaluable faculty of sobering up in a crisis. She pulled Billy off her old friend and tipped the colored porter ten dollars not to call in the law. She turned on all her southern charm and sweetness, trying to straighten things out. You darling, she said, you poor darling, to the bruised night clerk. The law was not called, but the outcome of the situation was far from pleasant. They had to check out, of course, and the hysterical old friend said he was going to write Cora's family in Alexandria, Louisiana, and give them a factual report on how she was living here in New York and how he supposed she was living anywhere else since she'd left home and he knew her.

At that time Billy knew almost nothing about Cora's background and former life, and he was surprised at her being so upset over this hysterical threat, which seemed unimportant to him. But all the next day Cora kept alluding to it, speculating whether or not the bitch would really do it, and it was probably on account of this threat that Cora made up her mind to leave New York. It was the only time, while they were living together, that Cora ever made a decision, at least about places to go and when to go to them. She had none of that desire to manage and dominate which is a typically American perversion of the female nature. As Billy said to himself, with that curious harshness of his toward things he loved, she was like a big piece of seaweed. Sometimes he said it irritably to himself, just like a big piece of seaweed washing this way and that way. It isn't healthy or normal to be so passive, Billy thought.

Where do you want to eat?

I don't care.

No, tell me, Cora, what place would you prefer?

I really don't care, she'd insist, it makes no difference to me.

Sometimes out of exasperation he would say, All right, let's eat at the Automat.

Only then would Cora demur.

Of course, if you want to, honey, but couldn't we eat some place with a liquor license?

She was agreeable to anything and everything; she seemed to be grateful for any decision made for her, but this one time, when they left New York, when they made their first trip together, it was Cora's decision to go. This was before Billy began to be terribly fond of Cora, and at first, when Cora said, Honey, I've got to leave this town or Hugo (the hotel queen) will bring up Bobo (her brother who was a lawyer in Alexandria and who had played some very unbrotherly legal trick on her when a certain inheritance was settled) and there will be hell to pay, he will freeze up my income—then, at this point, Billy assumed that they would go separate ways. But at the last moment Billy discovered that he didn't want to go back to a stag existence. He discovered that solitary cruising had been lonely, that there were spiritual comforts as well as material advantages in their double arrangement. No matter how bad luck was, there was no longer such a thing as going home by himself to the horrors of a second- or third-class hotel bedroom. Then there *were* the material advantages, the fact they actually did better operating together, and the fact that it was more economical. Billy had to be somewhat mean about money since he was living on savings that he wanted to stretch as far as he could, and Cora more than carried her own weight in the expense department. She was only too eager to pick up a check and Billy was all too willing to let her do it. She spoke of her income but she was vague about what it was or came from. Sometimes looking into her handbag she had a fleeting expression of worry that made Billy wonder uncomfortably if her finances, like his, might not be continually dwindling toward an eventual point of eclipse. But neither of them had a provident nature or dared to stop and consider much of the future.

Billy was a light traveler, all he carried with him was a three-suiter, a single piece of hand luggage and his portable typewriter. When difficulties developed at a hotel, he could clear out in five minutes or less. He rubbed his chin for a minute, then he said, Cora, how about me going with you?

They shared a compartment in the Sunshine Special to Florida. Why to Florida? One of Cora's very few pretensions was a little command of French; she was fond of using little French phrases which she pronounced badly. Honey, she said, I have a little *pied-à-terre* in Florida.

Pied-à-terre was one of those little French phrases that she was proud of using, and she kept talking about it, her little *pied-à-terre* in the Sunshine State.

Whereabouts is it, Billy asked her.

No place fashionable, she told him, but just you wait and see and you might be surprised and like it.

That night in the shared compartment of the Pullman was the first time they had sex together. It happened casually, it was not important and it was not very satisfactory, perhaps because they were each too anxious to please the other, each too afraid the other would be disappointed. Sex has to be slightly selfish to have real excitement. Start worrying about the other party's reactions and the big charge just isn't there, and you've got to do it a number of times together before it becomes natural enough to be a completely satisfactory thing. The first time between strangers can be like a blaze of light, but when it happens between people who know each other well and have an established affection, it's likely to be self-conscious and even a little embarrassing, most of all afterwards.

Afterwards they talked about it with a slight sense of strain. They felt they had gotten that sort of thing squared away and would not have to think about it between them again. But perhaps, in a way, it did add a little something to the intimacy of their living together; at least it had, as they put it, squared things away a bit. And they talked about it shyly, each one trying too hard to flatter the other.

Gee, honey, said Cora, you're a wonderful lay, you've got wonderful skin, smooth as a baby's, gee, it sure was wonderful, honey, I enjoyed it so much,

I wish you had. But I know you didn't like it and it was selfish of me to start it with you.

You didn't like it, he said.

I swear I *loved* it, she said, but I knew that *you* didn't like it, so we won't do it again.

He told Cora that she was a wonderful lay and that he had loved it every bit as much as she did and maybe more, but he agreed they'd better not do it again.

Friends can't be lovers, he said.

No, they can't, she agreed with a note of sadness.

Then jealousy enters in.

Yes, they get jealous and bitchy . . .

They never did it again, at least not that completely, not any time during the year and two months since they started living together. Of course, there were some very drunk, *blind* drunk nights when they weren't quite sure what happened between them after they fell into bed, but you could be pretty certain it wasn't a sixty-six in that condition. Sixty-six was Cora's own slightly inexact term for a normal lay, that is, a lay that occurred in the ordinary position.

What happened? Billy would ask when she'd had a party.

Oh, it was wonderful, she would exclaim, a sixty-six!

Good Jesus, drunk as he was?

Oh, I sobered him up, she'd laugh.

And what did you do, Billy? Take the sheets? Ha ha, you'll have to leave this town with a board nailed over your ass!

Sometimes they had a serious conversation, though most of the time they tried to keep the talk on a frivolous plane. It troubled Cora to talk about serious matters, probably because matters were too serious to be talked about with comfort. And for the first month or so neither of them knew that the other one actually had a mind that you could talk to. Gradually they discovered about each other the other things, and although it was always their mutual pursuit, endless and indefatigable, of "the lyric quarry" that was the mainstay of their relationship, at least upon its surface, the other things, the timid and tender values that can exist between people, began to come shyly out and they had a respect for each other, not merely to like and enjoy, as neither had ever respected another person.

It was a rare sort of moral anarchy, doubtless, that held them together, a really fearful shared hatred of everything that was restrictive and which they felt to be false in the society they lived in and against the grain of which they continually operated. They did not dislike what they called "squares." They loathed and despised them, and for the best of reasons. Their existence was a never-ending contest with the squares of the world, the squares who have such a virulent rage at everything not in their book. Getting around the squares, evading, defying the phony rules of convention, that was maybe responsible for half their pleasure in their outlaw existence. They were a pair of kids playing cops and robbers; except for that element, the thrill of something lawless, they probably would have gotten bored with cruising. Maybe not, maybe so. Who can tell? But hotel clerks and house dicks and people in adjoining hotel bedrooms, the specter of Cora's family in Alexandria, Louisiana, the specter of Billy's family in Montgomery, Alabama, the various people involved in the niggardly control of funds, almost everybody that you passed when you were drunk and hilariously gay on the street, especially all those bull-like middle-aged couples that stood off sharply and glared at you as you swept through a hotel lobby with your blushing trade—all, all, all of those were natural enemies to them, as well as the one great terrible, worst of all enemies, which is the fork-tailed, cloven-hoofed, pitchfork-bearing devil of Time!

Time, of course, was the greatest enemy of all, and they knew that each day and each night was cutting down a little on the distance between the two of them running together and that demon pursuer. And knowing it, knowing that nightmarish fact, gave a wild sort of sweetness of despair to their two-ring circus.

And then, of course, there was also the fact that Billy was, or had been at one time, a sort of artist *manqué* and still had a touch of homesickness for what that was.

Sometime, said Cora, you're going to get off the party.

Why should I get off the party?

Because you're a serious person. You are fundamentally a serious sort of a person.

I'm not a serious person any more than you are. I'm a goddam remittance man and you know it.

No, I don't know it, said Cora. Remittance men get letters enclosing checks, but you don't even get letters.

Billy rubbed his chin.

Then how do you think I live?

Ha ha, she said.

What does 'Ha Ha' mean?

It means I know what I know!

Balls, said Billy, you know no more about me than I do about you.

I know, said Cora, that you used to write for a living, and that for two years you haven't been writing but you're still living on the money you made as a writer, and sooner or later, you're going to get off the party and go back to working again and being a serious person. What do you imagine I think of that portable typewriter you drag around with you everywhere we go, and that big fat portfolio full of papers you tote underneath your shirts in your three-suiter? I wasn't born yesterday or the day before yesterday, baby, and I know that you're going to get off the party some day and leave me on it.

If I get off the party, we'll get off it together, said Billy.

And me do *what?* she'd ask him, realistically.

And he would not be able to answer that question. For she knew and he knew, both of them knew it together, that they would remain together only so long as they stayed on the party, and not any longer than that. And in his heart he knew, much as he might deny it, that it would be pretty much as Cora predicted in her Cassandra moods. One of those days or nights it was bound to happen. He would get off the party, yes, he would certainly be the one of them to get off it, because there was really nothing for Cora to do but stay on it. Of course, if she broke down, that would take her off it. Usually or almost always it's only a breakdown that takes you off a party. A party is like a fast-moving train—you can't jump off it, it thunders past the stations you might get off at, very few people have the courage to leap from a thing that is moving that fast, they have to stay with it no matter where it takes them. It only stops when it crashes, the ticker wears out, a blood vessel bursts, the liver or kidneys quit working. But Cora was tough. Her system had absorbed a lot of punishment, but from present appearances it was going to absorb a lot more. She was too tough to crack up any time soon, but she was not tough enough to make the clean break, the daring jump off, that Billy knew, or felt that he knew, that he was still able to make when he was ready to make it. Cora was five or maybe even ten years older than Billy. She rarely looked it, but she was that much older and time is one of the biggest differences between two people.

I've got news for you, baby, and you had better believe it.

What news?

This news, Cora would say. You're going to get off the party and leave me on it!

Well, it was probably true, as true as anything is, and what a pity it was that Cora was such a grand person. If she had not been such a nice person, so nice that at first you thought it must be phony and only gradually came to see it was real, it wouldn't matter so much. For usually queens fall out like a couple of thieves quarreling over the split of the loot. Billy remembered the one in Baton Rouge who was so annoyed when he confiscated a piece she had a lech for that she made of Billy an effigy of candle wax and stuck pins in it with dreadful imprecations, kept the candle-wax effigy on her mantel and performed black rites before it. But Cora was not like that. She didn't have a jealous bone in her body. She took as much pleasure in Billy's luck as her own. Sometimes he suspected she was more interested in Billy having good luck than having it herself.

Sometimes Billy would wonder. Why do we do it?

We're lonely people, she said, I guess it's as simple as that . . .

But nothing is ever quite so simple as it appears when you are comfortably loaded.

Take this occasion, for instance.

Billy and Cora are traveling by motor. The automobile is a joint possession which they acquired from a used-car dealer in Galveston. It is a '47 Buick convertible with a brilliant new scarlet paint-job. Cora and Billy are outfitted with corresponding brilliance; she has on a pair of black and white checked slacks, a cowboy shirt with a bucking broncho over one large breast and a roped steer over the other, and she has on harlequin sun-glasses with false diamonds encrusting the rims. Her freshly peroxided hair is bound girlishly on top of her head with a diaphanous scarf of magenta chiffon; she has on her diamond ear-clips and her multiple slave-bracelets, three of them real gold and two of them only gold-plated, and hundreds of little tinkling gold attachments, such as tiny footballs, liberty bells, hearts, mandolins, choo-choos, sleds, tennis rackets, and so forth. Billy thinks she has overdone it a little. It must be admitted, however, that she is a noticeable person, especially at the wheel of this glittering scarlet Roadmaster. They have swept down the Camino Real, the Old Spanish Trail, from El Paso eastward instead of westward, having decided at the last moment to resist the allure of Southern California on the other side of the Rockies and the desert, since it appears that the Buick has a little tendency to overheat and Cora notices that the oil pressure is not what it should be. So they have turned eastward instead of westward, with a little side trip to Corpus Christi to investigate the fact or fancy of those legendary seven connecting glory-holes in a certain tearoom there. It turned out to be fancy or could not be located. Says Cora: You queens know places but never know where places are!

A blowout going into New Orleans. That's to be expected, said Cora, they never give you good rubber. The spare is no good either. Two new tires had to be bought in New Orleans and Cora paid for them by hocking some of her baubles. There was some money left over and she buys Billy a pair of cowboy boots. They are still on the Wild West kick. Billy also presents a colorful appearance in a pair of blue jeans that fit as if they had been painted on him, the fancily embossed cowboy boots and a sport shirt that is covered with leaping dolphins, Ha ha! They have never had so much fun in their life together, the colored lights are going like pinwheels on the Fourth of July, everything is big and very bright celebration. The Buick appears to be a fairly solid investment, once it has good rubber on it and they get those automatic devices to working again . . .

It is a mechanical age that we live in, they keep saying.

They did Mobile, Pensacola, West Palm Beach and Miami in one continual happy breeze! The scoreboard is brilliant! Fifteen lays, all hitching rides on the highway, since they got the convertible. It's all we ever needed to hit the jackpot, Billy exults . . .

Then comes the badman into the picture!

They are on the Florida keys, just about midway between the objective, Key West, and the tip of the peninsula. Nothing is visible about them but sky and mangrove swamp. Then all of a sudden that used-car dealer in Galveston pulls the grinning joker out of his sleeve. Under the hood of the car comes a loud metallic noise as if steel blades are scraping. The fancy heap will not take the gas. It staggers gradually to a stop, and trying to start it again succeeds only in running the battery down. Moreover, the automatic top has ceased to function; it is the meridian of a day in early spring which is as hot as midsummer on the Florida keys . . .

Cora would prefer to make light of the situation, if Billy would let her do so. The compartment of the dashboard is filled with roadmaps, a flashlight and a thermos of dry martinis. The car has barely uttered its expiring rattle and gasp when Cora's intensely ornamented arm reaches out for this unfailing simplification of the human dilemma. For the first time in their life together, Billy interferes with her drinking, and out of pure meanness. He grabs her wrist and restrains her. He is suddenly conscious of how disgusted he is with what he calls her Oriental attitude toward life. The purchase of this hoax was her idea. Two thirds of the investment was also her money. Moreover she had professed to be a pretty good judge of motors. Billy himself had frankly confessed that he couldn't tell a spark plug from a carburetor. So it was Cora who had examined and appraised the possible buys on the used-car lots of Galveston and come upon this 'bargain'! She had looked under the hoods and shimmied fatly under the chassis of dozens of cars before she arrived at this remarkably misguided choice. The car had been suspiciously cheap for a '47 Roadmaster with such a brilliantly smart appearance, but Cora said it was just as sound as the American dollar! She put a thousand dollars into the deal and Billy put in five hundred which had come in from the resale to pocket editions of a lurid potboiler he had written under a pseudonym a number of years ago when he was still an active member of the literary profession.

Now Cora was reaching into the dashboard compartment for a thermos of martinis because the car whose purchase was her responsibility had collapsed in the middle of nowhere . . .

Billy seizes her wrist and twists it.

Let go of that goddam thermos, you're not gonna get drunk!

She struggles with him a little, but soon she gives up and suddenly goes feminine and starts to cry.

After that a good while passes in which they sit side by side in silence in the leather-lined crematorium of the convertible.

A humming sound begins to be heard in the distance. Perhaps it's a motorboat on the other side of the mangroves, perhaps something on the highway . . .

Cora begins to jingle and jangle as she twists her ornamented person this way and that way with nervous henlike motions of the head and shoulder and torso, peering about on both sides and half rising and flopping awkwardly back down again, and finally grunting eagerly and piling out of the car, losing her balance, sprawling into a ditch, ha ha, scrambling up again, taking the middle of the road and making great frantic circles with her arms as a motorcycle approaches. If the cyclist had desired to pass them it would have been hardly possible. Later Billy will remind her that it was *she* who stopped it. But right now Billy is enchanted, not merely at the prospect of a rescue but much more by the looks of the potential instrument of rescue. The motorcyclist is surely something dispatched from a sympathetic region back of the sun. He has one of those blond and block-shaped heads set upon a throat which is as broad as the head itself and has the smooth and supple muscularity of the male organ in its early stage of tumescence. This bare throat and the blond head above it have never been in a country where the sun is distant. The hands are enormous square knobs to the golden doors of Paradise. And the legs that straddle the quiescent fury of the cycle (called Indian) could not have been better designed by the appreciative eyes and fingers of Michelangelo or Phidias or Rodin. It is in the direct and pure line of those who have witnessed and testified in stone what they have seen of a simple physical glory in mankind! The eyes are behind sun-glasses. Cora is a good judge of eyes but she has to see them to judge them. Sometimes she will say to a young man wearing sun-glasses, will you kindly uncover the windows of your soul? She considers herself to be a better judge of good and bad trade than is Billy whose record contains a number of memorable errors. Later Cora will remember that from the moment she saw this youth on the motorcycle something whispered *Watch Out* in her ear. Honey, she will say, later, he had more Stop signs on him than you meet when you've got five minutes to get to the station! Perhaps this will be an exaggerated statement, but it is true that Cora had misgivings in exact proportion to Billy's undisguised enchantment.

As for right now, the kid seems fairly obliging. He swings his great legs off the cycle which he rests upon a metal support. He hardly says anything. He throws back the hood of the car and crouches into it for a couple of minutes, hardly more than that, then the expressionless blond cube comes back into view and announces without inflection, Bearings gone out.

What does that mean, asks Cora.

That means you been screwed, he says.

What can we do about it?

Not a goddam thing. You better junk it.

What did he say, inquires Billy.

He said, Cora tells him, that the bearings have gone out.

What are bearings?

The cyclist utters a short barking laugh. He is back astraddle the frankly shaped leather seat of his Indian, but Cora has once more descended from the Buick and she has resorted to the type of flirtation that even most queens would think common. She has fastened her bejeweled right hand over the elevated and narrow front section of the saddle which the boy sits astride. There is not only proximity but contact between their two parties, and all at once the boy's blond look is both contemptuous and attentive, and his attitude toward their situation has undergone a drastic alteration. He is now engaged in it again.

There's a garage on Boca Raton, he tells them. I'll see if they got a tow truck. I think they got one.

Off he roars down the Keys!

One hour and forty-five minutes later the abdicated Roadmaster is towed into a garage on Boca Raton, and Cora and Billy plus their new-found acquaintance are checking, all three, into a tourist cabin at a camp called The Idle-wild, which is across the highway from the garage.

Cora has thought to remove her thermos of martinis from the dashboard compartment, and this time Billy has not offered any objection. Billy is restored to good spirits. Cora still feels guilty, profoundly and abjectly guilty, about the purchase of the glittering fraud, but she is putting up a good front. She knows, however, that Billy will never quite forgive and forget and she does not understand why she made that silly profession of knowing so much about motors. It was, of course, to impress her beloved companion. He knows so much more than she about so many things, she has to pretend, now and then, to know *something* about *something*, even when she knows in her heart that she is a comprehensive and unabridged dictionary of human ignorance on nearly all things of importance. She sighs in her heart because she's become a pretender, and once you have pretended, is it ever possible to stop pretending?

Pretending to be a competent judge of a motor has placed her in the sad and embarrassing position of having cheated Billy out of five hundred dollars. How can she make it up to him?

A whisper in the heart of Cora: *I love him!*

Whom does she love?

There are three persons in the cabin, herself, and Billy and the young man from the highway.

Cora despises herself and she has never been much attracted to men of an altogether physical type.

So there is the dreadful answer! She is in love with Billy!

I am in love with Billy, she whispers to herself.

That acknowledgment seems to call for a drink.

She gets up and pours herself another martini. Unfortunately someone, probably Cora herself, has forgotten to screw the cap back on the thermos bottle and the drinks are now tepid. No drink is better than an ice-cold martini, but no drink is worse than a martini getting warm. However, be that as it may, the discovery just made, the one about loving Billy, well, after *that* one the temperature of a drink is not so important so long as the stuff is still liquor!

She says to herself: I have admitted a fact! Well, the only thing to do with a fact is admit it, but once admitted, you don't have to keep harping on it.

Never again, so long as she stays on the party with her companion, will she put into words her feelings for him, not even in the privacy of her heart . . .

Le coeur a ses raisons que la raison ne connaît pas!

That is one of those little French sayings that Cora is proud of knowing and often repeats to herself as well as to others.

Sometimes she will translate it, to those who don't know the French language, as follows:

The heart knows the scoop when the brain is ignorant of it!

Ha ha!

Well, now she is back in the cabin after a mental excursion that must have lasted at least a half an hour.

Things have progressed thus far.

Billy has stripped down to his shorts and he has persuaded the square-headed blond to do likewise.

Cora herself discovers that she has made concessions to the unseasonable warmth of the little frame building.

All she is wearing is her panties and bra.

She looks across without real interest at the square-headed stranger. Yes. A magnificent torso, as meaningless, now, to Cora as a jigsaw puzzle which put together exhibits a cow munching grass in a typical one-tree pasture . . .

Excuse me, people, she remarks to Billy. I just remembered I promised to make a long-distance call to Atlanta.

A long-distance call to Atlanta is a code message between herself and Billy.

What it means is this: The field is yours to conquer!

Cora goes out, having thrown on a jacket and pulled on her checkerboard slacks.

Where does Cora go? Not far, not far at all.

She is leaning against a palm tree not more than five yards distant from the cabin. She is smoking a cigarette in a shadow.

Inside the cabin the field is Billy's to conquer.

Billy says to the cyclist: How do you like me?

Huh . . .

(That is the dubious answer to his question!)

Billy gives him a drink, another one, thinking that this may evoke a less equivocal type of response.

How do you like me, now?

You want to know how I like you?

Yes!

I like you the way that a cattleman loves a sheepherder!

I am not acquainted, says Billy, with the likes and dislikes of men who deal in cattle.

Well, says the square-headed blond, if you keep messing around I'm going to give you a demonstration of it!

A minute is a microscope view of eternity.

It is less than a minute before Cora hears a loud sound.

She knew what it was before she even heard it, and almost before she heard it, that thud of a body not falling but thrown to a floor, she is back at the door of the cabin and pushing it open and returning inside.

Hello! is what she says with apparent good humor.

She does not seem to notice Billy's position and bloody mouth on the floor . . .

Well, she says, I got my call through to Atlanta!

While she is saying this, she is getting out of her jacket and checkerboard slacks, and she is not stopping there.

Instant diversion is the doctor's order.

She is stripped bare in ten seconds, and on the bed.

Billy has gotten outside and she is enduring the most undesired embrace that she can remember in all her long history of desired and undesired and sometimes only patiently borne embraces . . .

Why do we do it?

We're lonely people. I guess it's simple as that . . .

But nothing is ever that simple! Don't you know it?

::

AND SO THE STORY CONTINUES WHERE IT DIDN'T LEAVE OFF . . .

Trade ceased to have much distinction. One piece was fundamentally the same as another, and the nights were like waves rolling in and breaking and retreating again and leaving you washed up on the wet sands of morning.

Something continual and something changeless.

The sweetness of their living together persisted.

We're friends! said Cora.

She meant a lot more than that, but Billy is satisfied with this spoken definition, and there's no other that can safely be framed in language.

Sometimes they look about them, privately and together, and what they see is something like what you see through a powerful telescope trained upon the moon, flatly illuminated craters and treeless plains and a vacancy of light—much light, but an emptiness in it.

Calcium is the element of this world.

Each has held some private notion of death. Billy thinks his death is going to be violent. Cora thinks hers will be ungraciously slow. Something will surrender by painful inches . . .

Meanwhile they are together.

To Cora that's the one important thing left.

Cities!

You queens know places, but never know where places are!

No Mayor has ever handed them a gold key, nor have they entered under a silken banner of welcome, but they have gone to them all in the northern half of the western hemisphere, this side of the Arctic Circle! Ha ha, just about all . . .

Many cities!

Sometimes they wake up early to hear the awakening tumult of a city and to reflect upon it.

They're two on a party which has made a departure and a rather wide one.

Into brutality? No. It's not that simple.

Into vice? No. It isn't nearly that simple.

Into what, then?

Into something unlawful? Yes, of course!

But in the night, hands clasping and no questions asked.

In the morning, a sense of being together no matter what comes, and the knowledge of not having struck nor lied nor stolen.

A female lush and a fairy who travel together, who are two on a party, and the rush continues.

They wake up early, sometimes, and hear the city coming awake, the increase of traffic, the murmurous shuffle of crowds on their way to their work, the ordinary resumption of daytime life in a city, and they reflect upon it a little from their, shall we say, bird's-eye situation.

There's the radio and the newspaper and there is TV, which Billy says means 'Tired Vaudeville,' and everything that is known is known very fully and very fully stated.

But after all, when you reflect upon it at the only time that is suitable for reflection, what can you do but turn your other cheek to the pillow?

Two queens sleeping together with sometimes a stranger between them . . .

One morning a phone will ring.

Cora will answer, being the lighter sleeper and the quicker to rise.

Bad news!

Clapping a hand over the shrill mouthpiece, instinctive gesture of secrecy, she will cry to Billy.

Billy, Billy, wake up! They've raided the Flamingo! The heat is on! Get packed!

Almost gaily this message is delivered and the packing performed, for it's fun to fly away from a threat of danger.

(Most dreams are about it, one form of it or another, in which man remembers the distant mother with wings . . .)

Off they go, from Miami to Jacksonville, from Jacksonville to Savannah or Norfolk, all winter shuttling about the Dixie circuit, in spring going back to Manhattan, two birds flying together against the wind, nothing real but the party, and even that sort of dreamy.

In the morning, always Cora's voice addressing room service, huskily, softly, not to disturb his sleep before the coffee arrives, and then saying gently, Billy, Billy, your coffee . . .

Cup and teaspoon rattling like castanets as she hands it to him, often spilling a little on the bedclothes and saying, Oh, honey, excuse me, ha ha!

1954

JAMES PURDY

::

YOU MAY SAFELY GAZE

"DO WE ALWAYS HAVE TO BEGIN ON MILO AT THESE WEDNESDAY LUNCHES," Philip said to Guy. Carrying their trays, they had already picked out their table in the cafeteria, and Philip, at least, was about to sit down.

"Do I *always* begin on Milo?" Guy wondered, surprised.

"You're the one who knows him, remember," Philip said.

"Of course, Milo is one of the serious problems in our office, and it's only a little natural, I suppose, to mention problems even at one of our Wednesday lunches."

"Oh, forget it," Philip said. Seated, he watched half-amused as Guy still stood over the table with his tray raised like a busboy who will soon now move away with it to the back room.

"I don't dislike Milo," Guy began. "It's not that at all."

Philip began to say something but then hesitated, and looked up at the cafeteria clock that showed ten minutes past twelve. He knew, somehow, that it was going to be Milo all over again for lunch.

"It's his attitude not just toward his work, but life," Guy said, and this time he sat down.

"His life," Philip said, taking swift bites of his chicken à la king.

Guy nodded. "You see now he spares himself the real work in the office due to this physical culture philosophy. He won't even let himself get mad anymore or argue with me because that interferes with the development of his muscles and his mental tranquillity, which is so important for muscular development. His whole life now he says is to be strong and calm."

"A muscle ascetic," Philip laughed without amusement.

"But working with him is not so funny," Guy said, and Philip was taken aback to see his friend go suddenly very pale. Guy had not even bothered to take his dishes off his tray but allowed everything to sit there in front of him as though the lunch were an offering he had no intention of tasting.

"Milo hardly seems anybody you and I could know, if you ask me," Guy pronounced, as though the final decision had at last been made.

"You forget one of us *doesn't,*" Philip emphasized again, and he waved his fork as though they had finally finished now with Milo, and could go on to the real Wednesday lunch.

But Guy began again, as though the talk for the lunch had been arranged after all, despite Philip's forgetfulness, around Milo.

"I don't think he is even studying law anymore at night, as he was supposed to do."

"Don't tell me that," Philip said, involuntarily affecting concern and half-resigning himself now to the possibility of a completely wasted hour.

"Oh, of course," Guy softened his statement, "I guess he goes to the law library every night and reads a little. Every waking hour is, after all, not for his muscles, but every real thought, you can bet your bottom dollar, *is.*"

"I see," Philip said, beginning on his pineapple snow.

"It's the only thing on his mind, I tell you," Guy began again.

"It's interesting if that's the only thing on his mind, then," Philip replied. "I mean," he continued, when he saw the black look he got from Guy, "—to know somebody who is obsessed . . ."

"What do you mean by that?" Guy wondered critically, as though only he could tell what it was that Milo might be.

"You said he wanted to devote himself to just this one thing." Philip wearily tried to define what he had meant.

"I tried to talk to Milo once about it," Guy said, now deadly serious, and as though, with all preliminaries past, the real part of his speech had begun. Philip noticed that his friend had still not even picked up his knife and fork, and his food must be getting stone cold by now. " 'Why do you want to look any stronger,' I said to Milo. He just stared at me, and I said, 'Have you ever taken a good look in the mirror the way you are now,' and he just smiled his sour smile again at me. 'Have you ever looked, Milo?' I said, and even I had to laugh when I repeated my own question, and he kind of laughed then too . . . Well, for God's sake, he knows after all that nobody but a few freaks are going to look like he looks, or will look, if he keeps this up. You see he works on a new part of his body every month. One month he will be working on his pectorals, the next his calf muscles, then he will go in for a period on his latissimus dorsi."

Philip stopped chewing a moment as though seeing these different muscle groups slowly developing there before him. Finally, he managed to say, "Well at least he's interested in something, which is more than . . ."

"Yes, he's interested in *it,* of course," Guy interrupted, "—what he calls being the sculptor of his own body, and you can find him almost any noon in the gym straining away while the other men in our office do as they please with their lunch hour."

"You mean they eat their lunch then." Philip tried humor.

"That's right," Guy hurried on. "But he and this Austrian friend of his who also works in my office, they go over to this gym run by a cripple named Vic somebody, and strain their guts out, lifting barbells and throwing their arms up and around on benches, with dumbbells in their fists, and come back an hour later to their work looking as though they had been in a rock mixer. They actually stink of gym, and several of the stenographers have complained saying they always know when it's exercise day all right. But nothing stops those boys, and they just take all the gaff with as much good humor as two such egomaniacs can have."

"Why egomaniacs, for God's sake," Philip wondered, putting his fork down with a bang.

"Well, Philip," Guy pleaded now. "To think of their own bodies like that. These are not young boys, you know. They must be twenty-five or so, along in there, and you would think they would begin to think of other people, other people's bodies, at least." Guy laughed as though to correct his own severity before Philip. "But no," he went on. "They have to be Adonises."

"And their work suffers?" Philip wondered vaguely, as though, if the topic had to be continued, they might now examine it from this aspect.

"The kind of work young men like them do—it don't matter, you know, if you're good or not, nobody knows if you're really good. They do their work and get it out on time, and you know their big boss is still that old gal of seventy who is partial to young men. She sometimes goes right up to Milo, who will be sitting at his desk relaxed as a jellyfish, doing nothing, and she says, 'Roll up your sleeves, why don't you, and take off your necktie on a warm day like this,' and it will be thirty degrees outside and cool even in the office. And Milo will smile like a four-year-old at her because he loves admiration more than anything in the world, and he rolls up his sleeves and then all this bulge of muscle comes out, and the old girl looks like she'd seen glory, she's that gone on having a thug like that around."

"But you sound positively bilious over it," Philip laughed.

"Philip, look," Guy said with his heavy masculine patience, "doesn't it sound wrong to you, now seriously?"

"What in hell do you mean by wrong, though?"

"Don't be that way. You know goddamn well what I mean."

"Well, then, no, I can't say it is. Milo or whatever his name."

"You know it's Milo," Guy said positively disgusted.

"Well, he is, I suppose, more typical than you might think from the time, say, when you were young. Maybe there weren't such fellows around then."

"Oh there were, of course."

"Well, now there are more, and Milo is no exception."

"But he looks at himself all the time, and he has got himself tattooed recently and there in front of the one mirror in the office, it's not the girls who stand there, no, it's Milo and this Austrian boy. They're always washing their hands or combing their hair, or just looking at themselves right out, not sneaky-like the way most men do, but like some goddamn chorus girls. And oh, I forgot, this Austrian fellow got tattooed too because Milo kept after him, and then he was sorry. It seems the Austrian's physical culture instructor gave him hell and said he had spoiled the appearance of his deltoids by having the tattoo work done."

"Don't tell me," Philip said.

Guy stared as he heard Philip's laugh, but then continued: "They talked about the tattoo all morning, in front of all the stenogs, and whether this Austrian had spoiled the appearance of his deltoid muscles or not."

"Well, it *is* funny, of course, but I couldn't get worked up about it the way you are."

"They're a symbol of the new America and I don't like it."

"You're terribly worked up."

"Men on their way to being thirty, what used to be considered middle age, developing their bodies and special muscles and talking about their parts in front of women."

"But they're married men, aren't they?"

"Oh sure," Guy dismissed this. "Married and with kids."

"What more do you want then. Some men are nuts about their bowling scores and talk about that all the time in front of everybody."

"I see you approve of them."

"I didn't say that. But I think you're overreacting, to use the phrase . . ."

"You don't have to work with them," Guy went on. "You don't have to watch them in front of the one and only office mirror."

"Look, I've known a lot of women who griped me because they were always preening themselves, goddamn narcissists too. I don't care for narcissists of either sex."

"Talk about Narciss-uses," said Guy. "The worst was last summer when I went with Mae to the beach, and there *they* were, both of them, right in front of us on the sand."

Philip stiffened slightly at the prospect of more.

"Milo and the Austrian," Guy shook his head. "And as it was Saturday afternoon there didn't seem to be a damn place free on the beach and Mae wanted to be right up where these Adonises or Narciss-uses, or whatever you call them, were. I said, 'We don't want to camp here, Mae,' and she got suddenly furious. I couldn't tell her how those birds affected me, and they hardly even spoke to me either, come to think about it. Milo spit something out the side of his mouth when he saw me, as though to say *that for you.*"

"That was goddamn awful for you," Philip nodded.

"Wait till you hear what happened, for crying out loud. I shouldn't tell this during my lunch hour because it still riles me."

"Don't get riled then. Forget them."

"I have to tell you," Guy said. "I've never told anybody before, and you're the only man I know will listen to a thing like this. . . . You know," he went on then, as though this point were now understood at last between them, "Mae started staring at them right away. 'Who on earth are they?' she said, and I couldn't tell whether she was outraged or pleased, maybe she was a bit of both because she just fixed her gaze on them like paralyzed. 'Aren't you going to put on your sun tan lotion and your glasses?' I said to her, and she turned on me as though I had hit her. 'Why don't you let a woman relax when I never get out of the house but twice in one year,' she told me. I just lay back then on the sand and tried to forget they were there and that she was there and that even I was there."

Philip began to light up his cigarette, and Guy said, "Are you all done eating already?" and he looked at his own plate of veal cutlet and peas which was nearly untouched. "My God, you are a fast eater. Why, do you realize how fast you eat," he told Philip, and Philip said he guessed he half-realized it. He said at night he ate slower.

"In the bosom of your family," Guy laughed.

Philip looked at the cafeteria clock and stirred unceremoniously.

"But I wanted to finish telling you about these boys."

"Is there *more?*" Philip pretended surprise.

"Couldn't you tell the way I told it there was," Guy said, an indeterminate emotion in his voice.

"I hope nothing happened to Mae," Philip offered weakly.

"Nothing ever happens to Mae," Guy dismissed this impatiently. "No, it was them, of course. Milo and the Austrian began putting on a real show, you know, for everybody, and as it was Saturday afternoon, as I said, nearly everybody from every office in the world was there, and they were all watching Milo and the Austrian. So, first they just did the standard routine, warm-ups, you know, etc., but from the first every eye on the beach was on them, they seemed to have the old presence, even the life guards were staring at them as though nobody would ever dare drown while they were carrying on, so first of all they did handstands and though they did them good, not good enough for that many people to be watching. After all somebody is always doing handstands on the beach, you know. I think it was their hair attracted people, they have very odd hair, they look like brothers that way. Their hair is way too thick, and of course too long for men of our generation. . . ."

"Well, how old do you think I am?" Philip laughed.

"All right, of *my* generation, then," Guy corrected with surliness. He went on, however, immediately: "I think the reason everybody watched was their hair, which is a peculiar kind of chestnut color, natural and all that, but maybe due to the sun and all their exercising had taken on a funny shade, and then their muscles were so enormous in that light, bulging and shining with oil and matching somehow their hair that I think that was really what kept people looking and not what they did. They didn't look quite real, even though in a way they are the style.

"I kept staring, and Mae said, 'I thought you wasn't going to watch,' and I could see she was completely held captive by their performance as was, I guess, everybody by then on the goddamn beach.

" 'I can't help looking at freaks,' I told Mae, and she gave me one of her snorts and just kept looking kind of bitter and satisfied at seeing something like that. She's a great woman for sights like that, she goes to all the stock shows, and almost every nice Sunday she takes the kids to the zoo. . . ."

"Well, what finally did come off?" Philip said, pushing back his chair.

"The thing that happened, nobody in his right mind would ever believe, and probably lots of men and boys who saw it happen never went home and told their families."

"It should have been carried in the papers then," Philip said coolly and he drank all of his as yet untouched glass of water.

"I don't know what word I would use to describe it," Guy said. "Mae has never mentioned it to this day, though she said a little about it on the streetcar on the way home that afternoon, but just a little, like she would have referred to a woman having fainted and been rushed to the hospital, something on that order."

"Well, for Pete's sake now, what did happen?" Philip's ill humor broke forth for a moment, and he bent his head away from Guy's look.

"As I said," Guy continued quietly, "they did all those more fancy exercises then after their warm ups, like leaping on one another's necks, jumping hard on each other's abdomens to show what iron men they were, and some rough stuff but which they made look fancy, like they threw one another to the sand as though it was a cross between a wrestling match and an apache dance, and then they began to do some things looked like they were out of the ballet, with lots of things like jumping in air and splits, you know. You know what kind of trunks that kind of Narciss-uses wear, well these were tighter than usual, the kind to make a bullfighter's pants look baggy and oversize, and as though they had planned it, while doing one of their big movements, their trunks both split clear in two, at the same time, with a sound, I swear, you could have heard all over that beach.

"Instead of feeling at least some kind of self-consciousness, if not shame, they both busted out laughing and hugged one another as though they'd made a touchdown, and they might as well both been naked by now, they just stood there and looked down at themselves from time to time like they were alone in the shower, and laughed and laughed, and an old woman next to them just laughed and laughed too, and all Mae did was look once and then away with a funny half-smile on her mouth, she didn't show any more concern over it than the next one. Here was a whole beach of mostly women, just laughing their heads off because two men no longer young, were, well, exposing themselves in front of everybody, for that's all it was."

Philip stared at his empty water glass.

"I started to say something to Mae, and she nearly cut my head off, saying something like *why don't you mind your own goddamn business* in a tone unusually mean even for her. *Don't look damn you if you don't like it* was what my own wife said to me.

Suddenly Philip had relaxed in his chair as though the water he had drunk had contained a narcotic. He made no effort now to show his eagerness to leave, to hurry, or to comment on what was being said, and he sat there staring in the direction of, but not at, Guy.

"But the worst part came then," Guy said, and then looking critically and uneasily at Philip, he turned round to look at the cafeteria clock, but it showed only five minutes to one, and their lunch hour was not precisely over.

"This old woman," he continued, swallowing hard, "who had been sitting there next to them got out a sewing kit she had, and do you know what?"

"I suppose she sewed them shut," Philip said sleepily and still staring at nothing.

"That's exactly correct," Guy said, a kind of irritated disappointment in his voice. "This old woman who looked at least eighty went right up to them the way they were and she must have been a real seamstress, and before the whole crowd with them two grown men laughing their heads off she sewed up their tights like some old witch in a story, and Mae sat there as cool as if we was playing bridge in the church basement, and never said boo, and when I began to really let off steam, she said *Will you keep your big old ugly mouth shut or am I going to have to hit you over the mouth with my beach clogs.* That's how they had affected my own wife."

"So," Guy said, after a pause in which Philip contributed nothing, "this country has certainly changed since I grew up in it. I said that to Mae and that was the final thing I had to say on the subject, and those two grown men went right on lying there on the sand, every so often slapping one another on their muscles, and combing their hair with oil, and laughing all the time, though I think even they did have sense enough not to get up and split their trunks again or even they must have known they would have been arrested by the beach patrol."

"Sure," Philip said vacantly.

"So that's the story of Milo and the Austrian," Guy said.

"It's typical," Philip said, like a somnambulist.

"Are you sore at me or something," Guy said, picking up his and Philip's checks.

"Let me pay my own, for Christ's sake," Philip said.

"Listen, you *are* sore at me, I believe," Guy said.

"I have a rotten headache is all," Philip replied, and he picked up his own check.

"I hope I didn't bring it on by talking my head off."

"No," Philip replied. "I had it since morning."

1956

GORE VIDAL

pages from an abandoned journal

I

April 30, 1948

AFTER LAST NIGHT, I WAS SURE THEY WOULDN'T WANT TO SEE ME AGAIN BUT evidently I was wrong because this morning I had a call from Steven . . . he spells it with a "v" . . . asking me if I would like to come to a party at Elliott Magren's apartment in the *Rue du Bac.* I should have said no but I didn't. It's funny: when I make up my mind *not* to do something I always end up by doing it, like meeting Magren, like seeing any of these people again, especially after last night. Well, I guess it's experience. What was it Pascal wrote? I don't remember what Pascal wrote . . . another sign of weakness: I should look it up when I don't remember . . . the book is right here on the table but the thought of leafing through all those pages is discouraging so I pass on.

Anyway, now that I'm in Paris I've got to learn to be more adaptable and I do think, all in all, I've handled myself pretty well . . . until last night in the bar when I told everybody off. I certainly never thought I'd see Steven again . . . that's why I was so surprised to get his call this morning. Is he still hopeful after what I said? I can't see how. I was *ruthlessly* honest. I said I wasn't interested, that I didn't mind what other people did, etc., just as long as they left me alone, that I was getting married in the fall when I got back to the States (WRITE HELEN) and that I don't go in for any of that, never did and never will. I also told him in no uncertain terms that it's very embarrassing for a grown man to be treated like some idiot girl surrounded by a bunch of seedy, middle-aged Don Juans trying to get their hooks into her . . . him. Anyway, I really let him have it before I left. Later, I felt silly but I was glad to go on record like that once and for all: now we know where we stand and if they're willing to accept me on *my* terms, the way I am, then there's no reason why I can't see them sometimes. That's really why I agreed to meet Magren who sounds very interesting from what everybody says, and everybody talks a lot about him, at least in those circles which must be the largest and busiest circles in Paris this spring. Well, I shouldn't complain: this is the Bohemian life I wanted to see. It's just that there aren't many girls around, for fairly obvious reasons. In fact, except for running into Hilda Devendorf at American Express yesterday, I haven't seen an American girl to talk to in the three weeks I've been here.

My day: after the phone call from Steven, I worked for two and a half hours on Nero and the Civil Wars . . . I wish sometimes I'd picked a smaller subject for a doctorate, not that I don't like the period but having to learn German to read a lot of books all based on sources available to anybody is depressing: I could do the whole thing from Tacitus but that would be cheating, no bibliography, no footnotes, no scholastic quarrels to record and judge between. Then, though the day was cloudy, I took a long walk across the river to the Tuileries where the gardens looked fine. Just as I was turning home into the *rue de l'Université* it started to rain and I got wet. At the desk Madame Revenel told me Hilda had called. I called her back and she said she was going to Deauville on Friday to visit some people who own a hotel and why didn't I go too? I said I might and wrote down her address. She's a nice girl. We were in high school together back in Toledo; I lost track of her when I went to Columbia.

Had dinner here in the dining room (veal, french fried potatoes, salad and something like a pie but very good . . . I like the way Madame Revenel cooks). She talked to me all through dinner, very fast, which is good because the faster she goes the less chance you have to translate in your head. The only other people in the dining room were the Harvard professor and his wife. They both read while they ate. He's supposed to be somebody important in the English Department but I've never heard of him . . . Paris is like that: everyone's supposed to be somebody important only you've never heard of them. The Harvard professor was reading a mystery story and his wife was reading a life of Alexander Pope. . . .

I got to the *Rue du Bac* around ten-thirty. Steven opened the door, yelling: "The beautiful Peter!" This was about what I expected. Anyway, I got into the room quickly . . . if they're drunk they're apt to try to kiss you and there was no point in getting off on the wrong foot again . . . but luckily he didn't try. He showed me through the apartment, four big rooms one opening off another . . . here and there an old chair was propped against a wall and that was all the furniture there was till we got to the last room where, on a big bed with a torn canopy, Elliott Magren lay, fully dressed, propped up by pillows. All the lamps had red shades. Over the bed was a painting of a nude man, the work of a famous painter I'd never heard of (read Berenson!).

There were about a dozen men in the room, most of them middle-aged and wearing expensive narrow suits. I recognized one or two of them from last night. They nodded to me but made no fuss. Steven introduced me to Elliott who didn't move from the bed when he shook hands; instead, he pulled me down beside him. He had a surprisingly powerful grip, considering how pale and slender he is. He told Steven to make me a drink. Then he gave me a long serious look and asked me if I wanted a pipe of opium. I said I didn't take drugs and he said nothing which was unusual: as a rule they give you a speech about how good it is for you or else they start defending themselves against what they feel is moral censure. Personally, I don't mind what other people do. As a matter of fact, I think all this is very interesting and I sometimes wonder what the gang back in Toledo would think if they could've seen me in a Left-Bank Paris apartment with a male prostitute who takes drugs. I thought of those college boys who sent T. S. Eliot the record "You've Come a Long Way From St Louis".

Before I describe what happened, I'd better write down what I've heard about Magren since he is already a legend in Europe, at least in these circles. First of all, he is not very handsome. I don't know what I'd expected but something glamorous, like a movie star. He is about five foot ten and weighs about a hundred sixty pounds. He has dark straight hair that falls over his forehead; his eyes are black. The two sides of his face don't match, like Oscar Wilde's, though the effect is not as disagreeable as Wilde's face must've been from the photographs. Because of drugs, he is unnaturally pale. His voice is deep and his accent is still Southern; he hasn't picked up that phoney English accent so many Americans do after five minutes over here. He was born in Galveston, Texas about thirty-six years ago. When he was sixteen he was picked up on the beach by a German baron who took him to Berlin with him. (I always wonder about details in a story like this: what did his parents say about a stranger walking off with their son? was there a scene? did they know what was going on?) Elliott then spent several years in Berlin during the twenties which were the great days, or what these people recall now as the great days . . . I gather the German boys were affectionate: It all sounds pretty disgusting. Then Elliott had a fight with the Baron and he walked, with no money, nothing but the clothes he was wearing, from Berlin to Munich. On the outskirts of Munich, a big car stopped and the chauffeur said that the owner of the car would like to give him a lift. The owner turned out to be a millionaire ship-owner from Egypt, very fat and old. He was intrigued with Elliott and he took him on a yachting tour of the Mediterranean. But Elliott couldn't stand him and when the ship got to Naples, Elliott and a Greek sailor skipped ship together after first stealing two thousand dollars from the Egyptian's stateroom. They went to Capri where they moved into the most expensive hotel and had a wonderful time until the money ran out and the sailor deserted Elliott for a rich American woman. Elliott was about to be taken off to jail for not paying his bill when Lord Glenellen, who was just checking in the hotel, saw him and told the police to let him go, that *he* would pay his bill . . . here again: how would Glenellen know that it would be worth his while to help this stranger? I mean you can't tell by looking at him that Elliott is queer. Suppose he hadn't been? Well, maybe that soldier I met on Okinawa the night of the hurricane was right: they can always tell about each other, like Masons. Glenellen kept Elliott for a number of years. They went to England together and Elliott rose higher and higher in aristocratic circles until he met the late King Basil who was then a Prince. Basil fell in love with him and Elliott went to live with him until Basil became king. They didn't see much of each other after that because the war started and Elliott went to California to live. Basil died during the war, leaving Elliott a small trust fund which is what he lives on now. In California, Elliott got interested in Vedanta and tried to stop taking drugs and lead a quiet . . . if not a normal . . . life. People say he was all right for several years but when the war ended he couldn't resist going back to Europe. Now he does nothing but smoke opium, his courtesan life pretty much over. This has been a long account but I'm glad I got it all down because the story is an interesting one and I've heard so many bits and pieces of it since I got here that it helps clarify many things just writing this down in my journal. . . . It is now past four o'clock and I've got a hangover already from the party but I'm going to finish, just as discipline. I never seem to finish anything which is a bad sign, God knows.

While I was sitting with Elliott on the bed, Steven brought him his opium pipe, a long painted wooden affair with a metal chimney. Elliott inhaled deeply, holding the smoke in his lungs as long as he could; then he exhaled the pale medicinal-scented smoke, and started to talk. I can't remember a word he said. I was aware, though, that this was probably the most brilliant conversation I'd ever heard. It might have been the setting which was certainly provocative or maybe I'd inhaled some of the opium which put me in a receptive mood but, no matter the cause, I sat listening to him, fascinated, not wanting him to stop. As he talked, he kept his eyes shut and I suddenly realized why the lamp shades were red: the eyes of drug addicts are hypersensitive to light; whenever he opened his eyes he would blink painfully and the tears would streak his face, glistening like small watery rubies in the red light. He told me about himself, pretending to be a modern Candide, simple and bewildered but actually he must have been quite different, more calculating, more resourceful. Then he asked me about myself and I couldn't tell if he was really interested or not because his eyes were shut and it's odd talking to someone who won't look at you. I told him about Ohio and high school and the University and now Columbia and the doctorate I'm trying to get in History and the fact I want to teach, to marry Helen . . . but as I talked I couldn't help but think how dull my life must sound to Elliott. I cut it short. I couldn't compete with him . . . and didn't want to. Then he asked me if I'd see him some evening, alone, and I said I would like to but . . . and this was completely spur of the moment . . . I said I was going down to Deauville the next day, with a girl. I wasn't sure he'd heard any of this because at that moment Steven pulled me off the bed and tried to make me dance with him which I wouldn't do, to the amusement of the others. Then Elliott went to sleep so I sat and talked for a while with an interior decorator from New York and, as usual, I was floored by the amount these people know: painting, music, literature, architecture . . . where do they learn it all? I sit like a complete idiot, supposedly educated, almost a Ph.D. while they talk circles around me: Fragonard, Boucher, Leonore Fini, Gropius, Sacheverell Sitwell, Ronald Firbank, Jean Genet, Jean Giono, Jean Cocteau, Jean Brown's body lies a'mouldering in Robert Graves. God damn them all. I have the worst headache and outside it's dawn. Remember to write Helen, call Hilda about Deauville, study German two hours tomorrow instead of one, start boning up on Latin again, read Berenson, get a book on modern art (what book?), read Firbank. . . .

II

May 21, 1948

ANOTHER FIGHT WITH HILDA. THIS TIME ABOUT RELIGION. SHE'S A CHRISTIAN Scientist. It all started when she saw me taking two aspirins this morning because of last night's hangover. She gave me a lecture on Christ—Scientist and we had a long fight about God on the beach (which was wonderful today, not too many people, not too hot). Hilda looked more than ever like a great golden seal. She is a nice girl but like so many who go to Bennington feels she must continually be alert to the life about her. I think tonight we'll go to bed together. Remember to get suntan oil, change money at hotel, finish Berenson, study German grammar! See if there's a Firbank in a paper edition.

May 22, 1948

It wasn't very successful last night. Hilda kept talking all the time which slows me down, also she is a good deal softer than she looks and it was like sinking into a feather mattress. I don't think she has bones, only elastic webbing. Well, maybe it'll be better tonight. She seemed pleased but then I think she likes the idea better than the actual thing. She told me she had her first affair at fourteen. We had another argument about God. I told her the evidence was slight, etc. but she said evidence had nothing to do with faith. She told me a long story about how her mother had cancer last year but wouldn't see a doctor and the cancer went away. I didn't have the heart to tell her that Mother's days are unpleasantly numbered. We had a wonderful dinner at that place on the sea, lobster, *moules.* Write Helen.

May 24, 1948

A fight with Hilda, this time about Helen whom she hardly knows. She felt that Helen was pretentious. I said who isn't? She said many people weren't. I said name me one. She said *she* wasn't pretentious. I then told her all the pretentious things she'd said in the past week starting with that discussion about the importance of an aristocracy and ending with atonalism. She then told me all the pretentious things I'd said, things I either didn't remember saying or she had twisted around. I got so angry I stalked out of her room and didn't go back: just as well. Having sex with her is about the dullest past-time I can think of. I went to my room and read Tacitus in Latin, for practice.

My sunburn is better but I think I've picked up some kind of liver trouble. Hope it's not jaundice: a burning feeling right where the liver is.

May 25, 1948

Hilda very cool this morning when we met on the beach. Beautiful day. We sat on the sand a good yard between us, and I kept thinking how fat she's going to be in a few years, only fit for child-bearing. I also thought happily of those agonizing "painless" childbirths she'd have to endure because of Christian Science. We were just beginning to quarrel about the pronunciation of a French word when Elliott Magren appeared . . . the last person in the world I expected to see at bright noon on that beach. He was walking slowly, wearing sunglasses and a pair of crimson trunks. I noticed with surprise how smooth and youthful his body was, like a boy. I don't know what I'd expected: something gaunt and hollowed out I suppose, wasted by drugs. He came up to me as though he'd expected to meet me right where I was. We shook hands and I introduced him to Hilda who fortunately missed the point to him from the very beginning. He was as charming as ever. It seems he had to come to Deauville alone . . . he hated the sun but liked the beach . . . and, in answer to the golden Hilda's inevitable question, no, he was not married. I wanted to tell her everything, just to see what would happen, to break for a moment that beaming complacency, but I didn't . . .

May 27, 1948

Well, this afternoon, Hilda decided it was time to go back to Paris. I carried her bag to the station and we didn't quarrel once. She was pensive but I didn't offer the usual small change for her thoughts. She didn't mention Elliott and I have no idea how much she suspects; in any case, it's none of her business, none of mine either. I think, though, I was nearly as shocked as she was when he came back to the hotel this morning with that fourteen year old boy. We were sitting on the terrace having coffee when Elliott, who must've got up very early, appeared with this boy. Elliott even introduced him to us and the little devil wasn't faintly embarrassed, assuming, I guess, that we were interested in him, too. Then Elliott whisked him off to his room and, as Hilda and I sat in complete silence, we could hear from Elliott's room on the first floor the hoarse sound of the boy's laughter. Not long after, Hilda decided to go back to Paris.

Wrote a long letter to Helen, studied Latin grammar. . . . I'm more afraid of my Latin than of anything else in either the written or the orals: can't seem to concentrate, can't retain all those irregular verbs. Well, I've come this far. I'll probably get through all right.

May 28, 1948

This morning I knocked on Elliott's door around eleven o'clock. He'd asked me to pick him up on my way to the beach. When he shouted come in!

I did and found both Elliott and the boy on the floor together, stark naked, putting together a Meccano set. Both were intent on building an intricate affair with wheels and pulleys, a blueprint between them. I excused myself hurriedly but Elliott told me to stay . . . they'd be finished in a moment. The boy who was the color of a terra-cotta pot gave me a wicked grin. Then Elliott, completely unself-conscious, jumped to his feet and pulled on a pair of trunks and a shirt. The boy dressed, too, and we went out on the beach where the kid left us. I was blunt. I asked Elliott if this sort of thing wasn't very dangerous and he said yes it probably was but life was short and he was afraid of nothing, except drugs. He told me then that he had had an electrical shock treatment at a clinic shortly before I'd first met him. Now, at last, he was off opium and he hoped it was a permanent cure. He described the shock treatment, which sounded terrible. Part of his memory was gone: he could recall almost nothing of his childhood . . . yet he was blithe even about this: after all, he believed only in the present. . . . Then when I asked him if he always went in for young boys he said yes and he made a joke about how, having lost all memory of his own childhood, he would have to live out a new one with some boy.

May 29, 1948

I had a strange conversation with Elliott last night. André went home to his family at six and Elliott and I had an early dinner on the terrace. A beautiful evening: the sea green in the last light . . . a new moon. Eating fresh sole from the Channel, I told Elliott all about Jimmy, told him things I myself had nearly forgotten, had wanted to forget. I told him how it had started at twelve and gone on, without plan or thought or even acknowledgment until, at seventeen, I went to the army and he to the Marines and a quick death. After the army, I met Helen and forgot him completely; his death, like Elliott's shock treatment, took with it all memory, a thousand summer days abandoned on a coral island. I can't think now why on earth I told Elliott about Jimmy, not that I'm ashamed but it was, after all, something intimate, something nearly forgotten . . . anyway, when I finished, I sat there in the dark, not daring to look at Elliott, shivering as all in a rush the warmth left the sand about us and I had that terrible feeling I always have when I realize too late I've said too much. Finally, Elliott spoke. He gave me a strange disjointed speech about life and duty to oneself and how the moment is all one has and how it is dishonorable to cheat oneself of that. . . . I'm not sure that he said anything very useful or very original but sitting there in the dark, listening, his words had a peculiar urgency for me and I felt, in a way, that I was listening to an oracle. . . .

June 1, 1948

Shortly before lunch, the police came and arrested Elliott. Luckily, I was down on the beach and missed the whole thing. . . . The hotel's in an uproar and the manager's behaving like a mad man. It seems André stole Elliott's camera. His parents found it and asked him where he got it. He wouldn't tell. When they threatened him, he said Elliott gave him the camera and then, to make this story credible, he told them that Elliott had tried to seduce him. . . . The whole sordid business then proceeded logically: parents to police . . . police to Elliott . . . arrest. I sat down shakily on the terrace and wondered what to do. I was . . . I am frightened. While I was sitting there, a gendarme came out on the terrace and told me Elliott wanted to see me, in prison. Meanwhile, the gendarme wanted to know what I knew about Mr Magren. It was only too apparent what his opinion of *me* was: another *pédérast américain*. My voice shook and my throat dried up as I told him I hardly knew Elliott . . . I'd only just met him . . . I knew nothing about his private life. The gendarme sighed and closed his note book: the charges against Elliott were *très grave, très grave,* but I would be allowed to see him tomorrow morning. Then, realizing I was both nervous and uncooperative, the gendarme gave me the address of the jail and left. I went straight to my room and packed. I didn't think twice. All I wanted was to get away from Deauville, from Elliott, from the crime . . . and it *was* a crime, I'm sure of that. I was back in Paris in time for supper at the hotel.

June 4, 1948

Ran into Steven at the Café Flore and I asked him if there'd been any news of Elliott. Steven took the whole thing as a joke: yes, Elliott had called a mutual friend who was a lawyer and everything was all right. Money was spent; the charges were dropped and Elliott was staying on in Deauville for another week . . . doubtless to be near André. I was shocked but relieved to hear this. I'm not proud of my cowardice but I didn't want to be drawn into something I hardly understood.

Caught a glimpse of Hilda with some college boy, laughing and chattering as they left the brasserie across the street. I stepped behind a kiosk, not wanting Hilda to see me. Write Helen. See the doctor about wax in ears, also liver. Get tickets for Roland Petit ballet.

III

December 26, 1953

THE MOST HIDEOUS HANGOVER! HOW I HATE CHRISTMAS, ESPECIALLY THIS one. Started out last night at the *Caprice* where the management gave a party, absolutely packed. The new room is quite stunning, to my surprise: black walls, white driftwood but not artsy-craftsy, a starlight effect for the ceiling . . . only the upholstery is really *mauvais goût:* tufted velveteen in SAFFRON! . . . but then Piggy has no sense of color and why somebody didn't stop him I'll never know. All the tired old faces were there. Everyone was going to the ballet except me and there was all the usual talk about who was sleeping with whom, such a bore . . . I mean who cares who . . . whom dancers sleep with? Though somebody did say that Niellsen was having an affair with Dr Bruckner which is something of a surprise considering what a mess there was at Fire Island last summer over just that. Anyway, I drank too many vodka martinis and, incidentally, met Robert Gammadge the English playwright who isn't at all attractive though he made the biggest play for me. He's supposed to be quite dreary but makes tons of money. He was with that awful Dickie Mallory whose whole life is devoted to meeting celebrities, even the wrong ones. Needless to say, he was in seventh heaven with his playwright in tow. I can't understand people like Dickie: what fun do they get out of always being second fiddle? After the *Caprice* I went over to Steven's new apartment on the river; it's in a remodeled tenement house and I must say it's fun and the Queen Anne desk I sold him looks perfect heaven in his living room. I'll say one thing for him: Steven is one of the few people who has the good sense simply to let a fine piece go in a room. There were quite a few people there and we had New York champagne which is drinkable when you're already full of vodka. Needless to say, Steven pulled me off to one corner to ask about Bob. I wish people wouldn't be so sympathetic not that they really are of course but they feel they must *pretend* to be: actually, they're only curious. I said Bob *seemed* all right when I saw him last month. I didn't go into any details though Steven did his best to worm the whole story out of me. Fortunately, I have a good grip on myself nowadays and I am able to talk about the break-up quite calmly. I always tell everybody I hope Bob will do well in his new business and that I like Sydney very much . . . actually, I hear things are going badly, that the shop is doing *no* business and that Bob is drinking again which means he's busy cruising the streets and getting into trouble. Well, I'm out of it and any day now I'll meet somebody . . . though it's funny how seldom you see anyone who's really attractive. There was a nice young Swede at Steven's but I never did get his name and anyway he is being kept by that ribbon clerk from the Madison Avenue Store. After Steven's I went to a real brawl in the Village: a studio apartment, packed with people, dozens of new faces, too. I wish now I hadn't got so drunk because there were some really attractive people there. I was all set, I thought, to go home with one but the friend intervened at the last moment and it looked for a moment like there was going to be real trouble before our host separated us . . . I never did get the host's name, I think he's in advertising. So I ended up alone. Must call doctor about hepatitis pills, write Leonore Fini, check last month's invoices (re. missing Sheraton receipt), call Mrs Blaine-Smith about sofa.

December 27, 1953

I finally had tea with Mrs Blaine-Smith today . . . one of the most beautiful women I've ever met, so truly chic and well-dressed. . . . I'm hopelessly indebted to Steven for bringing us together: she practically keeps the shop going. She had only six or seven people for tea, very much *en famille,* and I couldn't've been more surprised and pleased when she asked me to stay on. (I expect she knows what a discount I gave her on that Heppelwhite sofa.) Anyway, one of her guests was an Italian Count who was terribly nice though unattractive. We sat next to each other on that delicious ottoman in the library and chatted about Europe after the war: what a time that was! I told him I hadn't been back since 1948 but even so we knew quite a few people in common. Then, as always, the name Elliott Magren was mentioned. He's practically a codeword . . . if you know Elliott, well, you're on the inside and of course the Count (as I'd expected all along) knew Elliott and we exchanged bits of information about him, skirting carefully drugs and small boys because Mrs Blaine-Smith though she knows everyone (and everything) *never* alludes to that sort of thing in any way, such a relief after so many of the queen bees you run into. Hilda, for instance, who married the maddest designer in Los Angeles and gives, I am told, the crudest parties with everyone drunk from morning till night. (Must stop drinking so much: nothing *after* dinner, that's the secret . . . especially with my liver.)

We were discussing Elliott's apartment in the *Rue du Bac* and that marvelous Tchelichew that hangs over his bed when a little Englishman whose name I never did get, turned and said: did you know that Elliott Magren died last week? I must say it was stunning news, sitting in Mrs Blaine-Smith's library so far, far away. . . . The Count was even more upset than I (could he have been one of Elliott's numerous admirers?) I couldn't help recalling then that terrible time at Deauville when Elliott was arrested and I had had to put up bail for him and hire a lawyer, all in French! Suddenly everything came back to me in a flood: that summer, the affair with Hilda . . . and Helen (incidentally, just this morning got a Christmas card from Helen, the first word in years: a photograph of her husband and three ghastly children, all living in Toledo: well, I suppose she's happy). But what an important summer that was, the chrysalis burst at last which, I think, prepared me for all the bad luck later when I failed my doctorate and had to go to work in Steven's office. . . . And now Elliott's dead. Hard to believe someone you once knew is actually dead, not like the war where sudden absences in the roster were taken for granted. The Englishman told us the whole story. It seems Elliott was rounded up in a police raid on dope addicts in which a number of very famous people were caught, too. He was told to leave the country; so he piled everything into two taxicabs and drove to the Gare St Lazare where he took a train for Rome. He settled down in a small apartment off the Via Veneto. Last fall he underwent another series of shock treatment, administered by a quack doctor who cured him of drugs but lost his memory for him in the process. Aside from this, he was in good health and looked as young as ever except that for some reason he dyed his hair red . . . too mad! Then, last week, he made a date to go to the opera with a friend. The friend arrived . . . the door was open but, inside, there was no Elliott. The friend was particularly annoyed because Elliott often would not show up at all if, enroute to an appointment, he happened to see someone desirable in the street. I remember Elliott telling me once that his greatest pleasure was to follow a handsome stranger for hours on end through the streets of a city. It was not so much the chase which interested him as the identification he had with the boy he followed: he would become the other, imitating his gestures, his gait, becoming himself young, absorbed in a boy's life. But Elliott had followed no one that day. The friend finally found him face down in the bathroom, dead. When the autopsy was performed, it was discovered that Elliott had had a malformed heart, an extremely rare case, and he might have died as suddenly at any moment in his life . . . the drugs, the shock treatments and so on had contributed nothing to his death. He was buried Christmas day in the Protestant cemetery close to Shelley, in good company to the end. I must say I can't imagine him with red hair. . . . The Count asked me to have dinner with him tomorrow at the Colony(!) and I said I'd be delighted. Then Mrs Blaine-Smith told the most devastating story about the Duchess of Windsor in Palm Beach.

Find out about Helen Gleason's sphinxes. Call Bob about the keys to the back closet. Return Steven's copy of "Valmouth." *Find out the Count's name before dinner tomorrow.*

1956

JOAN O'DONOVAN

::

JOHNNIE

A STRIP OF CEMENT-COLOURED COUNCIL HOUSES GLUED TO THE LANDSCAPE, a general store, a chapel with a tin roof, a pub with a waste of marshy ground behind: that was Freighting village, and the R.A.F. station stood on a dead river bed behind it. It was October when I first saw it, and I thought it was the end of the world. Tannoy masts broke through the low, perpetual fogs, and nissen huts crouched to the foul gummy earth that creaked when you walked on it. Everything that could rust did. Rust flaked from our stove, even from our bedsteads; and the barbed wire round the women's quarters was like a tangle of brown cotton hung with water drops. The Michaelmas daisies by the Officers' Mess, the cabbages outside S.H.Q., all turned black and rotted. Viridian weeds sprang up overnight, and disappeared as suddenly. A smell of decay hung everywhere: you could detect it even through the fatty odours of the cookhouse and the acrid soot that drifted down from Sharrington three miles away. And we, too, decayed. We were a ground station, tucked away in a remote corner of a non-operational Command, and the war had forgotten us. We fought only mud, cold and monotony . . . oh that corroding monotony!

There was nowhere to go in Freighting, so when we went off camp it was usually to Sharrington. The town centre, built in the eighteen-eighties, was a dour section of cobbled streets, factories and public buildings in Lancashire-Greek. The suburbs were feminine and flimsy, a toast-rack of arch villas stretching out to the first spurs of the Pennines. To get to Sharrington from camp one had to pass through the worst of them, row after genteel row in avenues, closes, crescents, lanes and drives. Each house had pebble-dashed walls, coloured glass in the front door, a cramped bay window and a low sunray gate; and every pavement was pegged at regular intervals with saplings in wire-netting tubes. Only once in the three miles was the regularity broken, and that was at the main crossroads where a timbered road-house sprawled like a drunken zebra.

But in spite of its size there wasn't much to do when you got to Sharrington, except drink or go to chapel. The library and cafés were closed in the evening and on Sunday . . . our day off. There was a cinema, of course, and we filled it; but that was all.

I have never been so wretched in my life as I was when I first went to Freighting. I had come into the Service straight from school, apparently for the purpose of pasting strips of paper over obsolete Air Ministry Orders. At first, I tried to read in the hut after work; but it was hard to concentrate with the radio on, and unpopular to turn it off. After a while, I no longer even tried; I felt too gross and stupid. I even ceased to notice the ugliness which, in the beginning, had been an almost physical pain. I was too bored, too dull, too miserable to care.

It went on like this for two months. Then Johnnie came.

I worked in the Orderly Room under Corporal Jimpson, a slight, petulant man with an acid little voice and a hairline moustache. His favourite job was writing out notices, notices about anything, and underlining the bad-tempered parts in red and green ink. 'Discipline, N.A.A.F.I. Hours: Airmen may not . . . *repeat NOT* . . . use the Canteen between 08.30 and 13.00 hours.' That sort of thing. The walls were plastered with them: Discipline, Fire Watching; Discipline, Duty Roster, and so on. Actually, Jimpson wasn't in charge of the Orderly Room. He only ran it because the Sergeant in charge wasn't interested. The Sergeant . . . I never knew his name . . . an elderly man with a brush of grey hair and medal ribbons from the First War, spoke only occasionally, and then to swear at Jimpson. He spent most of his time in the lavatory playing his flute. It was odd, going out of the Orderly Room where Jimpson was carrying on like a keen Head Girl, to hear snatches of Mozart coming from the Airmen Only.

From the beginning, to make matters worse, Jimpson disliked me; and he never forgave me for correcting a grammar mistake on one of his notices. After that I was known as *Teacher.*

::

ONE MORNING, SHORTLY BEFORE CHRISTMAS, THERE WAS A GREAT COMMOTION in the Orderly Room. Sergeant had been posted overseas and a woman . . . a woman! . . . was coming to fill the vacancy. Such a thing was unheard of, and Jimpson, who, naturally enough, was furious, prophesied that Freighting would now go completely to pieces. No sooner had the news struck than the postings took place. The gay little tunes ceased, and Sergeant Paston arrived. She was a small, neat body with greying cropped hair and merry eyes, and a voice so authoritative that it made Jimpson's sound even sillier than it was. With her pert nose and compact shape, she reminded me of a drummer boy; and the men at once dubbed her 'the wee Sergeant'. Knowing Jimpson, I was sorry for her; but I could have saved my pity. She had been with us only three days when she asked him to take down his notices. We couldn't believe our ears; you could have heard a mouse cough: but Sergeant Paston got on with her work and Jimpson obeyed. From that moment I was her slave. I felt my eyes follow her round the room, and I found myself making excuses to go and speak to her.

One lunch hour I was on telephone duty when she came in. She glanced round, then offered me a cigarette.

"You know," she said, screwing up her eyes in a way she had, "I'm sure I've met you somewhere before."

I was sure she hadn't. I should have remembered a woman like her, and I said so.

"Funny," she said. "I'm not often wrong. What's your name?"

"Janet Motson, Sergeant."

"Janet." She seemed to think about it. "Rather young, aren't you?"

"Eighteen, Sergeant," I said, and blushed. She made me feel very young indeed.

"And you don't like Freighting?"

"No I don't!" I burst out. "It's mouldy!" which sounded so silly that we both laughed.

"Poor kid," she said.

"Are they all like this, Sergeant?" I asked humbly.

"No they're not, thank God! And drop the 'Sergeant' business unless there's a crowd, Janet. My friends call me 'Johnnie' and I'm sickening to hear it again." She picked up the book that I had been trying to hide under my blotter. "Don't worry; they won't leave you here long. They never do, or so we're told. What's this; Ibsen? They recommended it at school, did they?" She grinned maliciously when I nodded. "Well, well! Not good reading for Freighting; you must come along to my bunk one evening and borrow some books."

"I'd love to!" I said eagerly. "When?"

"All right, come this evening if you've nothing better to do. Do you like Blake? I've some drawings you might enjoy."

After that I spent most of my free time in Johnnie's bunk, and if the other sergeants disapproved they never said so, for Johnnie had a way of frightening people. She let me read there, even when she was out; and she lent me books. Such books! Proust, Huxley, Joyce, Rimbaud . . . it was like rising from the dead to a new world. My inertia slid from me; I had energy for ten. Johnnie found me an interesting job, too, and then the horrors fell into place. I couldn't believe that I was still in Freighting. What's more, when Jimpson was posted I was made a corporal. Johnnie must have put in a word for me with the C.O.; nothing else could have done it. I shall always be particularly grateful to her for that.

Weekends were still the dullest times, for every Saturday Johnnie went home to a flat she shared with a girl called Brenda who was in the N.F.S. She came back late Sunday evening, and I always waited for her in her bunk after roll call and made tea, and we talked well into Monday morning, often about Brenda. Brenda sounded a delightful, crazy creature, and I longed to meet her, and, on more than one occasion, fished for an invitation. I remember once saying, just too casually, that I should be in Town on leave and had a good mind to call.

Johnnie didn't say anything, but she grinned.

"I was only joking! Don't look at me like that, Johnnie! I was pulling your leg."

I looked obliquely at Johnnie, who was still grinning.

"Come if you like," she said; "come by all means, but you mustn't mind if Brenda's jealous."

"Jealous? Why should Brenda be jealous?"

"She might get ideas; you never know!"

I was hurt. It was a feeble excuse, I thought. Johnnie was obviously putting me off. After a few minutes I made some pretext or other for going.

"What, already?" Johnnie was surprised. "It isn't late."

"I've one or two things to see to," I said stiffly.

I had hoped that she would press me to stay. I gathered up my cigarettes and coat in offended silence. Johnnie let me get as far as the door.

"Well," she said, "now that you've made your gesture, suppose you tell me what's the matter."

She put a hand on my arm and drew me gently down to sit by her.

"Come on, out with it!"

I gazed aloofly across the room. For the life of me I didn't know, now, what the trouble was. I took refuge in a look of dignified inscrutability. Johnnie watched me for a few minutes, then reached for her book. I felt foolish, and burst suddenly into tears. Johnnie at once put her arm around me, and I leaned against her and sobbed.

"Was it Brenda?"

"I suppose it was, i-in a way."

I dried my eyes and rolled my head against her, sniffing. Johnnie gave me a cigarette, then moved a little away.

"I'm sorry," I said. "I really don't know what's the matter with me."

"No," she said drily, "I don't believe you do."

We smoked in silence for a time.

"Well," Johnnie said, "run along now and get your beauty sleep!"

I could have hit her.

::

IT HAPPENED THAT JOHNNIE AND I TOOK OUR LEAVE AT THE SAME TIME. I spent mine at home; she went to her flat. I wrote to her the first day, a long letter . . . eighteen pages, I think . . . all about Life and Literature, but she didn't answer. Altogether it was a most frustrating leave. There was no pleasing me. My parents were irritating; my friends seemed dull. I longed for Johnnie and her half-maternal affection, her fun and her talk. Often I woke in the night, stirred by dreams that I couldn't quite recall, and lay for hours thinking of her. It was with a feeling of holiday relief that I returned to Freighting.

I went straight to Johnnie's bunk, meaning to wait for her and have tea ready; but the light was on, and she was curled on her bed writing a letter. It was a moment I had longed for for nine days. She glanced up when I opened the door, but she did not speak.

"Hello!" I cried joyously. "Had a good leave?"

"Fine," said Johnnie. "How's yourself?"

"Frozen. How long've you been in? I didn't expect you till midnight."

"Since three. Have a drink?"

I stared. Johnnie pulled a bottle of gin from under her bed, slopped a little in a mug and pushed it across to me.

"Isn't it forbidden . . . drinking?" I asked tentatively.

As Johnnie didn't bother to answer, I took a gulp. It was horrible. I choked and began to cough.

"Girlie's first drink," Johnnie remarked without looking up.

Her tone deadened me. All the things I had saved up to tell her seemed suddenly trivial, and I could think of nothing else. I knew that I was being dull, yet I couldn't go. After about twenty minutes, Johnnie looked at her watch and yawned. "I'm going to take a bath and turn in. You needn't finish your drink if you don't like it."

She stood up and put her letter on the table. It was addressed to Brenda.

"Johnnie," I said, "have I done anything to offend you?"

"Darling," she said, "you couldn't offend me, even if you tried. Now be a good child and run along!"

I didn't see Johnnie on the Monday, as she was working with the Adjutant; but all day I brooded over her snub, and instead of going to her bunk in the evening I went to the pictures. It was a musical film about a factory girl who began by singing at the lathe, and ended by singing the same songs in feathers, diamonds, hunting pink, a swim suit and . . . finally . . . her wedding dress: and I cried all the way through it, and came out before the second film, which was a comedy. It was still early. I had nothing to do and nowhere to go; so I returned to camp and dropped into the Corporals' Room of the N.A.A.F.I. for a cup of tea. For once, it was deserted; almost the entire station was at an E.N.S.A. show in the gym. The emptiness filled me with horror. The tiny spread of carpet scarcely broke the ice of the lino, and the coals in the narrow grate were more smoke than heat. I was drinking perhaps my third cup of tea, wishing I hadn't been so quick to take offence, when the door blew open, letting in a gust of sleet, and a moment later an R.A.F. Corporal appeared, lugging a kit bag. His cap was pulled down, his collar turned up. The bit of face that showed was beefy with cold.

He grunted, and dumped the heavy bag by the door; then he pulled off his cap and came over to the fire, shaking himself like a dog.

"What a night!" he grumbled. "My God, I'm frozen!"

"Posting?" I asked, though I wasn't interested.

"Yes. Does this hole live down to its reputation?"

"Easily."

He slapped his hands and held them in the smoke.

"Well, what's the tea like?"

"Awful."

But the rest of the evening wasn't so bad; in fact, I realised afterwards that I'd enjoyed it. Tim . . . that was his name; he was twenty-four . . . became quite friendly once he was warm, and I liked him. We found that we had quite a lot in common, and when we said good night he asked me to have dinner with him in Sharrington the following evening. I was enormously flattered.

I got back to my hut to find a note pinned to my pillow. Johnnie asked me not to go over that evening, as she had a headache and was going to bed early. I didn't give it a second thought.

Again, the next day, Johnnie was in the Adjutant's office; and by the end of the evening I should scarcely have noticed if she'd been posted. I had fallen in love.

::

THE FOLLOWING AFTERNOON, JOHNNIE CAME OVER TO SEE ME ABOUT SOME lists I was compiling for the C.O.

"You rat!" she murmured amiably, bending over my typewriter. "I made tea last night. Where did you get to?"

I didn't say anything. When she put her face so near mine, I saw that it was coarser than I remembered; and her collar wasn't clean.

"Anyway I'll expect you tonight, shall I?"

She touched my hand as she spoke, and for some reason it offended me and I drew away. Johnnie appeared not to notice.

"Very well," I said stiffly; "if you're sure I shan't be in the way."

Then I warmed to her again. I hadn't told her about Tim. I was longing to tell someone.

But I didn't get a chance that night. As soon as I was inside the door she burst out petulantly:

"Thank God you've come! I nearly went cuckoo!"

I threw my cap on to the cupboard and sat down.

"You weren't very inviting."

"You shouldn't have taken any notice; you know me! God, I've never been so depressed!"

"Poor Johnnie!"

She lit a cigarette and looked at the blacked-out window.

"What a hole!"

"Oh, it could be worse."

I bent down to tie up my shoelace while I thought up an impressive opening. I was still searching for the right words when she said, "As a matter of fact, as you've probably gathered, my leave went wrong."

I straightened my back and looked at her. Our leave seemed so long ago.

"That's right!" she cried shrilly. "Look at me! I'm forty-seven!"

"You don't look it, Johnnie," I said embarrassed. "Anyway that's not old . . . not really old. You're only middle-aged."

"Oh Christ!" she said, and laughed.

I didn't know what else to say. I daren't suggest that she went to the M.O. for a tonic.

"I'm getting a bit of a phobia about age." She scowled at her nails. "Silly, of course. One disgusting old woman is no worse than another."

"Sorry," she said at last.

"I didn't know you were feeling like this or I'd have looked in last night," I lied. "I mean, I just assumed you'd had a grand leave and hated being back."

"You know Brenda?"

I nodded. Johnnie went on smoking.

"Well," she said, "that's the trouble."

I waited.

"Oh for God's sake say something!" she snapped. "Even if it's only that you're shocked!"

"What do you mean?"

"Brenda!" she said savagely. "Brenda, Brenda, Brenda! Brenda and the barmaid, Brenda and the chorus girl, Brenda and her best friend the schoolteacher! And now Brenda and . . . oh, some bloody woman!"

I went on staring at her. It had never occurred to me before that she was jealous of Brenda's friends. Johnnie made a helpless gesture.

"And to think you've read Proust!"

I drank the tea she pushed across. It was no good. Everything I said seemed to be wrong.

"Then I don't suppose you'll be going to the flat this weekend?" I said, just to make conversation.

"You'd think not, wouldn't you?" she said lightly. "But I probably shall."

We were working overtime the next few evenings, so I didn't see Johnnie to talk to till late Sunday night. Tim and I had late passes, and it was after midnight when I hurried across to the bunk to see if Johnnie was still awake. I found her in bed, reading, a mug of cold tea and an ashtray full of stubs by her side. She raised her eyebrows at me when I opened the door.

"Come in, come in!" She spoke with elaborate politeness. "What a charming surprise!"

I felt suddenly guilty. It was the first time I had failed to make her tea on a Sunday evening since I had known her.

"I'm sorry I'm late, Johnnie," I said, "but Tim . . ."

"Tim?" she asked sharply.

"Yes, you see I . . . we . . . it wasn't the moment to tell you the other evening, and we've been so busy at work . . . well, good lord, I don't have to tell *you* that! . . ." I sank down. "Golly!" I said breathlessly. "I'm tired! But oh, Johnnie . . . we . . . Tim and I . . . we've been to Lichfield. I haven't enjoyed myself so much for years!"

"You might put the kettle on," said Johnnie. "You were saying?"

I lit the stove, my spirits subsiding like suds under a cold tap.

"And who is this *Tim?*" asked Johnnie. "Or mayn't I ask?"

"Only a corporal I met in the N.A.A.F.I." I mumbled.

Johnnie lit another cigarette. My words rang foolishly in my ears. Then I remembered Johnnie's troubles, and forced myself to ask if she had had a good weekend.

"Fine, fine!" she said. "I spent it in the Cumberley with a pick-up."

"A pick-up, Johnnie?"

"Yes, darling; a nice girl. No longer young, perhaps, but good enough for those of us who haven't had any luck in the N.A.A.F.I.!"

She spat the words at me as if they were acid.

"Don't be so mean!" I shouted, stung. "You could go out with dozens of men if you wanted to. The Adj is always pestering you; you've told me so yourself. So's Charlie, and the S.W.O. Oh there are dozens!"

"Oh, dozens!" Johnnie mimicked to the ceiling. *"Duzzins!"*

I made fresh tea, and refilled her cup in silence. I was trembling.

"I wish," she said at last in a low voice, "that at least you cared enough to quarrel."

What could I say? I sat there wondering how soon I could decently go.

"How was Brenda?" I asked when I could stand the silence no longer.

"Haven't I as good as told you," Johnnie screamed, "that the new bitch was in my half of the bed!"

She dropped her head to her knees and began to sob.

I put my arms around her, patting her shoulder, squeezing her tightly. After a while she quieted and lay back again, staring at the ceiling. I gave her a cigarette. It was late . . . gone one . . . and the silence of the camp seemed to ring round us like a bell.

"Pass my wallet," Johnnie said suddenly. "No, on the table."

She handed me a snap, a photograph of a little boy.

"My son. It's his birthday."

"Your *son?* He's lovely!" I added quickly.

She held out her hand and replaced the picture without a glance.

"I haven't seen him since I took this. That was ten years ago."

I made a noise in my throat.

"Do you know . . ." Johnnie was grinning. "I even had a white wedding to please my mother!" She looked hard at me and sat up. "I don't believe you think that's funny either!" she cried in despair.

"Oh Johnnie!" I was tremendously relieved. "I thought at first you meant you weren't married!"

::

THIS HAPPENED NEARLY TWELVE YEARS AGO. I'M TRYING TO SEE IT AS I SAW it then. It's easy enough to remember how Johnnie was, but I'm a stranger to myself. However . . .

::

IT WAS THE FOLLOWING WEEK, I THINK, THAT I HEARD THAT I WAS POSTED. This was a shock. I had got used to Freighting; and there was Tim.

I had dinner with Tim on my last evening; and after I had said goodbye to him I went to say goodbye to Johnnie. She had obviously been waiting a long time for me, but she greeted me cheerfully and got up at once to make tea. The kettle was steaming over a low flame.

"Sit down; you must be tired out." She threw me a pack of cigarettes. "Put that in your pocket; you'll need them tomorrow."

"Oh no, you keep them," I urged. "I've got plenty. Tim managed to scrounge a hundred."

"And mayn't I give you a present too?"

"Of course," I said awkwardly. "I didn't mean it like that. Thanks very much."

"Tea up!" Johnnie cried.

Johnnie lounged on her bed. She was wearing a new housecoat; and she had too much make-up on, I thought, though, in spite of it, she looked tired and strained. But she was in good form, full of the wild, improbable chatter that had so captivated me at first. I was amused for a little while; and then I began to feel uncomfortable. I couldn't detect what was wrong, but I knew something was. I became embarrassed, then tongue-tied; and the more silent I fell, the more feverishly Johnnie talked. Then, suddenly, she stopped. We looked at each other. It was like a physical shock.

"Am I boring you?"

"Don't be absurd!" I said loudly.

We were very still. The silence sang at us. I fidgeted with my feet to break the tension.

"Don't be frightened."

"Frightened?" I felt rather foolish, for oddly enough I was frightened.

"I'm lonely, that's all."

"Cheer up!" I said heartily. "I'll write."

Johnnie looked away.

"Write!"

And that's all Johnnie would say. She went dumb. She wouldn't even say goodbye. We sat in complete silence for nearly five minutes: it seemed like a day. I stared at the blackout until my eyes ached, and I listened to the wind getting up on the marsh. It was a wet night. I could picture the slanting wires of rain, flashing as the wind shifted. I could have drawn the view from that window, I knew it so well . . . the parade ground, the decontamination sheds, the R.A.F. quarters behind: and a warmth stole over me as I thought of those huts and knew that somewhere there Tim was asleep.

And then I became aware of Johnnie's breathing. It was laboured, as though the act itself were a conscious burden. I looked at her as she lay glaring at a spot on the ceiling, and I remembered Freighting as it had been before she came, and myself as I had been. Affection and gratitude welled up in me, but I was helpless. The book she had been reading lay face downward on the bed, and I asked her what it was. My question broke in pieces on the air.

I sat for a moment longer, then I got up.

"Johnnie, please!"

She continued to stare at the ceiling. I moved to the door.

"Goodbye, then, Johnnie."

And that, I felt, was the end of Johnnie. I was oppressed by something bigger than I could understand. I couldn't get this last impression out of my mind, and it mocked the gallant little sergeant. I felt deeply, illogically, guilty.

All the next day this sense of desolation was with me; then, the following evening, when I got to Woldham, my new station, I found a telegram waiting:

'Best luck darling' I read, 'wizard times ahead hope we meet soon what about leave all love Johnnie.'

My mood cracked like an eggshell. I screwed the wire up angrily and threw it away.

1958

HELEN ESSARY ANSELL

THE THREESOME

CLOVER AND JOEY MET ONE MORNING ON THE HOTEL BEACH. THE SAND LAY in the shape of a giant cuticle, enclosed on the inside by a wall of palms and on the outside by a submerged wall of coral. The bay between the beach and the reef reflected the stone porches and white awnings of the hotel perched like Noah's Ark on the rocks above.

The waiters had been flapping out white breakfast cloths over the round iron tables on the dining porch when Clover, in her bathing suit, ran down the hewn steps to the sand. She stopped abruptly, her face pinched tight with disappointment. Someone was there before her. She looked unkindly at him as he knelt with his diving hoses by the hem of the water. She had thought she would be alone on the beach and here was this boy, foolishly squatting there with his apparatus. She walked down to the edge of the water, and ignoring his bent, busy form, scooped up a shimmering handful of sea and wet her legs with it. He stopped what he was doing and examined her from under his bleached brows, then he said, "Hi," in a cheerful voice that grated on the soft morning like the metal screws he was untwisting.

Every morning after that she went down before breakfast and every morning he was there before her. She would stand still and frown at him, her close cap of curls burning red-gold in the sun, and her white skin, which never tanned, glowing peach-colored on her straight narrow back. Once she came an hour earlier than usual, but from the railing on the dining porch she saw him below on the sand, a single dark bug in a bin of sugar. He never failed to say good morning and she could not arm herself against his friendliness. Soon she was greeting him first, and one morning she filled a cup with drinking water from a table pitcher, carried it down and poured it on his hot back. After that they were friends; and with the clinks of the silverware being placed and the spurts of native voices coming down over the ledge, they worked together on his air hoses. He taught her to dive in the clear bay where the shallow coral caves held bright waving plants, and where vast sheets of tiny fish flashed through the filtered sun that pierced far into the water, shattering into fragments on the sandy bottom. Sometimes they spent whole mornings and afternoons together and the days were somehow spoiled if one of them did not appear.

Then Margaret came and everything was changed.

::

EVERYONE KNEW MARGARET FEW AND SOUGHT HER OUT FOR HER WITTY conversation, yet everyone was a little afraid of her. Her smile was beautiful and quick but it always rose with the same uplift of the mouth and always fell into the same hard mold, where her features lay trapped and immovable. She danced and drank with all the young men but the music could not loosen her and the wine could not flush her cheeks. Of all the men who had tried to kiss her none had succeeded more than once, and of the women who had tried to speak intimately with her none had succeeded at all.

One morning Margaret swung unexpectedly onto the dining porch to a table near the rail, and ordered breakfast. She sat upright and reserved on her chair, her face smooth, expressionless, her large, hard-muscled body moving slowly and deliberately as she turned the sheets of the morning paper. Over the open sheets she looked down to the beach that glowed pink in the early light.

She saw the figures of Joey and Clover as they moved together and she watched their two bodies as they stood and gestured and bumped together, the one very white, the other a dark cherry-brown. They were wet and the light shone off them as they raised their arms and bent their backs. The boy and the girl looked very much alike, curly brown head next to curly white head; and she watched them, her own head tilting toward them. Her eyes, plain brown eyes with brows like short crayon marks, eagerly took them in; Margaret was outspoken and confident, but she had eyes as timid and darting as little mice. Like small creatures that play dead, they could freeze under the enemy gaze of another. But now those timid eyes were bright and wide open and shining as brown marbles as she sat alone on the porch gazing over the paper at the beach and the figures there.

She had not seen either of them before. The girl had not been to any of the dances or buffets and the boy . . . he was very young.

After breakfast she put on her bathing suit and went down to the beach.

She could not swim, for the water had always filled her with an unreasonable sort of terror, but she spent hours lying lazy in the sun. Now she opened her chair on an empty spot of sand and stretched out on it, her long animal limbs overspreading the narrow aluminum frame, her straight dark hair hanging neatly over the curve of her broad bare shoulders. She put lotion on her bamboo-colored skin and closed her eyes. But the voices of the two youngsters lifted now and then over the sand and she was forced to look at them. They were quite close to her and she lay as quiet and engrossed as a bird-watcher.

The boy was as beautiful as the girl. He was small and smooth-limbed and shone as if he were made of polished wood, his chest hard-nippled and drum-tight, and the muscles in his arms thin and long like half-filled stretched balloons. His eyes, pale blue with blond lashes, were petaled flowers growing in his dark skin. He was a silent boy, his mind seemed fixed on the beautiful world of his little coral bank where there was no sound but only looking and touching; and his existence in the world was as hushed as the sea grass waving against the porous cliffs.

Margaret watched them go into the water and in twenty minutes come out again, unstrapping their little air tanks as they splashed up onto the dry sand. She watched them sit down, crossing their legs, one pair pale, the other dark, and she listened to the first words she had heard them say.

"It's too bad we haven't got a skiff," said Clover. "Then we could go out to the far reef where the big coral is."

"Who could give us a skiff?"

"I don't know anyone who could. I've never seen anyone but fishermen in them. I don't know any fishermen."

They were silent, looking out to the far ring of coral that divided the bay from the sea. White rolling waves broke against the rock that lifted its forehead an inch above the water line.

Margaret, too, looked out at the bank, her eyes almost glinting with her absorption in the two figures. Then she extricated her legs from the chair, unfolding them as a deer's legs unfold, and approached them across the sand.

"If you would like to go to the banks," she said in her deep quick voice, before she reached them, "I'll ride you out in my outboard."

Their faces were blank for a moment as they looked at her standing tall and square above them; then they accepted and thanked her in one gesture and leaped up to get the equipment.

The three of them walked down the beach toward the small pier at the end, Margaret striding a little ahead. And that is how they are remembered. People who come back to the hotel every season remember them clearly; they remember the threesome, always walking together. The tall one a mystery, especially her leaving so soon afterward and the children, not telling a thing, and the skipper as silent as any nigger ever was.

Margaret took them out and waited in the boat while they dove and dove again, shimmering bodies in the green sea. Then she brought them back.

"If you would like to go tomorrow, I'd be glad to take you again."

So they went the next day, too. And a third day. And it went on that way until it was no longer Joey and Clover. It was Joey and Clover and Margaret. The threesome.

::

THEY WENT MANY PLACES TOGETHER THAT SUMMER. THEY RODE BIKES TO nearby beaches, flying along narrow shore roads in their bathing suits, with blankets and shirts bundled over the back wheels. They drove in Margaret's open sports car to more distant towns, then left it and walked through the crowded smelly market streets, with Joey's white head bouncing along above the bright bandanna-bound skulls of the natives.

The gatherings at the hotel suffered from Margaret's absence. "Why don't you join us any more, Marg? Surely the two children can't keep you occupied all the time." But Margaret only answered with a shrug, impatient to be in the car, for they were starting out on an overnight trip to a coral formation on the other side of the island.

When Margaret finally bundled into the driver's seat, she jabbed the gas pedal with her bare foot as if it were a spur into a horse's flank, and they lurched off with Margaret's black flag of hair flapping over the thick bundle of dust they dragged behind them.

The trip did not at first seem to be any different from others they had taken together. The roads were the same—unpaved, strewn with natives on foot and on bicycles and in donkey carts, always inching along in the middle where it was dry and where there were not so many mosquitoes. Margaret honked at them as she always did and swore and stood up on the seat and yelled at them until they sidled off into the ditches and let her pass. Clover wore her same yellow scarf and Joey took his same position in the back seat, gazing silently between the two girls, his dark arms crossed on the seat in front, his chin on his folded hands. It was just another trip where they would eat their sandwiches together from wax-paper bags and sleep together on the car seats or on a blanket on the beach; and Clover and Joey would go out together in a rented boat to dive. That is how it had been, and this trip would not be different.

They arrived at the edge of the long narrow beach at nightfall, and Clover and Joey jumped over the doors of the car for the water, stripping off their shirts as they ran. Margaret followed slowly with the towels and prepared to sit on the sand.

"Margaret," Clover called, spreading her arms on the waist-deep water, "come in tonight. It's perfectly all right. No drops. No holes. Just come in and float with us."

Margaret shook her head as always and spread out a towel. But Joey was out of the water and beside her, touching her wrist with a warm wet hand. "Margaret, you have no idea how wonderful it is. Especially at night. Just once you must get more than your toes wet." His voice was tense and eager. She laughed and bent to sit down, but Clover was beside her. "Margaret, you must, you must," she coaxed, and the two took her by the arms and led her down to the edge of the sea. She was laughing and afraid, pulling back from their hands, but they led her straight in and up to her thighs.

"My shirt," she said, "wait, my shirt," turning to run back, but Joey lifted his arms, glistening in the dark, and unbuttoned it. She stood quietly and let him. He did it very delicately, taking it off her shoulders and carrying it up to the beach. Then they took her in up to her waist.

"You must learn to float," Clover said. "Lie on your back and we'll hold you."

Margaret's face broke its crust and was terrified.

"Margaret, the water will hold you," Clover encouraged, her voice soft, her round delicate face saddened and touched by Margaret's fear. "You mustn't be afraid."

"You weigh nothing in the water," Joey said. "You can't sink."

Gently they bent her backward and reached their arms under her. Her feet rose, she slapped the water, her neck craned. But they held her firmly and soon she was quiet and floating in their arms. Their faces looking down at her were gentle and smiling. The curve of their shoulders and the roundness of their wet cheeks and the dark hollows of their shadowed eyes in the night were almost identical. They could have been twins, either boys or girls, but for the small round bosom of the one facing the flat hard breastplates of the other.

Margaret, spread long between them, was all pale head on the black water, hair out to one side, her throat arched. Her eyes were half closed and her face was no longer strained with fear. Her lips were smiling a smile so soft, so vulnerable, that both Joey and Clover in the same movement reached out their hands toward her head to touch her floating hair and the wet nape of her neck.

Later, after they had eaten, they built a fire of brown fronds from the palms and dried themselves around it, kneeling on the spread blanket side by side. Margaret was much the largest of the three, as tall as a man, her sleek arms glowing orange in the firelight as she lifted them to comb her hair. And when the light went down she seemed to loom up like the slender tree she sat against, and her voice as she talked came soft and deep, as comforting and strong in the still night as a distant thunder roll. Dancing had never loosened her nor wine brought flush to her cheeks, but leaning damp and sleepy against the tall tree she was curved and heavy and her face shone warm long after the firelight had faded from it.

Joey lay on his side next to her as she and Clover talked, slowly and softly, about nothing in particular. The two had fallen to talking like that often, saying nothing either could remember later, but using the words like patches for a quilt, a quilt they made only to have something warm to pull about themselves. And Joey lay and listened to the sound and not the words, lay and listened and never took his eyes off Margaret. He turned to her boldly, shielded by the dark, and filled himself with looking at her as if he were the coral and she were the sea. He studied her face with its timid eyes and smooth square jaw; he looked long at her shoulders and the full breasts that moved slightly and softly with her breathing, that burned warm and half bare in the firelight. He watched her hands flex and shift and flatten on her thighs as she talked, broad and hard like the beautiful, calloused, long-used hands of a guitarist or a wood-carver.

He lay close to these hands, and once when they became still with the silence of an ended sentence, he reached over and touched the ridge of the knuckles, withdrawing his arm, but only halfway, so it lay against her thigh.

She looked down at him. His body lay curved and breathing full, with his face hidden in his shoulder. She bent slowly over him and tried to see his eyes.

"Are you asleep, Joey?" she said.

"Margaret," he whispered, as if he had not heard her, and his voice was trembling.

"What's the matter, Joey?" she asked, encircling his shoulders with her long arm.

"You're beautiful."

There was a hush, with Joey's words echoed in it, and Clover's mouth opening in the shadows. Margaret looked across at the girl, as though sensing the tiny twitch of the white cheek, then she reached down smoothly and took Joey up in her arms. His eyes were closed tight as he pressed his face against her. She rubbed her hand lightly over the white hair and the hill of his shoulder blade and the sharp cliff of the hip and the downy slope of the flank. He trembled and clung to her.

"You funny little boy," she whispered to him, "to tremble like that," and there was awe and sweetness in her voice.

::

THE NEXT DAY CLOVER AND JOEY EXPLORED THE REEF AND MARGARET waited, lying flat on the sand. Joey appeared on the surface before Clover and waded up quietly to where the girl lay stretched out, long and still. She had fallen asleep and her hand had slipped down by the side of her head. He scooped up a little sand and kneeled down to sprinkle it on her shoulder and wake her; but his hand remained suspended holding back the grains, and he crouched there with his long white forelock burning in the sun, the flower eyes wide and still, as if even their blinking might waken her. He crouched with his haunches raised, crouched in the sleeping heat of Margaret's body, bending close, locking his legs so the muscle bands stood in ridges. He was suspended there when Margaret's mouse eyes opened and met his, and they looked at one another. She lay, not speaking, as if in her sleep she had prepared herself to find him there.

"I was going to wake you," he said softly, and his voice rippled over her like fingers. "I was going to wake you with this sand, but here you are already awake."

Margaret lay with the white-headed boy close above her, and did not move even to blink when he spoke, and only closed her eyes slowly, as if she were in pain, when he bent and softly, quickly kissed her on the lips.

When their heads moved apart, Clover was there, her full pale legs apart, her air tank dripping in the sand.

No one said anything. The sandwiches were brought out and they ate. They talked about the reef. That is how it went for the rest of the trip. They never spoke of the new thing that had slipped in with them on that broad and deserted beach; but Joey never let Margaret out of his sight, looking quickly behind him sometimes to see if she was there, and Margaret only smiled, her face a little sad, exchanging no looks with his ardent eyes, but glancing now and then at Clover when her back was turned. And Clover had become very silent. She followed closely in their footsteps, her eyes quick and guarded, her face pinched and nearly blank. She no longer kept alive the conversations with Margaret, but answered questions quickly and in monotone like a morose and jealous servant girl.

::

TWO DAYS AFTER THEY ARRIVED BACK AT THE HOTEL THEY WERE PREPARING to leave again. Margaret had found a gentleman with a small launch, and she had persuaded him to loan it to her with its native skipper for the weekend. So on an airless, cloudless morning in August they filed aboard, the three of them in a line, with Margaret in the lead. The boat was old, with a stout varnished deck and a pilothouse that perched on the top of the squat cabin like a black top hat. There was a stove, a tiny sink-hole and four cotlike beds below. The skipper confined himself exclusively to his steerage, sleeping there and sitting unsmiling at the wheel with a bottle of rum and a grimy hunk of pork on the ledge beside him.

Clover, Joey and Margaret clustered at the broad stern the first day out, sunning themselves and gazing at the misty colorless horizon of the open sea. They spoke little, but the silence was not sleepy and languid as it had once been. It had a hard listening quality. It was a silence that sat poised and pulsing, ready to leap out.

"When will you be going home, Margaret?" Joey asked, swinging his legs over the low sill of the stern.

Clover looked around to see her face when she answered.

"Oh, the beginning of September sometime. It's a long way off."

"Not so long," Clover mumbled, and turned her head away.

"Shall I be seeing you sometime?" he asked.

"You live across the country from each other," Clover broke in sharply.

"I can write, then," Joey said, a spot of anger on either cheek, his eyes frowning into the surging foam below.

Clover rose and without looking at either of them took her towel and disappeared to the bow of the boat.

"She's tiresome," Joey said. "Tiresome and bad-tempered. We never used to quarrel . . . before; on the beach in the mornings, she never gave me those looks. She's very peculiar." He brooded over it a few moments, then came and knelt beside Margaret, smiling shyly at her as she sat staring at the deck, her arms around her knees.

"Don't bother about her," he said. "She's just put out because I'd rather sit with you than take her diving."

Margaret nodded abstractedly.

"Margaret," he said with sudden timidity in his voice, "Margaret, you do like me, don't you?"

"Of course, Joey." Her voice was clear and expressionless.

"It's only . . . it's only you seem rather peeved with me at times, rather cold." There was a silence while he waited for her to say something. Then he blurted quickly and earnestly, "I'm almost seventeen, Margaret. Seventeen is getting on. Seventeen is not so young."

"Of course it isn't, Joey," she said and looked him in the eyes. He put his hand out to touch her face, but she was getting up and slowly tossing her dark hair back like a fisherman casting his net. "Come on, Joey," she said, looking down at him kneeling there. "Come on and I'll fix us some dinner if you'll light the stove."

::

THE NIGHT WAS DARK AND MOONLESS. THE TINY STARS GAVE NO LIGHT, AND the boat had electric sockets without bulbs. Everyone went to bed early, and the old vessel swayed and creaked gently at its anchor in the black, smooth-rolling sea. The sense of wakefulness in the cabin mixed with the smell of sleep. No bed curtain moved for many hours, but sometime in the early-morning blackness there was a rustle and a crack of cot slats, then in the inky closeness, the presence of someone in the middle of the floor. A lithe figure moved noiselessly to Margaret's far bunk and pulled back the mosquito netting. The hands folded back the sheet from the broad shadow of Margaret's form and the shadow raised up.

"Who's that!"

"Hush, Margaret . . ."

At the sound of the voice Margaret was very still, sinking slowly down again.

"It's you . . ." she said, and the sound was part of the boat's sounds, was part of the washing, dripping sighs of the wooden hull. And the voice, as it lived in the narrow space between their two faces, was another part of the night, a whisper of water and air.

"Margaret . . . tomorrow we dock."

"Yes."

"And soon you'll be going back home."

"Yes," and the voice was faint in the shadows.

"Margaret . . ." and the sound was a weeping sound. "I came to tell you . . . I may never be able to tell you . . ."

An arm went up from the bunk and silenced the voice.

"You don't need to tell me."

The sea sounds hid the long soft cry of "Margaret . . . Margaret," from a throat overflowing and breathless, and the darkness hid the movement of the head and shoulders as they closed down upon Margaret's breast.

::

WHEN THE DAWN CAME GRAY INTO THE CABIN, THREE COTS SAGGED UNDER the weight of three outstretched forms. Two slept, but the largest, tall as a man, lay awake. Her hair hung disheveled on her forehead and she stared at the ceiling with fixed, unblinking eyes. She lay until the rumble and scrape of the motors started and rattled the floor under her. Then she rose, put on her suit and went out onto the stern. The boat was turning toward shore and the white carpet of foam had made almost a complete semicircle. The skipper stood in the black steerage, fingering the sliding wheel in his hands. Margaret looked up at him a full minute, but his long black back remained motionless.

At seven o'clock, with the sun full in the dingy cabin, Joey stretched and swung off his cot and noticed immediately that Margaret was not there. He went on deck and walked around it and came back to look once more in Margaret's bed.

"Clover!" He jogged her roughly, his face fallen with astonishment. "Clover, Margaret's not on the boat." The girl wavered in front of him, then slowly her body stiffened as she understood his words.

"Not in bed?" she asked, staring at the empty cot. "Not in bed?"

"I've gone up and back," he shouted, trying to make her understand, pulling at her to take her out on deck with him, but she broke away, heading for the cot. Joey caught her arm again and then dragged her out of the cabin and once around the deck until they stopped below the skipper. Without letting her go, he called, "Hey, hey, up there! Stop the engine. Cut off the engine! Margaret's not on the boat. Margaret's fallen off the boat!"

The engine died abruptly and the black man came down the ladder and all three of them went to the rail and stared over, four white hands clutching till their knuckles threatened to burst the skin, two huge black hands holding lightly, uncomprehending.

"Turn the boat around," Clover said, her voice small and rattling like a pebble being shaken in a can. The Negro's eyes popped out at them, fearful, as if they might be crazy. But there had been three of them yesterday and there were only two now; and he ran back up the ladder and ground the engine. They swung slowly around and started back through their foam path. Clover and Joey hung onto the bow and for twenty-five minutes there was nothing but chopped green sea and the heaving horizon with a low smear of land on it. The two faces thrust over the rail were wet and dripping with wave spray. They looked from one side of the water to the other. Then, beside him, Clover let her arms fall and she slid down on the deck.

"She can't swim, she can't swim at all. She'd have gone under—she'd have drowned by now. She'd have drowned . . ." The bronze head wavered and fell down on the varnished deck, and she sobbed.

But Joey kept his body arched out in the spray, not hearing her, not turning from the green sea; and he was the first to see the dark thing in the water, bobbing off to the side like a log. A long dark log rolling up and over the close waves, a log with two branches sticking out on either side.

He wheeled around on the deck and raised his arms to signal, but the skipper had seen already and had cut the engine and was sidling the boat over.

Joey wrenched Clover up by the arm and took her over to the rail as they puttered up gently. It was Margaret, lying on the waves, her arms outstretched. Joey was weeping now, standing, his white head bowed on his shiny chest, weeping for Margaret, who lay dead like a log.

The skipper leaned over the side rail and looked, his pink-lipped mouth open, his neck craned. Then slowly, loudly he declared, "She's not dead. She's floatin'. She's floatin' out there."

He ran on rubbery legs and got a rope ladder and climbed over the side, stretching far out for her. He grabbed her around the waist with his arm and hoisted her against him, climbing the ladder slowly, straining with her weight.

"Lawd, this is a big girl," he panted. "This is the biggest girl I ever saw."

Speechless, the two children followed him down to the cabin, where he put her on the bunk.

"She's not full awake, but she's not dead," he said, looking down at her. "No water inside either, 'cause she's breathin' easy." Then he turned and went up to his little steerage and started the motors. Joey and Clover did not leave Margaret once, but sat on the floor and watched her chest rise and fall with her breathing, as if it would stop if they took their eyes away. Clover moved once to cover the cold legs with an army blanket, then sat down again like a sleepwalker.

Margaret was the first of them to speak. She looked at them with washed, blank eyes as the boat finally slid up against the hotel dock.

"I float too well," she said, her voice strangely calm and natural coming from the mouth that opened in her gray face like a small black hole. "I tried but I can't sink. I just float. I can't do anything but float and float. If you hadn't taught me to float, you'd be Clover and Joey again. You'd be on the beach again, Joey and Clover, in the morning before breakfast." She closed her eyes and was still.

Then the black man came down and lifted her up from the cot. Even against his tremendous chest she looked large. He carried her out, with Clover and Joey behind. Clover walked ahead of Joey, her eyes on the one arm and the two legs that hung down limp as the skipper stepped up with her onto the dock. People were walking curiously toward them. Two beach boys in white shorts, and a woman, and three men in bathing suits. Clover saw them coming. They would crowd around. They would lead the Negro off to the hotel and perhaps call an ambulance. Clover's eyes looked after the limp legs and the one dangling arm, looked after the wet head on the black shoulder; and after the pale, tightly closed lips that had soothed her when she had cried "Margaret . . . Margaret" in the dark, whispering cabin.

1961

INGEBORG BACHMANN

A STEP TOWARDS GOMORRAH

THE LAST GUESTS HAD LEFT. ONLY THE GIRL IN THE BLACK SWEATER AND RED skirt was still sitting there, had not got up with the others. She's drunk, thought Charlotte, as she came back into the room, she wants to talk to me alone, perhaps she has something to tell me, and I'm dead tired. She shut the door in which she had been hesitantly standing to give the last guest a chance to notice that it was open, and picked up from the sideboard an ashtray over whose edge little films of ash trickled. In the room: the disarranged chairs, a crumpled table napkin on the floor, the hazy air, the devastation, the emptiness after the onslaught. She felt sick. She was still holding a burning cigarette in her hand and tried to stub it out in the pile of stumps and ashes. Now it was smouldering. She blinked across at the armchair in the corner, at the dangling hair with its reddish glint, at the red skirt which, spread out like a bullfighter's cape, fell over the girl's legs and in a semicircle covered feet, carpet and chair and trailed on the floor. More than the girl herself, she saw all these many clashing red tones in the room: the light that had to pass through a red shade with a flickering pillar of dust in front of it; a row of red book backs behind it on a shelf; the rumpled, wild skirt and the duller red hair. Just for a moment everything was as it could never be again—just for once the world was in red.

The girl's eyes became part of it, two moist, dark, drunken objects that met the woman's eyes.

Charlotte thought to herself: I'll say I feel ill and must go to bed. I have only to bring out this one polite, appropriate sentence to make her go. She must go. Why doesn't she go? I'm tired out. Why do guests never leave? Why didn't she leave with the others?

But the moment was past, she had stood there silent for too long; she walked quietly on into the kitchen, cleaned the ashtrays, quickly washed her face, washed away the long evening, all the smiling, the attentiveness, the strain of having eyes everywhere. Before her eyes there remained the wide skirt with its red death for which the big drums should have been beaten.

She's going to tell me a story. Why me? She is staying because she wants to talk to me. She has no money or can't settle down in Vienna, comes from down south, a Slovene, half Slovene, from the border, anyhow from the south, her name sounds like that too, Mara. There must be something, a request, a story, some story with which she wants to cheat me of my sleep. Of course she must be alone too much in Vienna or she has got mixed up in some affair or other. I must ask Franz about this girl tomorrow.

Tomorrow!

Charlotte started, quickly memorized her duties: meet Franz at the station tomorrow morning, set the alarm, be fresh, rested, give the impression of being pleased. There was no more time to lose. She quickly filled two glasses with mineral water and carried them into the room, handed one to the girl, who drank it in silence and then, as she put away the glass, said brusquely: 'So he's coming back tomorrow.'

'Yes,' said Charlotte. Offended too late, she added: 'Who?'—It was too late.

'He goes away often. So you're alone a lot.'

'Sometimes, not often. You know that.'

'Do you want me to go?'

'No,' said Charlotte.

'I had the feeling that the man who talked such a lot would also have liked to say . . .'

'No,' said Charlotte.

'I had the feeling . . .' Mara screwed up her mouth.

Charlotte was angry, but she still answered politely: 'No, definitely not.' She stood up. 'I'll make us some coffee. And then I'll call a taxi.'

Now she had managed to get out the sentence, she had solid ground under her feet again, had indicated to the girl that she would pay for the taxi, and above all she had shown that she objected to her remark.

Mara jumped up and grabbed Charlotte's arm.

'No,' she said, 'I don't want that. You've been into the kitchen often enough tonight. We can have a coffee out. Come on. Let's go away, far away. I know a bar. We'll go, shall we?' Charlotte freed her arm and, without a word, went to fetch their coats. She pushed the girl out through the door. She felt relieved. In the stair-well, which was dark and only faintly lit at every bend by the lamp in the courtyard, Mara's hand came towards her, grasping at her arm again. She was afraid the girl might fall, and simultaneously pulled and supported her till they were down below and had reached the gate.

The Franziskanerplatz lay quiet like a village square. The splashing of the fountain, quiet. One would have liked to smell woods and meadows nearby, to have looked up at the moon, at the sky that had become dense and midnight-blue again after a noisy day. There was no one about in the Weihburgstrasse. They walked quickly up to the Kärntner Strasse, and suddenly Mara took Charlotte's hand again, like a timid child. They held hands and walked even faster, as though they were being followed. Mara began to run and finally they ran like two schoolgirls, as though there were no other way of moving. Mara's bracelets clinked, and one pressed into Charlotte's wrist and hurt her, drove her on.

Seized with uncertainty, Charlotte looked round the airless and hot front room of the bar. Mara held open the door to the inner room. Again everything was red. Now the walls were red too, the red of hell, the chairs and the tables, the lights that were waiting like traffic lights to be released from duty by the green light of morning and were now holding up the night and trying to detain people in it, in smoke, in intoxication. But because they had not been arranged by chance, these red tones had a weaker effect than the first set of reds earlier on, they also weakened the memory of those earlier reds, and Mara's hair and her wide skirt were swallowed up in the gaping jaws of red.

People were drinking and dancing without pleasure; nevertheless Charlotte had the feeling that she had found her way into a room of hell, to be burned and made to suffer by tortures as yet unknown to her. The music, the din of voices tormented her, because she had ventured away from her own world without permission and feared to be discovered and seen by someone who knew her. With her head bent, she walked behind Mara to the table to which the waiter ushered them, a long table at which two men in dark suits were already sitting and, farther away, a young couple who did not look up for an instant, who were touching one another with the tips of their fingers. Round about them the dancers flowed and, as though sliding off the planks of a sinking ship, pressed against the table, stamped on the floor, on which the table also seemed to be precariously poised, as though they wanted to descend into the depths. Everything swayed, smoked, fumed in the red light. Everything wanted to descend into the depths, to go down deeper entangled in noise, to sink deeper without pleasure.

Charlotte ordered coffee and wine. When she looked up again Mara had stood up and started to dance a yard away from her. At first she seemed to be alone, but then the man who was dancing with her came into view, a heated, thin boy, an apprentice or student, who jerked his hips and legs, also dancing on his own and only occasionally grasping Mara's hands or taking her briefly in his arms, before pushing her away again and leaving her to her own inventive movements. Mara turned her face to Charlotte, smiled, turned away, threw her hair up with her hand. Once she jigged quite close up to Charlotte and bent down gracefully.

'You don't mind?'

Charlotte nodded stiffly. She turned away, drank in little sips; she didn't want to put the girl off by watching her. A man came up behind her chair and invited her to dance. She shook her head. She stuck to her chair, and her tongue, already dry again, stuck fast in her mouth. She wanted to get up and leave secretly when Mara wasn't looking. But she didn't leave because—though she didn't know this clearly until later—she didn't for a moment have the feeling that Mara was dancing for the sake of dancing, or that she wanted to dance with anybody here or to stay here or to enjoy herself. Because she kept looking across and was obviously performing her dance only so that Charlotte should watch. She drew her arms through the air and her body through space as though through water, she was swimming and displaying herself, and Charlotte, finally compelled to give her gaze an unmistakable direction, followed her every movement.

End of the music. A breathless, radiant Mara who sat down and reached for Charlotte's hand. Enlaced hands. Whispering. 'Are you angry?' Head-shake. A great dullness. To be able to get up now and go, to break free from these little burr-like hands. Charlotte freed her left hand with a jerk, reached for the wine glass and drank. The wine didn't come to an end either, no matter how much she drank. Time didn't come to an end; these looks, these hands didn't come to an end. The two men at the table turned to Mara, whispered with her, laughed at her in a friendly way.

'Shall we make a bridge, Fräulein?'

Mara raised her hands, played with the men's hands a brief game that Charlotte did not know.

'No, no bridge, no bridge!' she cried laughingly, turning her back on the men as suddenly as she had started to play with them and, returning home, plunged her hands under Charlotte's hands that were lying white and cold side by side on the table.

'Ah, the ladies want to be left to themselves,' said one of the men smiling good-naturedly at his friend. Charlotte closed her eyes. She felt the pressure of Mara's hard fingers and returned it, without knowing why and without wishing to. Yes, that was how it was. That was it. She came slowly to herself again, kept her eyes fixed unwaveringly on the table top in front of her and did not move. She didn't want ever to move again. She didn't care now whether they left or stayed, whether she would feel rested by morning or not, whether this music went on, anybody spoke to her, anybody recognized her . . .

'Charlotte, say something! Charlotte . . . don't you like it here? Don't you ever go dancing, ever go out drinking? . . . Say something!'

Silence.

'Say something. Laugh a bit. Can you stand it up there in your place? I couldn't stand it, wandering round alone, sleeping alone, alone at night and working during the day, always practising . . . Oh, Charlotte, that's terrible. Nobody can stand that!'

Charlotte said with an effort: 'Let's go.'

She was afraid of bursting into tears.

When they were out in the street she couldn't find the sentence that had saved her once already. Earlier the sentence had been possible: I'll call a taxi for you . . . But now she would have had to add 'Mara' to the sentence. She couldn't do that. They walked slowly back. Charlotte put her hands in her coat pockets. At least Mara shouldn't have her hand any more.

This time Mara found the stairs in the Franziskanerplatz without help, without question in the darkness. She went in front, as though she had often been up and down these stairs. Charlotte inserted the key in the lock and stopped. It could no longer be 'our apartment' if she really opened the door now, didn't push Mara down the stairs. I ought to push her down the stairs, thought Charlotte, turning the key.

Inside, next instant, Mara twined her arms round her neck, hung on her like a child. A small, touching body hung itself on hers, which all at once seemed to her bigger and stronger than usual. Charlotte freed herself with a quick movement, stretched out her arm and switched on the light.

They sat down in the room, as they had sat before, and smoked.

'That's madness, you're mad,' said Charlotte, 'how can you possibly . . . ?' She stopped, didn't go on speaking, she felt so ridiculous. She smoked and thought that this night would never come to an end, that this night was only just beginning and was perhaps endless.

Perhaps Mara would now stay there for ever and ever and ever, and she herself would now have to ponder for ever what she had done or said to be to blame for Mara being there and staying there.

When she looked helplessly across at the girl she noticed that tears were flowing from Mara's eyes.

'Don't cry. Please don't cry.'

'You don't want me. Nobody wants me.'

'Please don't cry. You're very sweet, very beautiful, but . . .'

'Why don't you want me? Why?' Fresh tears.

'I can't.'

'You don't want to. Why? Just tell me why you don't like me, then I'll go!' Mara slowly tipped out of the chair, came to rest on her knees and laid her head in Charlotte's lap. 'Then I'll go, then you'll be rid of me.'

Charlotte didn't move, as she smoked she looked down at the girl, studied every feature of her face, every expression that passed over it. She looked at her very long and very closely.

That was madness. She had never . . . Once, during her schooldays, when she had to take the exercise books to the history mistress in the staff room and there was no one else in the room, the mistress had stood up, put her arm round her and kissed her on the forehead. 'Dear girl.' Then Charlotte, scared because the mistress was normally so strict, had turned round and run out of the door. Long afterwards she had felt pursued by the two tender words. From that day on she was tested even more stringently than the others and her marks became even worse. But she didn't complain to anybody, she put up with the undeserved cold treatment; she had realized that this tenderness could only be followed by this harshness.

Charlotte thought to herself: but how can I touch Mara? She is made of the same stuff that I am made of. And she thought sadly of Franz, who was on his way to her; his train must already be at the frontier, and no one could now prevent him from travelling on, no one could warn Franz against coming back to a place where 'our apartment' no longer existed. Or did it still exist? Everything was still standing there in its place, the key had opened the door, and if Mara now disappeared by a miracle or simply changed her mind and left after all, then tomorrow everything would seem like a phantasm, it would become as though it had never been.

'Please be sensible. I've got to have some sleep, I have to get up early tomorrow.'

'I'm not sensible. Oh darling, beautiful darling, and you're only lying to me a little, aren't you?'

'Why? What do you mean?' Charlotte, sleepy, dizzy with smoke, empty, could no longer grasp anything. Her thoughts were still tramping to and fro like watchmen in her head, listening to the hostile words, they were on the lookout but couldn't raise the alarm, prepare for defence.

'You're lying! Oh, how you're lying!'

'I don't know what you're talking about. Why should I lie, and what do you take for a lie anyway?'

'You're lying. You called me, you made me come to you, you took me with you again in the night, and now I disgust you, now you don't want to admit that you called me to you!'

'You think I . . .'

'Didn't you invite me? What did that mean?'

Charlotte wept. She could no longer restrain the tears that came so suddenly. 'I invite lots of people.'

'You're lying.'

Mára's wet face, still wet while she was already starting to laugh, was pressed against Charlotte's, tender, warm, and their two streams of tears mingled. The kisses which the little mouth gave, the curls that were shaken over Charlotte, the little head that came up against her head—it was all so much smaller, more fragile, more insignificant than any head, any hair, any kisses that had ever come over Charlotte. She searched in her feelings for instructions, in her hands for an instinct, in her head for an announcement. She remained without instructions.

As a child, carried away by emotion, Charlotte had often kissed her cat on its little nose, the damp, cool, tender little object round which everything was so soft and strange—a strange region for kisses. The girl's lips were similarly moist, tender, unfamiliar. Charlotte couldn't help thinking of the cat and had to clench her teeth. And at the same time she tried to note what these unfamiliar lips felt like.

So that was what her own lips were like, this was how they met a man, thin, almost unresisting, almost without muscles—a little muzzle, not to be taken seriously.

'Just kiss me once,' begged Mara. 'Just once.'

Charlotte looked at her wrist-watch; she suddenly felt an urge to look at her watch, and she wanted Mara to notice.

'What time is it?' A new note was in the girl's voice, a kind of malicious, rebellious note such as Charlotte had never heard before.

'Four o'clock,' she said drily.

'I'm staying. Do you hear? I'm staying.' Again the undertone, threatening, vicious. But had she herself not also once said to somebody: I'm staying? She hoped fervently that she had never said it in that tone.

'In case you haven't grasped it yet, there's no point in your staying. And at six o'clock our home help comes.' She too must be malicious now, pay Mara back for that tone of hers, she said 'our' and moreover she was lying, because she had told the woman to come at nine.

Mara's eyes blazed. 'Don't say that, oh Charlotte, don't say that! You're mean, so mean. If you knew what you're doing to me . . . Do you think I shall let you go to the station and come back with him! Is he a good lover? Well, is he?'

Charlotte said nothing; she was so exasperated that she couldn't utter a word.

'Do you love him? No? People say . . . oh, people say all sorts of things . . .' She made a dismissive gesture with her hand. 'Oh, how I hate all that. How I hate Vienna! Hate this studying, these empty chatterers, these men, these women, the academy, everything. Only you, since I first saw you . . . You must be different. You must. Or you're lying.'

'Who is saying anything? And what?'

'I wouldn't have come, would never have come . . . I swear to you.'

'But that's . . .' Charlotte couldn't go on, she stood up reeling. Mara stood up. They stood facing each other. Quite slowly, and as her excitement already began to recede, Mara swept one glass from the table, then the other. She seized a vase and threw it at the wall, because the glasses had rolled on the carpet without a sound, then a casket, out of which shells and stones flew, landed with a crash and rolled over the furniture.

Charlotte sought strength for a great anger, for a scream, for rage, for insults. Her strength had left her. She simply watched the girl as she destroyed one object after another. The destruction seemed to go on for a long time like a fire, a flood, a demolition. Mara suddenly bent down, picked up two large fragments of the fruit bowl, held them together and said: 'Such a beautiful plate. Forgive me. I'm sure you were fond of the plate. Please forgive me.'

Without regret, without any emotion, Charlotte counted the things that had been smashed or damaged. There were only a few, but she would have liked to have counted in everything in the room, so that she could accurately express the real extent of the destruction, which was so much greater; everything might just as well have lain shattered. For she had watched, hadn't raised a finger, had kept quiet at every crash, every splintering.

She bent down and picked up the shells and stones, she pushed the fragments together, walked about bent so that she didn't have to look up and see Mara; then she dropped a few pieces again, as though there were no point in clearing up here. In the continued silence she cowered on the floor. Her feelings, her thoughts jumped off the normal rails, raced without a track into the open. She let them run wild.

She was free. Nothing seemed to her impossible any more. Why should she not begin to live with a creature just like herself?

But now Mara had knelt down beside her, had started speaking. She kept talking to her. 'My beloved, you must forgive me, Charlotte darling, I'm so sorry, I don't know what got into me, Charlotte be kind to me, I'm crazy, crazy for you, I should like, I believe I could. . . .'

Charlotte thought: I can't make out what she's talking about. The language of men at such moments was such that you could hold on to it. I can't listen to Mara, to her words without muscles, these useless little words.

'Listen, Mara, if you want to know the truth. We must try to talk together, really to talk together. Try it.' (I'm sure she doesn't want to know the truth at all, and then there is also the question of how the truth about us is to be put. There are no words for it yet.) 'I can't make out what you're saying. You're talking too vaguely for me. I can't picture how you think. Something in your head must run in the opposite direction from normal.'

'My poor head! You must take pity on it, must stroke it, tell it what to think.'

Charlotte obediently began to stroke Mara's head. Then she stopped. She had heard that once before—not the words, but the intonation. She had often talked like that herself, particularly during the early time with Franz, even before Milan she had lapsed into this intonation, had drawn her voice into frills; he had had to listen to that sing-song full of ignorance, she had chattered to him with a screwed up mouth, the weaker to the stronger, a helpless, ignorant woman addressing him, the one who knew. She had acted out the same weaknesses that Mara was now acting out to her, and had then suddenly held the man in her arms, had blackmailed tenderness from him when he wanted to think about something else, as she was now being blackmailed by Mara, being forced to caress her, to be kind to her, to be clever.

But this time she possessed insight. It didn't take effect on her. Or did it? Perhaps the fact that she understood and saw through the girl, because she suddenly remembered and caught sight of herself, didn't help at all. She merely felt much older all at once, because this creature in front of her was playing the child, was making herself small and her big for her own purposes. She timidly ran her hand through Mara's hair again, would have liked to promise her something. Something sweet, flowers, a night of love or a necklace. Just so that she would at last keep quiet. So that she, Charlotte, could at last get up and think about something else; so that this little bothersome animal should be shooed away. She thought of Franz and she asked herself whether he had sometimes been similarly bothered by her and would have liked to shoo her away, the little animal, so that there should be peace and quiet.

Charlotte stood up because she noticed that the curtains were not drawn. And yet she would have liked to have left the windows lit up, left them open so people could see in. She had nothing to fear. It was time that what counted was what she thought and felt, and no longer what she had been constrained to think and what she had been allowed to live.

If she began to live with Mara. . . . Then she would enjoy working more, for example. Although she had always liked working, her work had lacked the curse of compulsion, of absolute necessity. Also she needed somebody around her, beside her, beneath her, for whom she not only worked but for whom she was the approach to the world, for whom she set the tone, decided the value of a thing, chose a place.

She looked round the room. The furniture had been chosen by Franz, with the exception of the lamp in the bedroom and a few vases, bagatelles. There wasn't a single piece of her in this flat. It was unthinkable that anything would ever have anything to do with her in a dwelling so long as she was living with a man. After leaving home she had lived for a year with a student, in a room with dusty silk lampshades, plush chairs and walls plastered all over with posters and cheap reproductions of modern paintings. She would never have dared to change anything in it; it had been his environment. Now she lived in the lucid order that belonged to Franz, and if she were to leave Franz she would go into another order, into old curved chairs or into peasant furniture or into a collection of armour, anyhow into an order that wasn't hers—that wouldn't change. To be exact, she didn't know any longer what she wanted for herself, because there was nothing left to want. Naturally Franz had asked her, every time he bought something: 'Is that all right with you? What do you think? Or would you rather have it in blue?' And she had said what she thought, namely 'Blue'. Or, 'I'd prefer the table lower'. But she could only express a wish when he asked questions. She looked at Mara and smiled. She kicked the table with her toe. It was an act of abuse. She was abusing 'our table'.

She would be able to subjugate Mara, to guide and push her. She would have somebody who would tremble before her concerts, who would hold a warm jacket in readiness when she came out of the concert hall sweating, somebody for whom the only important thing was to take part in her life and for whom she was the measure of all things, somebody for whom it was more important to keep her linen in order, to turn back her bed, than to satisfy another ambition—somebody, above all, for whom it was more important to think with her thoughts than to have a thought of her own.

And she suddenly thought she knew what she had missed all these years and secretly looked for: the long-haired, weak creature on whom one could lean, who would always hold her shoulder ready when one felt disconsolate or exhausted or autocratic, whom one could summon or send away and whom, to be fair, one had to look after, about whom one was anxious and with whom one could be angry. She could never be angry with Franz, could never shout at him the way he sometimes shouted at her. She was never the one who decided. He decided (or they both decided, he would probably have said—but it was he who, without being aware of it, always decided, and she would not have wished it otherwise). Although he loved her independence and her work, her progress delighted him, he consoled her when she couldn't manage both her work and her housework and forgave her a great deal, as much as one could forgive in a partnership, she knew it was not in his nature to allow her the right to an unhappiness of her own, a different loneliness. She shared his unhappiness or pretended to share it; at times they were inseparable in her: hypocrisy, love, friendship. But it wasn't important how much honesty was in her and how much desire to conceal—the important thing was that only she was aware of this problem, that it often preoccupied her but that she had never been able to envisage a solution.

The arrogance to insist on her own unhappiness, her own loneliness, had always been in her, but only now did it venture to emerge; it blossomed, ran wild, smothered her. She was unredeemable and nobody should have the effrontery to redeem her, to know the millennium in which the red-blossoming rods that had grown inseparably entangled would spring apart and leave the path open. Come, sleep, come, thousand years, that I may be awoken by another hand. Come, let me awake when this is no longer valid—man and woman. When this has come to an end!

She mourned Franz like a dead man; he was awake or sleeping now in the train that was bringing him home and he didn't know that he was dead, that everything had been in vain, the subjugation that she herself, rather than he, had carried out, because he couldn't have had any idea what was to be subjugated. He had squandered too much strength on her as it was, had always expended so much consideration and concern on her. Whereas it had always seemed right that she had wanted to live with him, it had always seemed to her sad that he had had to burden himself with her, there was nothing in it for him; she would have wished him a wife who would have cared for and admired him, and he would not have become less on that account, nothing could diminish him—even as it was, her torments could not diminish him, but equally they could not be of any use to him, could not bring him any advantage, because they were of the illegitimate, incorrigible kind. He tackled the situation good-naturedly, he knew that he could have had an easier life, but he enjoyed living with her: she had become just as much of a habit with him as another woman would have done, and, wiser than Charlotte, he had long ago recognized marriage as a state that is stronger than the individuals who enter it, and which therefore also leaves more of a mark upon their partnership than they could have marked or even changed the marriage. However a marriage is conducted —it cannot be conducted arbitrarily, inventively, it cannot tolerate innovation or change, because to enter into marriage already means to enter into its form.

Charlotte was startled by a deep breath which Mara drew and saw that the girl had fallen asleep. She was now alone, watching over that which had become possible. At the moment she had no idea why she had ever been with men and why she had married one. It was too absurd. She laughed to herself and bit her hand to keep herself awake. She had to keep night-watch.

Suppose the old covenant were now rent asunder? She feared the consequences which this rending must have. Soon she would get up, wake Mara, go with her into the bedroom. They would take off their clothes; it would be troublesome, but it was part of it, things had to start like that. It would be a new beginning. But how is one to make oneself naked for the very first time? How is that to happen if one cannot rely on skin and smell, on a curiosity fed by many curiosities? How produce a curiosity for the first time, when nothing has yet preceded it?

She had often before stood in front of a woman half-naked or in thin underclothes. She had always found it embarrassing, at least for a moment: in the bathing-cabin with a friend; in the lingerie shop, in the dress shop when a salesgirl was helping her to try on corsets and dresses. But how was she to slip out of her dress in front of Mara, to let it fall, without leaving out the first step. But perhaps—and this suddenly seemed to her wonderful —the two of them wouldn't feel embarrassed at all, because they both wore the same articles of clothing. They would laugh, eye one another, be young, whisper. In the gymnasium, at school, there had always been this whirl of clothes, flimsy pink and blue and white fabric. As girls they had played with it, thrown the linen at each other's heads, laughed and danced like mad, hidden one another's clothes—and if heaven had had a use for the girls at that time it would certainly have placed them by the springs, in the forests, in the grottoes and chosen one of them to be Echo, in order to keep the world young and full of legends that were ageless.

Charlotte bent over Mara who, now that she was asleep, was no longer a danger, kissed her on the eyebrows that stood beautifully curved and festive in the pallid face, kissed the hand that hung down from the chair, and then, very furtively, shyly she bent down over the mouth from which the lipstick had disappeared in the course of the night.

If only mankind could once more reach for a fruit, once more arouse wrath, once more decide in favour of its earth! Experience another awakening, another shame! Mankind was never tied down. There were possibilities. The fruit was never consumed, had still not been consumed, not yet. The scent of all fruits, which were of equal value, hung in the air. There might be other knowledge to be grasped. She was free. So free that she could be led into temptation again. She wanted a great temptation and to answer for it and be damned, as it had been answered for once already.

My God, she thought, I'm not living today, I take part in everything, let myself be swept into everything that happens, in order not to be able to grasp an opportunity of my own. Time hangs on me in rags. I am no one's wife. I don't even exist yet. I want to decide who I am, and I also want to create my creature, to create my suffering, guilty, shadowy partner. I don't want Mara because I want her mouth, her sex—my own. Nothing of the sort. I want my creature; and I shall create it for myself. We have always lived on our ideas, and this is my idea.

If she loved Mara everything would change.

She would then have a being whom she could initiate into the world. She alone would bestow every criterion, every secret. Always she had dreamt of being able to transmit the world and had dodged when it was transmitted to her, had maintained a stubborn silence when anyone had tried to make her believe something and thought of the time when she was a girl and had still known how to be fearless and that there was nothing to be afraid of and one could lead the way with a high, piercing shout which others could follow.

If she could love Mara she would no longer be at home in this city, in this country, with a man, in a language, but in herself—and she would arrange the home for the girl. A new home. Then she would have to make the choice regarding the home, regarding the ebb and flow, the language. She would no longer be the chosen one and never again could she be chosen in this language.

Moreover, with all the joys that love of men had brought her, something had remained open. And although now, during the hour in which she watched, she still believed that she loved men, there was an untrodden zone. Charlotte had often been surprised that human beings, who ought to have known better than star, shrub and stone what caresses they could invent for each other, were so ill advised. In earlier times swan and golden laburnum must still have had an inkling of the greater scope for play, and the memory that the scope for play was greater and that the little system of caresses which had been formed and transmitted was not all that was possible could not have entirely vanished from the world. As a child Charlotte had wanted to love everything and be loved by everything, by the whirlpool in front of a rock, by the hot sand, the wood that felt good in the hand, the cry of the hawk—a star had got under her skin and a tree which she embraced had made her giddy. Now she had long since been instructed in love, but at what a price! In any case, most people's association with each other seemed a miserable act of resignation; they apparently considered it necessary because nothing else was available, and then they had to try to believe that it was right, that it was beautiful, that it was what they had wanted. And it occurred to her that only one of all the men she had known was perhaps really dependent on women. She thought of Milan, for whom she had not been enough, for whom nothing had been enough, for that very reason, and who for that same reason had known that nothing was enough for her, and had cursed himself and her because their already mis-trained bodies were an impediment on the departure towards already forgotten or as yet unknown caresses. It had been quite close, for instants actually present: ecstasy, intoxication, depth, surrender, delight. Afterwards she had united with a man again on the basis of kindness, being in love, benevolence, care, dependence, security, protection, of all sorts of admirable things which did not remain mere projects but could actually be lived.

Thus it had become possible for her to marry. She brought with her the precondition for entry into the married state and for settling down in it, in spite of occasional revolts, in spite of her desire to undermine the constitution. But whenever she had tried to undermine this she had quickly become aware that she had nothing to put in its place, that she had no idea of her own and that Franz with his smile, and with the pity he felt for her at such times, was right. She liked living in his indulgence. But she wasn't sure whether he too would have liked to live in her indulgence or what would have happened if he had ever noticed that she too was indulgent towards him. If he had known, for example, that secretly she could never believe that things had to be as they were between them and that above all she couldn't believe that he understood her body. Their good marriage —as they called it—was founded precisely upon the fact that he understood nothing about her body. He had certainly entered and wandered through this strange region, but he had quickly settled down where he found it most comfortable.

From a movement of the girl, who stretched out her hand to her as she dozed, clutched her knee with her fingers, stroked, tested and felt the back of her knee, she felt that this creature knew something about her which nobody had known, not even herself, because she had been dependent upon suggestions. Charlotte leant back trembling and dismayed, and stiffened. She was defending herself against the new suggestion.

'Leave me alone,' she said in an unfriendly tone. 'Stop that. At once.'

Mara opened her eyes. 'Why?'

Yes, why indeed? Why didn't she stop thinking, waking and burying the dead? Why, since it had gone that far, didn't she at last stand up, lift Mara up and go to bed with her?

Mara whispered with a conspiratorial look: 'I only want to take you to your room, put you to bed, watch you fall asleep. Then I'll go. I don't want anything. Just to watch you fall asleep . . .'

'Please be quiet. Don't talk. Be quiet.'

'You're simply afraid of me, of yourself, of him!' Again the intonation that made everything sink down, that made Charlotte sink down.

And Mara added triumphantly: 'How you lie! What a coward you are!'

As though that were the point! As though it would amount to no more than the breaking of a commandment, a little foolishness, the satisfaction of an additional curiosity!

No, not until she threw everything behind her, burnt everything behind her, could she enter her own. Her kingdom would come and when it came she would no longer be measurable, no longer estimable by an alien measure. In her kingdom a new measure was in force. Then it could no longer be said: she is like this, and like that, attractive, unattractive, sensible, silly, faithful, unfaithful, scrupulous or unscrupulous, unapproachable or consumed by adventures. She knew what it was possible to say and in what categories people thought, who was capable of saying this or that and why. She had always loathed this language, every imprint that was stamped upon her and that she had to stamp upon somebody—the attempted murder of reality. But when her kingdom came this language could no longer be valid, then this language would pass judgment on itself. Then she would have opted out, could laugh at every verdict, and it would no longer matter what anyone took her for. The language of men, insofar as it was applied to women, had been bad enough already and doubtful; but the language of women was even worse, more undignified—she had been shocked by it ever since she had seen through her mother, later through her sisters, girl friends and the wives of her men friends and had discovered that absolutely nothing, no insight, no observation corresponded to this language, to the frivolous or pious maxims, the jumble of judgments and opinions or the sighed lament.

Charlotte liked looking at women; they frequently moved her or they pleased her visually, but so far as possible she avoided talking to them. She felt separated from them, from their language, their suffering, their heart.

But she would teach Mara to speak, slowly, exactly and not to permit any clouding by the common language. She would educate her, hold her to something which very early on, because she had found no better word, she had called loyalty. She insisted on this alien word because she could not yet insist on the most alien of all words. Love. Since no one knew how to translate it.

Charlotte looked down at Mara; she admired in her something unheard of, all the hope she had cast upon this figure. All she had to do now was to know how to carry this unheard of element into every slightest act, into the new day, every day.

'Come. Listen to me,' she said, shaking Mara by the shoulder. 'I must know all about you. I want to know what you want. . . .'

Mara sat up with a surprised expression. She had understood. Could she not derive satisfaction from the very fact that the girl understood at this moment? Let her stand up to the test! Let her understand at last!

'Nothing,' said Mara. 'I don't want anything. I won't fall into the trap.'

'What do you mean, you don't want anything?'

'I mean what I mean. I have to do something. I'm gifted, they say, your husband says so too. But I don't care about that. They've given me this grant. But I shall come to nothing. And anyhow, nothing interests me.' She paused briefly and then asked: 'Does anything interest you?'

'Oh, yes. A great deal.' Charlotte felt that she could not go on talking;

the barriers had come down again. She had stammered, not found the courage to constitute herself an authority, to wipe away this stupid chatter and strike her own note again.

'You're lying!'

'Stop talking to me like that this minute,' Charlotte said sharply.

Mara obstinately folded her arms and stared at her impudently. 'Music, your profession, that can't possibly interest you. That's just a delusion. Loving—loving, that's the thing. Loving is everything.' She gazed gloomily and resolutely into space, no longer impudently.

Charlotte murmured awkwardly: 'That doesn't seem to me so important. I wanted to talk about something else.'

'Other things aren't important.'

'Are you trying to tell me that you know better than I what is important?'

Mara slid off the chair, sat down on the floor with her legs crossed and remained gloomily silent. Then she began again, like someone who has but few words at her disposal and must therefore throw these words into the fray all the more stubbornly, must help them to take effect. 'Absolutely nothing interests me. I think of nothing but loving. And therefore I don't believe you.'

Perhaps Mara really wanted nothing else, and at least she didn't pretend to be interested in anything, she was honest enough to admit it; and perhaps she was right and all the others who didn't admit it were lying to themselves and diligently hiding the truth from themselves in offices, factories and universities.

Something seemed to have occurred to Mara; she added shyly: 'I heard you on the radio last week. In that concert. You were very good, I think.'

Charlotte shrugged her shoulders defensively.

'Very good,' said Mara, nodding. 'Perhaps you can really do something and perhaps you're ambitious . . .'

Charlotte replied helplessly: 'I don't know. That's one way of putting it . . .'

'Don't be angry!' Mara sat up and threw her arms round Charlotte's neck. 'You're wonderful. I want to do everything, believe everything, that you want me to. Only love me! Love me! But I shall hate everything out of jealousy, music, the piano, people, everything. And at the same time I shall be proud of you. But let me stay with you.' She recollected herself and let her arms fall. 'Yes, do as you like. Only don't send me away. I shall do everything for you, I'll wake you in the mornings, bring you your tea, the post, answer the telephone, I can cook for you, run all your errands, see that no one bothers you. So that you can do what you want to do better. Only love me. And love only me.'

Charlotte seized Mara by the wrists. Now she had her where she wanted her. She assessed her prey and it was usable, was good. She had found her victim.

It was time for the change of shift, and now she could take over the world, name her companions, establish rights and duties, invalidate the old pictures and design the first new ones. For it was the world of pictures that remained when everything had been swept away that had been condemned by the sexes and said of the sexes. The pictures remained when equality and inequality and all attempts to define their nature and their legal relationship had long ago become empty words and been replaced by new empty words. Those pictures which, even when the colours faded away and mildew broke out, lasted longer and begot new pictures. The picture of the huntress, the great mother and the great whore, the good Samaritan, the decoy-bird, the will o' the wisp and the woman placed under the stars. . . .

I wasn't born into any picture, thought Charlotte. That is why I feel like breaking off. That is why I want a counterpicture, and I want to construct it myself. No name yet. Not yet. First make the leap, leap over everything, carry out the withdrawal when the drum is beaten; when the red cloth trails on the ground and no one knows how it will end. To hope for the kingdom. Not the kingdom of men and not that of women.

Not this, not that.

She could no longer see anything; her eyelids were drooping, heavy and tired. She did not see Mara and the room in which she was, but her last secret room which she must now lock up for ever. In this room, the lily banner waved, the walls were white and the banner was set up. Dead was the man Franz and dead the man Milan, dead a Luis, dead all seven whom she had felt breathing over her. They had breathed their last, those who had sought her lips and been drawn into her body. They were dead and all the flowers that had been given as gifts rustled drily in their folded hands; they had been given back. Mara would never learn, must never learn, what a room filled with dead was and under what sign they had been killed. In this room she walked round alone, a ghost, haunting her ghosts. She loved her dead and came to see them again in secret. There was a crackling in the rafters, the ceiling threatened to collapse in the howling morning wind that whirled the roof to pieces. The key to the room, she still remembered this, she was carrying under her vest. . . . She was dreaming but she was not asleep yet. Mara must never ask about it, or she too would be among the dead.

'I'm dead,' said Mara. 'I can't go on any longer. Dead, I'm so dead.'

::

'YOU'VE BEEN WANTING ME TO GO FOR A LONG TIME,' COMPLAINED MARA.

'No,' said Charlotte hoarsely. 'Stay. Drink with me. I'm dying of thirst. Go on, stay.'

'No, no more,' said Mara. 'I can't drink any more, can't walk any more, or stand. I'm dead.

::

'GO ON, SEND ME AWAY!'

Charlotte stood up; her paralysed, over-tired body scarcely obeyed her. She didn't know how she was going to get to the door or to her bed. Nor did she any longer want Mara to stay here. Nor that they should take time to think it over.

Time is no time to think it over. Morning was in the windows, with the first, not yet rosy light. A first sound could be heard, of a passing car, afterwards of footsteps—echoing, firm steps that moved away.

When they were both in the bedroom Charlotte knew that it was too late for everything. They undressed and lay down side by side—two beautiful sleepers with white shoulderstraps and close-fitting white slips. They were both dead and had killed something. With their hands they stroked one another's shoulders, breasts. Charlotte wept, turned over, reached for the alarm clock and wound it up. Mara looked at her indifferently. Then they tumbled down into sleep and into a stormy dream.

The red skirt lay crumpled and insignificant by the bed.

1961

TRANSLATED FROM THE GERMAN
BY MICHAEL BULLOCK

JOHN O'HARA

::

JURGE DULRUMPLE

ON LONG TRIPS—TO SEE THE CHERRY BLOSSOMS IN WASHINGTON, TO HEAR the music in the Berkshires, to visit relatives at distant points—Miss Ivy Heinz and her friend Miss Muriel Hamilton sang two-part harmony, not only because they loved to sing but as a safety measure. Muriel Hamilton had never learned to drive, and their singing kept Ivy Heinz from getting too drowsy. They sang well together, especially considering that both were natural altos. Muriel Hamilton carried the melody, since it was a little easier for her to get out of the lower register and also because she was more likely to know the words. Ivy Heinz could go awfully low, and sometimes for a joke she would drop down in imitation of a man's bass, and whenever she did that, just about *every* time she had done it, Muriel Hamilton would say, quickly, without a pause in the singing, "George Dalrymple."

"No, *no!*" Ivy would say, and they would laugh.

Any mention of George Dalrymple was good for a laugh when Ivy Heinz and Muriel Hamilton got together. It was an extremely private source of amusement, sure-fire or not. Shared with a third party it would have been an act of cruelty to George because an explanation of the laughter would have involved revealing a secret that concerned only George and the two women. It went back to a time when all three were in their middle twenties, the summer in which George Dalrymple proposed first to Muriel Hamilton and then, a month later, proposed to Ivy Heinz. Neither girl had been enormously complimented by a proposal from George Dalrymple, but they knew that from George's point of view it was a compliment, a terribly serious one that was no less serious or sincere because he had gone so soon from Muriel to Ivy. George Dalrymple was a serious man, a fact that made it fun to have a private joke about him, but in public you had to treat such seriousness seriously.

Other people, in discussing George Dalrymple or even in merely mentioning his name, would often lower the pitch as far down as they could get. They would pull their chins back against their necks, and the name would come out, "Jurge Dulrumple." His speaking voice was so deep, his enunciation so economical, that his vocal delivery was his outstanding characteristic, more distinctively his than those details of appearance and carriage and manners that he might share with other men. There were, for example, other men just as tall and thin; others who swayed their heads from side to side independently of their bodies when they walked; and others who were as quickly, instantly polite in such things as standing up when a lady entered the room, lighting a girl's cigarette, opening doors. George did all these things, but what set him apart was his way of talking, his words coming from down deep in his mouth and expelled with a minimal motion of his lips. His friends, such as Ivy Heinz and Muriel Hamilton, knew that he was not self-conscious about his teeth, which were nothing special but all right; and it was not in George Dalrymple's character to go around talking like a jailbird or a ventriloquist. George Dalrymple talked that way because he was serious and wanted people to realize that everything he said was serious.

When George came back from his army duties in the winter of 1919 he was twenty-three years old. His military service had largely consisted of guarding railroad bridges along the Atlantic Seaboard, a task he performed conscientiously with the result that he was discharged a corporal. If the woor—the war—had lasted six months longer he would have been a second lieutenant and probably sent to Brest, France, or some such point of debarkation; his congressman had been practically promised the commission by the War Department. But once the Armistice was signed George was anxious to get out of the army and resume work at the bank. He had already lost practically two years, and in the banking business it was wise to start early and stick to it. The time he had put in at the bank before he was drafted was now just about matched by the fifteen months he had spent protecting the railway systems from German spies. The bank took him back at a slight raise in pay and with full credit in seniority for the time he had been in the service of his country. It was a pleasant surprise to find that one of the newer bookkeepers at the bank was none other than his high school classmate, Muriel Hamilton.

Two of the women who had been hired during the hostilities were let go, as they had been warned they would be, but Muriel Hamilton was kept on. The recently inaugurated school savings plan, for children in the public and parochial schools, owed at least some of its success to Muriel Hamilton and her ability to get along with children. She was painstaking and patient, and the bank officials put her in complete charge. Once a year she went around and gave a talk to all the classes from seventh grade to senior high, and the bank could see the results immediately. No one was more surprised than Muriel herself.

In her four years at High she had been so near to failing in Public Speaking—which almost no one ever failed—that it had pulled down her general average and kept her out of the first third of her class. George Dalrymple's marks in Public Speaking were as bad as Muriel's, but his other subjects kept him in the first ten in a class of eighty-five boys and girls, the largest class in the history of G.H.S. It surprised no one that George Dalrymple, on graduation, had a job waiting for him at the Citizens Bank & Trust. His high school record merited the distinction, a fact that delighted his father, the assistant cashier. John K. Dalrymple was not a man who would have forced his son on the bank.

In his pre-army days as a runner at the bank George Dalrymple and his father always walked home together for noonday dinner. Each day John K. Dalrymple would take the opportunity to review George's morning activities in detail. The father had George repeat all the conversations he had had with the tellers at the other banks, and he would suggest ways of improving the impression he created in the banking community. "It's all very well to have the light touch," John Dalrymple would say. "But it can be carried too far. It's better to be all business at your age. Time enough for ordinary conversation later on." There was no actual danger that George might get a reputation for frivolity, but he was young and did not know all the ropes, and his father did not want George's natural gravity to be affected by nervous unfamiliarity with the work.

John Dalrymple, as assistant cashier, did not have to stay as late as his son, and they did not walk home together at the close of business. But as soon as George got home he would get into his overalls and join his father in the flower garden, or, during the cold months, in the odd jobs about the house that John Dalrymple claimed kept him from getting stale. Father and son had very little time together in the evenings; John Dalrymple liked to stay home and read, while George had choir practice one night, calisthenics and basketball at the "Y" two nights, stamp club another, Sunday evening services at the Second Presbyterian Church, and the remaining evenings he spent with his friend Carl Yoder. Sometimes the boys would be at the Yoders' house, sometimes at the Dalrymples', and once in a while they would take in a picture show if it was Douglas Fairbanks or a good comedy.

It was a terrible thing when Carl passed on during the influenza epidemic. George could not even get leave to come home for the funeral. In fact, there was no real funeral; the churches and theaters and all such public gatherings were prohibited during the epidemic; the schools were closed, and you could not even buy a soda at a soda fountain. The death rate was shockingly high in the mining villages, but death by the wholesale did not affect George Dalrymple nearly so much as the passing of funny little Carl, the Jeff of the Mutt-and-Jeff team of Dalrymple and Yoder in the Annual Entertainment at G.H.S., senior year. George Dalrymple knew that things would not be the same at home without Carl trotting along after him everywhere they went.

One of the first conversations he had with Muriel Hamilton at the bank was about Carl Yoder, their classmate, and George was quite surprised to discover how fond she had been of Carl. "I always thought it was mean to call him The Shrimp," she said. "He didn't like it, did he?"

"No, he certainly did not," said George. "But he wouldn't let on to anybody but me."

"I didn't like it either, because remember in the Annual Entertainment when he wore girl's clothes? I loaned him that dress. And if Carlie was a shrimp, then that made me one too."

"Oh, yes. I remember that dress. That's right, it was yours. But that wouldn't make you a shrimp, Mure. Girls aren't as tall. I never think of you as a short girl."

"Five feet two inches."

"That makes me ten inches taller than you and ten inches taller than Carl."

"Oh, I thought you were taller."

"No, it's because I'm skinny, and so much taller than Carl. Just six feet and maybe an eighth of an inch."

"I never saw you in your uniform."

"Well, you have that treat in store for you. I'm going to be marching in the parade, Decoration Day."

She was a girl, not a short girl, and soon after that first conversation he formed the habit of walking part way home with her after the bank closed for the day. He would say goodnight to her at Eighth and Market, slowing down but not stopping when she entered her house. His new duties at the bank included opening up in the morning, a full half hour before Muriel reported for work, and he did not see her in the evening after supper except by accident. His schedule also had been rearranged so that his and his father's lunch hours did not coincide, and George was not entirely displeased. His father's questions about army life indicated a belief that it had been far more exciting and sinful than was actually the case. Some aspects of army life had disgusted George and he hoped never again to see some of the men in his company; the bullies, the drunkards, the dirty talkers, the physically unclean. George Dalrymple had come out of the army a somewhat coarsened but still innocent young man; he had lived closely with men who really did so many of the things that George and Carl Yoder had only heard about. He had heard men tell stories that they could not possibly have made up, and some of the stories were told by men about their own wives. Nevertheless George Dalrymple had no inclination to discuss that sort of thing with his father. It would have been almost as bad as discussing them with his mother. The war was over, he was through with the army, he had not liked being a soldier, but the whole experience was his own, a part of him, and to speak of it to his father would be an act of disloyalty to himself and the army that he could not explain to himself but that he felt deeply. It was private.

The time would come, he knew, when it would be no more than the right thing to invite Muriel Hamilton to a picture show and a soda afterward. If, in those circumstances, she showed another side of her, he would start keeping company with her and, eventually, ask her to marry him. She was exactly his own age, but he did not know any younger girls. She was what some people called mousy, but she was very well thought of at the bank, and he liked her feminity and her neatness. As soon as there was a tiny daub of ink on her finger she would scrub it off; she never had a hair out of place; and he was sure she used perfume, although that may have been perfumed soap. He had watched carefully the tightening of her shirtwaists over her bosom, and concluded unmistakably that marriage to her would be a pleasure. She had not been one of the prettier girls at G.H.S., and yet she was not by any means homely, and it was remarkable that she was still single while other girls, less attractive, were already married. She belonged to a group that called themselves the H.T.P.'s, who went to the pictures and had sodas together and had been doing so since senior year. One of the group dropped out to get married, and shortly thereafter it became common knowledge that H.T.P. stood for Hard To Please. Now the only ones left of the original H.T.P.'s were Muriel Hamilton and Ivy Heinz.

Muriel so readily accepted George Dalrymple's first invitation to take in a show that he felt sorry for her. She was not really an H.T.P.; she was merely waiting to be asked. They went to the movies, they had a soda. "There'll be a trolley in about seven minutes," said George.

"A trolley, to go eight squares?"

"I forgot to ask you before," he said.

"The only time I ever take the trolley is if it's pouring rain and I'm going to be late to work," she said. "I like walking. It's good exercise."

"So do I, now. I got pretty tired of it in the army, but that was different."

Watching the movie, they had not had any conversation, and now, walking her home, he began a story, about his army duties, that he had not finished when they reached her house. She stood on the bottom of their front steps while he hurried the story to an ending. "Well, thank you for taking me to the movies, George. I enjoyed it very much," she said.

"The pleasure was all mine," he said.

"See you tomorrow," she said.

"Bright and early," he said. "Goodnight."

He said no more than good morning to her the next day. He was determined not to let their outside relationship alter their conduct at the bank. Nevertheless he waited for her when the bank closed, and he soon discovered that their relationship had been altered. "George, I, uh, maybe I ought to wait until you ask me again, but if you have any *intention* of asking me—to go to the movies, that is—then maybe we oughtn't to walk home together every day. Walking home from work, that's one thing. But having a date, that's another. And I don't think we ought to do both. Maybe that's rather forward of me, but if you had any intention of asking me for a date?"

"Yes. Yes, I see."

"Half the people at the bank knew we had a date last night."

"Oh, they did?"

"You can't do anything here without everybody finding out about it."

"Well, personally I don't mind if they find out about that."

"But I do, George. Walking home from work, that's just politeness, but when a fellow and a girl have dates at night in addition, then that's giving them something to talk about."

"I'd be willing to give them something to talk about, but that's up to you, Mure."

"It is and it isn't, if you know what I mean. It all depends on whether you were going to ask me to go out with you in the evening. But if you were, I'd have to say no. And I don't want to say no."

"On the other hand, I don't want to give up walking home with you."

"Then we haven't solved anything, have we?"

"Not exactly," he said. "But maybe I can solve it. How would it be if we kept on walking home every day, but didn't have *regular* dates? Most fellows and girls have date-night on Wednesday, and when they start going real steady, he goes to her house on Sunday."

"We're a long way from that," she said. "All right. We'll walk home after work, as usual, and if you want to take me to a picture, you say so and sometimes I'll say yes and sometimes I'll say no. Is that all right with you?"

"Anything's all right that you agree to."

They violated the agreement immediately. He saw her every Wednesday night, and on Sunday evenings he walked home with her and Ivy Heinz. He and Ivy would say good-night to Muriel, and he would then walk home with Ivy. But though Muriel had never invited him inside her house, Ivy simply opened the door and expected him to follow her, which he did, on the very first night he walked home with her. She called upstairs: "It's me, Momma. I have company."

"All right, but if you're going to play the Vic don't play it too loud. It's Sunday. And don't forget, tomorrow's Monday morning."

Ivy wound up the Victrola and put on Zez Confrey's "Kitten on the Keys."

"Do you still dance, George?"

"Oh, I'm terrible."

"Well, we can try," said Ivy.

He knew as soon as he put his arm around her waist that the dancing was only an excuse. She stood absolutely still and waited for him to kiss her. They kissed through three records, one of them a non-dance record of Vernon Dalhart's, and at the end of the third she stopped the machine and led George to the sofa, stretched out and let him lie beside her. She seemed to be able to tell exactly when he would be about to get fresh, and her hand would anticipate his, but she kissed him freely until the court house clock struck eleven.

"I-vee-ee? Eleven o'clock," her mother called.

"You have to go now," said Ivy.

Sunday after Sunday he got from Ivy the kisses he wanted from Muriel, and after several months it was more than kisses. "Next Sunday you come prepared, huh?" said Ivy, when their necking reached that stage.

"I am prepared, now," he said.

"No. But next Sunday Momma's going to be away and I'll be all alone. We won't have to stay down here."

He had grown fond of Ivy. From the very beginning she had understood that he was in love with Muriel and had never brought her into their conversations in any way that would touch upon her disloyalty to her friend or his weakness of character. Nor was she jealous of his feeling for Muriel. Nor was Muriel so much as curious about what might go on after they said goodnight to her on Sunday evenings. But fond as he was of Ivy, it was her taking him to bed with her—his first time with any woman—that compelled him to propose marriage to Muriel. He had no doubts about himself now, and among the doubts that vanished was the one that concerned his marital relations with Muriel. As husband he would be expected to know what to do, but before the night in Ivy's bed he had not been sure himself.

He took Muriel to the picture show on the Wednesday following the Sunday in Ivy's room, and when they got to Muriel's house he said, "Can we go inside a minute?"

"It's after eleven, George."

"I know, but I didn't have much chance to talk to you. I wish you would, Mure."

"Well, I guess they won't object, a few minutes. But you can't stay after half past eleven."

His manner did not show it, but he had never been so sure of himself or wanted Muriel so fiercely. He stood behind her as she was hanging up her things on the clothes-stand, and when she turned and faced him he did not get out of the way. "I want to kiss you, Muriel."

"Oh, George, no. I noticed all evening—is that what you were thinking about?"

"Much more, Muriel. I want you to marry me."

"Oh—goodness. You're standing in my way. Let's go in the parlor."

She switched on the parlor chandelier and took a seat on the sofa, where he could sit beside her. She let him take her hand. "Did you just think of this?"

"Of course not. I've been thinking about it for over a year," he said. "Maybe longer than that, to tell you the truth. You're an intelligent girl, and you know I've never dated anyone else."

"As far as I know, you didn't. But I never asked you and you never told me. You could have been having dates with other girls."

"Maybe I could have, but I never did. Ever since I got out of the army the only girl I wanted to be with was you. And that's the way I want it to be the rest of my life. I love you, Muriel."

"Oh, George. Love. I'm afraid of that word."

"You? Afraid of the word love? Why, you, you're so feminine and all, love ought to be—I don't know."

"Well, marriage, I guess. I guess it's marriage I'm afraid of."

"I guess a lot of girls are, but they get over it. Your mother did, my mother did, and look at them."

"You have so many wonderful qualities, George, but I don't think I could ever love you the way Mama loves Father. And your parents. It's nothing against you, personally, it's just me. And any fellow."

"My goodness, you love children."

"You mean when they come in the bank? But that's what they are. Children. You're a man, George."

"Don't tell me you're a man-hater."

"No, not a man-hater. Heavens. But I could never—I never want to get married! Why don't you help me? You know what I'm trying to say. I wouldn't like a man to—I was afraid you were going to kiss me, in the hallway. *That.* That's what I'm trying to tell you. I could never have children. When we were in High didn't you use to feel the same way about girls? I used to think you did. You never went out with girls, George. You and Carlie had more fun than anybody."

"But I always liked girls."

"Well, I liked boys, too, but I never wanted to be alone with a boy. You know how old I am, and I've never kissed a boy in my whole life. And I never will."

"You're wrong, Muriel. You'll fall in love with one some day. I wish it was going to be me."

"How wrong *you* are. I wouldn't let you sit here if I thought you were like the others." In the conversation she had taken away her hand, and now she put it back on his. "I want a man for a friend, George, but that's all. When I was little I read a story about a princess. She was forced to marry this king or else he'd declare war on her father. I couldn't do that. I'd sooner kill myself."

"Why?"

"Don't ask me why. I think all girls feel that way, underneath. I don't think they ever get used to some things, but they pretend to because they love their husbands for other reasons. I could love you that way, George, but you wouldn't love me. You wouldn't be satisfied with just being nice. You'd have to be a man and do those things that are so ugly to my way of thinking."

"But girls have desires, Mure."

She shook her head. "No. They only pretend. Most girls have to have a man to support them, but if they had a job they'd never get married. I have a job and Ivy has a job, so we didn't have to have a man to support us."

"The rich girls on Lantenengo Street, they don't need a man to support them."

"Not to support them, but that's the way they stay rich. The rich girls marry the rich boys and the money all stays together."

"I hear some pretty funny stories about some of those girls."

"Yes, but most of them drink, and the men take advantage of them. The girls are nice, but when they take too much to drink they're not responsible. That's why the men up there encourage them to drink."

"Well, I know very little about what goes on up there, but at the rate they're spending it, some of them won't have it very long."

"I feel sorry for the women. I don't really care what happens to the men, especially one of them."

"Did something to you?"

"Not to me, but to a girl I know. One of the H.T.P.'s. One night at the picture show, he did something. Don't ask me any more about it because I won't tell you. But they're all alike, up there."

"You'd better not say that at the bank."

"Oh, I should say not. But whenever that man comes in I think of what his wife has to put up with. And they're supposed to be the people everybody looks up to. Rich, and educated, the privileged class."

"I wouldn't be like that, Muriel."

"I know you wouldn't, George. But maybe men can't help themselves."

"It's a good thing we talked about this."

"Oh, I wouldn't have married you, George. Or anybody else."

"I was thinking of something else. You make me wonder about women, how they really feel. You're a woman, and I guess you ought to know."

"We just don't have the same feelings men do."

"Then if women all had jobs the whole race would die out."

"Yes, except that don't forget women love children and they'd still go through it all to have them."

"Would you?"

"No, I don't love children that much."

"What do you love, Mure?"

"What do I love? Oh, lots of things. And people. My parents. Some of my friends. The music in church. Singing with our old bunch. Nature. I love nature. I love scenery, a good view. Flowers. Nearly all flowers I love, and trees on the mountains. The touch of velvet, like this cushion. And I love to swim, not at the shore, but in a dam if the water's not too cold. And my one bad habit. Smoking cigarettes."

"Now I never knew you smoked."

"I don't get much chance to, except when I go to Ivy's. Mrs. Heinz has something the matter with her nose, some condition, and we can smoke one right after the other and she never catches on. If my parents knew I smoked they'd disown me."

He looked at her hand. "Muriel, some day the right fellow will come along, and all these things you said tonight, you won't even remember thinking them."

"Don't say things like that, George. You don't know me at all, what I really feel. Nobody does, not even Ivy."

"Your trouble is, you're just too good, too innocent."

"Oh, I don't like that, either. You meant it as a compliment, but it shows a great lack of understanding. Of me, that is. You think that some fellow with wavy hair—"

"Maurice Costello."

"Or Thomas Meighan. I'll meet somebody like that and forget the things I believe. But you're wrong. I'd love to have Thomas Meighan for a friend, but honestly, George, I'd just as soon have you. At least I know you better, and I don't know what I'd ever find to talk about with Thomas Meighan." She looked at him intently. "George, I don't want to put you off proposing to someone else. You'll make some girl a good husband. But when you do find the right girl, if you want to make her happy, don't be disappointed if she doesn't like the kissing part of married life. You know what I mean, and it isn't just kissing."

"I know."

"A friend of mine, a girl you know too, she got married, and now she comes to me and cries her heart out. 'You were right, Muriel,' she says. 'I hate the kissing.' I used to try to tell her that she wasn't going to like it, but she wouldn't believe me. She said if you love a person, you don't mind. Well, she loved the fellow she married but now he hates her. Isn't that awful? And I feel just as sorry for the fellow, George. He can't help it that he has those animal instincts. All men have them, I suppose. I guess even you, because I admit it, I had that feeling earlier that you were going to want to kiss me, and that's the first step. I've always known that about boys, and that's why I've never let one kiss me."

"Well, I guess we'd better not have any more dates."

"Oh, we couldn't now. And maybe you'd better not wait for me after work tomorrow. I've told you so much about myself, I don't know how I'm going to look at you in the morning."

"Do you feel naked?"

"George! Oh, why did you say that? Go home, go home. Please go, this minute." She was in angry tears, and he left her sitting on the sofa.

At the bank in the morning she seemed cool and serene, but he was not deceived. At moments when once she would have given him a bright, quick smile, she would not look at him. In the afternoon he stayed behind longer than usual, to give her a chance to leave well ahead of him. On Sunday night she was not at church, and he walked home with Ivy.

"You can't come in," said Ivy. "My mother's still downstairs."

"Then she must be sitting in the dark," he said.

"All right, you can come in, but it won't be any use," she said.

He put a record on the Victrola, but she braked the turntable. He put his arms around her, but she turned her face away and sat in a chair where there was not room for him. She lit a cigarette before he could get out his matches. "Muriel told you, huh?" he said.

"Sure. She tells me everything. I don't tell her everything, but she tells me. Now you'd better leave her alone."

"Oh, I will. She's a man-hater."

"Just finding that out? And what if she is?"

"At least you're not."

"Maybe I should be."

"Oh, she handed you some of her propaganda," said George.

"Think back to one week ago tonight, George Dalrymple. Then Monday, Tuesday, and Wednesday you proposed to Muriel."

"Ivy, you knew all along that some day I was going to ask Muriel to marry me."

"No I didn't. I thought you'd find out that she was never going to marry anybody. You had a lot of talks with her."

"Not about that subject. What's the matter with her?"

"Does there have to be something the matter with her?"

"Well, there's nothing the matter with you. You want to get married some day."

"Maybe I do and maybe I don't."

"Yes you do. What if I asked you to marry me?"

"You didn't ask me."

"Then I do ask you. Will you marry me?"

"No."

"Well, maybe that's because you're sore at *me.* But you're going to marry somebody."

"There you're wrong."

"You'll have to have somebody."

"I have somebody—now."

"Who?"

"Wouldn't you like to know?"

"That's why I'm asking you. Harry Brenner?"

"No, not Harry Brenner."

"Chick Charles?"

"Not him, either."

"Oh, that new fellow in the jewelry store."

"Wrong again."

"I can't think of anybody else you had a date with. Is it a married man?"

"Give up, stop trying."

"All right, I give up. Who is it?"

"That's for me to know and you to find out."

"Don't be sore at me, Ivy."

"I'm not really sore at you, George."

"Yes you are, but when you get over it, let's take in a movie next week?"

"No. Thanks for asking me, but I'm not going to see you any more."

"You're sore about Muriel. Well, I couldn't help it."

"Honestly, George, I'm not sore about Muriel. Not one bit."

"Well, I'm going to keep my eye on you. I want to find out about this mystery man."

"It's a free country, George."

On the next Wednesday night he happened to be at the movies with Harry Brenner's brother Paul, and sitting two rows in front of them were Ivy Heinz and Muriel Hamilton. Later, at the soda fountain, George walked over and reached down and picked up the girls' check. "Allow me, ladies?" he said.

"Oh, no, George, you mustn't," said Muriel.

"My treat," he said. "I guess thirty-two cents won't break me." He paid the cashier on the way out, and stood on the sidewalk. The girls stopped to thank him again, and Muriel, somewhat ill at ease, made some polite conversation with Paul Brenner. George, in his muttering way, spoke to Ivy. "Using Muriel as a disguise, eh?"

"Curiosity killed the cat," said Ivy.

It was a long time, many Wednesdays, before George Dalrymple allowed himself to believe that Ivy was not using Muriel as a disguise. But they were just as nice about his secrets, too.

1962

MAUDE HUTCHINS

::

THE WRECK

HE WAS FOURTEEN AND OUT OF THIS WORLD. HE LIVED IN A LIMBO OF violence and innocent obscenity. His imagination ranged from heroes of the better sort to thieves and cutthroats, from sailors alone at sea singing into the wind and munching hardtack, their square faces encrusted with salt, and engineers careening at top speed in long trains like strings of licorice through burning mesquite and red-hot timber, to peddlers of dope, skulking and cringing along outer edges, their forearms and thighs punctured and scarred, their eyes like windows, their lips bitten and bloody, and enormous men, obese, with lumpy parts, strangling their women and sucking oranges all day long, and four telephones; bankers, multimillionaires with matted hair on chests that bulged like women's breasts, pink tits on them, horrible.

With flushed cheeks he walked along the seashore, dreaming of men, teasing himself with horror, comforting himself with heroes. He could turn it on and turn it off at will and come home to his mother and his sisters as cool as a cucumber. Fatherless, he stuffed himself like a glutton with the muscular food of his dreams, meaty dreams, all male, carnivorous, protein. No pretty girls, no lovely women walked by his side along the strip of beach which was his empty page each day to people and plot and darken with the fine handwriting of his imagination, at each tide to be erased like a slate, cleaned like a plate. What if one day the bloated bodies of his accomplices were washed ashore by some evil undertow reversing its course, some strange sirocco flattening out the habit of natural things, and his dreams come true, his companions and heroes and pimps and rogues and thieves and multimillionaires pile up on the chaste expanse of sand like a lot of rotting stumps and logs and upholstered chairs? The corpus delicti of his dreams?

He walked lightly down the path he had trampled all summer long with his own sneakered feet, through the cutting beach grass and the blueberry, wild rose and bayberry. The strip of beach separating bay from ocean was deserted. Not even a fisherman at this fall of the year was in sight, casting the loop of his line like a lasso, dropping his plug into the sea and retrieving it and whistling under his breath, the lone contented male, hour after hour after hour, but real. The boy, this boy I am talking about who ten just such seasons as this ago hung around his mother's neck and screamed with pleasure as she dunked him again and again in the sea, the big waves, salty in his mouth, cold as ice in his ears, throwing him rhythmically against her bosom, gave her no more thought now than if she had been a tricycle he had outgrown. His sisters embarrassed and disgusted him by their animal femininity. He blushed at their calcimined pinkness where the sun hadn't browned them, when they immodestly raised their arms or crossed their legs. The brand new breasts of the elder that had not been there last week sickened him more than they mystified him and his mother's generous deeds, her everlasting housekeeping and her saddened eyes, her tired cheeks, her apron, infuriated him.

He clambered down the dunes, the heaped-up great clumps of sand fringed with sparse but hardy greenery that bent over in the wind tracing designs in the sand as if birds had walked beneath. He reached the hardened beach, pounded firm and smooth by the powerful surf, one could dance on it and see one's reflection as in a glass and it squeaked under his rubber sneakers so that he took them off and went along barefoot, hurling them back toward the path to be free of them. Hatless, empty-handed, barefoot, alone, free, the author.

The wind all the way from Spain slapped his cheeks and tugged at his fair hair and pulled at its roots. The waters of Egypt lapped and sucked at his feet and ankles and he turned up his jeans to just below his knees to feel their liquid caress. The calves of his legs were brown and tender, his ankles slight, his whole body with its still unthickened waist, narrow hips and round buttocks, his hollowed back, shaped like a V, his flat stomach, was as graceful and elegant as that of a highly bred animal. He was an unfortunately pretty boy. He had a long, smooth neck with a visible pulse at its base. His features were regular, not arresting, but his look, the expression of the whole, was what made one stare; the passionate self-centered gaze, without focus, of a nubile maiden: the parted sensuous lips, the flushed cheek, the melting eyes, almost molten, hot; in contrast, a cool expressionless forehead as chaste as white paper. His fair hair, bleached by the sun, seemed indecent, private; his look, let us say, was for the closet. It should not have gone abroad, it invited rape.

Where he left off yesterday he began this day: The powerful but benign male pressed into his palm a sheaf of bills, fifties, a couple of hundreds.

For your work last night, he said, don't thank me.

And tonight? said the pretty boy. He was dressed in a black trench coat and a white beret. People in the subway stared, as well they might have.

Not here, said the man; his iron-gray hair was pomaded and slicked down over his ears and his face was naked and gross, in the lobes of his ears were sapphires. Can you play the piano? he asked.

A little, said the boy, if I had the opportunity.

Here we are, said the man, his striped pants fit him so tight he walked as if he had a stomach-ache. They need music, he said, I will attend to the rest, give them everything you have.

The fair-haired virgin boy sat down at the luminous piano and ran his girlish fingers over the keys; a lovely and secret melody came out of the guts of the three-legged instrument and he raised his chin and sang in a penetrating, heartbreaking voice, that soprano one usually hears only in church, *voce di testa,* shameless, the swan song of innocence. Young men, beauties all, lay hands on each other's slender hips and danced, at least moved in unison to the strange, disassociated tune. The powerful but benign male moved his hips to the arbitrary and haunting rhythm that the boy beat out, and passed among the dancers, giving to each a folded white paper. A big Negro dressed in a crimson skirt, his breast bare and his buttocks locked, his feet in Turkish slippers and a diamond in his nose, poured each dancer a thimbleful of liquid into a tiny glass; all the little glasses shimmered like fireflies as the room grew dark as a hedge at night. The boy stopped playing but the harmony lingered. It seemed to be coming from upstairs, it crept into hollow places and down the banister.

Darling, don't stop, the boys cried. Sweetheart, go on, Baby, play to us.

The white powder slid into each glass like a doctor's prescription.

Lover, the powerful but benign male said, you were a great success, and he took the sapphires from his ears and gave them to him.

The pounding of the surf was insistent, incessant, ceaseless, the salt spray foamed in his mouth. The incoming tide dredged hollows under his feet and he could feel his hair curling, it hurt, and his ears ached. Enough, he whispered, tomorrow I will play for the boy dancers again and he, *he* will say, you are extraordinary, you are . . . and he will press into my hands what I have well earned and I shall go home with him and he will do it to me.

No, no, the boy shook his head, slowly, not yet, it must not end so soon. He was shaking with the cold and the sea at the horizon had a violet rim, the eel grass slithered and whined as if it were alive and very nervous, and mauve shadows lay in front of each hillock of sand on the eastern side as the sun set early and fast. The western sky turned orange right on time and the day was over, but the wind increased, it blew from behind him, smack out of the east and it carried him, almost, in the palm of its big hand, home. He scrambled up the uneven little path, his heart beating irregularly from his daydream which had been longer, much more prolonged, than I have described it and he felt a weakness in his knees and his head ached.

He lay quiet in his narrow bed, the girls were playing their silly records, and his mother's footsteps went back and forth, back and forth. The night was black as pitch and it was lighter when he closed his eyes where golden circles interlocked as in a plastic puzzle. He went to sleep, his fists against his face, his knees up, prenatal.

He woke to the rattle and bang of the wind in the cottage. He heard his mother slamming down the windows and the sleepy, irritable gibberish of his sisters. He got up and stood in the window from where he could see the lighthouse and he saw its light like an orange come and go, but the freshening wind seemed to blow its rays sideways, the beam scarcely penetrated the spray of the surf which was high and like a spangled fog.

Sonny, get up, it's a hurricane!

His heart leapt.

The wind increased and howled around the corners and edges of the house, it whined and mewed like a cat. It withdrew and slammed against the cottage like a truck. It sucked the air out of the chimney, it crept in and lifted the carpet an inch off the floor, it doused the candles his mother had lighted, it whispered of death and destruction and holocaust, it slunk away and returned, its force redoubled, its stubborn determination to uproot the earth perfectly ridiculous. Underneath it all like the tympanies in an orchestra, the tremendous natural roar of the surf, rhythmic, as if it were counting: one—two—three—four—wham! The cottage trembled and sighed. Erosion was in the air, the sand beat against the windowpanes with a message: Get out of here. An unearthly sobbing, a curious retching came out of the cellar, and in the attic, possibly from the ancient trunks and wardrobes, a cello-like chord, an anguished, desperate appeal for help. Giant steps resounded on the porch, and in the tiny vestibule the bell of the boy's bicycle began to ring as it sped away riderless, bounding over the dunes, possessed, in metamorphosis. The laundry that had been struggling all summer to get off the line escaped and finally would heap up where it wasn't wanted, torn to shreds, humiliated. The front door opposite the proper direction of the gale burst open while the door that the wind was pounding on like a madman remained adamant, even the slender key steadfast. Through the open door hanging against the suction of the crazy thermo came a deer from the dunes, carefully lowering his head, endowed with a new intelligence perhaps from catastrophe, to avoid the jamb. His antlers that looked like the branches of a stripped cherry tree, had no doubt acted as a complicated rudder and steered him to the cottage, up the steps and into the house, where he was greeted while not without amazement, still with little surprise on such a night of opposing logic or no logic at all as this. He might have been Jesus in disguise. The slick painting of the children's grandfather in the dining room that when he was naughty he had punctured with BB shot began to sing like an Aeolian harp.

His sisters whimpered on the couch. His mother, with a persistent cheerful look, belied by her trembling hands and twitching lips, went for a broom and began to sweep, as if a housewife could bring order out of chaos, from sheer feminine will power. The deer relieved itself as if dropping a sign for the hunters, the last gesture of the hunted, I am here, come and get me.

The boy's reaction was a still further removal from life, if this was life. He became remote to the point almost of physical disappearance.

Sonny! his mother called, sensing his withdrawal.

I am here, Mother, he said. He was fearless, as cool as a cucumber, but he turned his back on the womenfolk because his sex responded to the gale without his permission.

Well, the cottage, used to giving an inch in lesser gales every season, leaning, twisting, attenuating itself, crouching and feinting, never losing track of the calculus of the wind or the algebra of the sand, listening to every word the elements said, was still erect next morning. At low tide it stood as if on stilts, light airs stirring the curtains through shutterless windows, the chimney gone, the doors hanging off their hinges, the cellar door floating on its back a mile away.

The girls cheerfully helped their mother clean up, they were so glad not to be dead, and they gave her credit for it, but the boy was only in the way, absent-minded, moody, they let him go off to the beach.

He loped along over a brand new terrain, things that had been here were there and there, here; the dunes were turned upside-down as if plowed for spring planting, lumber from somewhere lay in his way, somebody's stove nestled in the sand, and a tennis racket, its strings curled up like his sister's hair, was hanging off a blueberry bush, a carpet of rosehips bled under his feet, juice for his mother's good jelly wasted. Dreaming, he leaned down and scooped up a handful of emeralds and slid them into the pocket of his jeans, they were weightless and soundless. He blushed at the theft. There would be diamonds glistening on the beach if he got there first, a hogshead-ful. He banished his fellow men and planned the elemental robbery alone. All the brainwashing in the world, even torture, would not loosen his tongue. The big cop stood over him with sweating brows, I found nothing, the beach was bare, he said. He beat his way down a new path, the sky was busy with gulls; heads down, they rode the updraughts, beady-eyed, necks outstretched, they, too, were out for plunder. One wonders where they had passed the fearful night. Maybe in the big fist of God. The moon hadn't been dislodged either, it looked, however, like a film of its former self, pale blue, almost transparent, a morning-after-the-storm moon.

The boy, from where he poised himself at last, surveyed the beach, and a sickening, fascinated horror made his heart stand still and the color leave his cheeks, only to return in an upsurge of blood, a blush that pounded in his ears, and the saliva glands in his mouth ejected a fine fountain of mist as if two thousand volts had passed through his slender body.

As far as he could see—the bloated, hideous, lifeless corpses of his dream men, an awful seraglio, harem, zenana, of males.

He dared descend; he knew no words to say. The continued story in his brain said, The End; the cheap and vulgar subject matter lay washed up on the beach for all to see, no longer the secret indulgence of a dream-ridden lad. Any vicious beauty with which he had endowed them was no longer theirs. The serpentine triple pile of them seemed to advance and retreat with the gentle movement of the still-outgoing tide; here and there it persuasively sucked at a discolored ankle or a fractured biscuit-colored elbow, but there was no returning of this doubly weighted mass of casualties to the depths. Soggy and disreputable, brutish, lascivious, lewd, in death as in life, their swollen cadavers nudged at each other and, giving very little to the undertow, nevertheless, as I have said, presented a slight rolling movement over all that made one's hair stand on end. This movement in death, this horrible inertia.

The boy made a tremendous effort and looked away, it would seem that he would always look and never stop looking at what he saw but he gazed out to sea, out over the expanse of pure and sparkling, silent water for a glimpse, a reason: a foundered ship, the wreck. There must have been a wreck, a big ship gone on the rocks, the lighthouse light had failed, the great tanker pounded to pieces on the cruel rocks and her cargo washed up on the beach.

No, it had been a passenger ship. And these were her passengers, he murmured.

Must I bury them all? he thought.

Hi! The jeep came up behind him. I almost ran over you, didn't see you, sun in my eyes.

The two Coast Guardsmen hopped out, pushed their caps back on their foreheads and, hands on their hips, took a good look at the beach.

Hell of a mess, said one.

And it was so pretty yesterday, said the other.

I think I'm going to throw up, said the boy in a childish voice, the awful smell of male perfume from the beach had got in his throat and he was sickened.

Hop in, the Coast Guards said, and ride along with us, it will do you good. Little fairy, they thought. They stared at his pretty throat, his fair, indecent hair, and they wondered and their lips curled.

I can't—all the *bodies*, the boy said. He wanted to, he wanted terribly to look at them all, even poke at them as if they were swollen toads, but his knees were turning to water, he shook all over.

Bodies! they laughed. It's just stuff, why it's just stuff, rotten stumps and logs and upholstered chairs. Funny all those upholstered chairs, where they came from every time. It's just stuff.

But they were mistaken; way down, a mile or so, they came upon the ribs of a fisherman's boat, embedded in the sand, and beside it the drowned sailor, his square face encrusted with salt, his mouth open as if he had been singing into the wind.

1962

EDMUND WHITE

::

THE BEAUTIFUL ROOM IS EMPTY

WHEN ED AND CHARLES WERE IN SAN JUAN FOR A WEEK'S VACATION, THEIR days were measured by Charles's pills: three kinds of tranquilizers four times a day. They would take the Number Ten from Condado Beach to the Plaza de Colón, wet towels rolled in their laps, and Charles's shaking fingers would be picking pills out of the cotton-stuffed cylinder; or they would sit over their breakfast at the Red Rooster, townspeople chattering at lunch beside them, and Ed would hear the familiar rattle of capsules on plastic. The sound would remind Ed to take a diet pill. Half an hour later their drugs took effect. Ed talked ceaselessly and Charles turned more and more taciturn and indifferent.

The first two days the Americans couldn't discover the rhythms of Puerto Rican life—they wanted to eat supper at six, hit the bars at ten, score by one; but San Juan ran four hours behind them, deep into the cool mornings. By Wednesday, after a few false starts, Charles was taking his last pills at midnight, content to stand at the Camino Real, one foot propped against the wall, until the bar began to swing at three in the morning.

The dim couples sitting along the wall sipping rum or attempting the latest dances under the slow fans scarcely knew how to swing by New York standards; Charles and Ed kept trying to discover where the action was. Hadn't Carlos said bar life in P.R. was wide open? And surely Jaime had mentioned something about a whorehouse full of nine-year-olds with perfect round asses. Some of the boys Ed talked to at Condado Beach only laughed when they heard about the *niños;* they shrugged and said San Juan was a big bore all the time, but particularly in October. Too early. The season doesn't start till December. Why, you're the only Americans in town.

"Wrong think!" Charles shouted like a commissar, frowning, then smiling. When they got back to Ed's room in the YMCA Charles explained: "It's boring for *them,* all right, but they've lived in New York for six months and want everything here to be like Third Avenue or the Village."

"But, Charles," Ed said, "that queen from San Francisco, you know, the one who's been here for six weeks, he says P.R. is a drag, too."

"And what does he go for?"

"Well, I don't know . . ."

"Americans!" Charles exploded, uncurling his legs and leaping off Ed's bed. "Those California fairies are always mooning over straight GI's. And can't get 'em! So they lie under the sun all day and add another layer of leather to their tans. Aren't tans disgusting on moony old queens?"

Charles had solved the problem; he sat down again, ran a hand through his long black hair and started drumming his fingers against his desert boots.

::

IT WAS ONLY ELEVEN O'CLOCK, BUT THE CITY SEEMED DESERTED. THE DIM lobby of the Y was empty except for two pool tables and an American soldier reading a newspaper close to the open doors. The narrow streets were empty except for policemen stationed every few blocks calmly pacing the blue brick pavement, seeming at once relaxed and formal, like morticians.

"This town is crawling with cops!" Charles hissed.

"Why are you walking so fast? Look at that woman." Ed pointed to a woman ambling slowly down the street, swinging her black pocketbook with every step. "That's the pace down here." A policeman passed on a cross street, refusing to look at them.

The square was lit in leafy patches by unfrosted light bulbs strung through the branches. A dozen old men and two or three little boys stood with their arms folded in the center of the white cement square watching the two public television sets placed high above ground in the crotches of old trees. The shirt-sleeved figures looked like a handful of extras on the immense stage of some opera house. On three sides of the plaza rose the khaki-colored façades of government buildings; on the fourth was the New York Department Store, its buzzing showcases filled with mannekins wearing kitchen aprons and pointing to bottles of clear Puerto Rican rum.

Charles pointed to the three stone steps leading down from a dais where two white statues stood holding sheaves of wheat—figures slightly smaller than life size which gave the disconcerting effect of their having been modeled on a forgotten race. "Do you want to sit down there?" Charles asked.

"Okay . . . What for?"

"We can watch a little TV."

I've exhausted him, Ed thought. My diet pills have made me talk too much. "It's an American movie—it's dubbed."

"Is this the main drag?" Charles asked.

"I don't know. Should I look at the map?"

"Let's not pull that out all the time."

"Why? Too touristy?"

Charles nodded absently and looked at his folded hands. Ed tried to adjust his voice so that it would sound casual. "How do you feel?"

Charles held out his hands—there was a faint line running across the knuckles on the left one, a scar from a knife fight. His right wrist, disguised by a heavy, old-fashioned ID bracelet, was smaller than the left, and the little finger curved inwards: a car accident. "Are my hands shaking as much?"

"You seem much calmer . . . And you seem to be in a better mood."

"I just hope there hasn't been any nerve damage." Charles's eyes widened as though startled by the term.

"No, I don't think so," Ed said. "It's like lifting weights: your arms shake when you curl more than you can handle. You've been under a strain." He'll never swallow that, Ed thought.

"Then you don't think there's been any permanent damage?"

"No."

"Look at me, I can't even hold a cigarette. In the morning I shake so bad I can't even shave. See?" He showed him a nick on his neck.

A young Puerto Rican boy, dressed in girl's white shantung pants zippered up the side, entered the square and walked toward them under the arcade of the city hall. "Look at that boy over there," Ed said, nodding.

Charles looked, smiled and dropped his eyes back to his hands. "Yeah . . . that's a nice one. There's not a bone in my arm that hasn't been broken. I don't know, Ed . . ."

Ed tried to count to ten. He must give Charles time to go on. But he only made it to six. "What's wrong?"

"I've had too many fuck-ups."

"That's ridiculous. If you think of yourself now and how you were two years ago . . ." Ed suddenly realized that he had to finish the sentence: "You'd see that you've made a lot of progress."

Charles smiled very slowly. Everyone remarked on his youthful looks. He once said he looked young only because he had studied boys' mannerisms and imitated them; for instance, boys never fall into a brown study but make countless eye adjustments every minute—close, far, left, right. Charles's eyes remained fixed on his hands.

"I'm glad you came to Puerto Rico with me," Ed said. "Right now I'd be sitting in my room at the Y reading a book if you hadn't come. You make me get out and do things."

"Come on," Charles said modestly; he received compliments as awkwardly as an athlete.

The boy in girl's pants hurried past with a friend whose hair was dyed red and stiffened with lacquer. "Do you think he's cute?"

"Yes," Charles sighed, visibly depressed again. "That's a nice one."

"He's been staring holes through you."

"Me?" He pressed the weight of his body against Ed's and put his hand on Ed's neck. Suddenly he let it fall away. His movements were strange. Which position he took, how long he held it and what he would do next always surprised Ed; Charles must have broken a lot of things when he was a little boy and never been scolded for it. "He's probably cruising *you,*" Charles said.

"No one looks at me."

"They do now that you're thin."

"That poor boy is pining away," Ed said. "Put him out of his misery."

"I'm staying in the wrong place!" Charles lurched forward, held Ed by the arm and looked into his eyes. "I can't take anyone to the Convento! Maybe"—he looked up at the black hands and numbers on the town hall's illuminated clock—"maybe we shouldn't try to score tonight."

"I don't think we should set any goals for ourselves," Ed agreed. The boy with girl's pants and his friend paused at a nearby tree and kept glancing at the Americans without once interrupting their stream of emphatic chatter.

"What should we do now?" Charles asked.

"That's just the point. We shouldn't *do* anything."

"You just want to sit here?" Charles asked. "I don't think I can do that yet." He took Ed's hands in his; Ed glanced at the crowd watching television. "Okay? I'm too buggy just to sit."

"You shouldn't take my hand like that, or people will think we're lovers and you'll never make out."

"Sorry." Charles shrugged, turned away and then stood up, tucking his shirt into his pants. He pulled the vial of pills out of his breast pocket and checked his watch. "If I take three now, that will give me one more dose before I go to bed, if I go to bed at three, let's say. Is that right? Yeah, that's right." He looked at Ed sheepishly. "You must be sick of seeing me take pills."

"Not at all; are you sick of seeing me take my diet pills?"

"I'm sick of all drugs. *All . . . drugs . . .* When I'm through with these tranquilizers, then that's it." Charles rested his hand on Ed's again; Ed could feel his rapid tremor. "I'm fed up with junk, with morphine, Benzedrine, Dexedrine, amphetamines, aspirin . . ."

"There they go," Ed said. As though they had plotted their route exactly and given each other a signal for leaving, the two boys hurried in perfect unison toward the jewelry shop, made a neat military turn and headed down the sidewalk. "I guess they got discouraged. Poor darlings . . ."

Charles insisted that Ed accompany him the three blocks to his hotel. He was afraid of getting lost, he said. He didn't know the city or the language.

A hand shot out of a doorway at them. Charles jumped. An old woman, sitting on a wooden crate, flexed her fingers and muttered something, then returned her hand to her lap. The policeman, the only other person on the street, looked probably for the hundredth time that night into a window full of lingerie as a breeze lifted his starched short sleeves.

When Ed had first imagined the week, he decided that Charles would be tricking right and left, and that he would not be making out at all. He had carefully fortified himself, but then, to his surprise, Charles seemed to avoid every opportunity. "He doesn't want me," Charles would say, or "He's too butch." At other times his excuse for not scoring would be, "The cops are looking."

And Ed, just as surely, would find an answer to each objection: "He does so want you—he's the one who kept swishing past you at the Concha"; "Butch? He could die with the secret . . ." Ed even flirted with a fat policeman just to prove to Charles that every man in Puerto Rico was available, even the cops.

"*Every* man?" Charles asked as they were ambling back to the Old City. He smiled, and Ed, pleased to see Charles's high spirits returning under his ministrations, declared flatly, "Every man."

"Let's test that theory of yours, mister. See those guys up there?" Charles nodded toward a gang of gleaming laborers swarming over the orange girders of a half-built hotel across the street. "Let's wave to them."

"Okay."

Charles lifted his right hand demurely and wiggled his fingers in the air; Ed watched and followed suit. "Boys, oh bo-o-oys," Charles sang in a fruity soprano. A laborer instantly whistled back through his fingers. In a moment the entire building was quick with bronze birds leaping from strut to strut, rending the air with their calls. Like angry birds, Ed thought, frightened by the mindless grin of one man who was pretending to jerk himself off.

But Charles didn't seem to notice that the other men were beginning to imitate the masturbator and to wield huge comic-book cocks, or if he did notice he failed to sense the derision in the act and the danger. "The theory's been proved," he said, "to *my* satisfaction," and he walked off toward the Hilton. The noise pursued them until they were well across the bridge.

Upon Charles's insistence they approached two middle-aged men at Condado Beach. "Maybe they'll take us up to their expensive room in this fabulous hotel and fuck us," Charles whispered, wide-eyed, as though he had just conceived the ad campaign of the century.

"What's so great about that?" Ed asked.

"They'll pay us and drive us around in their Cadillacs. I went to Miami last December with nothing but a toothbrush and came back with a hundred bucks. A Texas millionaire who weighed about three hundred pounds took me to the Eden Roc—I had to wear one of his Palm Beach jackets to get through the lobby. It was so big I wrapped it around me twice."

As it turned out, neither of these men owned a Cadillac or was particularly eager to pay for sex. They were vacationing Chilean businessmen, certainly not above sleeping with young Americans if the opportunity presented itself, but they were feeling much too casual to fit into the scenario Ed and Charles had plotted for them. While Ed was asking them about Chile, Charles concentrated on a Negro boy who had run out of the ocean and rolled in the sand; his black body was coated with sugar-white granules. The boy was lying motionless on his stomach, motionless except when he slowly contracted his buttocks and swiveled deeper into the warm rut he had hollowed out for himself.

Charles groaned. "Do you see that, Ed?"

"See what? Yeah. Nice."

Charles dropped his hand on Ed's bare back, his ID bracelet branding Ed with a thin bar of heat absorbed from the powerful sun. "Can you imagine *being* that boy?" Charles asked. He lifted his arm and moved his hand lightly down Ed's neck and shoulder. "To be that boy . . . I really think I'm going to pass out." He squinted, inhaled sharply and shook his head slowly from side to side. Finally he laughed and turned over on his stomach. "It's giving me a hard-on."

"Well," the swarthy Chilean said, turning his amethyst ring exactly once around his left little finger and smiling, "if you go for that, you'd like the public beach, the Playa Publica."

::

"THERE THEY ARE," CHARLES WHISPERED AS THEY APPROACHED THE WATER. He sat down on a rock. A tall boy was standing on a white raft, one leg relaxed, the other bearing his weight, a hand held to his waist. Another boy was straining to pull himself up onto the wooden dock that spanned the lagoon inside the breakwater. As he balanced on his hands, the sun gleamed on his hip: a flash of yellow shivering on his sleek white trunks. On the other side of the lagoon, quite close to Charles and Ed, a trio of boys lined up to dive off the cement wall. As each boy approached the edge his head eclipsed the late afternoon sun and his face was cast into a darkness relieved only by the pulsing reflections from the water below. Charles watched one of them dive and lowered his head.

"Are you depressed?" Ed asked.

"Yes," he sighed, "it's all here. I think we should go back."

Charles checked his watch, shook two pills into his hand and swallowed them mournfully. Ed followed suit by taking a large yellow diet pill.

One of the divers strolled past. He was short and slim, no more than fourteen. Rivulets of water streamed down his dark-brown chest; a drop swelled and hung from his earlobe for a second, catching the sun and turning as blue as a sapphire. His blue-black hair fit close to his head, forming two dripping points—one at the nape of his slender neck and one low on his forehead. He was wearing a bright yellow bathing suit with a thick blue band circling his body just below his waist.

He sauntered up to Ed and snapped "*Cigarillo!*" Ed pulled out his Pall Malls and shook them two or three times before one finally shot out of the pack and fell to the ground. Ed awkwardly offered another; as the boy took it he smiled and murmured "Sankyou."

"Me! Me!" shouted the other two divers who had been watching from a distance and who now came running up, as aggressive as their companion had been. But they, too, melted into grins as Ed offered them cigarettes and they, too, whispered "Sankyou."

"Should I have given in?" Ed asked Charles after the boys had strolled off.

"Of course," Charles said, watching his hands tremble.

"You don't think they'll laugh at us? Oh, who cares if they do."

The two Americans wandered slowly across the dock, stopping to look at the Caribe Hilton compound through a fence, stepping cautiously over the gaps where boards were missing, threading their way through the lines of boys. Ed picked out a hundred images Charles must have seen: the open, laughing mouth of this one; that one's patched trousers ripped short at the knee and slipping down below the suntan line to reveal an inch of lean stomach; this boy's eyebrows, thin and raised—the Japanese would call them "butterfly wings"; that boy's arm, resting unconsciously on his friend's shoulder; a little Negro adjusting his cock in his blue Jockey shorts; a flexed thigh; a gold tooth; the splatter from a bad dive, spraying plumes of water which rose, separated and gently fell as though filmed in slow motion.

Charles and Ed stripped down to their swimsuits and sat on the beach under three ratty palm trees; the broad leaves were curling and turning brown at the edges. The only other American on the beach was a pot-bellied man with hair on his shoulders. A Puerto Rican boy ran up to the man and ruffled his gray hair. The man smiled. The boy was wearing a white bathing suit with blue letters stenciled across the back: "MADE IN U.S.A." Out near the diving raft, a water fight erupted. One boy scrambled up a teen-ager's slippery back, hooked his legs around the other's neck and gave a shout of triumph in his clear, choir-boy's voice. Ed opened the book, Kafka's letters to his friend Milena, which he had been carrying to the beach for days. He liked having it beside him when he talked to Charles. It reminded him that he wasn't simply a listening-post—he was someone who read a lot, lived in New York, had other friends and interests. One of these other friends had lent the book to Ed; he glanced at a passage she had bracketed:

> Sometimes I have the feeling that we're in one room with two opposite doors and each of us holds the handle of one door, one of us flicks an eyelash and the other is already behind his door, and now the first one has but to utter a word and immediately the second one has closed his door behind him and can no longer be seen. He's sure to open the door again for it's a room which perhaps one cannot leave. If only the first one were not precisely like the second, if he were calm, if he would only pretend not to look at the other, if he would slowly set the room in order as though it were a room like any other; but instead he does exactly the

same as the other at his door, sometimes even both are behind the doors and the beautiful room is empty.

Charles had returned to studying his hands. "I could fall in love with one of these boys."

"I know . . ."

"It would be worth spending the rest of my life in prison just for one night with a perfect boy like 'Made in U.S.A.' "

Just then another boy, curly-headed and quiet, seemed to stand out from all the other noisy beauties. He saw Charles and Ed watching him and stood up in the water shouting *"Mira!"*

"What does that mean?" Charles asked apprehensively.

"Mira!" the boy repeated.

"He wants us to watch." Ed nodded at the swimmer.

The boy and a companion swam out to the raft, paused there for a moment and looked back to see if Charles and Ed had watched their performance. Then they raced back, lifting their small brown arms above their heads, locking each elbow into a V and then extending their hands stiffly forward—altogether, Ed thought, a rather pedantic rendition of free-style form.

Ed joined them at the edge of the beach. The boys, puffing hard, sat in the shallow water leaning back and supporting their weight on their hands. The curly-headed boy looked at Ed, squinted and asked him something in Spanish. Ed said slowly, *"Io no parlo español."*

"Ah . . . sí." He flashed a smile at the American and explained the problem to his friend. An embarrassing silence followed, the boys stood up, shrugged and swam off.

Ed looked back and saw that Charles was watching him. There was nothing Ed could do but wade out toward the boys. Again there was an awkward pause; the children, who were treading water beside him, kept spitting jets of salt water and studying his face. How did you say "What's your name?" *Mi chiamano Mimi* was the only phrase that came to mind; *tu chiamano questo?* If I say that they'll think I'm a madman. Ed finally settled for *"Como está?"*

The boys darted a glance at each other, smiled and whispered *"Bien."* Suddenly the curly-head asked Ed a long question in Spanish.

"Lentemente," Ed replied, hoping that meant "slowly." He added, *"Repetez, por favor."* High-school French and libretto Italian—how silly I am!

Trying another tack, the curly-head pointed to the raft and the shore and then to Ed.

"Swim? I swim?"

"*Sí.*" The curly-head nodded and touched Ed's chest.

"*Yo?*"

"*Sí!*"

"*Solo?*" Ed pulled a long clown face and turned his mouth down at the corners. The boys laughed. Encouraged, Ed sniffed, rubbed away an imaginary tear and sobbed, "*No! Non solo, por favor. Yo—*" How do you say "want"? Oh, I know. "*Yo quiero* swim *con usted.*" They laughed even harder and nodded.

Hadn't I better tell them in advance I'm a lousy swimmer?

The curly-head took a few strokes away from shore and waved for Ed to follow. When they all reached the raft they hung onto it for a few minutes, breathing hard and smiling. An older boy sitting cross-legged on the peeling white planks stared at them, his brown eyes so pale they looked blue. He sized up the situation—polite American fag snared by aggressive little tramps—and flashed Ed a confident, confiding grin.

Ed noticed that the older boy had made his little friends grow sober. Did they understand what the boy's smile meant? Perhaps nothing meant anything; it was so easy to sexualize situations when you were around Charles. In any event, Ed didn't want to discourage them, so he only nodded vaguely at the boy with pale eyes and paddled back toward Charles, who came down to meet them at the water's edge.

"*Hermano?*" the curly-head asked Ed, pointing at Charles.

"*Muy hermano,*" Ed agreed, thinking the word meant "beautiful." What a nice language, no silly distinctions like handsome for men and beautiful—but no, that was *hermoso.* "*Perdóname.* Charles *no es mi hermano.*"

"What does *hermano* mean?" Charles asked.

" 'Brother.' He wanted to know if we were brothers."

"*Amigo?*" the curly-head persisted. His companion looked bored; he was pressing wet black bangs over his forehead.

"*Sí, mi amigo.*" Ed felt a rush of emotion.

"What's your name?" Charles asked the curly-head, who didn't understand; he pushed his friend's bangs back from his face. The friend, who had turned solemn, perhaps because he was being ignored by the Americans, retaliated by pounding the curly-head on the shoulder. They wrestled and shrieked with laughter in the water. At last they subsided and looked at

Charles and Ed expectantly but also with a trace of frustration in their expressions—or so Ed imagined.

"I just can't make it down here," Charles said, sitting down beside Ed and letting the water swirl over his legs. "You know the language but I—"

"I know all of two or three words!" Ed protested. "I don't even know how to say 'What's your name?' "

The curly-head stood up and stretched; the skin under his arms was pale and smooth. Unlike his companion, who still had a baby's protruding belly, the curly-head had a stomach that was one long plane except where it was indented by his navel, a symmetrical dime-size twist of cartilage as pure and precise as a girl's ear. Small and underdeveloped, his chest looked insignificant below his knobby shoulders, which he squared, manifesting more pride in them than Ed could feel for his whole expensive barbell physique. The sun turned the boy's thick curls into tiny flames.

"*Su nome?*" Ed asked him, not remembering the correct expression.

"*Me llamo Pedro.*"

Pedro suddenly turned and looked up at the sun, perhaps to guage what time it was. He extended one arm and pressed his palm against the sky to shade his eyes. His other hand dangled so freely at his side that it grazed his leg when he moved.

"*Cómo se llama?*" Pedro asked, turning back to them.

"Ed."

"*Qué?*"

"Edmundo . . . uh, Eduardo."

"Oh! Eduardo . . ." Pedro shook Ed's hand; his skin was cool and his long fingers so flexible they seemed to be provided with extra joints.

"*Y tú?*" he asked Charles.

Charles smiled and shrugged, as though he were too old to understand Spanish, as though it were some sort of pig Latin invented by children. Ed felt a flicker of resentment; Charles wasn't entering into this at all, he was content to sit back and admire these children, he didn't care what their names were or what they were saying. Since they were beautiful, what *could* they say that mattered?

"He asked you what your name is."

"Oh," Charles said, starting out of his reverie. "My name is Charles." They didn't understand. "*Charles.*"

"Carlos," Ed murmured.

Charles scribbled "Carlos" in the sand. Pedro examined it and smiled.

"Scribo usted nome," Ed insisted. Pedro finally comprehended. He crouched between the Americans on his haunches, and with the gravity of a painter approaching his canvas, traced his name in long, elegant letters, so decorative that Ed started to laugh until he caught Charles's eye. The boy stood up and the four of them looked at the writing for a long moment, as though they had come upon a sign in the desert.

The boys started talking to an ominous type with a tattoo, greasy black d.a. and a scar across his cheek. "They'd clap us in jail, wouldn't they?" Charles asked.

"For what?"

"Fucking these boys."

"They're too young, anyway."

"How old do you think they are? Nine?"

"Nine or ten at the most. They're much too young."

"Why do you say that?"

"They're so innocent. Why go and do that to them?"

"I can't fuck up and land in jail for the rest of my life," Charles said, pursuing his own inner debate and ignoring Ed's remarks.

::

A MAN WITH A WHITE BEARD WAS STANDING ON TOP OF THE WALL HIGH above the beach, looking at them through binoculars. Ed went up to talk to him, stepping carefully over the half-buried tin cans and discarded clothes along the red-clay path. A tiny lizard scuttled out from under a fading red sock. The man was rubbing his crotch when Ed came up to him, but Ed was able to get him off that by asking how you scored with the little ones. The man smiled gently; his erection subsided and he agreed to join Charles down on the beach. They discovered he was a Peruvian Jew who had lived in New York for years until his wife got sick, when they had moved down here. He had built a big house nearby just so he could watch the boys. As Charles said, he was one of those "old men with beautiful manners" that Ezra Pound wrote about.

"Sure they know," he said. "Even the little ones know what you want."

"Can you make out with the nine-year-olds?" Charles asked.

"Oh, sure. Maybe you pay them a dollar or two, maybe not."

"Where do you take them?"

"Anywhere. Wherever you like." The man was amused by Charles's purposeful questioning.

"To the hotels?"

"Oh, no, that's no good. Take them up there, maybe." He pointed to the walls where he had been standing; they enclosed a grassy circle full of scraggly bushes and tall weeds.

"What can you do with them?" Ed asked.

"Fuck them!" Charles shouted, indignant at the question. But the Peruvian Jew smiled again, frowned and said, "Oh, sometimes. But, you know, they all want to be the man."

"Even the nine-year-olds?" Charles asked.

"Yes. They're very precocious down here. It's not that they really care what happens in bed; sometimes they'll let you. But they must save face with their friends. They always come out saying that they were the man, even the little ones." He smiled and ran the tip of his moist red tongue across his upper lip just beneath the meticulous line of his white mustache. The old man with beautiful manners left them and returned to his lookout. Ed dug his toes into the hot sand until it became damp and cold. He hummed a few notes.

"What's that song?" Charles asked.

"I don't know. Don't know."

"I do. It's 'I Wish You Love'—Gloria Lynne sings it."

"Funny. I don't know where I picked it up—I don't even know the words."

Charles lifted his eyebrows and sang in a high, soft voice: "*Friends forever, lovers never* . . . something, something, *I wish you bluebirds in the spring and then a song for you to sing* . . . And the last verse ends, *But most of all, when snowflakes fall, I wish you love* . . ." As though the speed of sound had just diminished, Ed waited a full minute before he heard everything Charles was saying.

"I guess I wish you love with these boys," Ed finally murmured. "Is that wrong?"

::

WHEN HE WAS ON HIS BEST BEHAVIOR ED WAS EAGER TO HELP CHARLES FIGHT the temptation the boys presented. Charles obviously wanted to stay faithful to his girl friend back in New York, no matter how much he talked about nine-year-olds. But when they visited the bars that night Ed was still matchmaking—"That one's looking at you."

"No, he's not."

"Yes, he is. Should I invite him over?"

"Let's not lose our cool, Ed."

Ed could feel his heart racing, but he forced his hand to stay wrapped around the cold glass of rum and soda and his eyes on the bottles lining the illuminated glass shelves behind the bar.

But it was no use; in a moment he would catch Charles glancing at one of the boys on the dance floor or notice a boy in a booth along the wall eying Charles—Ed's hand released the glass, tapped Charles, and he said, "That one's looking at you."

"He's with the old man."

"Charles, he's alone, I swear."

Charles turned wearily toward Ed and said, "*Please,* baby."

"I'm sorry." Damn my diet pills, they make me so obsessive; I must be unendurable. "Charles, I'm sorry."

Charles shrugged and looked back at the dance floor. The moments weighed more and more heavily until Ed felt compelled to point out some boy or other. "I'd better leave," he said.

"Why? You still have another ticket."

"I know," Ed said, "but I've got to go." He smiled. "I keep watching that poor boy staring at you, shifting from bun to bun, and—you know, I never could stand the pressure of other people's wants."

"I'll go with you. Let me finish my ginger ale."

::

ED WANTED TO DO THE RIGHT THING BY CHARLES. HE WANTED TO SERVE Charles's own better instincts and nothing else; he wanted to be the ideal friend, to allow Charles to experience his situation to the full, not to offer any easy, irresponsible solutions or to impose his own demands. Then why did he have to—yes, *have* to—nudge Charles and say, "That one's looking at you"?

"Me? Don't be ridiculous."

"Well, why don't you go talk to him and find out?"

"No, Ed."

Pause.

"What do you mean 'no'?"

"Ed, I made out fine in bars for years without your help, you know."

"Sorry."

::

THEY SAT FOR HOURS IN THE SQUARE WITH THE PUBLIC TELEVISION SETS, scarcely speaking. An old woman dozing beside a wooden pushcart of oranges and a policeman who strode on his beat down Calle San Francisco were the only other people in sight. The neon lights in the show windows of the New York Department Store buzzed. The policeman passed again, walking rather stiffly, as though he knew Ed was studying him. He turned up Calle San José and disappeared. A car several blocks away raced its motor. The old woman rearranged the black rebozo over her head.

Charles took Ed's hand and bent each finger back as though he were a masseur loosening joints. Then he let the hand drop. "Ed, what's going on between us?"

"I'm glad you brought it up."

"I think you're trying to destroy me."

"No, of course not . . . Could be."

"Why are you doing this, Ed?"

"I don't know."

"Tell me."

"Maybe I can't bear to see you go straight; after all, the homosexual must always tell himself that he has no choice, but now you're choosing straight life, and I must stop you. It's a life-or-death matter."

"So that's it."

"Could be. I don't know. After all, it is unconscious."

The policeman appeared, walked the length of the resounding arcade under a shuttered government building, turned, retraced his steps and vanished.

"We've got to get to the bottom of this," Charles said. The bottom seemed to be somewhere between the dozing orange lady and the buzzing windows, and Ed's eyes traveled back and forth from the cart to the department store.

"My group," Charles said, "thinks that homosexuality is a form of hate. We hate these boys, we don't love them. Oh, no, we hate them, we want to castrate them."

"Yes. Castrate. Yes, of course," Ed conceded hastily, as though nothing could be more obvious. "You are my executioner. I'm secretly arranging for you to murder them for me. That's why I keep trying to fix you up with them. My own hands will be clean."

"Or maybe you're afraid of these Spanish boys," Charles suggested. "Yes, you're afraid! They're so young and slender, but they want to be the man in bed; they're like slender matadors in silk suits, girlish, teasing the bull, but in the end the matador is the one. He's the one who stabs the bull with his long sword. Get it?"

"Gotcha."

"Well?"

"Charles! After all, it is unconscious . . ."

As dawn approached the air grew cool. Two or three men gathered around the orange cart and talked in low voices. Although his diet pill still kept him alert, Ed caught himself listening to the hushed, querulous voices and believing that he understood every word.

They fell into a new game.

"Maybe you think of me as your father," Charles said.

"Maybe."

"Or maybe your mother. Am I like your mother?"

"Possibly . . . No!"

"Maybe you fear I'll get married," Charles ventured.

"Could be . . . Do you think that's possible?"

"Maybe that's why your mother never remarried; you always stood in her way."

"Maybe I want to murder *you.*"

"Well," Charles announced proudly, "I'm out to castrate you, that seems evident."

If only there were someone else with us, Ed thought, someone excruciatingly conventional. He would oppose everything Charles and Ed said. They could sneer at his limitations, burst through them, congratulate themselves on their own originality. They would become a team again, championing the same cause—and the very act of trying to talk to such a philistine would impose on them a shared style, a united front.

But they were alone and outdoing each other's daredevil statements, working into an infinite regress of higher understandings, broader interpretations, deeper loneliness. "Well, what's wrong," Charles said, "is just that we're both so fucked-up we can't accept the friendship we're offering each other."

"I don't think that's it," Ed said. "I think it's just that we're both in transition, and we keep projecting our inner conflicts on each other."

But that didn't end it. Half a dozen times Ed or Charles would interject, "It's not that complicated. It's simply that—" and a new complexity would be added. If only the first were not precisely like the second, if he were calm, if he would only pretend not to look at the other, if he would slowly set the room in order as though it were a room like any other.

"Well," Charles said, standing and stretching, "I think we'd better not go to the bars together any more. We'll spend the days together and split up at night. Okay?" He took Ed's hand gently. "That's why we're not making out. You never make out when you cruise with someone else."

They walked in opposite directions back to their rooms. On the way Ed looked at the policeman standing in front of the penny arcade; would he please step into the alley and unzip his fly?

::

CRUISING SEPARATELY HAD ITS HUMOROUS SIDE. CHARLES AND ED DECIDED to check out the Voodoo Room at the Normandie. They took a cab there after dinner and split up at the door. At the horseshoe bar sat a bunch of tired Wichita types with white silk socks, brown baggy suits and browner ties. They hunched over their highballs in the dim orange light filtering down through black plastic palm leaves that looked as damp and heavy as dinosaur tongues. Ed and Charles lounged against the walls of woven rattan and avoided each other's eyes.

Nothing was happening here. Ed went to the juke box. Charles joined him. They conferred and departed.

El Camino Real. Ed was banished to his own corner, wanting to talk to Charles alone, to kiss him, take him in his arms—yet he was forced to exchange smiles with a stranger, join someone at his table, dance with someone else from Ohio, whirl past Charles, wink, compete. Alone for a moment, Ed punched J5—"My Guy." Charles came to him, put his hand on Ed's shoulder, and Mary Wells sang: *"No muscle-bound man's going to take my hand from MY Guy."*

They left.

Gino's. "He's your type, isn't he?" Ed asked.

"Ed, baby . . ."

They left.

A moment in the Plaza de las Armas, still echoing to the footsteps of last night's vigil. Tap. Tap tap tap. Silence. Then, far away, another tap. Both of them must have heard the echo of that terrible conversation, because they stood up quickly after resting only a moment, and hurried off.

The Olé. They entered separately. What sort of crowd is this? Black pointy shoes, the ubiquitous white shirts, short sleeves unrolled. Two Swedish sailors conspicuously snubbing Charles and Ed and turning their attention to the local product. Altogether not more than fifteen men in a small wood-paneled room behind painted glass doors that whispered in reversed red letters: "¡OLE!" and "IT'S DIFFERENT."

Three boys leaned against the juke box; its glare shone up through their loose cream-colored shirts, revealing the hard outline of their thin torsos, like an X-ray finding the dark bones within white flesh. Approaching them with exaggerated unconcern, Ed put a quarter in the machine. After studying the selections, he said to one of the boys, without really looking at him, "What shall I play?"

"Qué?"

"I don't know any of these songs," Ed explained, only now looking at the boy and smiling. "You choose for me."

"Yo?"

"Sí. Por favor."

The boy and one of his companions deliberated seriously before punching the red plastic buttons; they were self-conscious about choosing words and music for fifteen men at five in the morning. The third boy who was with them ambled over to the bar and wrapped an arm around a man who was obviously drunk and getting drunker.

The drunk man slowly revolved on his stool toward the boy and directed at him the same bombastic flow of Spanish he had been showering on his neighbor. The boy screwed his mouth up into an amused but not necessarily disdainful expression and asked the man to buy him a drink. Ed noticed with a start that the boy was not speaking Spanish but a heavily accented English. The man signaled the bartender by lifting his hand and exposing a purple patch of sweat under the arm of his blue suit. When the drink came, the boy ran his long fingers through the man's hair and turned on his quizzical smile again. The man thundered more thick Spanish bombast in reply, but the boy, far from showing annoyance, leaned an elbow on the man's shoulder and swirled the ice in his glass.

"Suficiente!" the man shouted.

"Don't be seely, Erasmo," the boy murmured in English; he handed his empty glass to the man.

"Suficiente, Ruben!" Erasmo shouted again.

"Erasmo, buy me a new drink, please."

Charles moved out of his corner and stood beside Ed. "That boy's beautiful."

"Ruben?"

"The boy at the—"

"Yes," Ed said, "his name is Ruben. Do you want Ruben?"

Charles swallowed. "Yes."

Once Charles gave permission, it was all executed smoothly and expertly. Ed sat next to the older man, Erasmo, rubbed legs with him, chatted, bought *him* a drink, asked him where he worked.

"In a bank," Erasmo said.

"The Banco Popular?"

"Yes. How did you know that name?"

"I guessed. I knew it was the best. You look like the sort of person they'd hire. Do you live alone?"

"Yes." Erasmo dropped his hand clumsily to Ed's knee.

"Far from here?"

Erasmo sat between Ed and Ruben, who was leaning his back against the bar and looking at Charles.

"Who's your friend?" Ed asked.

"Him? Ruben. Ruben, meet Ed." Putting aside his indolence for a moment, Ruben leaned forward and gave Ed a powerful handshake. "I buy Ruben drinks," Erasmo said. "*Many* drinks. His father is rich, a doctor, but they throw Ruben out. Now Ruben doesn't attend the school, he doesn't work, he won't speak Spanish, he only drinks."

"I drink too much," Ruben explained with a soundless chuckle and a glance toward Charles. After a moment Erasmo went to the toilet. As soon as Erasmo closed the door behind him, Ed quickly introduced Charles to Ruben. They studied each other; Charles was slow to release Ruben's hand. They both wore the same amused smile. Ed was suddenly struck by how much they looked alike—Ruben was Charles's darker, younger brother. Both of them had the same quiet dignity; Charles's tremor had miraculously disappeared, and Ruben, although unsteady on his feet, maintained his balance with ease as he lowered his head slightly in concentration and listened to Charles's low voice. They were the captains of rival teams conferring after the game, Ed thought. Not actually saying much but communicating mutual respect.

Charles asked Ruben to go home with him. Ruben nodded vaguely and placed his empty glass on the bar. No sooner had they left for the Convento, Charles taking Ruben's arm and guiding him along, than Erasmo returned. It took him a full twenty seconds before he realized that Ruben had gone.

"Where?" Ed said. "Oh, he left with my friend."

Erasmo absorbed the words slowly but reacted finally by shoving his way out the door after them.

"But you said *you* played around," Ed protested, trying to detain Erasmo at the corner.

"No little tramp does this to me. *Jamás.*"

"Are you mad at Charles?"

"No, not him. I kill Ruben. Never. *Jamás.*"

A block down Calle Cristo the two captains were heading home, unaware of the argument behind them, their white shirts lifting and billowing in the morning breeze, Ruben weaving and stumbling against Charles.

"I don't blame your friend," Erasmo repeated, walking quickly. "But I have pride. You Americans do not know this terrible Spanish pride. It is a curse for us, the Spanish. *Jamás.* Never."

"Oh, silly," Ed said, blocking Erasmo's path and resting one hand delicately against the avenger's chest. "This will cause a scandal; you'll lose your job at the bank."

"I don't care. I starve and beg in the streets. No one never insult me. *Jamás.*" And Erasmo pushed past and on toward the lovers.

"Oh, look at them!" Ed exclaimed, tears welling in his eyes. Charles and Ruben were now ambling through the Little Plaza of the Nuns; the sun was squirting pink all over the gray clouds that cruised slowly above the stiff white circles and squares of molding decorating the church's walls. A cold wind streamed up off the bay, pulling at their clothes, shaking the trees, bearing a smell of salt. Another sinister night was being swept away. The smell of spoiled oranges and oily rice dissolved in the briny air. "They're so beautiful," Ed almost shouted, shaking Erasmo violently and smiling. "Forget your stupid Spanish pride. Forget yourself. That"—and he held his hand out with drunken grandeur—"that is beauty! Those boys are going off with each other—look, they're climbing the stairs to the Convento, you see? You see? And now, look, they're going through the doors and into the lobby. Into the lobby, Erasmo, up the elevator, into Charles's room."

"*Jamás,*" Erasmo mumbled as the air hissed out of him and he shriveled up on the curb, squeezing his lungs to repeat a muffled, resigned "*Jamás . . .*"

"Always," Ed objected. "Always. Erasmo, they're together, right now, there's nothing we can do to stop them. And we shouldn't. We should *help* them. We should pray for them."

"*Jamás . . .*"

Down a side street out of sight, some late drinkers opened a bar door. Their slurred voices dipped and bobbed over the persistant snake rattle of a marimba.

Ed was swooning from alcohol, weariness and elation, but he shot a declamatory hand once more into the wind and cried, "Erasmo, they're together! I'll bet they're taking their first real good look at each other now. The room is dark," Ed whispered, bending over Erasmo, building up suspense. "They see the soft shadows under each other's eyes. They look down and see that their hands are touching. They kiss. They're together and everyone to each other now. Ruben is too drunk to get undressed. Charles helps him, not like a father, but like a brother."

"I kill Ruben."

"Kill him tomorrow, Erasmo. Wait for him all night here and stab him when he comes down at noon. But tonight," Ed said, crying harder now, "they are lying side by side."

1966

GRAHAM GREENE

Chagrin in Three Parts

I

IT WAS FEBRUARY IN ANTIBES. GUSTS OF RAIN BLEW ALONG THE RAMPARTS, and the emaciated statues on the terrace of the Château Grimaldi dripped with wet, and there was a sound absent during the flat blue days of summer, the continual rustle below the ramparts of the small surf. All along the Côte the summer restaurants were closed, but lights shone in Félix au Port and one Peugeot of the latest model stood in the parking-rank. The bare masts of the abandoned yachts stuck up like toothpicks and the last plane in the winter service dropped, in a flicker of green, red, and yellow lights, like Christmas-tree baubles, towards the airport of Nice. This was the Antibes I always enjoyed; and I was disappointed to find I was not alone in the restaurant as I was most nights of the week.

Crossing the road I saw a very powerful lady dressed in black who stared out at me from one of the window tables, as though she were willing me not to enter, and when I came in and took my place before the other window she regarded me with too evident distaste. My raincoat was shabby and my shoes were muddy, and in any case I was a man. Momentarily, while she took me in, from balding top to shabby toe, she interrupted her conversation with the *patronne,* who addressed her as Madame Dejoie.

Madame Dejoie continued her monologue in a tone of firm disapproval: it was unusual for Madame Volet to be late, but she hoped nothing had happened to her on the ramparts. In winter there were always Algerians about, she added with mysterious apprehension, as though she were talking of wolves, but none the less Madame Volet had refused Madame Dejoie's offer to be fetched from her home. "I did not press her under the circumstances. Poor Madame Volet." Her hand clutched a huge peppermill like a bludgeon, and I pictured Madame Volet as a weak timid old lady, dressed too in black, afraid even of protection by so formidable a friend.

How wrong I was. Madame Volet blew suddenly in with a gust of rain through the side door beside my table, and she was young and extravagantly pretty, in her tight black pants, and with a long neck emerging from a wine-red polo-necked sweater. I was glad when she sat down side by side with Madame Dejoie, so that I need not lose the sight of her while I ate.

"I am late," she said. "I know that I am late. So many little things have to be done when you are alone, and I am not yet accustomed to being alone," she added with a pretty little sob which reminded me of a cut-glass Victorian tear-bottle. She took off thick winter gloves with a wringing gesture which made me think of handkerchiefs wet with grief, and her hands looked suddenly small and useless and vulnerable.

"Pauvre cocotte," said Madame Dejoie, "be quiet here with me and forget awhile. I have ordered a bouillabaisse with langouste."

"But I have no appetite, Emmy."

"It will come back. You'll see. Now here is your porto and I have ordered a bottle of *blanc de blancs."*

"You will make me *tout à fait soûle."*

"We are going to eat and drink, and for a little while we are both going to forget everything. I know exactly how you are feeling, for I too lost a beloved husband."

"By death," little Madame Volet said. "That makes a great difference. Death is quite bearable."

"It is more irrevocable."

"Nothing can be more irrevocable than my situation. Emmy, he loves the little bitch."

"All I know of her is that she has deplorable taste—or a deplorable hairdresser."

"But that was exactly what I told him."

"You were wrong. I should have told him, not you, for he might have believed me, and in any case my criticism would not have hurt his pride."

"I love him," Madame Volet said, "I cannot be prudent," and then she suddenly became aware of my presence. She whispered something to her companion, and I heard the reassurance, *"Un anglais."* I watched her as covertly as I could—like most writers I have the spirit of a *voyeur*—and I wondered how stupid married men could be. I was temporarily free, and I very much wanted to console her, but I didn't exist in her eyes, now she knew that I was English, nor in the eyes of Madame Dejoie. I was less than human—I was only a reject from the Common Market.

I ordered two small *rougets* and a half bottle of Pouilly and I tried to be interested in the Trollope I had brought with me. But my attention strayed.

"I adored my husband," Madame Dejoie was saying, and her hand again grasped the pepper-mill, but this time it looked less like a bludgeon.

"I still do, Emmy. That is the worst of it. I know that if he came back . . ."

"Mine can never come back," Madame Dejoie retorted, touching the corner of one eye with her handkerchief and then examining the smear of black left behind.

In a gloomy silence they both drained their portos. Then Madame Dejoie said with determination, "There is no turning back. You should accept that as I do. There remains for us only the problem of adaptation."

"After such a betrayal I could never look at another man," Madame Volet replied. At that moment she looked right through me. I felt invisible. I put my hand between the light and the wall to prove that I had a shadow, and the shadow looked like a beast with horns.

"I would never suggest another man," Madame Dejoie said. "Never."

"What then?"

"When my poor husband died from an infection of the bowels I thought myself quite inconsolable, but I said to myself, Courage, courage. You must learn to laugh again."

"To laugh!" Madame Volet exclaimed. "To laugh at what?" But before Madame Dejoie could reply, Monsieur Félix had arrived to perform his neat surgical operation upon the fish for the bouillabaisse. Madame Dejoie watched with real interest; Madame Volet, I thought, watched for politeness' sake while she finished a glass of *blanc de blancs.*

When the operation was over Madame Dejoie filled the glasses and said, "I was lucky enough to have *une amie* who taught me not to mourn for the past." She raised her glass and, cocking a finger as I had seen men do, she added, *"Pas de mollesse."*

"Pas de mollesse," Madame Volet repeated with a wan enchanting smile.

I felt decidedly ashamed of myself—a cold literary observer of human anguish. I was afraid of catching poor Madame Volet's eyes (what kind of a man was capable of betraying her for a woman who took the wrong sort of rinse?) and I tried to occupy myself with sad Mr. Crawley's courtship as he stumped up the muddy lane in his big clergyman's boots. In any case, the two of them had dropped their voices; a gentle smell of garlic came to me from the bouillabaisse, the bottle of *blanc de blancs* was nearly finished, and, in spite of Madame Volet's protestation, Madame Dejoie had called for another. "There are no half bottles," she said. "We can always leave something for the gods." Again their voices sank to an intimate murmur as Mr. Crawley's suit was accepted (though how he was to support an inevitably large family would not appear until the succeeding volume). I was startled out of my forced concentration by a laugh: a musical laugh: it was Madame Volet's.

"Cochon!" she exclaimed.

Madame Dejoie regarded her over her glass (the new bottle had already been broached) under beetling brows. "I am telling you the truth," she said. "He would crow like a cock."

"But what a joke to play!"

"It began as a joke, but he was really proud of himself. *Aprés seulement deux coups . . ."*

"Jamais trois?" Madame Volet asked and she giggled and splashed a little of her wine down her polo-necked collar.

"Jamais."

"Je suis saoule."

"Moi aussi, cocotte."

Madame Volet said, "To crow like a cock—at least it was a *fantaisie.* My husband has no *fantaisies.* He is strictly classical."

"Pas de vices?"

"Hélas, pas de vices."

"And yet you miss him?"

"He worked hard," Madame Volet said and giggled. "To think that at the end he must have been working hard for both of us."

"You found it a little boring?"

"It was a habit—how one misses a habit. I wake now at five in the morning."

"At five?"

"It was the hour of his greatest activity."

"My husband was a very small man," Madame Dejoie said. "Not in height, of course. He was two meters high."

"Oh, Paul is big enough—but always the same."

"Why do you continue to love that man?" Madame Dejoie sighed and put her large hand on Madame Volet's knee. She wore a signet ring which perhaps had belonged to her late husband. Madame Volet sighed too, and I thought melancholy was returning to the table, but then she hiccupped and both of them laughed.

"Tu es vraiment saoule, coccotte."

"Do I truly miss Paul, or is it only that I miss his habits?" She suddenly met my eye and blushed right down into the wine-coloured wine-stained polo-necked collar.

Madame Dejoie repeated reassuringly, *"Un anglais—ou un américain."* She hardly bothered to lower her voice at all. "Do you know how limited my experience was when my husband died? I loved him when he crowed like a cock. I was glad he was so pleased. I only wanted him to be pleased. I adored him, and yet in those days—*j'ai joui peut-être trois fois par semaine.* I did not expect more. It seemed to me a natural limit."

"In my case it was three times a day," Madame Volet said and giggled again. *"Mais toujours d'une façon classique."* She put her hands over her face and gave a little sob. Madame Dejoie put an arm round her shoulders. There was a long silence while the remains of the bouillabaisse were cleared away.

II

"MEN ARE CURIOUS ANIMALS," MADAME DEJOIE SAID AT LAST. THE COFFEE had come and they divided one *marc* between them, in turn dipping lumps of sugar which they inserted into each other's mouth. "Animals too lack imagination. A dog has no *fantaisie.*"

"How bored I have been sometimes," Madame Volet said. "He would talk politics continually and turn on the news at eight in the morning. At eight! What do I care for politics? But if I asked his advice about anything important he showed no interest at all. With you I can talk about anything, about the whole world."

"I adored my husband," Madame Dejoie said, "yet it was only after his death I discovered my capacity for love. With Pauline. You never knew Pauline. She died five years ago. I loved her more than I ever loved Jacques, and yet I felt no despair when she died. I knew that it was not the end, for I knew by then my capacity."

"I have never loved a woman," Madame Volet said.

"Chérie, then you do not know what love can mean. With a woman you do not have to be content with *une façon classique* three times a day."

"I love Paul, but he is different from me in every way . . ."

"Unlike Pauline, he is a man."

"Oh Emmy, you describe him so perfectly. How well you understand. A man!"

"When you really think of it, how comic that little object is. Hardly enough to crow about, one would think."

Madame Volet giggled and said, *"Cochon."*

"Perhaps smoked like an eel one might enjoy it."

"Stop it. Stop it." They rocked up and down with little gusts of laughter. They were drunk, of course, but in the most charming way.

III

HOW DISTANT NOW SEEMED TROLLOPE'S MUDDY LANE, THE HEAVY BOOTS of Mr. Crawley, his proud shy courtship. In time we travel a space as vast as any astronaut's. When I looked up Madame Volet's head rested on Madame Dejoie's shoulder. "I feel so sleepy," she said.

"Tonight you shall sleep, *chérie.*"

"I am so little good to you. I know nothing."

"In love one learns quickly."

"But am I in love?" Madame Volet asked, sitting up very straight and staring into Madame Dejoie's sombre eyes.

"If the answer were no, you wouldn't ask the question."

"But I thought I could never love again."

"Not another man," Madame Dejoie said. *"Chérie,* you are almost asleep. Come."

"The bill?" Madame Volet said as though perhaps she were trying to delay the moment of decision.

"I will pay tomorrow. What a pretty coat this is—but not warm enough, *chérie,* in February. You need to be cared for."

"You have given me back my courage," Madame Volet said. "When I came in here I was *si démoralisée. . . .*"

"Soon—I promise—you will be able to laugh at the past. . . ."

"I have already laughed," Madame Volet said. "Did he really crow like a cock?"

"Yes."

"I shall never be able to forget what you said about smoked eel. Never. If I saw one now . . ." She began to giggle again and Madame Dejoie steadied her a little on the way to the door.

I watched them cross the road to the car-park. Suddenly Madame Volet gave a little hop and skip and flung her arms around Madame Dejoie's neck, and the wind, blowing through the archway of the port, carried the faint sound of her laughter to me where I sat alone *chez* Félix. I was glad she was happy again. I was glad that she was in the kind reliable hands of Madame Dejoie. What a fool Paul had been, I reflected, feeling *chagrin* myself now for so many wasted opportunities.

1967

ELIZABETH TAYLOR

MISS A. AND MISS M.

A NEW MOTORWAY HAS MADE A DIFFERENT LANDSCAPE OF THAT PART OF England I loved as a child, cutting through meadows, spanning valleys, shaving off old gardens, and leaving houses perched on islands of confusion. Nothing is recognizable now: the guest-house has gone, with its croquet-lawn; the cherry orchard; and Miss Alliot's and Miss Martin's week-end cottage. I should think that little is left anywhere, except in *my* mind.

I was a town child, and the holidays in the country had a sharp delight which made the waiting time of school term, of traffic, of leaflessness, the unreal part of my life. At Easter, and for weeks in the summer, sometimes even for a few snatched days in winter, we drove out there to stay—it wasn't far—for my mother loved the country, too, and in that place we had put down roots.

St. Margaret's was the name of the guest-house, which was run by two elderly ladies who had come down in the world, bringing with them quantities of heavily riveted Crown Derby, and silver plate. Miss Louie and Miss Beatrice.

My mother and I shared a bedroom with a sloping floor and threadbare carpet. The wallpaper had faint roses, and a powdery look from damp. Oil lamps or candles lit the rooms, and, even now, the smell of paraffin brings it back, that time of my life. We were in the nineteen twenties.

Miss Beatrice, with the help of a maid called Mabel, cooked deliciously. Beautiful creamy porridge, I remember, and summer puddings, suckling pigs and maids-of-honour and marrow jam. The guests sat at one long table with Miss Louie one end and Miss Beatrice the other, and Mabel scuttling in and out with silver-domed dishes. There was no wine. No one drank anything alcoholic, that I remember. Sherry was kept for trifle, and that was it, and the new world of cocktail parties was elsewhere.

The guests were for the most part mild, bookish people who liked a cheap and quiet holiday—schoolmasters, elderly spinsters, sometimes people to do with broadcasting, who, in those days, were held in awe. The guests returned, so that we had constant friends among them, and looked forward to our reunions. Sometimes there were other children. If there were not, I did not care. I had Miss Alliot and Miss Martin.

These two were always spoken of in that order, and not because it was easier to say like that, or more euphonious. They appeared at luncheon and supper, but were not guests. At the far end of the orchard they had a cottage for weekends and holidays. They were schoolmistresses in London.

"Cottage" is not quite the word for what was little more than a wooden shack with two rooms and a veranda. It was called Breezy Lodge, and draughts did blow between its ramshackle clapboarding.

Inside, it was gay, for Miss Alliot was much inclined to orange and yellow and grass-green, and the cane chairs had cushions patterned with nasturtiums and marigolds and ferns. The curtains—and her clothes—reflected the same taste.

Miss Martin liked misty blues and greys, though it barely mattered that she did. She had a small, smudged-looking face with untidy eyebrows, a gentle, even submerged, nature. She was a great—but quiet—reader and never seemed to wish to talk of what she had read. Miss Alliot, on the other hand, would occasionally skim through a book and find enough in it for long discourses and an endless supply of allusions. She wrung the most out of everything she did or saw and was a great talker.

That was a time when one fell in love with who was *there.* In my adolescence the only males available for adoration were such as Shelley or Rupert Brooke or Owen Nares. A rather more real passion could be lavished on prefects at school or the younger mistresses.

Miss Alliot was heaven-sent, it seemed to me. She was a holiday goddess. Miss Martin was just a friend. She tried to guide my reading, as an elder sister might. This was a new relationship to me. I had no elder sister, and I had sometimes thought to have had one would have altered my life entirely, and whether for better or worse I had never been able to decide.

How I stood with Miss Alliot was a reason for more pondering. Why did she take trouble over me, as she did? I considered myself sharp for my age: now I see that I was sharp only for the age I *lived* in. Miss Alliot cultivated me to punish Miss Martin—as if she needed another weapon. I condoned the punishing. I basked in the doing of it. I turned my own eyes from the troubled ones under the fuzzy brows, and I pretended not to know precisely what was being done. Flattery nudged me on. Not physically fondled, I was fondled all the same.

::

IN THOSE DAYS BEFORE—MORE THAN FORTY YEARS BEFORE—THE MOTORway, that piece of countryside was beautiful, and the word "countryside" still means there to me. The Chiltern Hills. Down one of those slopes below St. Margaret's streamed the cherry orchard, a vast delight in summer of marjoram and thyme. An unfrequented footpath led through it, and every step was aromatic. We called this walk the Echo Walk—down through the trees and up from the valley on its other side to larch woods.

Perched on a style at the edge of the wood, one called out messages to be rung back across the flinty valley. Once, alone, I called out, "I love you," loud and strong, and "love you" came back, faint and mocking. "Miss Alliot," I added. But that response was blurred. Perhaps I feared to shout too loudly, or it was not a good echo name. I tried no others.

On Sunday mornings, I walked across the fields to church with Miss Martin. Miss Alliot would not join us. It was scarcely an intellectual feast, she said, or spiritually uplifting, with the poor old vicar mumbling on and the organ asthmatic. In London, she attended St. Ethelburga's in the Strand, and spoke a great deal of a Doctor Cobb. But, still more, she spoke of the Townsends.

For she punished Miss Martin with the Townsends too.

The Townsends lived in Northumberland. Their country house was grand, as was to be seen in photographs. Miss Alliot appeared in some of these, shading her eyes as she lay back in a deck-chair in a sepia world or —with Suzanne Lenglen bandeau and accordion-pleated dress—simply standing, to be photographed. By whom? I wondered. Miss Martin wondered, too, I thought.

Once a year, towards the end of the summer holiday (mine: theirs) Miss Alliot was invited to take the train north. We knew that she would have taken that train at an hour's notice, and, if necessary, have dropped everything for the Townsends.

What they consisted of—the Townsends—I was never really sure. It was a group name, both in my mind and in our conversations. "Do the Townsends play croquet?" I inquired, or "Do the Townsends change for dinner?" I was avid for information. It was readily given.

::

"I KNOW WHAT THE TOWNSENDS WOULD THINK OF HER," MISS ALLIOT SAID, of the only common woman, as she put it, who had ever stayed at St. Margaret's. Mrs. Price came with her daughter, Muriel, who was seven years old and had long, burnished plaits, which she would toss—one, then the other—over her shoulders. Under Miss Alliot's guidance, I scorned both Mrs. Price and child, and many a laugh we had in Breezy Lodge at their expense. Scarcely able to speak for laughter, Miss Alliot would recount her "gems," as she called them. "Oh, she *said* . . . one can't believe it, little Muriel—Mrs. Price *insists* on it—changes her socks and knickers twice a day. She likes her to be nice and fresh. And"—Miss Alliot was a good mimic—" 'she always takes an apple for recess.' What in God's name is recess?"

This was rather strong language for those days, and I admired it.

"It's 'break' or . . ." Miss Martin began reasonably. This was her mistake. She slowed things up with her reasonableness, when what Miss Alliot wanted, and I wanted, was a flight of fancy.

I tried, when those two were not there, to gather foolish or despicable phrases from Mrs. Price, but I did not get far. (I suspect now Miss Alliot's inventive mind at work—rehearsing for the Townsends.)

All these years later, I have attempted, while writing this, to be fair to Mrs. Price, almost forgotten for forty years; but even without Miss Alliot's direction I think I should have found her tiresome. She boasted to my mother (and no adult was safe from my eavesdropping) about her hysterectomy, and the gynaecologist who doted on her. "I always have my operations at the Harbeck Clinic." I was praised for that titbit, and could not run fast enough to Breezy Lodge with it.

I knew what the medical words meant, for I had begun to learn Greek at school—Ladies' Greek, as Elizabeth Barrett-Browning called it, "without any accents." My growing knowledge served me well with regard to words spoken in lowered tones. "My operations! How Ralph Townsend will adore that one!" Miss Alliot said.

A Townsend now stepped forward from the general family group. Miss Martin stopped laughing. I was so sharp for my years that I thought she gave herself away by doing so, that she should have let her laughter die away gradually. In that slice of a moment she had made clear her sudden worry about Ralph Townsend. Knowing as I did then so much about human beings, I was sure she had been meant to.

Poor Miss Martin, my friend, mentor, church-going companion, mild, kind and sincere—I simply used her as a stepping-stone to Miss Alliot.

I never called them by their first names, and have had to pause a little to remember them. Dorothea Alliot and Edith Martin. "Dorothea" had a fine ring of authority about it. Of course, I had the Greek meaning of that, too, but I knew that Miss Alliot was the giver herself—of the presents and the punishments.

::

MY MOTHER LIKED PLAYING CROQUET AND CARDS, AND DID BOTH A GREAT deal at St. Margaret's. I liked going across the orchard to Breezy Lodge. There, both cards and croquet were despised. We sat on the veranda (or, in winter, round an oil-stove which threw up petal patterns on the ceiling) and we talked—a game particularly suited to three people. Miss Alliot always won.

Where to find such drowsy peace in England now is hard to discover. Summer after summer through my early teens, the sun shone, bringing up the smell of thyme and marjoram from the earth—of the melting tar along the lane and, later, of rotting apples. The croquet balls clicked against one another on the lawn, and voices sounded lazy and far-away. There were droughts, when we were on our honour to be careful with the water. No water was laid on at Breezy Lodge, and it had to be carried from the house. I took this duty from Miss Martin, and several times a day stumbled through the long grass and buttercups, the water swinging in a pail, or slopping out of a jug. As I went, I disturbed clouds of tiny blue butterflies, once a grass snake.

Any excuse to get to Breezy Lodge. My mother told me not to intrude, and I was offended by the word. She was even a little frosty about my two friends. If for some reason they were not there when we ourselves arrived on holiday I was in despair, and she knew it, and lost patience.

In the school term I wrote to them and Miss Martin was the one who replied. They shared a flat in London, and a visit to it was spoken of, but did not come about. I used my imagination instead, building it up from little scraps as a bird builds a nest. I was able to furnish it in unstained oak and hand-woven rugs and curtains. All about would be jars of the beech leaves and grasses and berries they took back with them from the country. From their windows could be seen, through the branches of a monkey-puzzle tree, the roofs of the school—Queen's—from which they returned each evening.

That was their life on their own where I could not intrude, as my mother would have put it. They had another life of their own in which I felt aggrieved at not participating; but I was not invited to. After supper at St. Margaret's, they returned to Breezy Lodge, and did not ask me to go with them. Games of solo whist were begun in the drawing-room, and I sat and read listlessly, hearing the clock tick and the maddening, mystifying card-words—"*Misère,*" "Abundance"—or "going a bundle," "prop and cop," and "*Misère Ouverte*" (which seemed to cause a little stir). I pitied them and their boring games, and I pitied myself and my boring book—imposed holiday reading, usually Sir Walter Scott, whom I loathed. I pecked at it dispiritedly and looked about the room for distraction.

Miss Louie and Miss Beatrice enjoyed their whist, as they enjoyed their croquet. They really were hostesses. We paid a little—astonishingly little—but it did not alter the fact that we were truly guests, and they entertained us believing so.

"Ho . . . ho . . . hum . . . hum," murmured a voice, fanning out a newly dealt hand, someone playing for time. "H'm, h'm, now let me see." There were relaxed intervals when cards were being shuffled and cut, and the players leaned back and had a little desultory conversation, though nothing amounting to much. On warm nights, as it grew later, through the open windows moths came to plunge and lurch about the lamps.

Becoming more and more restless, I might go out and wander about the garden, looking for glow-worms and glancing at the light from Breezy Lodge shining through the orchard boughs.

On other evenings, after Miss Beatrice had lit the lamps, Mrs. Mayes, one of the regular guests, might give a Shakespearean recital. She had once had some connection with the stage and had known Sir Henry Ainley. She had often heard his words for him, she told us, and perhaps, in consequence of that, had whole scenes by heart. She was ageing wonderfully—that is, hardly at all. Some of the blond was fading from her silvery-blond hair, but her skin was still wild-rose, and her voice held its great range. But most of all, we marvelled at how she remembered her lines. I recall most vividly the balcony scene from *Romeo and Juliet.* Mrs. Mayes sat at one end of a velvet-covered chaise-longue. When she looped her pearls over her fingers, then clasped them to her bosom, she was Juliet, and Romeo when she held out her arms, imploringly (the rope of pearls swinging free). Always she changed into what, in some circles, was then called semi-evening dress, and rather old-fashioned dresses they were, with bead embroidery and loose panels hanging from the waist. Once, I imagined she would have worn such dresses *before* tea, and have changed again later into something even more splendid. She had lived through grander days: now, was serenely widowed.

Only Mrs. Price did not marvel at her. I overheard her say to my mother, "She must be forever in the limelight, and I for one am sick and tired, *sick* and *tired*, of Henry Ainley. I'm afraid I don't call actors 'Sir.' I'm like that." And my mother blushed, but said nothing.

Miss Alliot and Miss Martin were often invited to stay for these recitals; but Miss Alliot always declined.

"One is embarrassed, being recited *at*," she explained to me. "One doesn't know where to look."

I always looked at Mrs. Mayes and admired the way she did her hair, and wondered if the pearls were real. There may have been a little animosity between the two women. I remember Mrs. Mayes joining in praise of Miss Alliot one day, saying, "Yes, she is like a well-bred race-horse," and I felt that she said this only because she could not say that she was like a horse.

Mrs. Price, rather out of it after supper, because of Mrs. Mayes, and not being able to get the hang of solo whist, would sulkily turn the pages of the *Illustrated London News*, and try to start conversations between scenes or games.

"*Do* look at *this*." She would pass round her magazine, pointing out something or other. Or she would tiptoe upstairs to see if Muriel slept, and come back to report. Once she said, *à propos* nothing, as cards were being redealt, "Now who can clasp their ankles with their fingers? Like *that*—with no gaps." Some of the ladies dutifully tried, but only Mrs. Price could do it. She shrugged and laughed. "Only a bit of fun," she said, "but they do say that's the right proportion. Wrists, too, that's easier, though." But they were all at cards again.

One morning, we were sitting on the lawn and my mother was stringing red-currants through the tines of a silver fork into a pudding-basin. Guests often helped in these ways. Mrs. Price came out from the house carrying a framed photograph of a bride and bridegroom—her son, Derek, and daughter-in-law, Gloria. We had heard of them.

"You don't look old enough," my mother said, "to have a son that age." She had said it before. She always liked to make people happy. Mrs. Price kept hold of the photograph, because of my mother's stained fingers, and she pointed out details such as Gloria's veil and Derek's smile and the tuberoses in the bouquet. "Derek gave her a gold locket, but it hasn't come out very clearly. Old enough! You are trying to flatter me. Why my husband

and I had our silver wedding last October. Muriel was our little afterthought."

I popped a string of currants into my mouth and sauntered off. As soon as I was out of sight, I sped. All across the orchard, I murmured the words with smiling lips.

The door of Breezy Lodge stood open to the veranda. I called through it, "Muriel was their little afterthought."

Miss Martin was crying. From the bedroom came a muffled sobbing. At once, I knew that it was she, never could be Miss Alliot. Miss Alliot, in fact, walked out of the bedroom and shut the door.

"What is wrong?" I asked stupidly.

Miss Alliot gave a vexed shake of her head and took her walking-stick from its corner. She was wearing a dress with a pattern of large poppies, and cut-out poppies from the same material were appliqued to her straw hat. She was going for a walk, and I went with her, and she told me that Miss Martin had fits of nervous hysteria. For no reason. The only thing to be done about them was to leave her alone until she recovered.

We went down through the cherry orchard and the scents and the butterflies were part of an enchanted world. I thought that I was completely happy. I so rarely had Miss Alliot's undivided attention. She talked of the Townsends, and I listened as if to the holy intimations of a saint.

::

"I THOUGHT YOU WERE LOST," MY MOTHER SAID WHEN I RETURNED.

Miss Alliot always wore a hat at luncheon (that annoyed Mrs. Price). She sat opposite me and seemed in a very good humour, taking trouble to amuse us all, but with an occasional allusion and smile for me alone. "Miss Martin has one of her headaches," she explained. By this time I was sure that this was true.

::

THE HOLIDAYS WERE GOING BY, AND I HAD GOT NOWHERE WITH *Quentin Durward.* Miss Martin recovered from her nervous hysteria, but was subdued.

Miss Alliot departed for Northumberland, wearing autumn tweeds. Miss Martin stayed on alone at Breezy Lodge, and distempered the walls primrose, and I helped her. Mrs. Price and Muriel left at last, and a German governess with her two little London pupils arrived for a breath of fresh air. My mother and Mrs. Mayes strolled about the garden. Together they did the flowers, to help Miss Louie, or sat together in the sunshine with their *petit point.*

Miss Martin and I painted away, and we talked of Miss Alliot and how wonderful she was. It was like a little separate holiday for me, a rest. I did not try to adjust myself to Miss Martin, or strive, or rehearse. In a way, I think she was having a well-earned rest herself; but then I believed that she was jealous of Northumberland and would have liked some Townsends of her own to retaliate with. Now I know she wanted only Miss Alliot.

Miss Martin was conscientious; she even tried to take me through *Quentin Durward.* She seemed to be concerned about my butterfly mind, its skimming over things, not stopping to understand. I felt that knowing things ought to "come" to me, and if it did not, it was too bad. I believed in instinct and intuition and inspiration—all labour-saving things.

Miss Martin, who taught English (my subject, I felt), approached the matter coldly. She tried to teach me the logic of it—grammar. But I thought "ear" would somehow teach me that. Painless learning I wanted, or none at all. She would not give up. She was the one who was fond of me.

::

WE RETURNED FROM OUR HOLIDAY, AND I WENT BACK TO SCHOOL. I WAS moved up—by the skin of my teeth, I am sure—to a higher form. I remained with my friends. Some of those had been abroad for the holidays, but I did not envy them.

Miss Martin wrote to inquire how I had got on in the *Quentin Durward* test, and I replied that as I could not answer one question, I had written a general description of Scottish scenery. She said that it would avail me nothing, and it did not. I had never been to Scotland, anyway. Of Miss Alliot I only heard. She was busy producing the school play—*A Tale of Two Cities.* Someone called Rosella Byng-Williams was very good as Sydney Carton, and I took against her at once. "I think Dorothea has made quite a discovery," Miss Martin wrote—but I fancied that her pen was pushed along with difficulty, and that she was due for one of her headaches.

Those three "i's"—instinct, intuition, inspiration—in which I pinned my faith were more useful in learning about people than logic could be. Capricious approach to capricious subject.

Looking back, I see that my mother was far more attractive, lovable, than any of the ladies I describe; but there it was—she was my mother.

::

TOWARDS THE END OF THAT TERM, I LEARNED OF A NEW THING, THAT MISS Alliot was to spend Christmas with the Townsends. This had never been done before: there had been simply the early autumn visit—it seemed that it had been for the sake of an old family friendship, a one-sided one, I sharply guessed. Now, what had seemed to be a yearly courtesy became something rather more for conjecture.

Miss Martin wrote that she would go to Breezy Lodge alone, and pretend that Christmas wasn't happening—as lonely people strive to. I imagined her carrying pails of cold water through the wet, long grasses of the orchard, rubbing her chilblains before the oil-stove. I began to love her as if she were a child.

My mother was a little flustered by my idea of having Miss Martin to stay with us for Christmas. I desired it intensely, having reached a point where the two of us, my mother and I alone, a Christmas done just for me, was agonizing. What my mother thought of Miss Martin I shall never know now, but I have a feeling that schoolmistresses rather put her off. She expected them all to be what many of them in those days were—opinionated, narrow-minded, set in their ways. She had never tried to get to know Miss Martin. No one ever did.

She came. At the last moment before her arrival I panicked. It was not Miss Alliot coming, but Miss Alliot would hear all about the visit. Our house was in a terrace (crumbling). There was nothing, I now saw, to commend it to Miss Martin except, perhaps, water from the main and a coal fire.

After the first nervousness, though, we had a cosy time. We sat round the fire and ate Chinese figs and sipped ginger wine and played paper games which Miss Martin could not manage to lose. We sometimes wondered about the Townsends and I imagined a sort of Royal-Family-at-Sandringham Christmas with a giant tree and a servants' ball and Miss Alliot taking the floor in the arms of Ralph Townsend—but then my imagination failed, the picture faded: I could not imagine Miss Alliot in the arms of any man.

After Christmas, Miss Martin left and then I went back to school. I was too single-minded in my devotion to Miss Alliot to do much work there, or bother about anybody else. My infatuation was fed by her absence, and everything beautiful was wasted if it was not seen in her company.

The Christmas invitation bore glorious fruit. As a return, Miss Martin wrote to ask me to stay at Breezy Lodge for my half-term holiday. Perfect happiness invaded me, remembered clearly to this day. Then, after a while of walking on air, the bliss dissolved. Nothing in the invitation, I now realized, had been said of Miss Alliot. Perhaps she was off to Northumberland again, and I was to keep Miss Martin company in her stead. I tried to reason with myself that even that would be better than nothing, but I stayed sick with apprehension.

At the end of the bus-ride there on a Saturday morning, I was almost too afraid to cross the orchard. I feared my own disappointment as if it were something I must protect myself—and, incidentally, Miss Martin—from. I seemed to become two people—the one who tapped jauntily on the door, and the other who stood ready to ward off the worst. Which did not happen. Miss Alliot herself opened the door.

She was wearing one of her bandeaux and several ropes of beads and had a rather gipsy air about her. "The child has arrived," she called back into the room. Miss Martin sat by the stove mending stockings—an occupation of those days. They were Miss Alliot's stockings—rather thick, and biscuit-coloured.

We went over to St. Margaret's for lunch and walked to the Echo afterwards, returning with branches of catkins and budding twigs. Miss Alliot had a long, loping stride. She hit about at nettles with her stick, the fringed tongues of her brogues flapped—she had long, narrow feet, and trouble with high insteps, she complained. The bandeau was replaced by a stitched felt hat in which was stuck the eye part of a peacock's feather. "Bad luck," said Miss M. "Bosh," said Miss A.

We had supper at Breezy Lodge, for Miss Alliot's latest craze was for making goulash, and a great pot of it was to be consumed during the weekend. Afterwards, Miss Martin knitted—a jersey of complicated Fair Isle pattern for Miss Alliot. She sat in a little perplexed world of her own, entangled by coloured wools, her head bent over the instructions.

Miss Alliot turned her attention to me. What was my favourite line of poetry, what would I do if I were suddenly given a thousand pounds, would I rather visit Rome or Athens or New York, which should I hate most—being deaf or blind; hanged or drowned; are cats not better than dogs, and wild-flowers more beautiful than garden ones, and Emily Brontë streets ahead of Charlotte? And so on. It was heady stuff to me. No one before had been interested in my opinions. Miss Martin knitted on. Occasionally, she was included in the questions, and always appeared to give the wrong answer.

I slept in their bedroom, on a camp-bed borrowed from St. Margaret's. (And how was I ever going to be satisfied with staying *there* again? I wondered.)

Miss Alliot bagged (as she put it) the bathroom first, and was already in bed by the time I returned from what was really only a ewer of water and an Elsan. She was wearing black silk pyjamas with D.D.A. embroidered on a pocket. I bitterly regretted my pink nightgown, of which I had until then been proud. I had hastily brushed my teeth and passed a wet flannel over my face in eagerness to get back to her company and, I hoped, carry on with the entrancing subject of my likes and dislikes.

I began to undress. "People are kind to the blind, and impatient with the deaf," I began, as if there had been no break in the conversation. "You are so right," Miss Alliot said. "And people matter most."

"But if you couldn't see . . . well, this orchard in spring," Miss Martin put in. It was foolish of her to do so. "You've already *seen* it," Miss Alliot pointed out. "Why this desire to go on repeating your experiences?"

Miss Martin threw in the Parthenon, which she had *not* seen, and hoped to.

"Still people matter most," Miss Alliot insisted. "To be cut off from them is worse than to be cut off from the Acropolis."

She propped herself up in bed and with open curiosity watched me undress. For the first time in my life I realized what dreadful things I wore beneath my dress—lockknit petticoat, baggy school bloomers, vest with Cash's name tape, garters of stringy elastic tied in knots, not sewn. My mother had been right. . . . I should have sewn them. Then, for some reason, I turned my back to Miss Alliot and put on my nightgown. I need not have bothered, for Miss Martin was there between us in a flash, standing before Miss Alliot with Ovaltine.

::

ON THE NEXT DAY—SUNDAY—I RENOUNCED MY RELIGION. MY DOUBTS made it impossible for me to go to church, so Miss Martin went alone. She went rather miserably, I was forced to notice. I can scarcely believe that any deity could have been interested in my lack of devotion, but it was as if, somewhere, there were one who was. Freak weather had set in and, although spring had not yet begun, the sun was so warm that Miss Alliot took a deck-chair and a blanket and sat on the veranda and went fast asleep until long after Miss Martin had returned. (She *needed* a great deal of sleep, she always said.) I pottered about and fretted at this waste of time. I almost desired my faith again. I waited for Miss Martin to come back, and, seeing her, ran out and held a finger to my lips, as if Miss Alliot were royalty, or a baby. Miss Martin nodded and came on stealthily.

::

IT WAS BEFORE THE END OF THE SUMMER TERM THAT I HAD THE DREADFUL letter from Miss Martin. Miss Alliot—hadn't we both feared it?—was engaged to be married to Ralph Townsend. Of course, that put paid to my examinations. In the event of more serious matters, I scrawled off anything that came into my head. As for questions, I wanted to answer them only if they were asked by Miss Alliot, and they must be personal, not factual. As usual, if I didn't know what I was asked in the examination paper, I did a piece about something else. I imagined some *rapport* being made, and that was what I wanted from life.

Miss Martin's letter was taut and unrevealing. She stated the facts—the date, the place. An early autumn wedding it was to be, in Northumberland, as Miss Alliot had now no family of her own. I had never supposed that she had. At the beginning of a voyage, a liner needs some small tugs to help it on its way, but they are soon dispensed with.

Before the wedding, there were the summer holidays, and the removal of their things from Breezy Lodge, for Miss Martin had no heart, she said, to keep it on alone.

During that last holiday, Miss Martin's face was terrible. It seemed to be fading, like an old, old photograph. Miss Alliot, who was not inclined to jewelry ("Would you prefer diamonds to Rembrandts?" once she had asked me), had taken off her father's signet ring and put in its place a half hoop of diamonds. Quite incongruous, I thought.

I was weeks older. Time was racing ahead for me. A boy called Jamie was staying at St. Margaret's with his parents. After supper, while Mrs. Mayes' recitals were going on, or the solo whist, he and I sat outside the drawing-room on the stairs, and he told me blood-chilling stories, which I have since read in Edgar Allan Poe.

Whenever Jamie saw Miss Alliot, he began to hum a song of those days —"Horsy, keep your tail up." My mother thought he was a bad influence, and so another frost set in.

Sometimes—not often, though—I went to Breezy Lodge. The Fair Isle sweater was put aside. Miss Martin's having diminished, diminished everything, including Miss Alliot. Nothing was going on there, no goulash, no darning, no gathering of branches.

"Yes, she's got a face like a horse," Jamie said again and again.

And I said nothing.

::

"BUT HE'S OLD." MISS MARTIN MOVED HER HANDS ABOUT IN HER LAP, regretted her words, fell silent.

"Old? How old?" I asked.

"He's seventy."

I had known that Miss Alliot was doing something dreadfully, dangerously wrong. She could not be in love with Ralph Townsend; but with the Townsends entire.

::

ON THE DAY THEY LEFT, I WENT TO BREEZY LODGE TO SAY GOOD-BYE. IT looked squalid, with the packing done—something horribly shabby, ramshackle about it.

Later, I went with Jamie to the Echo and we shouted one another's names across the valley. Our names came back very clearly. When we returned, Miss Alliot and Miss Martin had gone forever.

::

MISS ALLIOT WAS MARRIED IN SEPTEMBER. MISS MARTIN TRIED SHARING HER London flat with someone else, another schoolmistress. I wrote to her at once, and she replied.

Towards Christmas my mother had a letter from Miss Louie to say that she had heard Miss Martin was dead—"by her own hand," she wrote, in her shaky handwriting.

"I am *horrified,*" I informed my diary that night—the five-year diary that was full of old sayings of Miss Alliot, and descriptions of her clothes.

::

I HAVE QUITE FORGOTTEN WHAT JAMIE LOOKED LIKE—BUT I CAN STILL SEE Miss Alliot clearly, her head back, looking down her nose, her mouth contemptuous, and poor Miss Martin's sad, scribbly face.

1972

INSIDE: TOWARD NEW DEFINITIONS

DORIS BETTS

::

burning the bed

ISABEL TAPPED LIGHTLY ON HER BRAKES TO KEEP FROM RAMMING THE LONG ambulance which was bringing her father home. Its taillights winked and the painted cross on the rear doors swayed down the clay road which had washed ragged with winter rains, then frozen in lumps and craters. Now the last snow had sunk into the soil. The mud was cold, rust-colored.

Isabel rolled down her car window, leaned out, pressed her horn. The ambulance turned left. One minute, Isabel thought. That's all it would take to check the mailbox. It seemed to her the aluminum door was cracked, that even as she drove by something white with her name on it could be seen. She braked harder, and the rear wheels floated slightly to one side on the slick mud.

"Goddamnit," she said aloud, pulling into the ruts left by the ambulance. She'd probably have to walk back for her letter, through the mire and after dark.

While she parked in the far corner of the yard, the hospital driver rocked back and forth, then swung in a slippery crescent and backed toward the front steps. Both attendants got out, opened the ambulance doors. Then they looked toward her car.

"I'm coming," Isabel said. She put her key ring in her pocketbook next to Brenda's postcard. She checked the hand brake.

When she was halfway to the house, the driver said, "If you'll just hold open the front door." Isabel did not like his tone.

Into the ambulance the other man said, "Get you right inside, Mr. Perkins." They slid him out as carefully as a pane of glass. Isabel was looking down at his head. A skull thrust through his face.

"How deep was the snow?" he said to them all. His smile looked raw. Isabel was carrying his false teeth in her pocketbook.

"You rest, Papa."

"A couple of inches." The orderly moved to the foot of the stretcher, looking at Isabel.

Quickly she said, "It's all gone now except in the shady places." She could have gnawed off her tongue. Now, of course, he would want the men to carry him around the north side of the house and show him those last patches.

"Papa!" she said, even while he was pointing. "Lay back and hush! Let's get you inside. You'll catch your death of cold."

She ran ahead of the bearers onto the porch, held open the door. Her eyes felt cold in her head, like silver spoons. She could have cried. Turning away, she looked down the hall where they would carry him, through a doorway to the old bed which filled the room like an abandoned river barge, washed up askew and catty-cornered. The counterpane was turned back, the pillow as white as a square of snow below the eaves, or somebody's flat grave marker.

The two men maneuvered the stretcher past, grazing her waist.

"That room straight ahead," Isabel said, standing thin against the wall. The men did not like her. She could tell that.

Then they carried him beyond her, toward the bed where he had jerked with joy when he fathered her, the same bed in which she had been wetly born, and Jasper, too. Twice her father had stood and looked down into that bed at what would survive him, and half the time he'd been wrong. Now he had a month or two of dying to do in that mammoth bed. After that, Isabel thought, she might burn the thing. Might leave it burning in the back field, below the old orchard. Might fly through the smoke of it, headed north, and not even look out the airplane window. She pressed her pocketbook where the stretcher had touched her, and followed them down the hall. Brenda can help burn it. Brenda wouldn't let me go through that funeral all alone. I doubt I can carry the bed outside by myself.

They laid him down and drew the sheets to his chin. Isabel signed the slip which said Marvin Perkins had been delivered with due care by the county ambulance service. On the way out, the short man pulled a small jar of pear preserves from his hip pocket. "Mama sent it," he said, and thrust it toward Isabel's front. "She's in his church. She said he liked pear preserves."

Isabel caught the jar against her purse. She'd forgotten what Papa liked and didn't like in the years she had been gone. Between now and Easter, she could not learn it all again. She was more grateful for the information than the fruit. She wanted to smile at the man, but she was a head taller and he kept his face down.

She held out her hand to the big one. "I believe you were in school with my brother."

"I played basketball with Jasper." The handshake was quick. "Got boys of my own playing now."

"That's fine," said Isabel, though really she thought it was depressing. "Thank you both."

Her father had gone instantly to sleep, the way a tired child will when at last he is dropped someplace familiar. Isabel stopped with her mouth open on the cheery word there was no need to say. On the pillow, his face even looked like a child's face, one which had been slightly crumpled. There were only a few wisps of hair on the pale scalp. Isabel laid his false teeth on the bedside table. He snuffled juicily in his sleep, like a baby or a bulldog. If she hurried, she could be back from the mailbox before he even wanted supper. She set the pear preserves beside the teeth.

The telephone rang in the hall.

It was Papa's preacher. She craned to see the clock. "Yes, he's asleep right now." Isabel felt through both pockets of her corduroy coat but could find no cigarettes. The preacher said something about food left on the kitchen table. By the churchwomen. Isabel said that was very nice. She braced the telephone on her shoulder and poured out her pocketbook and found cigarettes but no matches. "You'll tell them how much we appreciate it? Since I don't know the names? . . . Oh. Yes. Certainly."

Isabel made an ugly face at the framed picture of "Washington Crossing the Delaware" on the opposite wall. George, the boat, the tumbling waves: all painted in snuff, tar, nicotine. There was a pencil in the clutter from her bag and she wrote on the telephone book names the preacher spelled for her. With the eraser she poked Brenda's postcard into view. Cypress Gardens, for Christ's sake. "Yes." She thanked him again.

In the kitchen she found chicken broth and potato salad, two loaves of yeast bread, jars of beets and spiced apples, a bowl of ambrosia, a tall coconut cake on a cut-glass pedestal. They can't mean all that for a man who has cancer of the stomach, she thought. Most of that is for *me.* Deep in her throat there rose something smooth and solid, like a hard-boiled egg. They must have seen the coffee cups stacked in the sink, maybe even smelled the sticky glasses. What do I care if they poked through the kitchen? At home, Brenda won't even let me make toast.

Isabel poured the broth into a small pan, set it on the front burner of the stove, and looked at it. Globes of fat skated on the surface as if they were alive. Pushing the other food to one end of the table, she took her stationery box from a chair seat. There was a pack of matches inside with her pen. She wondered if the Baptist women had opened her stationery box and read the letter which still lay inside, face-down. She took out the two sheets and, lighting a cigarette and clicking her pen, read what she had written.

Dear Brenda,

Here I am in this ghastly hospital; I wish you could see it. No matter what waiting room I pick, somebody always sits beside me with a running sore, a bloody bandage, or a scar on his face where the skin was burned and snatched off. They don't get sick here, they get hurt. Axes and car jacks and hunting accidents. Even Papa still thinks it was carrying hay bales and feed that gave him his cancer. First he got hernia and then the hernia got mean.

But today they're sending Papa home and I have to feed and nurse him to death. I do believe in mercy killing, I do. How could you watch this day after day and not believe in it? But if I had that power I don't know where I would stop. Two perfectly healthy boys have just walked through smelling of beer and motor oil, and I could poison them both.

I can't tell yet when I can come home. You can't imagine how far away from you I feel. This is some other planet. Papa's preacher is in and out, talking in whatever his language is—it can't be English. I never liked it here and it's worse now, at my age, when I've been living my own life so long. Nights I've been leaving the hospital to sleep in that house I never wanted to live in anymore. It's cold and empty. Everything you do in it makes a loud noise and everything Papa owns is made of tin and falls down in the night.

Nothing here is comfortable to me, and I don't mean the old plumbing or the mattresses that have fallen in. Even the parts of the house I thought I liked aren't there anymore. Four of us lived here and two are dead and one is dying, and it makes me nervous. The people who used this furniture don't use it anymore.

Isabel pinched off a piece of the cake icing and pushed it back in that space on her gum where a wisdom tooth should be. She drew a line across the page, deliberately sloping it upward in case Brenda should be looking for clues about her mood. Then she began to add in a firm, angular hand:

That reminds me of what I wanted to tell you about the bed.

She put out her cigarette. No point in pressing on with this letter when, even now, a long one from Brenda might lie in the mailbox. She buttoned her coat, hurried out the back door. As soon as she had gone halfway, Isabel began to fear Papa was calling, or the chicken broth had boiled all over the stove. She tried to run, mud spattering on her broad shoes and freckling her ankles. I must look like a grizzly bear, she thought, aching. The mailbox was empty.

She took her time walking back. Let him call. He'd be calling in an empty house if she was home in Baltimore where she belonged. Her shoes were such a mess she unlaced them at the back steps and left them there. The broth still waited over an unlit burner on the gas range. Isabel took off her coat. She ate a tablespoon of ambrosia. The linoleum was cold on her bare feet.

It was too soon to tell Brenda about the bed, how they could burn it together in the back field. At night. With Isabel pointing out the constellations. Save that for a surprise. Brenda would say, "What makes you think of such things!" And Brenda would giggle, carrying the slats out just the way Isabel said, and backing downstairs with her end of the stained old mattress.

Isabel sat down again to her letter. "That reminds me of what I wanted to tell you about the bed." She wrote:

> Now we're at home and Papa's asleep in his big bed. I've moved it at an angle because the footboard is too tall to see over. God knows what makes Papa so cheerful, even about the snow he couldn't really see from the hospital. He's happy to have me here and says daughters will always come home when you need them. You know what a lie that is. But I want you to see this bed. It's a hundred years old, maybe two, and somebody built it out of trees cut down on the farm. It's put together with wooden pegs and they made it to last forever.

She got up and put some more ambrosia into a bowl and spooned it between sentences. There was a little sherry stirred into the juice.

> Brenda, I wish you'd write more often. I need your letters. I don't see why you're going to the movies with Katherine Moose even if she is lonesome and has trouble getting her support checks. When did you ever have anything in common with Katherine Moose? (Which I mean as a compliment to you.) I thought you were going to make a decoupage table while I was gone, for the living room? After this house, I'll be glad to see something colorful. All Mama ever hung on these walls was that fellow hoeing in the fields, the Horse Fair, cathedrals, that St. Bernard in the woods with the children, George Washington, and Gainsborough's Blue Boy. All of them, even the blue boy, painted in brown gravy. I am so depressed. . . .

Papa was calling. Isabel flicked on the gas under his broth and hurried to the bedroom.

"Who's that?" he cried when she came in. More and more, Isabel thought, he comes out of sleep into a world he's half forgotten. Maybe the world was for him like this house to Isabel. Not even the good parts looking like they used to.

"It's Isabel," she said, as gently as she could. She knew her voice was too loud for a sickroom. The nurses had said so. Even the doctor whispered, while touching her father with rapid, hairy hands.

"Isabel? That you?"

"You're home." She eased to his side and laid one hand on his arm, to show she was real. If he asks about Jasper, I don't know what I'll say.

"You've got things fixed up real nice. Even the cobwebs swept down. You've not been washing this old woodwork?" He struggled higher on the pillow. Isabel shook her head. "It looks whiter. What time is it?"

"I'll bring you some soup. You never saw so much food. Mrs. . . . Mrs. Bradford. And two others. And somebody sent you pear preserves." She nudged the jar but he reached beyond it for his teeth in their gauze wrapping. "I'll get your supper now. You need anything first? You need the bedpan?" Isabel didn't know why she asked, since by now she knew he was like any other animal and did not defecate until after a meal. She and Brenda had an Airedale at home the same way. "You get your teeth in," she said, although he was already settling his jaws with a few bites of empty air.

She arranged his tray carefully by the bed, then sat in a chair where the high footboard hid him. She did not like to watch him eat. Tonight she looked at the room itself, improved somehow just because it had Papa to belong to. The wide floorboards had mellowed from years of traffic. Two braided rugs were faded gray. Under the bed the lint curled back, and softly under Mama's treadle sewing machine, behind her domed tin trunk stamped with flowers, then under the bureau with its three-foot mirror.

The mirror was in such a condition nobody was safe looking into it. Its surface had peeled and bubbled along jagged stripes of gold and gray. Isabel had glanced in it her first day home and discovered a face that, for all its broadness, looked frail and insane.

Neither she nor Papa could see themselves in the mirror now, after her struggle to move the furniture. Getting ready to bring him home, Isabel had lain in the big bed where he would lie, just to be certain. No need, she'd thought, for Papa to see how his skin had yellowed, his eyes shrunk away from their bony cups. Papa's fine black eyes lay now in their sockets like two butter beans. Isabel smiled. Brenda wouldn't know what a butter bean was. The Baptist women will bring some when Papa dies; Brenda can taste them then. She'll feel sorry for all I've had to bear these last weeks. She'll be sorry she didn't write more letters.

In front of the mirror on an embroidered spread was Papa's stopped cookie of a watch, two combs, shaving mug, brush. A china heart which held buttons, cuff links, and moldering tieclasps. In the bottom corners of the leprous mirror two photographs were stuck: one of Isabel, age 10, riding a mule; and one of Jasper in his army uniform. She'd been tempted to put these in a drawer but decided she didn't have the right. From where Papa lay, they wouldn't look much larger than postage stamps.

Behind the high wall of his bed, Papa said, "How's it feel to be home? Not counting me sick and all?"

"Not the way I remember it," Isabel said. She was glad she could not see the way he siphoned up his soup.

"You never did come home much. You sure you can get off work this long?"

"I'm sure. I'm good at my job, you know."

"I hate costing you money. You was always tight about money, not like Jasper." The slurping stopped. He said, "And that's a good thing. Here you are, independent. No worries. Nobody telling you what to do. I'm that way myself."

He did not know how long ago his insurance money had been used up, couldn't guess how much Isabel had paid the hospital. With her cruise money. She and Brenda had meant to go to Greece this summer. She said, "Your preacher called, wants to come see you. I told him tomorrow morning. Get you over the trip. Get your strength up." She could not tell whether he laughed or choked.

Then at last came the question she had dreaded. "When's Jasper coming?" He had already asked it once, just after the operation.

"Papa," she said, but he was ahead of her.

"That's right, Jasper's dead. It's the fault of the medicine. With the medicine I can't tell what time it is."

Isabel said it was seven o'clock. "Soon be time for . . . well, not for bed. For sleep."

"I don't mean clocks," he said crossly, and the dishes rattled when he put the tray on the table. "They's not a thing wrong with my mind and don't you forget it. The medicine flattens things out, that's all. It can send you into any year it damn well pleases."

Isabel thought this was not a good time to remind him to take another dose. She cleared the dishes, slid the bedpan under his blanket, and went to the kitchen to put food away. She carried her cigarettes to the back steps, because when he was awake smoke made Papa cough, and coughing made Papa hurt. The mud had hardened on her shoes like concrete. When she put them on, the earth dragged at her soles. She clumped around the yard. I told Brenda it was like another planet here. Even gravity pulls harder.

She could barely see the mailbox in the growing dark. Tomorrow, at least, one of Brenda's damned postcards. Brenda taught third grade in a private school for Jewish children, and all year long she made them bring in postcards showing vacation spots in fifty states. Brenda would never have to buy a postcard in her entire life. Especially being so stingy with them. So far, Isabel had only received Natural Bridge, Virginia, and the Cypress Gardens, both with a hole where they had once been thumbtacked to a display board. Both said much the same.

Busy at school. Had to get new battery your car. Hope things aren't too bad. Letter follows love Brenda. Can't write going to movie with Katherine but got your letter and will answer soon.

Isabel had jammed that one inside her pocketbook so hard the shiny surface folded and made a long crease up the Southern belle in her hoop skirt.

She flattened her cigarette with a weighted foot. When she padded in bedroom shoes to Papa's room, carrying the medicine bottle and spoon, he was already asleep and the bedpan waited for her on the table, as neatly covered with the napkin as a plate of cooling rolls. It won't be long, thought Isabel, before I'll be giving him a needle in his arm, the way the doctor showed me. "You've got a real knack for this," he had said when she plunged distilled water into the orange. "You'd have made a good nurse."

"I don't talk soft enough," Isabel had said.

She woke her father and made him take the medicine, though he swore he didn't need it tonight. They had an argument. In the end, she jammed the spoon into his mouth while he was still fussing, and made a small reddening dent on his upper gum. He pulled back, stiff, on the pillow and held the liquid in his mouth. His cheeks blew out like a squirrel's.

"You swallow that now," she said. He would not.

"I didn't mean to hurt you. Please swallow it down."

Still he lay rigid, his eyes black, neck hard, chin sharp.

She said, "Jasper would want you to take the medicine." Her father closed his eyes. The bulb jerked in his throat. His face relaxed. Isabel laid her hand on his forehead, but he would not move and he was not going to open his eyes. "Good night, Papa," she said, trying to make her voice soft, and thinking, Goddamn him, damn Jasper, damn Brenda, damn them all.

::

JASPER'S BEDROOM WAS THE MOST COMFORTABLE PLACE IN THE OLD FARM-house and that was the only reason Isabel was sleeping there. A late addition, the room had electrical outlets in the baseboards and less bulky, gloomy furnishings. Jasper's old books still lined the shelves he and Papa had built, and she and Jasper had painted.

A broad map of Korea was tacked on one wall, a green peninsula touching the Sea of Japan, Manchuria, and the Yellow Sea. A snaky line of black crayon marked the places Jasper might have been, battles in which he might have fought. Papa had kept this record against the day Jasper came home to tell them everything. Near Wonju, the black line broke off. Once Jasper died, in February, 1951, the whole Eighth Army, the war itself, stopped dead and hung uncompleted on Jasper's wall.

Isabel looked at the fading map while she put on pajamas. She plugged in Jasper's reading lamp and ran one finger along his books. *Tom Swift.* Zane Grey. *Tarzan and the Jewels of Opar. Kidnapped. Wuthering Heights. Boy Scout Handbook.* Dog and horse stories. True stories of the F.B.I. *Tobacco Road. Dutchess Hotspur.* Frank Harris.

From the flyleaf of *Robin Hood,* she read the blurred lines scrawled across the treetops of Sherwood Forest:

You steal my book
And I can tell
You'll go to Hell.
Marvin Jasper Perkins, Jr. Age 9½

Sometimes on the map of her own mind Isabel tried to draw the rest of Jasper's life—to crayon him home across the Pacific, over the continent to Carolina, to some good Northern college on the G.I. Bill and what money Isabel would have given him. What was a cruise to Greece compared to that investment?

And now Jasper would be . . . forty-one years old, two more than Isabel was now. And they might be sitting here tonight, in Papa's house, waiting out Papa's death together.

She had always been larger than Jasper. By now he, too, would have added weight. Maybe his pale hair would have thinned, the capillaries begun to surface in his cheeks. Her income would have been higher than his—and how Jasper would have hated that! He'd have told her for the hundredth time to let her hair grow long. Isabel took a bottle of Scotch and a glass from a drawer. They could have shared a drink, talked about things. About Brenda. About whoever Jasper might have had to talk about.

Papa called out. Isabel put her drink behind the photograph of Jasper in his high-school mortarboard. She went to the back bedroom, but he was asleep again from the medicine that could send him into any year it pleased.

"I'm still here, Papa," she said, just in case he could hear.

Then she went to bed.

. . . *Jasper moves swiftly ahead of me through the thick forest. Sometimes he swings from vines; at others, he is simply thrown lightly from one great tree to another. I am riding more slowly behind him on the ground, on the back of something shaped like a mule but much larger. Nearly the size of an elephant. I am happy, but I wish he would wait for me. We are going to a cleared space he knows, to build our house. He calls down to me that the Indians are coming. He calls down that we will need help in building our house. I am to choose some Indian to help us. Now I see the line of natives marching, a column in single file. All are women, very dark brown, young, healthy, as tall as the animal which carries me. They wear nothing but short skirts made of black feathers. I pick a girl I think Jasper will like. She looks very strong. Now I see another who resembles her; she says the two of them are sisters. Perhaps they are even twins. I decide to choose both girls to help us in the clearing where Jasper is waiting for me.* . . .

When Isabel woke, the thick forest turned into a network of tree-branch shadows thrown by the morning sun on the walls and floor and across the four-legged bed. Her mouth was dry. Her head ached and seemed to be full of fungus. She got up, feeling tired, and put the Scotch back inside Jasper's bureau. She decided to wear her wool slacks because the preacher probably wouldn't like slacks.

She made Papa's oatmeal and soft-boiled egg and woke him. He looked into her face as if he had never seen it before.

She said it twice. "Time for breakfast."

His eyes slowly remembered what breakfast was. She put another pillow behind his head and shoulders. "Want you to eat early and get cleaned up. Your preacher's coming."

"Good morning, Isabel," he finally said. In a minute he smiled.

He ate as if he were really hungry. It depressed her to think of all that good food, falling down into that internal ruin. "You're not a bad cook, Isabel," he said, not noticing, as she did, the oatmeal spilling onto the sheets. "For somebody that always hated cooking. You fix your own meals in Baltimore?"

"Anybody can make oatmeal." She stored his empty suitcase in the closet, under the suit he would likely be buried in. "Maybe we'll have time to change those sheets."

"You should of got married," Papa said.

"I'm better off than plenty married people. Tomorrow you want a poached egg?"

"I never could stand an egg looked like it had just fell out of the nest. You really don't miss it? Your friends married and all?"

"My friends aren't married."

"You're not old yet. Maybe you're courting? You and your roommate go out much? You and Sheila?"

Isabel gave him the yellow capsule. "I haven't lived with Sheila for over a year now. Sheila turned out to be somebody I couldn't respect. I don't even see her anymore. Want some more water?"

"What are you getting so mad for? You and the new one, then. You find any bachelors to take you to supper?"

"Brenda. Her name is Brenda." She decided to brush the sheets off and leave them. Why make the preacher think a dying man was neat? "Anything else?"

"Open the window," Papa said. "Maybe it's started to smell like spring."

Isabel took the preacher to Papa's bedroom, waited politely while they talked about Easter, baseball, plans for the new church—none of which Marvin Perkins would live to see. She had never met so tactless a man as that preacher, and she stood behind the high footboard and made disapproving faces until even her scalp was tired. He kept right on telling Papa what a fine time the youth club would have camping by the river when it got warm, and how they'd moved the revival to August.

At last he began to read Scripture—which was all he was supposed to do in the first place, thought Isabel. He started the Sermon on the Mount, but Papa said he'd like something older than that, something sterner.

"I've got to like the Old Testament again," he said, sounding embarrassed, as if this were a breach of taste. "What I really like is the wars against the Philistines."

"I see." The preacher began leafing back.

"After Moses, though," said Papa. He settled back and spread his arms wide on the counterpane, palms up. Like a horizontal shrug. "I never thought it was right Moses got shut out of the Promised Land."

That would have tickled Brenda! The preacher began to read about armies, battles, the fear of the Lord. Isabel excused herself, took down her coat from its peg in the hall, and went into the yard, knocking clay off her shoes. The jonquils were already up, their buds like cartridges. There were red knots on the twigs of the maple she and Jasper had climbed. Jasper once climbed to the very top of that tree because it had been his ambition to spit down the house chimney; and he did, but he missed.

Through Papa's half-open window she could hear that the story was about Moab, the Canaanites, and Deborah the prophetess: ". . . for the Lord shall sell Sisera into the hand of a woman," the preacher read.

Isabel circled to the back yard. Here the orchard spread downhill to the back field, bottomland, a winding creek. There were broken limbs still caught in the fruit trees, jelly-filled wounds in trunks where peach borers waited out the winter. Last year's caterpillar webs flapped on the cherries like wet old flags.

"You've quit tending the orchard?" She'd asked Papa that in the hospital, on some choking, long, steam-heated afternoon.

"Not much point after your mama died. Too much to eat raw, and nobody to make jam or cobbler." Talk of the orchard revived him, though he was very weak from surgery. "I never liked sprays and poisons. Used to go out and kill everything by hand. That way, a worm knew who it was and I knew who I was." His cheeks grew red as apples. At that time, the doctor was saying he would live either a day or two months, depending on which his heart decided and how fast his stomach ate itself. "It still blooms, though, down that whole hillside. Not as much fruit, but how it does bloom!"

Now she paced downhill, wondering if he would wait to see it blossom one more time, ducking her head under the limbs of the Bartlett pear. Bartlett was self-sterile; she'd heard him say you needed another variety to cross-pollinate. He'd set another pear far down the hill. Isabel looked for it, but all the bare trees looked alike at a distance.

When Papa's done with the bed, I'll burn it there. In the bottomland. Primitive ritual, I'll tell Brenda. Like putting a Viking to sea on his flaming barge. It'll be just pagan enough to suit an anti-Semite Jewess like Brenda. She'll shiver while she's laughing. "Isabel, there's nobody like you in the world!" she'll say. But she'll be uneasy about it, too, and we'll need a drink when we get back inside, in Jasper's room.

Then Isabel thought one more step: she saw herself home and telling the other women in their apartment building. Katherine Moose. And Rhonda. She imagined how easy it would be to boast, to repeat when she was drunk and maudlin. "So the country Baptists got the body to bury, but the real ceremony was mine. Father and offspring, just like that." Offspring. I could make a pun on bedspring if I was sober. And Brenda would echo the telling in mock horror. "I said, Isabel, you can't do that! But you know Isabel, she'd been down there till she needed to be *cauterized*, or something, so I took one end and . . ."

In the distance, Isabel heard the preacher's car. Hurrying to the house, she forgot to bend her head and some tree—the pear?—raked a limb through her short hair.

There was still no letter and that night Isabel tried to call Brenda Goldstein. The telephone in their Baltimore apartment was first busy, and later unanswered. She tried the number several times. When she finally got through at eleven-thirty, there seemed to be a party going on.

"Brenda? It's Isabel. What in the world is all that noise?"

"Turn that thing down. Hello?"

"I said it's Isabel! I've been calling for hours."

"I went to an art lecture. What's the matter? Has he died?"

Isabel was angry and said, too loud, "NO, HE HAS NOT DIED!" She wondered if Papa could have heard. "He's about the same. I just wanted to talk to you. I haven't had a letter for two weeks."

"Well, I mailed you one." A crowd was milling around that apartment, talking, laughing, shaking ice cubes.

"Listen, it gets lonesome down here." Isabel decided she must speak softer, much softer. She stared at George Washington, who seemed to her afloat in rapids of Scotch and seltzer. She eyed the canal in Venice on the other wall, painted in shades of bourbon whiskey thinned down with spit. "Listen," she hissed, "where were you all night long with me calling and calling?"

"I told you. I went with Katherine Moose to an art lecture."

Isabel said it sounded like they were having a goddamn party.

"Well, Ron's here from next door. And Sheila. We ran into Sheila at the museum."

Isabel paced up and down on the gleaming heart-pine boards. "It's all right for Rhonda to be there, but you know, Brenda, you *know* Sheila's not to set foot in that apartment! Brenda, you know that! As many times as I've said . . ."

"Yes," came a stiff, polite voice. "It was a *very* good lecture. Manet."

"Oh, Christ," said Isabel. "And Sheila just can't wait to see what changes you've made in the apartment. Rode her home in my car, I'll bet! I can imagine. She can't wait to tell you all my faults while I'm down here keeping a deathwatch. You hear me, Brenda? A deathwatch! I never thought the minute my back was turned . . ."

"Well, you try to get some sleep and not break your own health over it," Brenda said, and hung up.

Isabel couldn't sleep at all. She rolled from one edge of Jasper's bed to the other. She was almost grateful when Papa cried out with pain in the night, but the hurt was gone before she got to him. He was sleeping. The gray folds of skin under his neck hung loose. He breathed in and out, in and out.

I meant to offer him those pear preserves for supper, thought Isabel. I'd have thought of it if Brenda had stayed home where she belonged, and my mind had been easy. In and out he breathed. She moved her arm toward his tall mirror where reflected light showed up her wristwatch. Three-thirty. Isabel wound the watch. She did not look at her image.

She went into the hall and dialed, direct, the number of their apartment. Out of a dry and swollen mouth, Brenda said, "Hello?"

Isabel said nothing.

"Hello? Who is this?"

Isabel breathed heavily into the telephone. In and out. In and OUT.

"What number are you calling?" said Brenda.

(She's sitting up in bed now and reaching for her robe. She covers up with that fluffy robe even to talk on the phone. Her throat's probably scratching. In the morning her head will ache right over both mastoid bones. Oh, I know her. She'll look older than thirty-five in the morning, and there'll be lines on her face where the pillowcase wrinkled. . . .)

Shaking with the laugh she was holding back, Isabel blew two hard puffs of air into the mouthpiece.

Then she heard a second voice, a woman's voice, say, ". . . answers, just hang up."

There was a single click, then the long singing as emptiness rushed along the black highway, beside the asphalt road, by the rutted road, down the wires to Isabel, across the state of Virginia, humming inland over the muddy yard, into the house and through her ear and into her brain, like that old tent peg the Hebrew woman nailed through the brain of Sisera when he took refuge in her tent.

1973

JANE RULE

::

middle children

CLARE AND I BOTH COME FROM BIG FAMILIES, A BOSSY, LOVING LINE OF voices stretching away above us to the final authority of our parents, a chorus of squawling, needy voices beneath us coming from crib or play pen or notch in tree. We share, therefore, the middle child syndrome: we are both over earnest, independent, inclined to claustrophobia in crowds. The dreams of our adolescent friends for babies and homes of their own we privately considered nightmares. Boys were irredeemably brothers who took up more physical and psychic space than was ever fair. Clare and I, in cities across the continent from each other, had the same dream: scholarships for college where we would have single rooms, jobs after that with our own apartments. But scholarship students aren't given single rooms; and the matchmakers, following that old cliche that opposites attract, put us, east and west, into the same room.

Without needing to discuss the matter, we immediately arranged the furniture as we had arranged furniture with sisters all our lives, mine along one wall, hers along the other, an invisible line drawn down the center of the room, over which no sock or book or tennis racket should ever stray. Each expected the other to be hopelessly untidy; our sisters were. By the end of the first week, ours was the only room on the corridor that looked like a military barracks. Neither of us really liked it, used to the posters and rotting corsages and dirty clothes of our siblings, but neither of us could bring herself to contribute any clutter of her own. "Maybe a painting?" Clare suggested. I did not know where we could get one. Clare turned out to be a painter. I, a botanist, who could never grow things in my own room before where they might be watered with Coke or broken by a thrown magazine or sweater, brought in a plant stand, the first object to straddle the line because it needed to be under the window. The friends each of us made began to straddle that line, too, since we seemed to be interchangeably good listeners, attracting the same sort of flamboyant, needy first or last or only children.

"Sandra thinks she may be pregnant," I would say about Clare's friend who had told me simply because Clare wasn't around.

"Aren't they all hopeless?" Clare would reply, and we middle children would shake our wise, cautious heads.

We attracted the same brotherly boys as well who took us to football games and fraternity drunks and sexual wrestling matches on the beach. We used the same cool defenses, gleaned not from the advice of our brothers but from observing their behaviour.

"Bobby always told me not to take the 'respect' bit too seriously if I wanted to have any fun," Clare said, "but I sometimes wonder why I'd want 'respect' or 'fun'. Doesn't it all seem to you too much trouble? This Saturday there's a marvelous exhibit. Then we could just go out to dinner and come home."

We had moved our desks by then. Shoved together, they could share one set of reference books conveniently and frugally for us both. We asked to have one chest of drawers taken out of the room. Neither of us had many clothes, and, since we wore the same size, we had begun to share our underwear and blouses to keep laundry day to once a week. I can't remember what excuse we had for moving the beds. Perhaps by the time we did, we didn't need an excuse, for ourselves anyway.

I have often felt sorry for people who can't have the experience of falling in love like that, gradually, without knowing it, touching first because pearls have to be fastened or a collar straightened, then more casually because you are standing close together looking at the same assignment sheet or photograph, then more purposefully because you know that there is comfort and reassurance for an exam coming up or trouble in the family. So many people reach out to each other before there is any sympathy or affection. When Clare turned into my arms, or I into hers—neither of us knows just how it was—the surprise was like coming upon the right answer to a question we did not even know we had asked.

Through the years of college, while our friends suffered all the uncertainties of sexual encounter, of falling into and out of love, of being too young and then perhaps too old in a matter of months, of worrying about how to finance graduate school marriages, our only problem was the clutter of theirs. We would have liked to clear all of them out earlier in order to enjoy the brief domestic sweetness of our own sexual life. But we were from large families. We knew how to maintain privacy, a space of our own, so tactfully that no one ever noticed it. Our longing for our own apartment, like the trips we would take to Europe, was an easy game. Nothing important to us had to be put off until then.

Putting off what was unimportant sometimes did take ingenuity. The boys had no objection to being given up, but our corridor friends were continually trying to arrange dates for us. We decided to come back from one Christmas holiday engaged to boys back home. That they didn't exist was never discovered. We gave each other rings and photographs of brothers. Actually I was very fond of Bobby, and Clare got on just as well with my large and boisterous family. Our first trip to Europe, between college and graduate school, taught us harder lessons. It seemed harmless enough to drink and dance with the football team traveling with us on the ship, but, when they turned up, drunken and disorderly at our London hotel, none of our own outrage would convince the night porter that we were not at fault. Only when we got to graduate school did we find the social answer: two young men as in need of protection as we were, who cared about paintings and concerts and growing things and going home to their own bed as much as we did.

When Clare was appointed assistant professor in art history and I got a job with the parks board, we had been living together in dormitories and student digs for eight years. We could finally leave the clutter of other lives behind us for an apartment of our own. Just at a time when we saw other relationships begin to grow stale or burdened with the continual demands of children, we were discovering the new privacy of making love on our own living room carpet at five o'clock in the afternoon, too hungry then to bother with cocktails or dressing for dinner. Soon we got quite out of the habit of wearing clothes except when we went out or invited people in. We woke making love, ate breakfast and made love again before we went to work, spent three or four long evenings a week in the same new delight until I saw in Clare's face that bruised, ripe look of a new, young wife, and she said at the same moment, "You don't look safe to go out."

In guilt we didn't really discuss, we arranged more evenings with friends, but, used to the casual interruptions of college life, we found such entertainment often too formal and contrived. Then for a week or two we would return to our honeymoon, for alone together we could find no reason not to make love. It is simply not true to say such things don't improve with practice.

"It's a good thing we never knew how bad we were at it," Clare said, one particularly marvelous morning.

When we didn't know, however, we had had more sympathy for those around us, accommodating themselves to back seats of cars or gritty blankets on the beach. Now our friends, either newly wed in student digs where quarreling was the only acceptable—that is, unavoidable—noise, or exhausted by babies, made wry jokes about missing the privacy of drive-in movies or about the merits of longer bathtubs. They were even more avid readers of pornography than they had been in college. We were not the good listeners we had been. I heard Clare being positively high minded about what a waste of time all those dirty books were.

"You never used to be a prude," Sandra said in surprise.

That remark, which should have made Clare laugh, kept her weeping half the night instead. I had never heard her so distressed, but then perhaps she hadn't had the freedom to be. "We're too different," she said, and "We're not kind any more."

"Maybe we should offer to baby sit for Sandra and lend them the apartment," I suggested, not meaning it.

We are both very good with babies. It would be odd if we weren't. Any middle child knows as much about colic and croup as there is to know by the time she's eight or nine. The initial squeamishness about changing diapers is conquered at about the same age. Sandra, like all our other friends, had it all to learn at twenty-three. Sometimes we did just as I had suggested, sitting primly across from each other like maiden aunts, Clare marking papers, I thumbing through books that could help me to imagine what was going on in our apartment. Or sometimes Sandra would call late at night, saying, "You're fond of this kid, aren't you? Well, come and get him before we kill him." Then we'd take the baby for a midnight ride over the rough back roads that are better for gas pains than any pacing. I didn't mind that assignment, but I was increasingly restless with the evenings we spent in somebody else's house.

"You know, if we had a house of our own," I said, "we could take the baby for the night, and they could just stay home."

I realize that there is nothing really immoral about lending your apartment to a legally married couple for the evening so that you can spend a kind and moral night out with their baby, but it seemed to me faintly and unpleasantly obscene: our bed . . . perhaps even our living room rug. I was back to the middle child syndrome. I wanted to draw invisible lines.

"They're awfully tidy and considerate," Clare said, "and they always leave us a bottle of scotch."

"Well, we leave them a bottle of scotch as well."

"We drink more of it than they do."

I didn't want to sound mean.

"If we had a house, we could have a garden."

"You'd like that," Clare decided.

Sandra's husband said we could never get a mortgage, but our combined income was simply too impressive to ignore. We didn't really need a large house, just the two of us, though I wanted a studio for Clare, and she wanted a green house and work shop for me. The difficulty was that neither of us could think of a house that was our size. We weren't used to them. The large, old houses that felt like home were really no more expensive than the new, compact and efficient boxes the agent thought suitable to our career centered lives. Once we had wandered through the snarled, old garden and up into the ample rooms of the sort of house we had grown up in, we could not think about anything else.

"Well, why not?" I asked.

"It has five bedrooms."

"We don't have to use them all."

"We might take a student," Clare said.

We weren't surprised at the amount of work involved in owning an old house. Middle children aren't. Our friends, most of whom were still cooped up in apartments, liked to come out in those early days for painting and repair parties, which ended with barbecue suppers on the back lawn, fenced in and safe for toddlers. Our current couple of boys were very good at the heavy work of making drapes and curtains. They even enjoyed helping me dig out old raspberry canes. It was two years before Clare had time to paint in the studio, and my green house turned out to be a very modest affair since I had so many other things to do, cooking mostly.

We have only one room left now for stray children. The rest are filled with students, boys we decided, which is probably a bit prudish, and it's quite true that they take up more physical and psychic space than is ever fair. Still, they're only kids, and, though it takes our saintly cleaning woman half a day a week just to dig out their rooms, they're not bad about the rest of the house.

Harry is a real help to me with the wine making, inclined to be more careful about the chemical details than I am. Pete doesn't leave his room except to eat unless we've got some of the children around; then he's even willing to stay with them in the evening if we have to go out. Carl, who's never slept a night alone in his life since he discovered it wasn't necessary, doesn't change girls so often that we don't get to know them, and he has a knack for finding people who fit in: take a turn at the dishes, walk the dogs, check to see that we have enough cream for breakfast.

Clare and I have drawn one very careful line across the door of our bedroom, and, though it's not as people proof as our brief apartment, it's a good deal better than a dormitory. We even occasionally have what we explain as our cocktail there before dinner when one of Carl's girls is minding the vegetables; and, if we don't get involved in too interesting a political or philosophical discussion, we sometimes go upstairs for what we call the late news. Both of us are still early to wake, and, since Pete will get up with any visiting child, the first of the day is always our own.

"Pete's a middle child," Clare said the other morning, hearing him sing a soft song to Sandra's youngest as he carried her down the stairs to give her an early bottle. "I hope he finds a middle child for himself one day."

"I'd worry about him if he were mine," I said.

"Oh, well, I'd worry about any of them if they were mine. I simply couldn't cope."

"I just wouldn't want to."

"There's a boy in my graduate seminar . ." Clare began.

I was tempted to say that, if we had a family of our own, we'd always be worrying and talking about them even when we had time to ourselves, but there was still an hour before we had to get up, and I've always felt generous in the early morning, even when I was a kid in a house cluttered with kids from which I dreamed that old dream of escape.

CONTRIBUTORS

HELEN ESSARY ANSELL (1940–) is both a writer and a photographer. She won the O. Henry Short Story Award for "The Threesome," published a novel called *Lucy* in 1969, and is currently working on another tentatively titled *The Queen Bee.* She lives in San Francisco.

INGEBORG BACHMANN (1926–) is a native of Austria. Besides her short-story collection, *The Thirteenth Year,* she has written two volumes of poetry, numerous plays for radio, and the libretti for two operas by Henze.

DORIS BETTS (1932–), a native of North Carolina, has published three collections of short stories and three novels, most recently *The River to Pickle Beach.*

PAUL BOWLES (1910–) was born in New York City and now lives in Morocco. He is a composer as well as the author of *The Sheltering Sky* and *The Delicate Prey.*

JOHN HORNE BURNS (1916–1953), born in Massachusetts, died of a cerebral hemorrhage in Italy at age thirty-six. Besides *The Gallery,* he wrote *Lucifer with a Book* and *A Cry of Children.*

JAMES T. FARRELL (1904–), like Dreiser, has been associated with American naturalism since the publication of *Studs Lonigan* in 1932. His huge body of work has been translated into more than twenty languages.

WILLIAM FAULKNER (1897–1962) is regarded by many as America's foremost novelist and short-story writer. In 1949 he won the Nobel Prize for literature for such novels as *The Sound and the Fury, Sanctuary, Light in August,* and *Absalom, Absalom.*

E. M. FORSTER (1879–1970), one of the leading British writers of the twentieth century, stopped publishing fiction in 1924 after achieving great success with *A Passage to India,* an action explained in the preface to his posthumously released novel, *Maurice.*

GRAHAM GREENE (1904–) has written poetry, short stories, dramas, novels, essays, literary criticism, and screenplays, and is one of the important figures in British letters today.

RADCLYFFE HALL (1886–1943), born in England, is famous as the author of *The Well of Loneliness,* published in 1928. She also wrote *Adam's Breed* and *The Unlit Lamp.*

ERNEST HEMINGWAY (1899–1961), one of the most influential American writers of this century, won the Nobel Prize in 1954. Among his best-known works are *A Farewell to Arms, For Whôm the Bell Tolls, The Sun Also Rises,* and *The Old Man and the Sea.*

MAUDE HUTCHINS, a native of Connecticut, has exhibited widely as a sculptor and written numerous books, among them *The Elevator* (1962).

CHRISTOPHER ISHERWOOD (1904–) was born in England but has made his home in many places. After his sojourn in Berlin in the twenties, which provided the material for *Berlin Stories,* he has lived fairly continuously in California. Besides his fiction, he is known for his autobiographical writings and his collaborations with W. H. Auden.

D. H. LAWRENCE (1885–1930) mastered every literary genre, and spent his life wandering the world. Among his most famous books are *Lady Chatterly's Lover* and *Sons and Lovers.*

MARRIS MURRAY (1908–) was born in South Africa and has, in addition to her short stories, written a novel, *The Fire Raisers* (1953).

JOAN O'DONOVAN (1914–) is the author of five novels, her latest being *She, Alas!* (1965). She lives in London.

JOHN O'HARA (1905–1970) wrote many volumes of short stories, essays and novels, notably *Appointment in Samarra, Butterfield 8,* and *Pal Joey.*

MARCEL PROUST (1871–1922), the great French novelist, arrived at his crowning achievement, *Remembrance of Things Past,* through a series of experiments of which the text in this volume is one of the earliest (1893).

JAMES PURDY (1923–) counts among his works *Color of Darkness, Malcolm, Cabot Wright Begins,* and most recently, *I Am Elijah Thrush* (1972).

JANE RULE (1931–) was born in New Jersey and currently lives and teaches in British Columbia. She has written five books, among them *Theme for Diverse Instruments* and *Lesbian Images.*

GERTRUDE STEIN (1874–1946) was born in America but spent most of her life in France. Although she is perhaps best known for *The Autobiography of Alice B. Toklas* and *Three Lives, Q.E.D.* remains one of her surest, if earliest, achievements (1903).

ELIZABETH TAYLOR (1912–1975) published many collections of short stories and novels.

GORE VIDAL (1925–) wrote his first novel, *Williwaw,* when he was nineteen. In 1960 he ran for Congress as a Liberal Democrat in a severely Republican district of New York City and lost the election by the narrowest margin in fifty years. He is the author of, among many other novels, *Julian, Burr,* and *1876.*

EDMUND WHITE (1940–) is the author of *Forgetting Elena* (1973). He lives in New York City.

TENNESSEE WILLIAMS (1911–), best known as a playwright, is also the author of a novel, *The Roman Spring of Mrs. Stone,* three volumes of short stories, and his recent autobiography.

WILLIAM CARLOS WILLIAMS (1883–1963) was born in New Jersey and practiced medicine there throughout his life. One of America's major poets, he also wrote novels, short stories, and essays.

ABOUT THE EDITOR

SEYMOUR KLEINBERG was born in 1933 in Brooklyn. He teaches English literature at Long Island University and is a critic of film and dance, a founding member of the Gay Academic Union and currently lives in New York City.

V-380 **JOYCE, JAMES** / Ulysses
V-991 **KAFKA, FRANZ** / The Castle
V-484 **KAFKA, FRANZ** / The Trial
V-841 **KANG-HU, KIANG AND WITTER BYNNER** / The Jade Mountain: A Chinese Anthology
V-508 **KOCH, KENNETH** / The Art of Love
V-915 **KOCH, KENNETH** / A Change of Hearts
V-467 **KOCH, KENNETH** / The Red Robbins
V-82 **KOCH, KENNETH** / Wishes, Lies and Dreams
V-134 **LAGERKVIST, PAR** / Barabbas
V-240 **LAGERKVIST, PAR** / The Sibyl
V-776 **LAING, R. D.** / Knots
V-23 **LAWRENCE, D. H.** / The Plumed Serpent
V-71 **LAWRENCE, D. H.** / St. Mawr & The Man Who Died
V-329 **LINDBERGH, ANNE MORROW** / Gift from the Sea
V-822 **LINDBERGH, ANNE MORROW** / The Unicorn and Other Poems
V-479 **MALRAUX, ANDRE** / Man's Fate
V-180 **MANN, THOMAS** / Buddenbrooks
V-3 **MANN, THOMAS** / Death in Venice and Seven Other Stories
V-297 **MANN, THOMAS** / Doctor Faustus
V-497 **MANN, THOMAS** / The Magic Mountain
V-86 **MANN, THOMAS** / The Transposed Heads
V-36 **MANSFIELD, KATHERINE** / Stories
V-137 **MAUGHAM, W. SOMERSET** / Of Human Bondage
V-720 **MIRSKY, D. S.** / A History of Russian Literature: From Its Beginnings to 1900
V-883 **MISHIMA, YUKIO** / Five Modern Nō Plays
V-151 **MOFFAT, MARY JANE AND CHARLOTTE PAINTER** / Revelations: Diaries of Women
V-851 **MORGAN, ROBIN** / Monster
V-926 **MUSTARD, HELEN (trans.)** / Heinrich Heine: Selected Works
V-925 **NGUYEN, DU** / The Tale of Kieu
V-125 **OATES, WHITNEY J. AND EUGENE O'NEILL, Jr. (eds.)** / Seven Famous Greek Plays
V-973 **O'HARA, FRANK** / Selected Poems of Frank O'Hara
V-855 **O'NEILL, EUGENE** / Anna Christie, The Emperor Jones, The Hairy Ape
V-18 **O'NEILL, EUGENE** / The Iceman Cometh
V-236 **O'NEILL, EUGENE** / A Moon For the Misbegotten
V-856 **O'NEILL, EUGENE** / Seven Plays of the Sea
V-276 **O'NEILL, EUGENE** / Six Short Plays
V-165 **O'NEILL, EUGENE** / Three Plays: Desire Under the Elms, Strange Interlude, Mourning Becomes Electra
V-125 **O'NEILL, EUGENE, JR. AND WHITNEY J. OATES (eds.)** / Seven Famous Greek Plays
V-151 **PAINTER, CHARLOTTE AND MARY JANE MOFFAT** / Revelations: Diaries of Women
V-907 **PERELMAN, S. J.** / Crazy Like a Fox
V-466 **PLATH, SYLVIA** / The Colossus and Other Poems
V-232 **PRITCHETT, V. S.** / Midnight Oil
V-598 **PROUST, MARCEL** / The Captive
V-597 **PROUST, MARCEL** / Cities of the Plain
V-596 **PROUST, MARCEL** / The Guermantes Way
V-600 **PROUST, MARCEL** / The Past Recaptured
V-594 **PROUST, MARCEL** / Swann's Way
V-599 **PROUST, MARCEL** / The Sweet Cheat Gone
V-595 **PROUST, MARCEL** / Within A Budding Grove
V-714 **PUSHKIN, ALEXANDER** / The Captain's Daughter and Other Stories
V-976 **QUASHA, GEORGE AND JEROME ROTHENBERG (eds.)** / America a Prophecy: A New Reading of American Poetry from Pre-Columbian Times to the Present

V-80 **REDDY, T. J.** / Less Than a Score, But A Point: Poems by T. J. Reddy
V-504 **RENAULT, MARY** / The Bull From the Sea
V-653 **RENAULT, MARY** / The Last of the Wine
V-24 **RHYS, JEAN** / After Leaving Mr. Mackenzie
V-42 **RHYS, JEAN** / Good Morning Midnight
V-319 **RHYS, JEAN** / Quartet
V-2016 **ROSEN, KENNETH (ed.)** / The Man to Send Rain Clouds: Contemporary Stories by American Indians
V-976 **ROTHENBERG, JEROME AND GEORGE QUASHA (eds.)** / America a Prophecy: A New Reading of American Poetry from Pre-Columbian Times to the Present
V-366 **SARGENT, PAMELA (ed.)** / Bio-Futures: Science Fiction Stories about Biological Metamorphosis
V-876 **SARGENT, PAMELA (ed.)** / More Women of Wonder: Science Fiction Novelettes by Women about Women
V-41 **SARGENT, PAMELA (ed.)** / Women of Wonder: Science Fiction Stories by Women About Women
V-838 **SARTRE, JEAN-PAUL** / The Age of Reason
V-238 **SARTRE, JEAN-PAUL** / The Condemned of Altona
V-65 **SARTRE, JEAN-PAUL** / The Devil & The Good Lord & Two Other Plays
V-16 **SARTRE, JEAN-PAUL** / No Exit and Three Other Plays
V-839 **SARTRE, JEAN-PAUL** / The Reprieve
V-74 **SARTRE, JEAN-PAUL** / The Trojan Women: Euripides
V-840 **SARTRE, JEAN-PAUL** / Troubled Sleep
V-443 **SCHULTE, RAINER AND QUINCY TROUPE (eds.)** / Giant Talk: An Anthology of Third World Writings
V-607 **SCORTIA, THOMAS N. AND GEORGE ZEBROWSKI (eds.)** / Human-Machines: An Anthology of Stories About Cyborgs
V-330 **SHOLOKHOV, MIKHAIL** / And Quiet Flows the Don
V-331 **SHOLOKHOV, MIKHAIL** / The Don Flows Home to the Sea
V-447 **SILVERBERG, ROBERT** / Born With the Dead: Three Novellas About the Spirit of Man
V-945 **SNOW, LOIS WHEELER** / China On Stage
V-133 **STEIN, GERTRUDE** / Autobiography of Alice B. Toklas
V-826 **STEIN, GERTRUDE** / Everybody's Autobiography
V-941 **STEIN, GERTRUDE** / The Geographical History of America
V-797 **STEIN, GERTRUDE** / Ida
V-695 **STEIN, GERTRUDE** / Last Operas and Plays
V-477 **STEIN, GERTRUDE** / Lectures in America
V-153 **STEIN, GERTRUDE** / Three Lives
V-710 **STEIN, GERTRUDE & CARL VAN VECHTEN (ed.)** / Selected Writings of Gertrude Stein
V-20 **STEINER, STAN AND MARIA-THERESA BABIN (eds.)** / Borinquen: An Anthology of Puerto-Rican Literature
V-770 **STEINER, STAN AND LUIS VALDEZ (eds.)** / Aztlan: An Anthology of Mexican-American Literature
V-769 **STEINER, STAN AND SHIRLEY HILL WITT (eds.)** / The Way: An Anthology of American Indian Literature
V-768 **STEVENS, HOLLY (ed.)** / The Palm at the End of the Mind: Selected Poems & A Play by Wallace Stevens
V-278 **STEVENS, WALLACE** / The Necessary Angel
V-896 **SULLIVAN, VICTORIA AND JAMES HATCH (eds.)** / Plays By and About Women
V-63 **SVEVO, ITALO** / Confessions of Zeno
V-178 **SYNGE, J. M.** / Complete Plays
V-601 **TAYLOR, PAUL B. AND W. H. AUDEN (trans.)** / The Elder Edda
V-443 **TROUPE, QUINCY AND RAINER SCHULTE (eds.)** / Giant Talk: An Anthology of Third World Writings
V-770 **VALDEZ, LUIS AND STAN STEINER (eds.)** / Aztlan: An Anthology of Mexican-American Literature

V-710 **VAN VECHTEN, CARL (ed.) AND GERTRUDE STEIN** / Selected Writings of Gertrude Stein
V-870 **WIESEL, ELIE** / Souls on Fire
V-769 **WITT, SHIRLEY HILL AND STAN STEINER (eds.)** / The Way: An Anthology of American Indian Literature
V-2028 **WODEHOUSE, P. G.** / The Code of the Woosters
V-2026 **WODEHOUSE, P. G.** / Leave It to Psmith
V-2027 **WODEHOUSE, P. G.** / Mulliner Nights
V-607 **ZEBROWSKI, GEORGE AND THOMAS N. SCORTIA (eds.)** / Human-Machines: An Anthology of Stories About Cyborgs

V-594 **PROUST, MARCEL** / Swann's Way
V-599 **PROUST, MARCEL** / The Sweet Cheat Gone
V-595 **PROUST, MARCEL** / Within a Budding Grove
V-899 **SAMUEL, MAURICE** / The World of Sholom Aleichem
V-415 **SHATTUCK, ROGER** / The Banquet Years (revised)
V-278 **STEVENS, WALLACE** / The Necessary Angel
V-761 **WATTS, ALAN** / Behold the Spirit
V-923 **WATTS, ALAN** / Beyond Theology: The Art of Godmanship
V-853 **WATTS, ALAN** / The Book: On the Taboo Against Knowing Who You Are
V-999 **WATTS, ALAN** / Cloud-Hidden, Whereabouts Unknown: A Mountain Journal
V-665 **WATTS, ALAN** / Does it Matter?
V-951 **WATTS, ALAN** / In My Own Way
V-299 **WATTS, ALAN** / The Joyous Cosmology
V-592 **WATTS, ALAN** / Nature, Man and Woman
V-609 **WATTS, ALAN** / Psychotherapy East & West
V-835 **WATTS, ALAN** / The Supreme Identity
V-298 **WATTS, ALAN** / The Way of Zen
V-870 **WIESEL, ELIE** / Souls on Fire

VINTAGE WORKS OF SCIENCE AND PSYCHOLOGY

V-286 **ARIES, PHILIPPE** / Centuries of Childhood
V-292 **BATES, MARSTON** / The Forest and The Sea
V-267 **BATES, MARSTON** / Gluttons and Libertines
V-994 **BERGER, PETER & BRIGITTE AND HANSFRIED KELLNER** / The Homeless Mind: Modernization & Consciousness
V-129 **BEVERIDGE, W. I. B.** / The Art of Scientific Investigation
V-837 **BIELER, HENRY G., M. D.** / Food Is Your Best Medicine
V-414 **BOTTOMORE, T. B.** / Classes in Modern Society
V-742 **BOTTOMORE, T. B.** / Sociology: A Guide to Problems & Literature
V-168 **BRONOWSKI, J.** / The Common Sense of Science
V-419 **BROWN, NORMAN O.** / Love's Body
V-877 **COHEN, DOROTHY** / The Learning Child: Guideline for Parents and Teachers
V-972 **COHEN, STANLEY AND LAURIE TAYLOR** / Psychological Survival: The Experience of Long-Term Imprisonment
V-233 **COOPER, DAVID** / The Death of the Family
V-43 **COOPER, D. G. AND R. D. LAING** / Reason and Violence
V-918 **DAUM, SUSAN M. AND JEANNE M. STELLMAN** / Work is Dangerous to Your Health: A Handbook of Health Hazards in the Workplace & What You Can Do About Them
V-638 **DENNISON, GEORGE** / The Lives of Children
V-671 **DOMHOFF, G. WILLIAM** / The Higher Circles
V-942 **DOUGLAS, MARY** / Natural Symbols
V-157 **EISELEY, LOREN** / The Immense Journey
V-874 **ELLUL, JACQUES** / Propaganda: The Formation of Men's Attitudes
V-390 **ELLUL, JACQUES** / The Technological Society
V-802 **FALK, RICHARD A.** / This Endangered Planet: Prospects & Proposals for Human Survival
V-906 **FARAGO, PETER AND JOHN LAGNADO** / Life in Action: Biochemistry Explained
V-97 **FOUCAULT, MICHEL** / Birth of the Clinic: An Archaeology of Medical Perception
V-914 **FOUCAULT, MICHEL** / Madness & Civilization: A History of Insanity in the Age of Reason
V-935 **FOUCAULT, MICHEL** / The Order of Things: An Archaeology of the Human Sciences
V-821 **FRANK, ARTHUR, & STUART** / The People's Handbook of Medical Care
V-866 **FRANKL, VIKTOR D.** / The Doctor & The Soul: From Psychotherapy to Logotherapy
V-132 **FREUD, SIGMUND** / Leonardo da Vinci: A Study in Psychosexuality
V-14 **FREUD, SIGMUND** / Moses and Monotheism
V-124 **FREUD, SIGMUND** / Totem and Taboo
V-491 **GANS, HERBERT J.** / The Levittowners
V-938 **GARDNER, HOWARD** / The Quest for Mind: Piaget, Levi-Strauss, & The Structuralist Movement
V-152 **GRAHAM, LOREN R.** / Science & Philosophy in the Soviet Union
V-221 **GRIBBIN, JOHN AND STEPHEN PLAGEMANN** / The Jupiter Effect: The Planets as Triggers of Devastating Earthquakes (Revised)
V-602 **HARKINS, ARTHUR AND MAGORAH MARUYAMA (eds.)** / Cultures Beyond The Earth
V-372 **HARRIS, MARVIN** / Cows, Pigs, Wars, and Witches: The Riddles of Culture
V-453 **HEALTH POLICY ADVISORY COMMITTEE** / The American Health Empire
V-283 **HENRY, JULES** / Culture Against Man
V-73 **HENRY, JULES & ZUNIA** / Doll Play of the Pilaga Indian Children
V-970 **HENRY, JULES** / On Sham, Vulnerability & Other Forms of Self-Destruction
V-882 **HENRY, JULES** / Pathways to Madness
V-663 **HERRIGEL, EUGEN** / Zen in the Art of Archery
V-879 **HERSKOVITS, MELVILLE J.** / Cultural Relativism

V-566 **HURLEY, RODGER** / Poverty and Mental Retardation: A Causal Relationship
V-953 **HYMES, DELL (ed.)** / Reinventing Anthropology
V-2017 **JUDSON, HORACE FREEDLAND** / Heroin Addiction: What Americans Can Learn from the English Experience
V-268 **JUNG, C. G.** / Memories, Dreams, Reflections
V-994 **KELLNER, HANSFRIED AND PETER & BRIGITTE BERGER** / The Homeless Mind: Modernization & Consciousness
V-210 **KENYATTA, JOMO** / Facing Mount Kenya
V-823 **KOESTLER, ARTHUR** / The Case of the Midwife Toad
V-934 **KOESTLER, ARTHUR** / The Roots of Coincidence
V-361 **KOMAROVSKY, MIRRA** / Blue-Collar Marriage
V-144 **KRUEGER, STARRY** / The Whole Works: The Autobiography of a Young American Couple
V-906 **LAGNADO, JOHN AND PETER FARAGO** / Life in Action: Biochemistry Explained
V-776 **LAING, R. D.** / Knots
V-809 **LAING, R. D.** / The Politics of the Family & Other Essays
V-43 **LAING, R. D. AND D. G. COOPER** / Reason and Violence
V-280 **LEWIS, OSCAR** / The Children of Sánchez
V-634 **LEWIS, OSCAR** / A Death in the Sánchez Family
V-421 **LEWIS, OSCAR** / La Vida: A Puerto Rican Family in the Culture of Poverty —San Juan and New York
V-370 **LEWIS, OSCAR** / Pedro Martinez
V-727 **MANN, FELIX, M. D.** / Acupuncture (rev.)
V-602 **MARUYAMA, MAGORAH AND ARTHUR HARKINS (eds.)** / Cultures Beyond the Earth
V-816 **MEDVEDEV, ZHORES & ROY** / A Question of Madness
V-427 **MENDELSON, MARY ADELAIDE** / Tender Loving Greed
V-442 **MITCHELL, JULIET** / Psychoanalysis and Feminism
V-672 **OUSPENSKY, P. D.** / The Fourth Way
V-524 **OUSPENSKY, P. D.** / A New Model of The Universe
V-943 **OUSPENSKY, P. D.** / The Psychology of Man's Possible Evolution
V-639 **OUSPENSKY, P. D.** / Tertium Organum
V-558 **PERLS, F. S.** / Ego, Hunger and Aggression: Beginning of Gestalt Therapy
V-462 **PIAGET, JEAN** / Six Psychological Studies
V-221 **PLAGEMANN, STEPHEN AND JOHN GRIBBIN** / The Jupiter Effect (Revised)
V-6 **POLSTER, ERVING & MIRIAM** / Gestalt Therapy Integrated: Contours of Theory & Practice
V-70 **RANK, OTTO** / The Myth of the Birth of the Hero and Other Essays
V-214 **ROSENFELD, ALBERT** / The Second Genesis: The Coming Control of Life
V-301 **ROSS, NANCY WILSON (ed.)** / The World of Zen
V-441 **RUDHYAR, DANE** / The Astrology of America's Destiny
V-464 **SARTRE, JEAN-PAUL** / Search for a Method
V-806 **SHERFEY, MARY JANE, M. D.** / The Nature & Evolution of Female Sexuality
V-918 **STELLMAN, JEANNE M. AND SUSAN M. DAUM** / Work is Dangerous to Your Health
V-440 **STONER, CAROL HUPPING** / Producing Your Own Power: How to Make Nature's Energy Sources Work for You
V-972 **TAYLOR, LAURIE AND STANLEY COHEN** / Psychological Survival
V-289 **THOMAS, ELIZABETH MARSHALL** / The Harmless People
V-800 **THOMAS, ELIZABETH MARSHALL** / Warrior Herdsmen
V-310 **THORP, EDWARD O.** / Beat the Dealer
V-588 **TIGER, LIONEL** / Men in Groups
V-810 **TITMUSS, RICHARD M.** / The Gift Relationship From Human Blood to Social Policy
V-761 **WATTS, ALAN** / Behold the Spirit
V-923 **WATTS, ALAN** / Beyond Theology: The Art of Godsmanship

V-853 **WATTS, ALAN** / The Book: On the Taboo Against Knowing Who You Are
V-999 **WATTS, ALAN** / Cloud-Hidden, Whereabouts Unknown
V-665 **WATTS, ALAN** / Does It Matter?
V-299 **WATTS, ALAN** / The Joyous Cosmology
V-592 **WATTS, ALAN** / Nature, Man, and Woman
V-609 **WATTS, ALAN** / Psychotherapy East and West
V-835 **WATTS, ALAN** / The Supreme Identity
V-904 **WATTS, ALAN** / This Is It
V-298 **WATTS, ALAN** / The Way of Zen
V-468 **WATTS, ALAN** / The Wisdom of Insecurity
V-813 **WILSON, COLIN** / The Occult
V-313 **WILSON, EDMUND** / Apologies to the Iroquois
V-197 **WILSON, PETER J.** / Oscar: An Inquiry into the Nature of Sanity
V-893 **ZAEHNER, R. C.** / Zen, Drugs & Mysticism